The Runaway Wife

Also by Rowan Coleman

Lessons in Laughing Out Loud

The Home for Broken Hearts

The Accidental Family

Mommy by Mistake

Another Mother's Life

The Accidental Mother

The Runaway Wife

ROWAN COLEMAN

GALLERY BOOKS
New York London Toronto Sydney New Delhi

Gallery Books
A Division of Simon & Schuster, Inc.
1230 Avenue of the Americas
New York, NY 10020

This book is a work of fiction. Any references to historical events, real people, or real places are used fictitiously. Other names, characters, places, and events are products of the author's imagination, and any resemblance to actual events or places or persons, living or dead, is entirely coincidental.

Originally published in 2012 in Great Britain by Arrow Books.

Manufactured in the United States of America

ISBN 978-1-61129-016-5

For Stanley Edward and Aubrey John,
born April 10, 2012

Dearest Rose,

Our meeting, though brief, has stayed with me and I wanted to write and thank you for your hospitality when I came to see you a few days ago. You didn't have to be so kind to a stranger turning up unannounced, but you were and I am so grateful. Although you were not able to help me find the painting, everything you told me about your father was both fascinating and heartbreaking. Why is it, I wonder, that artists are so often capable of creating such beauty whilst doing such harm to themselves and others? I hope that one day you will perhaps be able to reconcile with him and find the answers to all of your questions.

I hope you will forgive me when I write that you are a remarkable woman and you deserve all the happiness, contentment, and love in the world. I, for one, know that I have never met anyone quite like you.

Yours,

Frasier

Chapter One

"Do you know what time it is?" An irritated woman's muffled voice was just about audible from the other side of the door.

"I . . . I know, but this is a B and B, isn't it?" Rose asked. Her seven-year-old daughter, Maddie, snuggled into her neck, weighing heavily on her hip as she shivered against the cold. Despite it being the height of summer, fine needles of icy rain were driving down into the tops of their heads, and Rose had forgotten to bring Maddie a coat. There hadn't been time to think about coats; there hadn't been time to do anything but leave, grabbing a few damp and muddled items from the wash basket in the kitchen, and one oddly wrapped package, bundled up and secreted long ago, perhaps waiting for just this moment.

"Doors are locked at nine p.m. sharp!" the voice called back. "It's in all the literature. It's three o'clock in the morning. I've got a good mind to call the police."

Rose gasped in a ragged breath, determined not to cry. She'd made it this far without crying; she wasn't going to let this disembodied voice break her when nothing else had.

"I know, but, please, I've come a long way and I've got a

little girl with me. We just need a place to stay. I would have booked ahead, but I didn't know I was coming."

There was some more muttering, a man's voice too, Rose thought, drawing Maddie even nearer into her body, trying to suppress the child's shivers with her embrace. As she did so, she tightened her arm on her other, less precious package, which was tucked underneath it: a smallish rectangular object that Rose had hurriedly wrapped in a blanket.

"A child?" The woman's voice came again.

"Yes, she's only seven."

With a mixture of fear and trepidation, Rose waited as she heard bolts being drawn back and locks being released. Finally the heavy-looking, thickly painted wooden door drew back to let a slant of yellow light cut through the rain, making the drops dazzle and glitter. A woman of indeterminate age peered through the gap at the sodden pair, and then after a moment took a step back and opened the door wider.

"This is really most irregular," she told Rose as she hurried into the hallway. "Knocking on the front door at all hours of the day and night. I've got my other guests to think of."

"There *are* no other guests." The owner of the male voice, a well-built bearded man in his late fifties, sporting a vest and jogging bottoms, smiled at Rose. "Don't you fret about it, love. It's no bother. I'm Brian and this is my wife, Jenny. Jenny, you take them up, give them towels, and I'll bring you both up a nice warm drink. Hot chocolate do you, little one?"

Maddie drove her face deeper into Rose's chest, her frozen fingers clinging on for all they were worth. Maddie was not a child who settled easily into strange surroundings, particularly when the circumstances that had brought them here had already been so traumatic.

"That really is so kind," Rose said gratefully. "We'd love a hot chocolate, wouldn't we, Maddie?"

"Like I said, no bother." Brian smiled. "Now, got any luggage you want me to bring in for you?"

"I . . . don't. No. There's no luggage." Rose smiled weakly, lifting one elbow awkwardly to reveal her oddly wrapped package. "Just us and this."

Jenny raised a skeptical brow, and clearly saw that nothing good could come of her latest and only guest. "I usually ask for cash up front, twenty-five a night. Presumably you've got cash?"

"Yes, I . . ." Rose attempted to reach into her pocket while still cradling Maddie and the package.

"For God's sakes, woman," Brian said, shaking his head, "let the lass be. We'll sort the payment in the morning. Right, now . . . ?" He looked at her questioningly.

"Oh, I'm Rose, Rose Pritchard, and this is Maddie."

"Right then, well, Rose here needs to get little Maddie into bed!"

"For all you know she might be an axe murderer," Jenny muttered not entirely under her breath.

"Well, if she is, I'll wager she's too tired to chop us up tonight. Now stop going on and get up them stairs."

It was only as Rose followed Jenny's considerable behind up the narrow stairs that she realized her landlady was wearing a rather risqué pink negligee, which floated above her on the steep incline like a jellyfish, showing flashes of her ample dimpled thighs. Dimly it occurred to Rose that perhaps Jenny and Brian were the axe murderers, but she was so tired, her body exhausted by the hours of driving and her mind reeling from everything that had happened, that if they were, she didn't think she could be bothered to run away twice in one day. After all, it had taken her most of her life to find the courage to make this first escape. Millthwaite, without any particular renown or importance, lost deep in the heart of the

Lake District, was a village very few people had heard of. Except it was here, in a place that could perhaps most accurately be described as the middle of nowhere, that Rose was hoping against hope to find her second chance.

Jenny opened the door on a room at the top of the house, flicking on the light. It was a neat, clean little room, with narrow twin beds set about a foot apart, covered with pink candlewick bedspreads. The small rose pattern on the wallpaper was repeated on the curtains and on the swags that hung over them, a style that had been fashionable about thirty years earlier.

"I've put you in here because it's got its own loo," Jenny said as Rose sat down on a bed, still holding Maddie tightly as she laid her package down beside her. "There's clean towels there, and I'll put the immersion on, I suppose, if you want a shower."

"Really, all I want to do is sleep," Rose said, closing her eyes for a moment.

"And you've got no luggage but that thing?" Jenny asked her, standing in the doorway, her nightie floating around her with a life of its own. "Where have you come from again?"

"Broadstairs, in Kent," Rose said, easing Maddie onto the bed and taking one of the folded towels from the pillow to rub her wet hair. Rolling onto her tummy, Maddie refused to show her face to the strange woman, or even the strange room.

"All that way and not even an overnight bag?" Jenny asked, her curiosity almost as naked as her considerable cleavage.

"No," Rose said, hoping she was making it clear that she would not be drawn on the subject.

"Well, then, as you've ruined my and Brian's special night, anyway, I'll go and find you something to wear . . ."

"Oh, please, don't go to any trouble," Rose called after

Jenny, but she had already left, leaving the door open so that Rose could get the full effect of her righteous stomp down the stairs.

When she returned, minutes later, she had a few clothes over one arm, and two mugs of hot chocolate in the other hand.

"My youngest one, Haleigh," she said, dropping a pink nightshirt with the words "Sex Bomb" emblazoned across the front in glitter. "She's on a gap year in Thailand, although don't ask me what a gap year is, as if you get time off from having a proper life to mess around in a foreign country. Anyway, she's only a slip of a thing, so about your size. And these belong to my grandson, my eldest's boy. They've got Spider-Man on but I shouldn't think she'll mind." Jenny set down the mugs of chocolate on the bedside table. "She all right? Very quiet."

"Very tired," Rose said, stroking Maddie's dark hair. "And confused."

"Right, well, breakfast's between eight and eight thirty. I don't take orders, you get what you're given, and if you want coffee you'll have to go to the shop and buy it. I don't hold with the stuff. Unnatural. Oh, and here's a key for the front door. *Do not lose it.*"

"Thank you," Rose said, breathing a sigh of relief as Jenny gave her one more look of disapproval and then closed the door. Leaving Maddie sitting huddled on the bed for a moment, Rose went over and locked it, and then, turning back to her daughter, eased the little girl's damp top off over her head.

Maddie squealed in protest, resolutely keeping her eyes closed, refusing to acknowledge her radical change in circumstances. Change was the very thing that Maddie hated the most, and yet a few hours ago Rose had decided to rip her out of her home, away from everything she knew, and bring her here. Had she done the right thing? At the time it had felt like the only thing she could do, but was that ever true?

"Come on, darling, let's get you changed and we can get some sleep," Rose said, doing her best to keep the tension and uncertainty out of her voice.

"Where's Bear?" Maddie asked, opening one eye.

"Bear's here. We never go anywhere without Bear, do we?" Bear was in fact a very flea-bitten rabbit that Maddie had been given as a baby, but Bear he had always been known as and Bear he would remain.

"Where's my book?" Maddie was referring to her history book on Ancient Egypt, which she'd begged Rose to buy after a day trip to the British Museum. Maddie had become obsessed by mummies, pyramids, and everything else Egyptian, poring over anything she could find on the subject, until she became almost as expert as any curator at the museum. She had read the book she was referring to literally hundreds of times and knew it by heart, but still Rose knew she would read it hundreds of times more. It was just one of her myriad rituals that she had developed recently that Rose had scarcely had time to dwell on or worry about. Young children were eccentric, that's what everyone said. This same everyone said that Maddie's obsessive behavior was nothing to worry about, and Rose chose to believe them, even though her instinct told her otherwise.

"It's here," Rose said, pulling the tatty book out of her bag. Thank God it had been in there already, from when she'd taken Maddie to have an asthma checkup that afternoon, otherwise Rose was sure she wouldn't have remembered to take it with her.

Content for the book to lie unread on the pillow beside her head, Maddie let Rose pull off her crumpled and damp clothes and put on the pajamas. "I don't like Spider-Man," she protested dimly, her lashes dropping with every rise and fall of her chest. Carefully, Rose eased her daughter under the covers, turning off the overhead light that glared from beneath a pink fringed lampshade, and after waiting for a moment to let her eyes adjust to the lack of light, she slipped the package, still wrapped in its ancient blanket—one that had used to grace Rose's cot when she was a very small child—under Maddie's bed, took one lukewarm cup of chocolate, and climbed into the other bed, the smooth cool sheets very welcome against her hot, aching skin. Hoping that sleep would come quickly, Rose closed her eyes, yet even though her body shuddered with exhaustion and her eyes screamed to be shut, sleep would not come. Wearily, Rose leant back against the quilted-velour headboard, stared out the window into the dense wet night, and wondered, not for the first time since she'd started the ignition of the car and pulled away from home, what on earth she was doing.

A persistent knocking at the door finally forced Rose to drag her eyelids apart. She wasn't sure when she had finally fallen asleep, but it felt like only a few seconds ago as she rubbed her eyes and looked around, her memory of where she was, and why, coming back to her in heavy persistent thuds, in time with the beat of her heart.

"Hello?" she called out, dragging herself up in bed.

"Rose? Love, it's Brian. It's gone ten, darling. We didn't like to wake you before. But Jenny'll still do you a bit of bacon and toast if you're hungry?"

"Oh, sorry!" Rose called back, climbing out of bed and looking around for her clothes.

"I'll tell her ten minutes, then?" Brian checked, having obviously done some expert diplomatic work to secure her and Maddie breakfasts to go along with their beds.

"We'll be there in five!" Rose called, pulling on her knickers and skirt. Maddie was regarding her from her position partially hidden by the bedspread, her large blue eyes peering out over the top.

"Come on, darling, toast!" Rose said, beaming at her daughter, hoping the promise of her favorite food would lure her out from under the covers.

"It might not be my bread," Maddie said, pulling the cover below her chin. "What if it's not my special bread? I like toast at home, not toast . . . here."

"Well, it might be a different, nicer sort of bread. You won't know what you are missing unless you try it. Here, shall I help you put your dress on?"

"I don't want it if it isn't my bread," Maddie said, referring to the only brand of sliced bread that she liked to eat.

Rose closed her eyes for a moment and took a breath. Really, when she'd decided to run away from her home and husband, she perhaps should have given more thought to Maddie's very particular dietary requirements. "Fussy" was how her teacher referred to her at school, but what she didn't realize was that anything different on her plate caused Maddie real anxiety.

"Just try it, for me. You never know, you might like it." Rose smiled encouragingly.

"I won't if it's not my bread," Maddie said miserably, adding as she trailed after Rose down the stairs, "When will it be OK to go home again? Before school starts back, after the holidays?"

Rose didn't have the heart to tell her the answer was never.

They discovered the dining room after opening a series of doors that led off the main hallway, finding first a guest sitting room dominated by a huge doll's house encased in glass, which Rose had to drag Maddie away from, and then an office containing a desk covered in piles of paper, with an ancient, almost historical PC sitting on top of it.

"This isn't a hotel, you know," Jenny greeted Rose and Maddie as they finally made it into the small dining room, with about six tables all neatly laid, despite the absence of other guests.

"Well, it sort of is," Brian said, winking at Rose as he picked up his keys and kissed Jenny goodbye before heading for the door.

"I've got too much to do without waiting around for people to deign to get up!"

"We didn't expect you to wait," Rose said. "I'd have just taken Maddie out for breakfast."

"You will not," Jenny said, pointing at the table next to the window in a clear command to sit. "Can you imagine? No, tea and toast will be through in a minute. And what about you, young lady? Would you like a glass of milk?"

"I don't like milk," Maddie said.

"Well, orange juice, then?" Jenny asked her, and Maddie nodded.

"Do you mean yes please?" Jenny chided her. Maddie nodded again.

Rose rubbed her hands over her face, pushing her long hair back as she reached into her skirt pocket and took out the postcard. Pushing Maddie's book across the table towards the little girl, hoping its contents would distract her from her toast, she let herself read the short message on the back for a moment, following the familiar swirls and loops of the handwriting that she had come to know by heart over the years. And then she turned it over and looked at the picture on the front, which had become just as familiar. A reproduction of an oil painting, *Millthwaite from a Distance* by John Jacobs.

This small, slight piece of card with a neatly written note inscribed on the back of it was the only reason she had run away to here, which seemed crazy if she even thought it, let alone said it out loud, but it was true.

Frasier McCleod, the person who had written the note, was the reason that she had come to Millthwaite, although she had no idea where he was, or even who he was really. That card, this place, were the only links she had with him and the possibility that had been haunting her since she had met him once, more than seven years ago, for less than an hour: that he might, just might, feel the same way about her as she did about him. That in the one and only meeting of less than an hour, when Rose had been long married and very pregnant, she might just have met the love of her life.

Rose held her breath as Jenny plonked down a plate of toast, and Maddie picked it up, eyeing it suspiciously as she touched it to her lips, licked it, and then nibbled the tiniest crumb off the corner, before taking a full bite.

"Delicious!" Maddie said, nodding at Jenny, who also put down a small glass of juice. "Thank you very much, you are most kind."

"You are very welcome," Jenny said, a little put off by Maddie's sudden burst of good manners, but that was Maddie. It wasn't that she didn't know how to behave, it was just that most of the time she didn't see the point.

"Do you know this postcard?" Rose plucked up the courage to ask Jenny before she bustled back to the kitchen to resentfully fry bacon. "The painting of the village?"

Jenny nodded and then pointed at the wall above Rose's head, where an exact, but larger, reproduction of the same painting was hanging.

"You'll find one like that in most houses round here," Jenny said. "It's the closest Millthwaite's ever come to being famous—well, unless you count that one time we were on *Escape to the Country*. Still, it's made Albie Simpson more money than he needs."

"How do you mean?" Rose asked her, twisting in her chair to get a better look at the print. It was a bold and confident painting, almost as if the artist had been bored when he painted it, restless and eager to be onto the next thing, dashing it off as an afterthought, and yet, for all its carelessness, it was very beautiful.

"The artist, John Jacobs, he was a heavy drinker, a real boozer, never sober. A few years back he turned up at the pub and offered Albie his painting of the village in exchange for a bottle of whiskey. Albie—who's no better than he should be, if you ask me—took it because he fancied the look of it over his bar. And that's where it sat, until about four years ago. Then all of a sudden this fancy-looking feller from over the border turned up and offered Albie five thousand for it! Pounds!"

Jenny waited for Rose to be either scandalized or shocked, her face registering clear disappointment when she was neither.

"Well, Albie turned him down, don't know why—he must have been drunk as a dog. Or not, because the bloke doubled his offer on the spot without blinking an eye. And he said he'd throw in a print of it to replace the original if Albie shook on the deal there and then. So Albie did the deal, the man got the painting, and Albie got his money." Jenny pressed her lips together, shaking her head.

Rose looked down from the painting, running the tips of her fingers over the writing on the postcard. A well-dressed man with an interest in John Jacobs, willing to pay what it took to secure one. That could be him. That could be Frasier McCleod. All she had to do to be one step nearer to finding out where he was, was to talk to the landlord, who might still have a number or an address for him, and then . . . And then what?

Rose bit her lip as Jenny talked on over her head, entirely oblivious of whether or not Rose was listening.

And then turn up on Frasier's doorstep, and say, what? "Hello, remember me? You came to my house once, years ago, looking for some information. I was crying, you were kind to me. We talked for a while, and the only other thing I ever heard from you is written on the back of a postcard. A postcard that I have treasured every single day since. Oh, and by the way, I think I love you. You can take out a restraining order on me now, if you like."

Rose blinked as the foolishness of what she was doing washed over her with a wave of icy-cold reality. This was madness, a crazy teenage wild-goose chase, in which she'd selfishly involved her daughter. Frasier McCleod hadn't written her a coded love letter, he'd written her a thank-you note, a polite little formality that somehow she'd turned into some grand forbidden passion. What on earth was she doing here? And yet she couldn't go home, she couldn't take Maddie back to the home that she knew, where she could eat her favorite bread, or back to the nice teaching assistant in school who sat next to her and helped her keep up, and played with her at break time when no one else would. There was no way she could go home. A postcard, a painting of Millthwaite, might be why she was here, so far from home and following the thread of a fantasy that was bound to unravel to nothing as soon as it was pulled, but it was not the reason she'd run away.

"Anyway, old Albie was laughing on the other side of his face when the painting sold for four times as much, a year or so later. Turned out that the man who sold it was some arty-farty type from Edinburgh. Made a packet on it, and has made a ton more besides since he started selling the old git's other stuff. That bloody John Jacobs, sitting pretty on all that money. You know what I say? I say it's a shame that he sobered up, otherwise maybe we all would have had a chance of getting hold of one of his paintings. I know I'd have swapped him a hot breakfast for one."

"What do you mean?" Rose asked her, suddenly hooked back into her stream of words, a cold wash of shock drenching her in sudden shudders.

"Well, he lives up the road, doesn't he?" Jenny said, her expression mirroring the look of shock on Rose's face, as she saw the impact that piece of information was having on her guest. "John Jacobs, he's lived up there for almost ten years now, the last three of them sober, by all accounts. We used to see him a lot in the village, in the pub, but not so much anymore, which is a good job, if you ask me, the miserable old bugger. He's rolling in cash, he is, but does he ever do anything for his community? This village is dying on its feet and he's quite content to sit up there like a king in his castle, not caring what other people are thinking."

"That sounds like him," Rose said slowly, turning away from Jenny's hawklike eyes to watch Maddie, her head close over her book, Bear sitting demurely on the table as Rose took the news in, reeling and dizzy. Why it had never occurred to her that the artist might paint the place he lived in, she didn't know, but it hadn't. Not until that moment. And now she had no idea how to react.

"Why, do you know him, then? Old Jacobs?" Jenny asked her.

"Do I know him?" Rose said thoughtfully. "No, I don't suppose I do. Although perhaps I ought to. He is my father, after all."

Chapter TWO

When Rose was very little, her father used to take her for walks on the beach, in the summer, just as the sun was setting. They'd sit on the sand and pick out the colors in the sky, making up names for every nuance between red and gold. Rose remembered knowing, with total certainty, that John loved her the best, more than anyone else in the world, more than her mother, even. And she remembered what a wonderful feeling that was, that closeness between them filling her with a sense of complete safety, so that nothing ever frightened her. John was a tall man, with long arms and legs, and fingers that seemed to flay wildly and splay as he talked, animating his words, continually wanting to tell the world what he was thinking, because he was certain that the world would care. Rose cared, Rose listened to every word he said, drinking in his wisdom; she was his acolyte.

His thick black shock of hair was long and unbrushed, and there was always stubble on his chin, which Rose liked to rub her cheek against when she hugged him. He wore the same pair of glasses that he'd had since he was fourteen years old, round Lennon spectacles, which didn't suit his angular face at all, and his clothes and skin were always smeared and stained with paint. Their embraces were always scented with the linseed oil he used to mix with his pigments and Rose remembered how the three of them—John, her mother, Marian, and she—would spend Saturday mornings in her parents' big bed, laughing and talking, eating toast and making crumbs. Like in most childhood memories, the sun always seemed to be shining, the sky was always blue, Marian was always smiling, and John was endlessly fascinating, weaving a world around them that made Rose feel special. She wasn't like the other little girls at school, the ones whose dads had jobs and came home after bedtime. Her father was magical, beguiling, exciting, and adoring. Yes, for the early part of her life, Rose certainly felt like the luckiest little girl in the world to have a father who was so very interesting. Of course, she hadn't known until later, much later, that John was drunk most of the time.

The last time she had seen him, Rose was nine years old.

The idyll that she believed she existed in didn't blow up overnight; rather, it wore away, week after week, year after year, and as Rose grew a little older she noticed that the layer of gilt that John had painted over their lives was gradually rubbing away, revealing the rough darkness beneath. He no longer smelt of paint, but instead the sour scent of whiskey was always on his breath. His outbursts of joy had become dark, dangerous episodes when he was just as likely to lash out at Rose for being in the wrong place at the wrong time as he was at her mother. Rose became accustomed to turning up the TV when her parents were screaming at each other, and she went into the garden to play when her mother was weeping, her head buried in her arms, at the kitchen table. And she never climbed into their bed anymore on a Saturday morning, because her father wasn't there.

The morning he had left was just as bright and as sunny as every other day that Rose remembered. The sun streaming in through the stained-glass window in the door imprinted a hazy shimmering colored pattern on the floorboards in the hall. John had sat her down on the bottom of the stairs, and, crouching in front of her, taken her hands in his.

"I've got to go, Rosie," he said.

Rose remembered mostly being irritated with him: he never called her Rosie, not ever. Why start now?

"Go where?"

"I'm going away, to live in a different place. Me and your mum, we just . . . well, I've got to go. So . . . but . . . you will still be my Rosie and—"

"I'm not your Rosie," Rose said, frowning deeply. There was nothing about this red-eyed, slurring man that she recognized, not even his voice. "When are you coming back?"

"I'm not coming back," he said, holding her gaze, unflinching in that moment.

"But I'll see you?" Rose remembered the tremble in her voice, as the reality of what was happening began to dawn on her. Yet she was determined not to cry. John hated it when she cried.

"Course you will," John said. "You'll see me all the time, Rosie-Ro."

He leant forward and kissed her wetly in the center of her forehead. Rose wanted to put her arms around him, cling onto him and beg him not to go. But even then, even at nine years old, she had known that her father would not stay for her. That, as much as he loved her, he did not love her enough for that.

"I'll see you really soon." He'd winked and pointed at her as he'd picked up his bag and closed the front door behind him.

That was the last time that Rose had seen her father.

"Who'd have thought that miserable old beggar would have a daughter?" Jenny had abandoned any pretense of being a hostess and had sat down at the table with Maddie and Rose and a fresh pot of tea. "I can't imagine any woman letting that miserable old sod get close enough. He looks like a tramp, smells like one too."

"I wouldn't really know," Rose said, intensely uncomfortable about having to talk about something that still hurt her so deeply. The news that her father was nearby was shocking, terrifying, eclipsing everything else that had happened in the last few hours, and even her postcard. If she'd pictured him at all after he'd left, which she'd tried very hard not to do, it was as a nebulous thing, more of an idea of the man she had used to know and trust, existing somewhere, but nowhere real or solid. She never thought of him with a home, a house, and even though she knew he'd left with another woman, she never thought of them as enduring, of the chances of him having another life, another family, more children, even. Rose took a sharp inward breath as the realization that she could have half sisters and brothers dawned on her.

"So, John Jacobs is your father, but he's not the reason you came here?" Jenny questioned her, her head tilted to one side.

"Not really." Rose shifted in her seat. "Well, I knew that he'd painted this postcard. But I didn't expect to actually find him here. I don't really know what I expected to find."

"So why are you here, then?" Jenny asked her, clearly not one for tiptoeing around an issue.

"I just had to get away, and I've been looking at this painting for so long. This was the first place I thought of. It seems random, I know . . ." How could Rose explain that there was only ever one place she would be able to run away to, even if it was one she knew so little about?

"Get away, as in on the run, or get away, as in needed a bit of a break?"

Rose thought that strictly speaking both of those things were true.

"You know how things can get sometimes," Rose said, nodding at Maddie, in the hope that Jenny would take the hint and change the subject. Jenny beamed, hugging her mug of tea to her chest, clearly delighted to have something so fascinating land literally on her doorstep.

"I wish my Brian was here. He'll be gobsmacked when I tell him we've got John Jacobs's daughter staying. He will. You'll be able to knock him down with a feather. So he abandoned you, did he, the old bastard? When you were little?"

"I suppose he did," Rose said reluctantly, not used to talking about it.

"And you never saw a penny of all that money, I'll bet, did you?" Jenny said, arming herself for a morning of gossip. "The tight old git."

"When he left, his work didn't make him any money. We lived on my mum's salary, mostly."

"So he bled the poor woman dry and then dumped her for a new model." Jenny was compiling her version of events at lightning speed.

Rose thought about Tilda Sinclair, the "new model," also an artist, who had posed for her father. Statuesque, stunning, with a mass of midnight hair and navy blue eyes. She wasn't a newer model, she wasn't younger, thinner, or more beautiful than Marian had been. She was just different, in every way. Where Marian worked in an office nine to five, Tilda was a creator who sat for her father during the day and worked on her own art all night. Marian was always neatly turned out, slender and fair-haired. Tilda was a voluptuous woman, who oozed fleshy curves that looked like they might envelop you entirely. Rose had never known Tilda, so when she thought of her it was as this siren, this irresistible creature that had lured her father away from his family without a backward glance. Had her father bled Marian dry? In a way, Rose thought, feeling her stomach clench as it always did when she thought of her mother. After all, in fewer than ten years after he'd left, she was dead.

"I suppose so," she said to Jenny, who was pouring her yet another cup of tea.

"So are you going up there to confront him? I could give you a lift, if you like? I don't mind, if you need some moral support. Or immoral, I'm easy either way."

Maddie lifted her head from her book. "Going up where?" she asked. "Where are we, again?"

It occurred to Rose that since they'd left in a blaze of confusion, Maddie hadn't even really looked out the window. She'd cried herself to sleep on the journey up and it had been dark when they finally arrived. She had absolutely no idea how far she was from home, which was probably a good thing as it would only frighten her. Maddie was not a child who liked to be far from the things she knew.

"We are in Millthwaite," Rose told her. "For a little summer break."

"And then . . . what then?" Maddie asked her uncertainly. Rose thought of John's last words to her the morning that he kissed her goodbye as she sat on the bottom stair, that he would see her soon—the first lie of many—and now she had to tell Maddie another one.

"And then everything will be fine again," she said. How was she ever going to explain that to Maddie?

"I'm free after I've done the vacuuming," Jenny offered again eagerly.

"No, thanks, Jenny," Rose said firmly. "I didn't come here to find him. I'm not sure I want to find him at all."

"Find who?" Maddie asked.

"A man I used to know who lives nearby," Rose said.

"Your daddy," Maddie stated. She had clearly been listening to everything. "Your daddy lives near here but you don't want to see him because he is mean."

Maddie had an uncanny knack for sensing that something was up in a way that belied her years. As if, even at the age of seven, she was well aware that the world was short of happy endings.

"Not at the moment," Rose said, telling her as much of the truth as she was able to.

Just at that moment Rose's phone went off, shrilling noisily in her pocket. Without even looking at it, Rose rejected the call and then turned it off.

"But you will," Jenny insisted. "Because it's fate, isn't it? You come all this way, in the middle of the night, for no apparent reason, and find your father, who you've not seen for years! That's fate, that is. That's God telling you something."

"Fate." Rose repeated the word slowly. "Fate makes it sound like you have no choice about what happens to you, but I don't think that's true. I think if I left everything up to fate, then I wouldn't be here. It was going against fate that brought me here."

Jenny regarded her for a moment as she chewed her final corner of toast.

"But you will go up there eventually, won't you? Give the old buzzard a heart attack!"

"I'd like to look at your doll's house." Much to Rose's relief, Maddie interrupted Jenny midinterrogation. "I like small things."

"Do you, dear?" Jenny said. "It's not for playing with, I'm afraid."

"Why not?" Maddie asked her.

"Well, it's old and precious. It might get broken."

"So it's never been played with, ever?" Maddie asked her insistently.

"Well, yes, when I was a girl, and my Haleigh used to love it. But not now. It's an antique, you know."

Maddie sighed and spent a long moment examining the ceiling. And then she turned to Jenny and fixed her with her own peculiarly unnerving stare.

"What is the point of a doll's house if it can't be played with?"

Rose scowled at herself in the almost full-length mirror that was glued to the back of the wardrobe door in the tiny room. Since Jenny had received the news that Rose was John Jacobs's abandoned daughter, her attitude had transformed from one of resentful hostess to most eager helper. The first thing Jenny had done when Rose told her she wanted to go to the pub and find out more about the art dealer was to insist that she find her fresh clothes to wear.

"These will do for another day," Rose had said, looking down at her crumpled skirt and worn, creased blouse.

"No," Jenny said. "I'm not having my guests going out into the town looking like a pair of tramps. What will people think of me? There's a wardrobe full of clothes that Haleigh's left behind, which will do you just fine, and as for madam here, I'm sure I can rustle her something up from the stuff my grandchildren leave here when they come for visits. Although they are all boys. But you don't mind a few boys' things, do you, madam?"

"Yes, actually, I do. I don't like boys," Maddie told her, not that Jenny heard her as she bustled off, already intent on her mission.

As a result, Rose, who after more than a decade of marriage to a doctor, had become accustomed to wearing nice skirts, sensible tops, always dresses and never trousers, found herself sporting a pair of low-rise jeans with a rip at the knee, jeans that would have exposed the lower half of her stomach if she had not managed to find a longish black T-shirt to cover it, one with a slash neck that sloped off one shoulder. Rose wasn't old—she was only thirty-one—and she knew plenty of women of around her age who dressed like Haleigh obviously did and didn't give it a second thought. And she knew some—for example, her friend Shona—who dressed like a fifteen-year-old with questionable morals.

Rose had always been conservative, though, at least since she stopped being simply Rose and started being a wife, not long after her eighteenth birthday. Richard was always very insistent that she should take care not to attract the wrong sort of attention, telling her that as his wife she had a certain standing in the community, that there would be certain expectations. And Rose, whose teenage years had been chaotic and confusing, had been not only happy, but grateful to comply. Marrying Richard had been like stepping out of the glaring heat into a deep cool pool of calm. Rose didn't even own a pair of jeans, let alone hipster ones, and it came as quite a shock to her to find that unless she was completely delusional—which, considering where she was and why, was entirely possible—nineteen-year-old Haleigh's clothes rather suited her.

Sweeping her long, smooth curtain of hair over one shoulder, Rose turned round to find Maddie on the bed regarding her, clearly not entirely satisfied with the boy's jeans that she had been given but somewhat mollified by a very tiny pink Las Vegas T-shirt that Rose had found in the pile of Haleigh's clothes. On Haleigh the skimpy article surely had to reveal more than was appropriate, but on Maddie it came to just above her knees and had just enough glitter on it to make the boy's jeans bearable. As soon as she had her bearings she'd find the nearest town and buy them some more clothes, other than the few bits of underwear she'd managed to scoop up under her arm as they left, but for now these hand-me-downs would have to do.

"What do you think?" Rose asked her, smiling, smoothing the T-shirt down over her slender hips. Maddie looked thoughtful.

"Daddy wouldn't like it," she said.

"No, I know." Rose turned back to the mirror, pulling at the neck until both of her shoulders were covered, if only briefly. "But Daddy's not here."

"Mummy?" Rose met her daughter's eyes in the reflection. "Does Daddy still like me?"

Biting her lip, Rose swirled to engulf Maddie in a hug that the child instinctively resisted, her body tensing, just as it always did when anyone touched her.

"Of course he likes you. He loves you, darling," Rose told her, kissing Maddie's screwed-up face. "You're the apple of his eye, you know that."

"I don't think I do," Maddie said. "Why would anyone want an apple in their eye? It would hurt."

"What I mean is, whatever has happened between Daddy and me, it's not to do with you. It's not because of you. Daddy loves you."

Maddie turned her face from Rose, her lips pressed together in a thin pale line. It was clear that she found it hard to reconcile what she'd witnessed, what had happened, with Rose's version of events, and Rose had no idea how to fix that, only that she was certain she didn't want Maddie to blame herself.

"He didn't act like it, did he, though?" Maddie said.

"Before . . . when . . . and when we got in the car and came here. He was very, very angry."

"I know," Rose said, stroking Maddie's heavy fringe back from her face. "But that wasn't because of you, it was me. It was because of something *I* had done."

"What did you do?" Maddie asked her.

"It's not important," Rose said. "All that is important is that you remember that Daddy loves *you*."

"Do we . . . will we have to go back? If we don't go back, Daddy will be cross again," Maddie persisted.

Rose considered another lie, but only for a moment. "I don't want to see Daddy for a while."

"What shall we do instead?" Maddie asked, her voice ragged with anxiety. "I want to see him. This Saturday we are supposed to go swimming at two forty-five. And on Sunday we have lunch at one o'clock. Chicken and potatoes, and I always have the breast with no skin. The last time I saw Daddy, he was angry. What if he's still angry?"

"I know, darling, I know," Rose said, watching Maddie's taut expression. "Well, you and I can go swimming somewhere near here, I'm sure. And we'll go to a pub for lunch. They are bound to have chicken. I'll take the skin off for you."

"But that isn't what we do!" Maddie protested anxiously. "We go swimming at home and you cook chicken. You know how I like it, without the gravy touching."

"Maddie, listen," Rose said gently, crouching down next to her frightened daughter, keeping her hands carefully folded to her own body so as not to panic her further. "Just for now things will be a little bit different. But it will be OK, you'll see. I'll protect you. I know it's hard, I know you don't like things to be different. But trust me, I promise I won't let anything bad happen to you."

"That's what Daddy said," Maddie muttered. "He lied."

"I've been thinking." Jenny appeared at the door without any warning and beckoned to Maddie. Rose wondered irritatedly how long she had been standing outside. "You are right, madam, what *is* the point of a doll's house that no one plays with? My great-grandfather made it, you know, in his spare time for his daughters. I used to play and play with it when I was a girl, but other than Haleigh my lot never showed any interest, so I had my Brian make me a display case for it so that I didn't have to dust it every day. Would you like to play with it this morning, while Mummy is out and about? I can open it up just for you."

"Thank you but—" Rose was about to explain to Jenny that Maddie did not like to be left with strangers, but her daughter cut across her.

"Yes, thank you, I would," she said, the model of good manners.

"Are you sure, sweetheart?" Rose asked her a little warily.

"Yes," Maddie said confidently. "I really like miniature things, don't I, Mummy? And I would like to do something that isn't thinking about home."

"Are you sure?" Rose asked Jenny. "I mean, babysitting's outside your remit, isn't it?"

"Yes, it is," Jenny said, making it clear how very kind she was being, before her expression softened a little. "But, well, I haven't seen my grandsons for getting on for a year. Haleigh's on the other side of the world and can't even be bothered to email. And I don't know what is going on with you two, but I don't like to see a child look as lost as that one. It'll be nice for me to spend a bit of time with a little 'un. And when you get back, you can tell me all about how it went and when you are going to see your dad and what you are going to say to him."

Rose smiled. She found Jenny's motivation of sheer nosiness much easier to accept than her sudden gesture of kindness, although she had to concede Jenny *was* being kind, and she obviously did worry about Maddie, caught in the middle of some drama she could only guess at.

"I will be fine, Mummy, with the miniature things," Maddie assured her. "I don't want to go. I'm not sure I will like it."

"Well, OK," Rose said, wondering if she would ever understand her daughter. "I will just be down the road. If you need me you can call me . . ." Rose thought of her mobile phone, which lay dormant in her pocket. She really had no desire to switch it back on, to see the number of calls from Richard that she had missed, listen to his messages, or read his texts. He would be angry with her, that much was a given, and everything that had happened to drive her out of the door, that would be her fault, he'd be adamant about that. The trouble was, Rose thought, there was a good chance he might be right.

"Love," Jenny said, brushing her concerns away, "the pub's five minutes down the road. If I need you, I'll phone Ted and he can give you a shout."

"Ted?" Rose had visions of some ancient local who was permanently situated in the corner of the bar, slowly sipping a pint of real ale and stuffing his pipe.

"My middle one. He's a live-in barman over there—not a proper job, but he likes it. Keeps him in beer money while he works on being a rock star. One day he'll grow up and realize life isn't about having fun, although God knows his father never has."

"Ted." Rose smiled. "I'll look out for him."

"Oh, you won't have to," Jenny said, pursing her lips and looking Rose up and down in her new get-up. "He'll find you like a shot."

• • •

The Bull was quiet when Rose pushed her way in through the door. A traditional pub with flagstone flooring, ancient-looking furnishings, and walls still stained with nicotine, it was almost empty at midday except for a couple of hikers and an old lady sitting in the corner sipping beer from a bottle. Just as Jenny had told her, another reproduction of John Jacobs's painting of Millthwaite hung over the impressive stone mantelpiece that surrounded a cold grate, and a young man, possibly Ted, was leaning over the bar, examining a magazine.

"Ted?" Rose approached the bar, smiling uncertainly.

Ted looked up, grinning wickedly. "Rose! I've been waiting for you all my life."

"How did you . . . ?"

"Mum texted me that you were on your way," he told her warmly. "I'm to try and listen in on your conversation and find out what you want with Albie. Don't worry, I don't care what you're doing here, unless you are planning to ask me out for a drink, in which case the answer is yes, day after tomorrow is my night off, although I am gigging, but you can come and be my groupie."

"I beg your pardon?" Rose half spluttered, half laughed, uncertain if he was teasing her or not.

"Sorry," Ted said, smiling ruefully. "I was trying to be funny. I do play in a band, though, that much is true. And there's a live music night on. If you've got nothing on you should come down and check me out. Once a girl's seen me sing, she's powerless to resist my charms."

Rose blinked at him.

"Trying to be funny again," Ted said. "And failing again."

Ted was indeed quite charming to look at. In his early twenties and brimming with confidence, he had Jenny's coppery brown hair, which he wore with a long fringe that flopped into his brown eyes, and a swagger that he shouldered as confidently as his pristine white shirt, which was unbuttoned down to at least the middle of his chest.

"Well, as I am very far from being a girl, I think I'll turn down your invite, as friendly as it was," Rose said, unable to hide her amusement. "And you are quite funny, although probably not in the way that you intended."

"Ouch!" Ted grinned, holding his hands over his heart. "OK, I can take rejection. For now. But for the record, you look like a girl to me, Rose. So, you want to see Albie, right?"

"Yes, please," Rose said, her heart rate picking up as she looked around her. Unconsciously her fingers closed around the phone in her jeans pocket. Richard might be trying to phone her now; he might be trying to find out where she'd gone, if she'd told anyone. He'd be so angry, so frustrated that she wasn't within his reach, so furious that he'd lost control of the situation, and of her. And, oddly, it gave Rose a sense of real discomfort knowing that she was somewhere in the world where Richard could not reach her. He'd been there every day of her life since she was eighteen years old. And yet now here she was, standing in this pub, hundreds of miles away from her husband, hoping to make contact with the only man she had ever met in her life, albeit fleetingly, who'd made her feel . . . so much.

"Nice to meet you, Rose." Albie, who was an athletic-looking man in his late middle age, and not at all what Rose expected from a village landlord, extended his hand across the bar.

"Did Jenny text you too?" Rose smiled, taking his hand.

"She's not been this excited since Mrs. Harkness's au pair got knocked up by Mr. Harkness," Albie told her with a wry smile. "Poor old Jenny, she lives for news in a place where almost nothing ever happens."

"Except to you," Rose said. "An art dealer walks in off the street and gives you ten thousand pounds?"

"Well, he didn't give it to me. He got my painting in return, which was worth a lot more than ten grand."

"Were you upset," Rose asked him, "when you heard how much he sold it for?"

Albie shook his head, "Frasier—that's the dealer—called me up when it sold. Gave me another five, a finder's fee. He offered, I never asked for it. And I thought, well, you can't say fairer than that, can you?"

Rose's heart leapt at the sound of Frasier's name so casually dropped into the conversation. She attempted to collect herself.

"No . . . so do you have his number, Frasier's? His contact details, I mean."

"I do." Albie nodded, crossing his arms.

"Well, she wants you to give it her, you old fool," Ted said, rolling his eyes at Rose.

"Oh, right, of course. Wait there a minute, love."

Albie had to duck to make it under the low threshold that led to whatever room lay beyond the bar.

"So what's this Frasier got that I haven't?" Ted said casually, leaning a little closer to Rose. "You know, apart from tons of money and a flash car. Oh, and hair that looks like it gets done in a salon, darling."

"You know him?" Rose asked, intrigued.

"He comes in," Ted said with a shrug. "Listen, I've seen him and I've seen me, and I'm thinking if you want a holiday romance, then I'm your best bet. I'm younger, I've got more stamina, you see."

"You're hilarious." Rose laughed, finding it easy to warm to the young man who seemed intent on mischief, his eyes dancing with suppressed laughter. "Life around here must be very dull if you have to throw yourself at old ladies like me. Or is that how you get extra tips?"

"I work under the basic delusion that I am irresistible to all women." Ted grinned at her. "I won't lie, it mostly leads to disappointment, but I'm a glass-half-full sort of bloke. And you are not old. You are very pretty."

"Do you mind?" Rose snapped, turning her face away from him, feeling suddenly acutely uncomfortable under his gaze, trained by years of disapproval to shy away from any kind of male attention.

"Sorry!" Ted apologized, caught off guard by her discomfort. "I didn't mean to fluster you. I was just trying to have a laugh. I'm an idiot. Everyone says so."

"I'm not flustered, I'm thirty-one," Rose assured him, angry more at herself for overreacting to his lightheartedness than she was at him. Richard always got so angry if he thought other men were paying her attention, furious if he even suspected that she liked it. The fear of being seen talking to any male had been drummed into her so hard that it was difficult not to react now in exactly the way that Richard had taught her. Taking a breath, she steadied herself. "I'm just not here to flirt with a boy like you, that's all."

"I'm twenty-four," Ted told her, tipping his head to one side, perplexed by her strong reaction. "Seven years, that's not too big an age gap, is it? Look, I'm sorry. I've obviously upset you. I never meant to. I'm not evil, really; I'm a nice bloke."

"Don't believe the hype," Albie said as he returned, clutching a piece of paper. "Ted here is all talk and no trousers. I keep waiting for him to leave and get a proper job, but he still seems to be here."

"You love me." Ted grinned at Albie, patting him on the back. "The day me and the band finally go to London is the day your takings drop like a stone."

"I'll risk it," Albie said cheerfully.

"Seriously, though," Ted told Rose, his dark eyes sparkling with a charm he was acutely aware of, "anything I can do to help while you're here—show you round, put you in touch with people, take you out—then let me know. I don't bite, I promise. Not unless you ask me to."

"I don't think so, but thank you," Rose said, utterly at a loss as to why Ted would be so interested in her.

"Here you go, love." Albie handed out a page torn from a notebook, which Rose took with trembling fingers. Along with a couple of contact numbers and an email address, Albie had written: "Frasier McCleod—Dealer" and "Agent in Fine Art—Edinburgh." "But I was thinking, you don't have to go over the border to see him. He'll be at your dad's later this week."

"What?" Rose blinked, any trace of color that Ted's clumsy attempts at flirting had ignited in her complexion quickly draining away.

"Oh, yeah. Frasier's up there most weeks, more sometimes. He's his agent, isn't he? He keeps old John on the straight and narrow. It was Frasier who found him Storm Cottage and helped him get sober. I'm not going to say that wasn't a sad day for me—I never get any pleasure out of serving a man a glass of tap water—but still Frasier takes care of him. And he often pops in here for some refreshment, so you're bound to run into him sooner or later."

Chapter Three

The day that Rose first and last met Frasier McCleod, the house had been quiet, as it always was midafternoon. Richard would be at the surgery until at least six, if not much later, and Rose found herself with very little to do now that the maternity leave had kicked in and she was only a few weeks away from becoming a mother. Rose had wanted to go on working part time as his receptionist for longer, but Richard was adamant. Every day he checked her blood pressure, her urine, looking for signs that she was doing too much. In the end it had been neither of those things that had compelled him to send her home for what might quite possibly be for good, if he had his way. It was her swollen ankles.

Richard said he refused to be the kind of man who worked his pregnant wife so hard that her ankles ballooned up like an old woman's. What would people think of him if she looked all puffy and swollen, when they must know that she didn't need to work? Rose had thought that actually she did need to work, she did need to do anything that wasn't being at home, walking around the house looking for something to polish. But she hadn't said anything out loud, because she knew that Richard was only trying to do what he thought was best for her and their baby, and that was something she should be grateful for.

That morning had been the end of Rose's second week at home, and after she'd cleaned the already spotless house, prepped for dinner, put away the laundry, and made herself walk down to the seafront and back, in the searing heat of a late August day, she still found herself with several hours of nothing to do except trying to imagine the house, her childhood house, which had become hers when her mother died, full of a child's—her child's—laughter again. Somehow it seemed impossible that this place, where she had once been so happy, would ever be a place of light and love again. The deep sadness that was never very far from the surface welled up inside her once again, quiet tears rolling down her cheeks, and she cradled her belly, simultaneously longing for her baby to hold in her arms and yet wanting to keep her safe from all the unpleasantness that the world could contain, that this house could contain.

When the doorbell sounded, Rose hesitated, wiping the tears away with the edge of her sleeve, peering out the living room door to look at the silhouetted figure behind the stained glass. Richard did not like her to answer the door to cold callers, who he said were con men at best, or downright predators and thieves at worst. Nor did he like people to see her upset, telling her their private business was theirs alone and not to be shared with gossips.

And yet it was only just gone three; Rose had hours of silence stretching ahead of her before Richard got home. Hours more like this, overwhelmed and helpless by the emotions that racked her body. And, after all, before Richard had sacked her, she had, in her time, maneuvered drunks, drug addicts, and determined old ladies out of the surgery, so what harm could a salesman do her? Richard underestimated her, Rose was all too aware of that. It wasn't exactly that she wanted to show him he was wrong—far from it—but she liked to show herself every once in a while, just to remind herself who she really was.

Tucking a strand of hair behind her ear, she squared her shoulders and opened the door, shielding most of her body, allowing just her head and shoulders to show. And there were several seconds when she and Frasier just looked at each other, as if they had each just come across a very old friend. That's how it was in her memory.

"Are you OK?" were the first words that Frasier McCleod ever spoke to her, his soft well-spoken Scottish accent melodic and gentle. "Have you been crying?"

"Oh?" Rose touched her hand to her face, caught off guard by his unfamiliar concern. "No, no. Not crying. Not really. I've got a cold, that's all."

Frasier studied her face for a moment longer, his clear green eyes so compelling that Rose did not turn away from his gaze, as she was used to doing with men. Instead she let him look at her, as she looked at him, finding some solace in the concern on his face. How long had it been since anyone had regarded her that way?

"Can I help you?" Rose said after a few moments, prompting Frasier to collect himself as if he were waking from a trance.

"I'm sorry to bother you, I'm an art dealer . . ." He handed her his card. "I'm trying to find the whereabouts of an artist called John Jacobs? I don't know if you are aware, but he lived here for a while, in the late eighties. It's a bit of a long shot, but I was hoping perhaps you might have some contact details for the previous owners?"

Rose looked at the card. "You've come all the way from Edinburgh to knock on my door?" she asked him, looking up with a tentative smile. It seemed so ludicrous, and yet here he was, and she discovered she was glad of it. Glad to hear his voice, and see his face, its expression that reminded her she still existed in the world beyond these doors.

"Yes." Frasier smiled ruefully in return. "I found a piece by him recently, picked it up at auction. Sold it on for ten times what I paid. I've been looking into him and there's a growing interest in his work, so I know it sounds mad but, believe it or not, this is what I do. I chase hunches around the country hoping to make that one great find that's going to change my life."

Rose remembered the ease with which she could look into his pale green, almost aqua eyes. There was something about him that seemed inherently decent and kind. Which were strange things to notice first about a man—the kindness, the gentleness that showed in the contours of his face, the way he spoke, softly, hesitantly—when there were so many more obvious things to admire: his flaxen hair, his height and broad, safe-looking shoulders, the fullness of his mouth, the easy elegance of his hands. But all those things seemed secondary compared to the qualities that Rose discovered she was unexpectedly drawn to, taking enormous pleasure in feeling so instantly comfortable with another person.

"John Jacobs is my father," she told him, secretly thrilled by his expression of amazement and delighted to be so connected to his object of interest. "He lived here, with me and my mother, until I was nine. When he left, Mum got the house, and when she died, her life insurance paid off the mortgage and it became mine."

"Rose." Frasier breathed her name in wonder, making the tiny hairs on the back of her neck bristle. "You must be Rose. I never expected to find you here."

"You know my name?" Rose felt a little unnerved.

"Know it?" Frasier smiled at her. "I've dreamt your name every night for weeks."

There was a moment between them, a moment when Rose thought that maybe he'd come here to find her after all, and, perhaps seeing the hope in her face, Frasier had been anxious to put her right.

"Here." Frasier reached into a briefcase he was carrying and drew out a photocopied sheet. "It's a sketch. I bought it on eBay for a few hundred pounds. A sketch of a painting by your father."

A little reluctantly, Rose reached through the gap in the door and took the piece of paper, looking at the drawing, a tangle of thick, black, chaotic lines that somehow came together as a drawing of a small girl, leaning her chin on her hand as she peered out of the window. The title of the drawing was *Dearest Rose*.

"It's drawn with such love," Frasier said, taking a step closer so that they could look at it together. "I assumed that Rose had to be his daughter, although there is barely any biographical information about him. I only know that he lived here because I found a clipping in the local press about an incident where he was arrested for being drunk and disorderly."

"That sounds like Dad," Rose said, unable to look at the image anymore. "Look, come in. I'll tell you what I know about John Jacobs, but honestly, it isn't very much. I haven't heard from him since the day he left."

Rose pulled open the door and saw the look of surprise on Frasier's face when he saw the swell of her belly.

"You're pregnant," he said quietly. "Very, very pregnant. Congratulations."

"Thank you," Rose said, feeling self-conscious of her girth as she led him toward the kitchen. "I can't say I really believe it, even now. I'm not sure I will know what to do or how to be a mother. Everyone says it's instinct, but I don't know how it can be. I don't feel any instinct now. Just . . . oh, so many things. I get overwhelmed sometimes by it all."

"Is that why you were crying when you opened the door?" Frasier asked her carefully, as he studied the generic prints with which Richard lined the walls of the hallway as they made their way to the kitchen at the back of the house. The house, as it was then, was so different from the one of Rose's childhood. Then, it had been an explosion of chaos and color, her father's work very often painted directly onto the wall, as well as hanging in every possible space. Now each room was painted in varying shades of beige, white, and cream. It had been one of the first things that Richard had done after they were married, as if he were determined to erase any trace of Rose's life before she became his wife, and Rose had been glad of it, glad of the serenity of the blank canvas that her husband had made for her. Wrinkling his nose a little, Frasier redirected his gaze to her once more. "Were you crying because all of this overwhelms you?"

Rose nodded, sensing she didn't need to explain to Frasier what "all of this" was, that somehow he just knew; he simply understood her. It was the strangest feeling to be standing in her kitchen with a man she'd only just met and feeling the strongest sense of peace and belonging that she'd had since she was a very small girl. It had to be that her aching heart was clutching at straws, clinging to any glimmer of kindness, even polite concern, and blowing it out of all proportion. And yet that wasn't how it felt. To Rose it felt like she had somehow discovered her soul mate standing on the doorstep.

Feeling strangely elated, Rose filled the kettle, gesturing for Frasier to take a seat at the table. She thought of Richard, sitting in his office at the surgery, nodding sympathetically at old ladies, diagnosing the common cold over and over again.

If he could see her now . . . Rose found herself smiling at her act of quiet rebellion, at the joy she was finding in this unexpected encounter.

Sitting down, she passed a cup of tea to Frasier.

"I haven't seen Dad since he left us," she repeated. "When he went, the house, the studio at the back, was full of his work. One night Mum had a bonfire. It was the first Christmas after he went, I think. She put all of his stuff that she could find in a huge pile in the middle of the lawn, poured a load of lighter fuel over it, and burnt it to a crisp. There was nothing left, and if this painting was in that pile then it's gone now."

The look of pain on Frasier's face as he listened to her story was palpable.

"All that work, up in flames, it's sacrilege," he said quietly.

"I suppose you would see it like that," Rose said. It hadn't occurred to her before how sad it was that all she had left of her father had been so wantonly destroyed, but then she'd never seen him the way that Frasier obviously did, as a talented, intriguing man. A man to be admired and revered. Rose had only loved him and lost him, been left with the destruction he'd dealt in his wake. Suddenly, she wanted very much for Frasier to understand why her mother had done what she had. "Life was very difficult for us, alone. For Mum especially. She loved him so much; she gave up a lot to be with him—her life, her family, who never approved of him. When he left, when he threw all that back in her face, he hurt her so badly she never recovered. She'd put a brave face on it—or at least she'd try to every now and then—but in the end she just couldn't go on without him. I think she started to kill herself the day he left. It took her eight more years to finish the job, but she did it in the end. Burning the paintings was part of that. An expression of her pain."

As she finished speaking, Rose unconsciously rested the fingers of her right hand over her mouth, unable to remember the last time she'd spoken so many words at all to anyone, even Richard, let alone words of such an intensely personal nature. She felt she'd better stop herself from talking somehow, before she said more than she should to this strange man she felt so compelled by and frightened him away.

Frasier was silent for a moment, his long fingers wrapped around the mug of tea. "Are you saying your mother died of a broken heart?" he asked Rose quietly.

"I suppose I am," Rose said from between her fingers, her gaze directed inwardly as she remembered that last day with her mother. Marian had been so happy, as if the weight of the world had suddenly been lifted off her shoulders, and she was finally able to be at peace. She had persuaded Rose to skip school, and the two of them had gone for a walk along the seafront, stopping for ice cream and to play the games in the arcade. Rose had gone to sleep that night believing that at last the storm clouds that had plagued Marian for so long were clearing, sleeping truly peacefully for the first time in months. When she'd got up the next morning and found Marian had already gone out, Rose hadn't given it much thought. And she hadn't been that concerned when her mum still wasn't home when she got in from school. It had been just after eleven that night, just as Rose was wondering about whether or not she should tell someone her mother hadn't been at home all day, when the doorbell sounded, and a very kind policewoman told her that her mother's body had been washed ashore a few miles down the coast. She was wearing a swimming costume; there had been no note. So they had every reason to believe it was a simple, tragic accident. But Rose knew that her mother had walked into the sea that morning without ever planning to come back, and she realized that the final perfect day they had spent together was Marian's goodbye gift to her daughter.

"I'm so sorry, Rose." Frasier's voice made her start, as his fingers slid across the table towards hers, stopping millimeters away from making contact.

"Don't be." Rose smiled weakly, retrieving her hand from the proximity of Frasier's and resting it on the crest of her tummy. "The way I look at it, the best thing I can do for this baby is to make sure that I don't live life like my mum, don't let my circumstances beat me down. Don't get me wrong, she was an amazing person and a really great mother—no one could have loved me more than she did—but I never wanted to be caught forever in the things that have happened to me. I don't want to be the victim. My dad is a prick and my mum is gone, but I don't have to be ruined by that. Not at all."

Neither one of them spoke for a moment and, a little flustered by the unexpected passion that had overtaken her as she spoke, Rose looked away from Frasier, feeling the heat in her cheeks. Everything she had told him was true, but she hadn't known exactly how she felt until just that moment. She certainly had never had the guts to say it out loud. Here she was, trapped in this immaculate kitchen, with Richard's baby in her womb, and the rest of her life, a successful life, mapped out for her. And yet Rose wanted to scream out loud, she felt so imprisoned.

"You are a remarkable person, Rose," Frasier said, tentatively reaching out again, this time touching her arm. "I turn up here unannounced, looking for the man that's hurt you so badly, and you ask me in, give me tea and . . . well, show me how life should be lived."

"Not really." Rose twisted her mouth into a wry knot. "I'm sorry I just got a bit carried away, and I haven't been at all useful about helping you find Dad."

"You have," Frasier said, watching her intently, his fingers resting on her bare skin. "You've reminded me that art is just that. It's not real life. Sometimes I'm afraid I do get rather carried away and forget that."

"But you will keep looking for him?" Rose asked him, hopeful, for some reason that she didn't really understand, that he would. Perhaps because as long as he was looking for her father, he might still think of her from time to time, and she would like that very much.

"I will," Frasier said with certainty. "In my experience, being a terrible person rarely stops you from being a brilliant artist. And I care about the work too much to let it go unnoticed. If I do find him, do you want me to let you know where he is or tell him about you?"

Rose shook her head without hesitation, the thought of having to face John again after all these years unbearable.

"No, no. I'm done with him and he's done with me, and that's the way I want to keep it," she said, quietly adamant.

Frasier nodded, looking regretful.

"My father loves to fish, he loves it more than he loves breathing, I think sometimes," he said, as if casting around for something personal to share with her in exchange. "Fly-fishing is his thing, standing up to his waist in waders in the loch, do you know what I mean?" Rose nodded, smiling. "Every few weeks I go home to see my folks. Mum cooks for five thousand, even though there are only three of us, and Dad and I fish. And I bloody hate fishing. I hate the water, the hooks, the mess, the cold, the boredom, I don't even like fish. But I still go, because Dad loves fishing and it's the only thing we do together." Frasier looked a little perplexed. "And I don't know why I told you that."

"I'm glad that you did," Rose said, smiling, glancing up at

the clock as she always did, habitually checking the minutes she had left until Richard got home.

"Well, I'd better go." Frasier stood up, taking it as a hint. "It's been so nice to meet you." He took her hand on impulse, holding it for a few moments.

"You too," Rose said, pulling her fingers from his with some effort, walking hurriedly to the door, anxious that he shouldn't see the bright spots of color that were flaring on her cheeks.

"Good, that's us officially friends, then," Frasier beamed at her, diffusing the sadness and tension in an instant.

Rose laughed, not realizing in nearly enough time that he was leaning forward to kiss her on the cheek. It was the briefest of kisses, over in one fraction of a chaste second, the warmth of his lips grazing her skin for the shortest of moments, and yet it made her heart pound.

"Goodbye, dearest Rose," Frasier said and, seeing Rose's eyes widen in alarm, added, "The sketch title, I will always think of you as 'dearest Rose' now. You may think of me however you choose, or not at all, I wouldn't blame you."

"I think that I've been very glad to meet you," Rose said a little formally. "Goodbye, Frasier."

Her heart had been light with happiness as she had closed the door on him, leaning back against it, forcing herself to take a little time to work out what had just happened. Rose believed she might have flirted just a little, although it had been a long time since, as a teen, she used to bat her lashes at the boys on the promenade and flick her hair over her shoulder to make them look at her. No, it hadn't been flirting, it had been a . . . connection. A moment of contact with another person who wasn't Richard, or the people he worked with, one of the very small number of people that Rose came across in her daily life, and that was what had been so exhilarating. That, and the way he'd held her hand and kissed her on the cheek. Rose had found herself laughing out loud, humming as she danced back to the kitchen, carefully washing and drying the teacups and returning them to the cupboard. Smoothing her hands over her smocked top, she had smiled to herself as she turned round to examine the kitchen, returning the chair Frasier had sat on to its exact position. Which was when it hit her that nothing, actually nothing at all, had changed. So why did it feel like everything had?

Chapter Four

"We thought you might like to join us for dinner," Jenny said as soon as Rose let herself in through the front door.

"Dinner?" Rose said. "Are you sure?"

It was a kind offer, but Rose suspected it had more to do with Jenny's insatiable need to find out everything about John Jacobs's long-lost daughter than it did with being benevolent.

"Yes," Maddie said, appearing behind Jenny, wearing an oversized apron. "We are making dumplings, Mummy. I don't even know what a dumpling is. It looks quite icky."

"Have you ever heard the like?" Jenny muttered, shaking her head and returning to the kitchen, with Maddie trotting behind.

"So was everything OK?" Rose called after them, pausing by the living room, where the door of the glass cabinet that encompassed the doll's house was still open, as was the front of the house itself. Tiny lights twinkled, and Maddie had taken great care arranging tiny people around a dining room table laden with pretend food.

"Fine," Jenny said, as Rose joined them in the busy kitchen. "Speaks as she finds, your Maddie. I like that in a person."

"Yes, she can be rather candid," Rose said, thinking of

Maddie's innate ability to rub people the wrong way in seconds, never shying away from pointing out that they were fat or short, or badly dressed in her opinion. It had been funny when she was two and three and four, but now that she was seven people were a little less forgiving.

"Was it amazing playing with the doll's house?" Rose asked Maddie, squeezing the little girl's shoulders as she stood on a stool, crumbling butter and flour together. Maddie shrugged her touch off, just as she usually did.

"It was," Maddie said. "They are having dinner now, and then later they are going to watch TV, although there isn't a TV, but Jenny says Brian will make one when he gets in."

"Oh, well, I'm sure there's no need to bother him . . ."

"He'll make one," Jenny assured her. "Thirty years of marriage, he's learnt what's good for him."

"And you didn't miss me?" Rose said. "Or get worried?"

"No," Maddie said, completely blasé. "I don't worry when things are interesting, and things were very interesting. I like Jenny, she talks a lot and is quite bossy, but she is mainly nice. I told her all about Daddy."

"Did you?" Rose said uncertainly.

"Speaks as she finds," Jenny repeated, raising a brow as she browned what Rose assumed were cubes of beef in a pan. Just what had Maddie told her? Had she said anything about those last few minutes at home before she'd been forced to leave? Rose didn't think so. The things that Maddie found the most distressing were also the things she studiously ignored, determined to act as if they didn't exist. And if Jenny knew, then there would be no way she'd be able to refrain from letting Rose know.

"So how did you get on with my Ted?" Jenny asked.

"He's very . . . boisterous," Rose said, not sure how to describe her first encounter with Ted.

"He's a waste of space, that's what he is," Jenny said fondly, rolling her eyes at Maddie. "How he's got to his age without getting a proper job and a proper girlfriend, I'll never know. He's too good-looking, that's his trouble. My oldest, he looks like his dad, so there was never going to be a problem there. And Haleigh, well, she's a right looker, the spit of me, and she's got a good head on her shoulders, like her mother. The trouble with Ted is he's a dreamer, a romantic, always waiting for the love of his life to walk through the door. He pretends he's all bluster and front, but really he's a sensitive soul, my Ted, even if he does have too much of a nice time, working in that pub, messing around with his so-called band."

"What's a right looker?" Maddie asked her.

"Someone who's pretty, like you," Jenny said, flicking a smudge of flour onto the end of Maddie's nose, which the child vigorously wiped off at once.

"I don't think that you are a right—"

"He really is very handsome," Rose said, preventing Maddie from speaking in the nick of time, even if sounding somewhat inappropriately overenthused about Jenny's son.

"Well, you wouldn't be the first married woman he's had dealings with." Jenny pursed her lips, more than a hint of pride mixed in with the disapproval. "My Brian had to stand between Ted and Ian Wilkins and his shotgun for fifteen minutes, talking him down from castrating the lad. It was the talk of the town for months."

"Oh, I don't mean that *I'm* attracted to him . . ." Rose said, horrified, realizing a little too late that Jenny clearly expected every woman with a pulse to be exactly that, and that any other response was simply bad manners.

"Well, most are," Jenny said, clearly a little offended that Rose hadn't been more overwhelmed. "Anyway, get peeling those apples. I'm thinking of making a crumble."

"I look forward to meeting this Ted," Maddie said. "He sounds most interesting."

As it turned out, Maddie didn't have long to wait to meet Jenny's younger son, as he turned up uninvited for dinner, grinning at Rose as he appeared around the dining room door.

"All right, Mum?" he said, just as Jenny was serving up beef stew and dumplings. "Room for a little one?"

"Oh, yes, and to what do we owe this pleasure?" Jenny asked him, tucking her chin in. "You haven't been round for your dinner in weeks, and then you just stroll in off the street, treating the place like a—"

"B and B? Thought I'd pop in, say hello to my lovely mother, that's all," Ted said, putting his arms around Jenny and kissing her on the cheek, making her giggle like a girl.

"Get on with you," she chided him. "Sit down and don't be rude to our guests. You've met Rose, and this is her daughter, Maddie."

"Hiya." Ted smiled at Maddie, who observed him from beneath her fringe, clearly feeling it wasn't necessary to return the greeting.

Unoffended, Ted grinned across the table at Rose, who couldn't help returning the smile. He looked like he was always in on some private joke, a smile constantly playing round his eyes and lips. Maybe it was her he was laughing at in her mutton clothes, Rose thought, self-consciously pulling up the off-the-shoulder top again. It had been a long time since she wondered what anyone, let alone men, thought of her, mostly because she was certain that they didn't think of her at all, not as an individual. She was the doctor's wife, the odd child's mother, the nice one behind reception. Now, of course, putting aside the dreadful mess that she had left behind, pretending it didn't exist in exactly the same way as Maddie did, Rose realized she had no idea how men—how Frasier—would see her, or what he would think of her, dropping everything and following him on a whim. He'd think she was insane, someone he'd met briefly years ago who was fixated and obsessed, and he'd be right. Acutely aware of her situation, Rose watched Maddie chewing her way diligently through beef stew, scowling at Ted. This wasn't right, dragging her this far from home on such a spurious whim. This was not Rose, this wasn't how she did things. Rose always did the right thing, the best thing, the safest thing. This was none of those. She couldn't go on pretending nothing had happened, because soon there would be consequences. It was more than twenty-four hours now since she'd left Richard. He could be calling the police, reporting her missing. Very soon the real world would be crashing after her, catching up with her and forcing her to face what she had done.

"How's work, son?" Brian asked Ted, glancing up from finishing the matchbox that he was meticulously turning into a TV with the aid of some silver foil and a black marker. "They're looking for some summer help over in Keswick, you know."

"Work's fine, Dad. We had a hen night last week. Those girls were scary. At one point I thought they were going to rip me to shreds," Ted said, inhaling the scent of the food that his mother set before him. "Besides, I can't do manual work. Got to look after these hands; they're going to make us a fortune one day."

"How?" Maddie asked him, testing a dumpling with the tip of her tongue and then carefully placing it on her side plate.

"With my music." Ted grinned at her. "I'm going to conquer the world with my song!"

"Which song? What does it go like?" Maddie said.

"Well, when I say song, I mean all of my songs, my entire opus," Ted told her.

"Hum one," Maddie said. "Hum a song."

"Maddie," Rose began, knowing how tenacious her daughter could be when she got her teeth into something. "Leave Ted alone."

"I'm just saying, if he's going to take over the world with a song then it had better be a really good one . . ."

"Anyway," Ted said, "what are you two girls up to tomorrow?"

Rose looked at Maddie, who returned her gaze.

"What are we up to?" she asked, suddenly unsettled.

"Nothing yet, especially," Rose said. "I've got a few more things to do here, and then . . ." Rose had no idea about the "and then" part. What would it change if she went to see her father, or if she met Frasier McCleod again? And as for what would happen afterwards, what she and Maddie would do next, Rose didn't have the courage to think about that.

"I could take you out for a sightseeing trip," Ted offered. "Not got much on in the afternoon. We can go up the mountain, look at the view and stuff."

"I don't like walking much," Maddie said.

Ted looked at her, nodding. "I know what you mean, but the thing is, walking up a mountain isn't the same as walking to school or to the shops. It's like walking in the clouds. And like you are looking down on a world of ants."

"I do like miniature things," Maddie conceded thoughtfully. "And clouds."

"So pick you up at lunch?" Ted nodded at Rose, who really could not understand why this strange young man would be so keen to spend time with a married woman and her daughter. Maybe Jenny had put him up to this; perhaps she was deploying him as her secret information-gathering weapon.

"I could pack us a picnic," Ted went on. "One I've prepared myself, something to save you from the terrible food you'll get here."

He winked at his mother and earned a stiff punch in the arm for his cheek.

"Brian, say something!" Jenny told her husband, who set a perfect miniature television down in front of a delighted Maddie.

"Say what, woman?" Brian grumbled. "It's your fault he's like this. You've always been too soft on him and now he thinks he's God's gift."

"I'm just being friendly!" Ted protested.

"It's why you're being friendly that worries me. If you were a real man," Jenny scolded Brian, "he wouldn't have grown up so unruly."

Brian chuckled, shaking his head as he tucked into his dinner, entirely unoffended by Jenny's jibes. "Only a real man could be married to you for thirty years, my love. You ask anyone hereabouts and they'll tell you, I'm a hero."

"And what's that supposed to mean?" Jenny exclaimed, half cross, half laughing.

"It means you're damn lucky I agreed to marry you all those years ago," Brian told her with an affectionate smile. "Disagreeable old bird that you are."

"That is more true than the 'right looker' thing." Maddie nodded in agreement, apparently entertained by the friendly banter, even though this was the sort of gentle joking and teasing within a family that neither Rose nor her daughter were used to. Cross words at home were always cross, and barbed comments were always meant to be cruel. It came as something of a welcome surprise to Rose that Maddie seemed completely at home and relaxed here. Her precious book was looking neglected on the bed upstairs, and even

Bear was looking rather put out as he sat unattended on the sofa in the living room, staring unblinkingly at the TV.

"I think," Rose said, interrupting a kiss between husband and wife that Maddie thought was hilariously revolting, "I think that, actually, tomorrow I will be busy."

"And that's the brush-off!" Brian said, slapping Ted on the shoulder.

"No, it's not that," Rose said. "It's just I came here for a reason, and I don't know how long I've got to see it through."

"You make it sound like you're on a deadline," Ted said, tilting his head curiously.

"I am, sort of," Rose said. "And so I think tomorrow I'd better just do it. I'd better just go and see my father."

Rose had not come here to find her father; she had come chasing a specter, a half-dreamt ideal that might be as far away from reality as her hundreds and hundreds of daydreams of Frasier. And yet, here her father was, real and solid and for certain, and he couldn't very well be ignored, no matter how much she might want to. And somehow the prospect of seeing her father, which she knew would be painful and most likely disappointing, was not nearly as frightening as actually, really seeing Frasier, who in reality could be so very different from all the dreams that had sustained her for so long. Rose wasn't ready to find out if that was the case, not quite yet.

Rose left Maddie sitting on the floor of the small en-suite shower cubicle, with a drizzle of warm water pouring down on her, as she chatted away to Bear, who was sitting safely on the sink. Leaving the door into the bedroom open, Rose sat on the edge of her bed and switched on her phone. It chirruped angrily into life immediately, buzzing with a throng of text messages and her voice mail service ringing. Her stomach filling with dread, Rose collected her messages.

He had left the first one just after she had bundled Maddie into the car and gone. It was quiet, apologetic, reasonable, kind. There was that ever-present implication that she was overreacting again, that she was irrational, tired, doing too much, needed help.

"Just come home, darling," Richard's voice nestled in her ear. "Come home and let me take care of you. We can sort this out."

Rose deleted it and listened to the next message, and the next. He'd left more than twenty in all, filling her voice mail, each angrier and more frustrated than the last. Rose listened to a part of each and then deleted it, knowing what was coming next, knowing his patterns and habits inside out. For most of her married life she'd learnt to defuse his fury in its early stages, to back down, to agree, to nod and smile and keep her mouth shut. But this time she was not there, and her voice mail was taking the brunt of his wrath. Rose knew if she wanted to hear how her husband was really feeling then she needed to listen to his most recent message, left at seven twenty-two p.m., when they had been eating dinner. That's when the real Richard had finally shown his hand.

"I've had it with you this time, Rose." His voice was tight, thick with rage. "I try, and I try to deal with all your . . . stupidity, but this time you've gone too far. You can't take our child and disappear without expecting repercussions. Everyone *knows* that you haven't been yourself, everyone *knows* how difficult and unbalanced you are. And that Maddie has a delicate disposition. Let me tell you there are serious question marks over your fitness to be a parent. If you don't contact me today I will have no choice but to inform the police, and social services, if need be. Because believe me, Rose, I will find you and when I do, I'll make sure you never see Maddie again. You have until midnight, and if I haven't heard from you by then, well, gloves are off, Rose."

Stifling the sob of anxiety that clogged her throat, Rose deleted the call and stared at the phone sitting so benignly in the palm of her hand. This was how Richard always won, by persuading her she was being foolish, that she was overreacting, being irrational, seeing things all wrong, and finally, most recently, by implying that she was losing it altogether, that her fragile mind was finally cracking, disintegrating. She was the daughter of an alcoholic father and a suicidal mother, so it was hardly surprising really that her mental health was finally giving in to genetics, despite the care that Richard had taken of her.

"You see me as the enemy," Richard had said to her on that final afternoon. "But don't you see, Rose, you are your own worst enemy? Without me to protect you, you have no idea how to survive."

What if he was right? After all, here she was, hiding in a picture postcard, chasing a signature on a letter that was nothing more than a half-formed memory, a delusion. What if she was more like her mother than she ever realized? Anyone looking at this situation from the outside would be on Richard's side. She knew anyone sensible would be, and that's what frightened her the most. A trusted and respected GP, Richard had it well within his powers to carry out his threat to the letter, and the whole world would be on his side. And yet, there was *one* person who knew the truth.

Peering round the door to check that Maddie was still happy composing songs to conquer the world under the drizzle of the shower, Rose dialed the number of the only person in the world she could truly call a friend. She phoned Shona.

"Fuck's sake," Shona greeted her. "I thought he'd done for you. I thought you were under the floorboards, babe. I tried phoning you, but all it said was that your voice mail was full. Full of that shit, no doubt."

"How did you know I'd gone?" Rose asked. She'd had no plans to meet Shona that she hadn't turned up for; they rarely spoke on the phone or texted, always making their arrangements in person, face-to-face.

"He came here looking for you this morning," Shona told her. "All polite concern, sweetness and light, 'It's Maddie I'm worried about, Rose hasn't been herself for weeks, there's no telling what she might do,' and all that bollocks. I told him I haven't seen you in months, so why would I know anything about you?"

Rose wasn't sure when her friendship with Shona became a secret that both of them kept from their partners, she only knew that it seemed like the only way of keeping it intact. Richard didn't like her to have friends he didn't approve of, and as for Shona's boyfriend . . . he hated Rose with a passion, blaming her completely for his and Shona's breakup. Shona often joked that all the sneaking around they did to see each other was just as complicated as having an affair, and without any of the sex.

"So you've left him, then?" Shona said. "What happened to make you finally go, what did he do?"

"He . . ." Rose closed her eyes, images and words flashing behind them too quickly to make any sense, things she couldn't face seeing or hearing, even in memory, just yet. "I just couldn't take another minute. Before I knew what I was doing I had the car keys, Maddie and I were gone. He ran down the street after us. I didn't think it through, Sho. I just went and . . . and now I don't know what to do next."

The gnawing fear at the empty chasm that represented

Rose's future bit fiercely at her heart again, as Rose remembered she had nothing like a plan that stretched beyond the next few hours.

"I don't blame you for getting out. About time too," Shona said. She'd hated Richard from the moment she set eyes on him, more than fourteen years ago, when the two of them waitressed in Marley's Famous Ice-Cream Parlour on the front as teenagers, Shona a bolshie, mouthy, sexy girl with more front than the town, and Rose, an alternative, Gothic, odd-looking girl, with a scowl that could turn anything to stone. They shouldn't have hit it off; Rose, pale, thin and glowering in her candy-striped uniform, and buxom Shona nonchalantly making sure she left more buttons undone than she should, a surefire way of boosting her tips from harassed dads. And yet the two of them had become instant friends, making each other smile when they least expected it, and as Rose began to find her feet in the world as an adult, it was Shona who made her realize that her life wasn't going to be an endless stream of nights alone in her big empty house, that if she wanted it there would be travel, university, boys, fun, a whole world waiting for her whenever she was ready to explore it. That there was more to her than her family, more to her future than her past. It had been exactly at that moment of realization that Rose had met Richard and fallen madly in love with him. Within months she had left the café to get married. Caught up in her husband and the life he created for the two of them alone—where Rose existed only for him, where for most of those early years she had wanted to exist only for him, allowing him to decide they weren't ready for children, what she did, where she worked, what she wore, even how she felt and thought—Rose had embraced every single one of his desires willingly. As a consequence she had barely seen Shona for years. When they had come across each other again, it was at exactly the right time for both of them, each equally grateful and in need of the other, each changed by the life she'd learnt, too late, had conquered her instead of vice versa.

"I suppose he wants you to get in touch. Trot back home like a good little wifey."

"Yes," Rose said. That was something of an understatement.

"Where are you, babe?" Shona asked her softly, hesitantly, as if she didn't really want to know.

Rose understood her friend's reservations. Listening to Richard's messages and speaking to Shona was making all this real. Up until this point it had been a sort of a dream, a flit in the night, an eccentric landlady, finding her father and Frasier all at once. Even Maddie settling in and getting on with people she barely knew. It was as if as soon as she stepped away from Richard, her life just fell neatly into place, and everything was as it should be. But that wasn't how it was; she couldn't just pretend she hadn't been married for thirteen years and now she'd changed her mind. Richard was coming, he would find her, and when he did, Rose couldn't imagine what would happen next, but she knew it would be bad.

"If I tell you where I am, you'll think I'm insane."

"Well, according to your darling husband, that's a given," Shona said. "Where are you? Say it's somewhere good, without an extradition treaty."

"I'm in Millthwaite," Rose said, bracing herself.

"Millthwaite? Which part of the Costa del . . . fucking hell, Rose, you went to your fucking postcard!" Rose braced herself against the string of expletives that blasted into her ear, as Shona tried to come to terms with what she had done.

"Well, yes, I know but . . . I had to go somewhere, Shona, somewhere far away, and it was the only place I could think of."

"Not, you know, London or Leeds or New York?" Shona asked her, before adding, "*Millthwaite,* Rose? What, did you think Mr. Perfect, whatever his name is, would be sitting on a bench in the village green waiting for you?"

"Well, the thing is," Rose said, biting her lip, "he sort of is."

"What the fuck!" Shona exclaimed.

"He's in Millthwaite a lot . . . visiting my dad, who lives up the road."

"Did Dickhead give you those antipsychotic drugs he's been threatening you with?" Shona asked her, with her usual acidic bluntness.

Rose was used to Shona's way, knowing that no matter how harsh Shona might sound, it was only because she was, as far as Rose knew, the only person in the entire world who really cared about her. And that was Shona in a nutshell: she spent her life roaring at the world, but in reality there could not be a kinder, sweeter, more loyal, or more thoughtful best friend. It was just hard to spot that sometimes when Shona was in full sail.

"You know, the ones that make you hallucinate," Shona continued. "Are you sure you're in Millthwaite, not gibbering on the floor of the ladies' loo in some service stop, staring at your postcard?"

"I know it sounds crazy," Rose said, smiling at Shona's outrage. "It *is* crazy, isn't it? I came here expecting . . . well, nothing really. I just wanted to be here and not there. And they are both here. Frasier and my father."

"Fucking ridiculous," Shona said, sighing with obvious frustration. "Babe, this is only going to make things worse. This Frasier, he's not going to know who you are, and if he does, he's going to be freaked out by you. And as for your dad, well, I think you and I both know what he is, even if you have made me promise to stop using the C-word. He cut you out of his life and you've moved on without a second glance. How's any of this going to help you now, when you've finally got away from him? You need to be finding your feet, not setting yourself up to be knocked down. You've made a clean break, so make it a fresh start too and run away from your past, not back to it."

"So where should I go?" Rose asked. In her heart she knew Shona was most likely right, but Shona didn't understand everything. She had been the only person Rose had ever confided in about the postcard, about how much of an impression Frasier had made on her, but Rose couldn't tell even Shona how much he'd lived in her heart every single moment of every single day since. That was something too precious, too special, and quite possibly too insane to share with anyone, even Shona. "I can't come to you. I've got no family, no friends anywhere else that aren't really Richard's. Only the cash that's in my secret account to live on. My only family is here, even if I have found him by accident, even if I'm pretty sure I don't want to see him. This is a sign, right? This is the universe telling me in ten-foot-high neon-flashing letters exactly what to do. I can't ignore it."

"You can't handle this on your own," Shona said. "You're not strong enough."

"Now you're sounding like him," Rose said unhappily, hoping for more support from her friend. "I'm not crazy, Shona. I see what this looks like, but it's not how it is. You weren't there, you don't know how I feel. I've got to see Frasier again—I just have to—before I can do anything else. I'm not expecting anything to happen, or for him to sweep me into his arms and ask me where I've been all his life, but I have to see him. I have to know if what happened for me, happened for him too, because even if he's moved on and forgotten me, if I know it was real for him too, then I'll know. And I know there is something out there for me that's better than Richard."

"Hannibal Lecter would have been better than Richard," Shona said bitterly.

"What's wrong?" Rose asked her. "I mean apart from me and all this mess. Are you OK?"

Shona was silent, which could mean only one thing. Ryan was somehow back, wanting to be in her life again.

"What does he want?" Rose asked, her chest filling with heavy dread. The key difference between Shona and Rose was that Rose hadn't loved Richard for a long, long time, if she ever truly had. Shona never stopped loving Ryan, no matter what he did to her.

"He wants me back," Shona said quietly. "He wants another chance, he wants to give it a go. For us and the boys to be a family again."

"But you know that can never happen," Rose said slowly, to be sure that Shona was hearing her. "Not after the last time. He never changes, Sho."

"But he sounds so sad," Shona said softly, her strident tone now gentle, fragile almost. As far as Ryan was concerned she would always be like a moth to a flame, only ever seeing the light and never the danger. "He sounded so lonely and lost, and I . . . I miss him, Rose. Maybe he's had enough of other women now. Maybe this time he means it."

Not this time, Rose thought, not ever. She couldn't drag herself away from darkness only to let her best friend fall back into the arms of the man who never tired of hurting her. There had to be some way of stopping Shona from making the same mistake again; telling her how wrong she was never worked. There was only one thing that Rose thought might be powerful enough to influence Shona, and that was loyalty. Shona's unswerving loyalty to her.

"Come here." Rose said the words out loud at exactly the moment the idea formed in her head. "Come here to me, please."

"What?" Shona asked, incredulous. "What are you talking about?"

"Come here. You say I'm not strong enough to deal with this alone, and you're right. I need you, Shona, I need you with me, and even if you don't want to admit it, you need some time to think about what you're going to do next. Run away too, come here and bring the boys and we can both hide for a while. I can help you clear your head, and you can make sure I don't make a total fool of myself with Frasier or my father."

"Mate, I can't just disappear like you," Shona said, distracted enough by the idea to sound like her old self again. "People will worry about me."

"Oh, thanks very much," Rose said.

"You know what I mean. My mum, my job, Ryan . . ."

"Ryan doesn't care about you, Shona," Rose said brutally, unable to contain herself any longer. "He wants you, maybe he does love you in his own particular, twisted way, but he doesn't care about you. If he did, he wouldn't have a bevy of women and four more children scattered across Kent. You know he only ever comes back to you when he's broke and has nowhere else to go."

There they were, the facts laid bare, the reasons why Rose couldn't bear for Shona to make the same mistake again, and Rose had said them out loud, even though she felt like a hypocrite, even though she knew she could never tell anyone, not even Shona, what it was Richard did to her. But this wasn't about her, it was about saving Shona.

"I know it sounds bad from the outside, but you don't know . . ." Shona trailed off, aware that she was repeating exactly what Rose had just said to her. "No one knows, do they, what it's like inside? How you feel stuff you don't want, think things you shouldn't. It's like . . . it's like you're two people—the person who knows what to do, and the one who does what she wants, whatever the consequences."

"Come here, Shona, please," Rose begged, concern flooding her voice. "Please, come and escape with me for a bit. I've decided I'm not going to call Richard. I'm not going to let him get inside my head again. He'll find me eventually, but not yet. We've got time, you and me, not much, but a little bit of time before everything catches up with us, and I'm determined to make the best of it. I'm sure there is room here—I'm the only guest—but I'll book you in as soon as I get off the phone, and you can help me get my head straight and strong before I have to face him again. And I can help you finally move on from Ryan. Besides, if you come here, then I'll look a whole lot less like a stalker when I 'bump' into Frasier."

"OK," Shona said, so quietly that Rose was unsure she'd heard her. "OK, I'll borrow Mum's car and drive up tomorrow. But I'm only coming because you need me, you bloody loser. And you better tell me where the hell the godforsaken shit hole of Millthwaite actually is."

Chapter Five

Rose sat in Jenny's living room, the weak August sunshine battling through the silver clouds to illuminate the spotless room. Maddie was sitting on a dining room chair, her head buried in the enormous doll's house where she was happily arranging its occupants around the new technological arrival of television into their nineteenth-century lives. She felt curiously at peace considering the hurricane of a day she was about to step into, Richard snapping somewhere at her heels, her father alone somewhere in the hills, oblivious to her just as he had been every single day for more than twenty years. And one step closer to seeing Frasier again.

After giving it some thought, Rose had decided not to wait for Shona to arrive before making the short drive to her father's cottage. It would mean wasting another precious day before Richard found her and, besides, Shona had this curious effect on her life, reflecting back a true image of herself, of the way things really were, that Rose rarely enjoyed looking at. Shona was the one adult in her life who never lied to Rose, who was always straight with her. If Shona said something was wrong or insane or deeply misguided, then Rose knew she was right. Rose didn't want that lens focused on her too closely on the day she first set eyes on her father again. It had been a brief, chance encounter with Shona years before they truly found each other that had made Rose see her marriage for what it was for the first time, an unveiling that Rose would have been content to live without.

Rose was twenty-three and had been a married woman for five years. She was walking back from her daily trip to the supermarket a little later than usual, and was almost home when she'd bumped into Shona, walking down the road where Rose lived, underdressed for the freezing weather in a flimsy cotton jacket. And heavily pregnant.

Panicking at the sight of her former friend, Rose ducked her head down, hoping to make it past the other woman without being spotted. It wasn't that she didn't want to talk to Shona, it was more that she had no idea what she would say to her.

"Babe? Rose, babe, it is you?" Shona stopped her by putting a hand on her arm. "Rose, fuck me, I've been wondering about what happened to you since you left Harley's. You disappeared! What happened to you? One minute you were there, next you were gone."

Rose caught her breath as Shona hugged her, slapping her on the back for good measure when she finally released Rose from her grip.

"Hello, Shona," Rose said quietly. "It's good to see you. You haven't changed, well, apart from the obvious."

"This fucking thing?" Shona laughed, hugging her belly. "I know, it's nuts, right? I wasn't planning on kids just yet, but I've met this bloke. The father, fuck, Rose. He's perfect. He loves me so much, and I just know he's going to be a brilliant dad. I'm so happy!"

Shona squealed and hugged Rose again with sheer joy, which Rose felt radiating through her bones. It was an unfamiliar sensation.

"Listen to me, I haven't let you get a word in. So, what have you been up to?"

"Me? I got married! Have been for five years," Rose smiled, trying to emulate a little of Shona's ebullience. She had felt that way once about marrying Richard, she had felt that way for a long time, reveling in a sense of belonging, of being wanted and cherished, of feeling safe. It was only seeing Shona's own fresh excitement about life that made her realize she didn't really feel that way anymore.

"Married, at eighteen! Well, that's better than being dead in a ditch, I suppose," Shona said cheerfully. "We all thought that creep that used to stalk you had murdered you!"

"What creep?" Rose asked her, smiling uncertainly at a joke she didn't quite get.

"You know, that weird-looking bloke that hung around for weeks. The one that looked like he should be on *Crimewatch*. Used to take you for drinks after work. Ooh, he gave me the shudders."

"That . . . *creep*?" Rose had been momentarily at a loss for words. It never occurred to her that anyone could look at her handsome, respectable doctor husband and think of the word "creep." She forced a laugh. "That 'creep' was the one who I married, and I'm very happy, thank you very much!"

"Oh fuck!" Shona giggled, her laughter bubbling through the fingers with which she covered her mouth. "Really sorry! You married him, the one that looked like a serial killer? All piercing black eyes and long murdery raincoats?"

Shona was so amused that Rose couldn't help but smile.

"I don't think he looks like a serial killer at all," she insisted weakly. "He's tall, dark, handsome, *and* a doctor."

"Seriously, I'm pleased for you." Shona grinned, when she eventually got back her composure. "There's nothing like finding the right man, is there? Honestly, Rosie, I thought it was all bollocks, I really did, love. I mean my mum and dad hated each other, yours did too. And then it happened. Ryan, he's my knight in shining armor. Hey, do you still live here? I couldn't have stayed here if I knew my mum had topped herself. I'd be too worried about bumping into her ghost, but anyway, I'm desperate for a piss. This little bastard is dancing on my bladder. Can I come in?"

Unconsciously calculating the time she had left before Richard would be back from the surgery, Rose glanced over her shoulder at her house, the lawn neatly manicured, the privet hedge trimmed to within an inch of its life. There had been no ghosts in the house after her mother had died; it had been a singularly empty place, even when she was in it. Now it was Richard's house, her and Richard's home, and he filled every corner of it with his presence, even in his absence.

"Yes, yes, of course," she said hesitantly, knowing instinctively how Richard would hate it if he knew there was a stranger in his house.

"You're a lifesaver. Any chance of a cuppa while you're at it?" Shona asked her brightly. "I'm gasping and fucking freezing. I got sacked from Harley's when I couldn't squeeze through the tables anymore. I said to him, what about my rights? He said, when was the last time you paid any tax? He had a point. Ryan's getting me a coat, though. I've seen the perfect one."

Shona continued to talk as she followed Rose up the garden path.

"Actually, Shona, I'm not sure . . ." Rose looked at her watch as she reached the front door. It was almost five. Richard would be home in an hour, ready for a scotch, or more likely two, and his dinner. After a day of talking over minor ailments with patients, making small talk with old ladies, and fielding the latest furious row instigated by his prickly receptionist, who seemed to feel she had the diagnostic skills to know if a patient really needed an emergency appointment, the woman whose job Rose had been begging Richard to give to her, the last thing he would want was a house full of noise and chatter. They never invited people round for a reason.

"Oh, go on, I'm dying for a slash," Shona told her. "I'll pee my pants right here if you say no!"

"OK, just a quick cup of tea, though," Rose said. "I have to go out in a little while."

As Rose opened the front door and set her keys in the little dish on the smoked-glass-topped telephone table, which Richard had chosen, she wondered why she'd felt the need to lie. And it was then that she realized that her marriage wasn't totally normal, that she knew instinctively that if Richard found out she'd invited an old friend into their home he would be angry with her, even if Shona was gone by the time he came back.

"There's a loo under the stairs," Rose told Shona, as she went into the kitchen and put the kettle on. Pork chops and mash were what she'd been planning for tea, with frozen peas. She could peel the potatoes while Shona drank her tea and still be on schedule, just as long as Shona left well before six o'clock.

"Two sugars, cheers," Shona said as she returned from the loo, with decidedly dry-looking hands, nodding at the mug of weak tea that Rose had hurriedly made her.

"So no kids, then?" Shona asked, looking round the spotless kitchen.

"No, not yet. We're enjoying each other," Rose said, repeating what Richard always said in response to similar inquiries.

"Ew," Shona said, wrinkling her nose. "I can't wait to be a mum. It's going to be so perfect. I'm down for a flat, when one comes up, so I have to keep quiet about Ryan for a bit. I'll get one quicker if it's just me. I'd feel bad about it, but they hand out housing to flipping Poles like there's no tomorrow. I mean, what do I pay my taxes for?" Shona grinned. "If I paid any, that is."

She looked tired for a moment, the unsympathetic strip lighting on the winter afternoon adding depth to the shadows under her eyes and around her mouth, making her look much older than her twenty-something years. "Anyway, Ryan will see us right, I know he will."

Shona beamed again, and Rose smiled, self-consciously taking the peeler from the drawer and beginning to peel the potatoes.

"You're a proper little housewife, aren't you?" Shona said, nodding at the pile of vegetables. "Don't you work at all, then?"

"No." Rose shrugged, uncertain why the admission made her feel uncomfortable. She'd been working up for several months to asking Richard to let her look for a part-time job, but whenever she attempted to raise the subject, he promptly changed it or cut her off with, "Why? There's no need."

"Lucky cow! You've really fallen on your feet, haven't you? I'll have to go back to work when I can, even with Ryan's wages. Who knows if that old perv Harley will give me my job back when I'm a mummy. I only got it the first time round because I let him look down my top. Do you remember that time he had me trapped in the office, saying he wanted to make sure my uniform fitted? He had his hands all over me. Thank God you walked in when you did!"

Rose did remember that Mr. Harley was rather inappropriately taken with Shona's and many of the other girls' physiques, always thinking of reasons to touch them in places that he shouldn't. She had been so slight and slim that apart from one fleeting palm grazing across her backside one afternoon, she had fortunately escaped his attentions.

"Right, I'd better get back. I'm staying with my mum until a flat comes up, and she still gets a strop on if I'm not home for tea. Thanks for the use of your bog."

"No problem," Rose said, feeling a flood of relief as she checked the clock. Richard wasn't due home for ten more minutes. She'd have plenty of time to wash up Shona's mug and make it look as if no one had been here at all.

"Hey, you know what, you and me should go out for a drink some time, have a laugh!"

"Yes, great—we should," Rose said, although she knew it was unlikely she'd ever see Shona again.

"I'm going to need your number, then." Shona stopped dead in the hallway, so that Rose walked into her back. "Steady! Got a pen?"

"A pen?" Aware that her precious ten minutes were ticking away, Rose went and fetched the pen Richard liked always to be present beside the telephone and handed it to Shona.

"And a bit of paper?" Shona raised an eyebrow and smiled. "The lights are on, but there's no one in, is there?"

"Sorry I . . ." Rose glanced at the notepad next to the telephone. Richard would know if she'd torn out a sheet, and then he'd want to know why. "Hang on, just a second . . ." She ran into the loo and ripped off a piece of toilet paper.

"Are you mental?" Shona asked, amused as Rose took the pen and scribbled down not her home number but the number of the dry cleaners that she had memorized, absolutely certain that moment that not only did she never want to see Shona again, she simply wanted her out of the house now.

"Well," Shona said pleasantly enough, taking the flimsy piece of tissue without looking at it. "You're still a weirdo. See you, then."

"See you," Rose said as she anxiously opened the door.

But it was too late. Richard was walking up the garden path. The look of fury on his face as he'd spotted Shona on his doorstep had been less than fleeting, gone in an instant, but Rose had seen it.

"Well, hello," Richard said. "Who do we have here?"

"This is Shona," Rose told him nervously. "I worked with her at the café. We bumped into each other just now, and she needed to use the loo, so I invited her in . . . just for a second."

"I'm just off anyway," Shona said, clearly sensing Rose's discomfort.

"Oh, there's no need," Richard said. "Come on in, join us for dinner, check the TV pages, see what's on, why not?" He was smiling, but there was no humor there.

"Jesus, all right." Shona frowned, forced to edge past him as he refused to step aside to make room for her. She held up the tissue paper and waved it at Rose. "I'll call you, yeah? We'll go out, have a laugh."

Rose said nothing, letting go of the front door and walking quickly back into the kitchen, where she put the dirty mug into the sink and began peeling potatoes again.

"You're home early," she said, without looking up when Richard came into the room, carrying his scotch.

"Yes," he said. "I was hoping for a bit of peace and quiet in my own home, not a houseful."

"Shona is hardly a houseful," Rose said uncertainly, cutting a potato carefully into quarters and dropping it into a pan of cold water. "And she was just here for a minute, not even that."

"It takes longer than a minute to drink a cup of tea," Richard said, picking up the mug and slamming it down on the counter.

"Does it matter?" Rose asked him, briefly defiant, before

lowering her eyes to quarter the next potato. She winced as Richard pushed her away from the worktop and into the cooker, its metal edges biting into her spine.

"I've been up to my neck in sick old ladies, filthy kids, and malingering shirkers all day long, and what for? To keep this place, to keep you in it so that when I get home I have just a few hours of calm to myself! So yes, I would say it does matter, it matters a lot, Rose!"

He picked up the pan of water and potatoes and threw it hard against the opposite wall, where it clanged with a metallic thud before bouncing off the tiles and leaving a pool of water and neatly quartered potatoes on the floor. Gasping, Rose remembered sensing it would be best to stay completely still, not making eye contact with her husband, as he finished his scotch in one swig, his shoulders heaving from the exertion. When he spoke again, his voice was soft. Gentle.

"See, see what you made me do?" he said.

"I'm sorry," Rose said. "I won't do it again."

"Good girl." Richard leant over and kissed her on the cheek. "You'd better peel some more potatoes, hadn't you? I'm starving."

Rose had left her phone on so she could get updates from Shona on her whereabouts, and by midmorning Shona was still trying to organize her sons and secure the loan of a car, which was tricky because her mum had gone off the radar with her latest flame. It came as no surprise to Rose that Richard texted her again. His deadline of midnight had come and gone with no response, and she knew that his lack of control over her, what she was doing, how she was responding to him, would be killing him. If there was one thing he couldn't bear it was losing his grip on anything that he considered belonged to him. Rose thought for a moment about deleting the text unread, but even though she knew what it said, still she had to be sure. It was a simple, short message, quite benign in most other circumstances. All it said was, "I am coming to get you."

That he would find her somehow, Rose had no doubt. It was more a question of what she did with the uncertain amount of time she had left until he got here. It was time to go and see her father.

"Maddie," she said to her daughter's back. Maddie was chatting away quite happily in the voices of several small family members.

"Yes?" Maddie sighed in her own voice without turning to look at her.

"I have to go out. Do you want to stay here and play if Jenny says it's OK?"

Maddie thought for a moment and then swiveled on her chair to look at Rose. "You're going to see your dad," she stated, with a single nod.

"Yes," Rose affirmed. "Which might be a bit tricky as I haven't seen him for a long time. I expect there might be a lot of talking." Or no talking at all, Rose thought. "Anyway, I don't think it's the best time for you to meet him, so you'll be OK here, won't you, for a little while?"

Maddie stared at her for a long time in that unnerving way she had, as if she knew something that Rose didn't.

"What will happen when Daddy comes?" Maddie asked her at last, her expression pinched and uncomfortable.

"We will talk things over," Rose said.

"And then what?" Maddie asked, so uncertainly that Rose wasn't sure which answer she was hoping for.

"To be honest, I don't really know," Rose said. "Except that you and I will stick together, like we always do."

Maddie was silent for a long time, watching Rose from

her chair next to the doll's house. Then, as Rose thought she might be about to say something, she turned back to the house and began to play again.

"I think I'll be OK here for now," she said over her shoulder.

Rose was getting into her car, wondering how much petrol it had left in its tank, when a stupidly big Toyota truck pulled up alongside her, blocking her in.

"Excuse me!" she was about to complain when she saw Ted in the driver's seat grinning down at her, which made her all the more exasperated as she felt it would be impolite to be rude to her hosts' son.

"Morning," he said. "What you up to, then?"

"I'm going to see my father, as if it's any of your business!" Rose exclaimed, as all her anxieties—about Richard's text, about leaving Maddie, about seeing John—came to a head. "Maybe round here you all live in each other's pockets, but I don't, so mind your own. Get out of the way, please."

The smile on Ted's face faded. "All right, whatever, I was just asking," he said, looking offended.

"Well, don't," Rose snapped as she climbed into her car. "I am perfectly capable of managing on my own!" She tried the engine, which spluttered and choked on the trace of petrol fumes that were left in the tank.

"Damn it!" She smashed the steering wheel with the heel of her hand, closing her eyes as she braced herself to have to ask Ted for help after all. Rolling down the window, she signaled to him as he was about to pull his truck out of her way.

Raising an eyebrow, he lowered his window. "What?" he asked.

Rose sighed heavily. "Do you have a can of petrol on that truck? I'm out."

"Well, I wouldn't want to interfere . . ." Ted said.

"Look, have you or haven't you?" Rose asked. "If you haven't, point me in the direction of the nearest petrol station and I'll walk there and get some."

"It's miles," Ted told her. "Look, let me give you a lift. I'll wait and you can pick up some petrol on the way back."

"No." Rose squirmed uncomfortably at his magnanimous gesture when she had, after all, been rather rude to him. "Anyway, why are you so keen to be nice to me?"

Ted looked nonplussed, as if she'd asked him the most ridiculous question. "Or I could just leave you stranded here? I don't know why I'm being nice to you, but I tell you what, the urge is rapidly running out. Do you want a lift or not?"

"Sorry," Rose said, suddenly sensitive to her inherent sense of mistrust coloring everything, as well as the churning of acid in her guts and the speed of her heartbeat. To not go now, when she'd prepared herself to, would be an anticlimax, and besides, perhaps it would be good to have someone there, someone who was just willing to help her out. It was a concept so alien to her life that she found it hard to believe, even when she encountered it face-to-face. It was Richard who had done that to her: instilled in her a sense of mistrust, isolating her from everyone around her, and putting her trust in Ted's unexpected offer of friendship was one way of defying him. "I'm stressed-out and snappy. Yes, thank you, I'd appreciate a lift." Rose was rewarded with a dazzling smile, which was hard not to return. "Just as long as you promise me this wasn't your mother's idea, and you aren't really only working undercover as a spy."

"You've been here five minutes, and yet you know Mum so well." Ted chuckled, jumping out of the truck and going around to the passenger side to open the door for Rose, holding out a hand and helping her up the high step into her seat.

"But if you stick around long enough to really get to know her, you'll see her bark is much worse than her bite. Nosy, yes, but she cares about people. That must be where I get it from."

"What does a barman need a great big thing like this for anyway?" Rose asked him as he jumped into the driver's seat beside her. She found his willingness to be so openly affectionate for his mother very charming.

"This is not a barman's car," he told her with a smirk. "It's a rock star's."

Rose stopped listening to Ted's stream-of-consciousness chatter, which as far as she could gather seemed to be mostly about himself, as soon as they left the village and began to follow the road that cut into the mountains. Having arrived in the dark and spent her first day here in the shelter of the village, Rose was unprepared for the landscape that surged up around her. Even on this damp August day, with the sky heavy and leaden, and the heat that should have signaled a burning hot day turning the air humid and close, the peaks and valleys of the Lake District were something to behold. It was so unlike what Rose was used to: flat, mild-mannered Kent, gently slipping into the sea. This landscape looked like it had been churned up just minutes earlier by some angry giant, searching for something he'd lost, mountains thundering skyward leaving rocks flung asunder in their wake, white water hurtling down their slopes. There were no lakes on the short drive up to Storm Cottage, but nevertheless Rose was pressed into silence by the sheer scale of her surroundings. No wonder her father had found his natural home in the country. Its wild unpredictability, its cold hard beauty, suited him very well.

Ted pulled the truck into a wide and muddy yard where on one side there stood a large barn, its door propped open. To the left, sitting in the crook of the mountain, situated behind a low derelict-looking drystone wall, was an overgrown garden fringing what had to be Storm Cottage.

As she climbed out of the truck, without speaking or acknowledging Ted, Rose looked up at the cottage—a dim, squat, toadlike silhouette against the thunderous late summer afternoon, hunched against the inclement border weather. Ramshackle and unkempt, it embodied its name—or perhaps that was just Rose, turning the building into her image of her father. The strangeness of the situation did not escape her. Here she was, finally standing outside her father's house, willing if perhaps not ready to face him again. And, stranger still, he was somewhere in that small building utterly unaware that she was here. Rose was about to change his life, one way or the other.

Fat, slow drops of rain finally began to spatter down from the threatening clouds. "Knock, be brave," Rose told herself. "Don't take no for an answer. This is your dad, your dad, remember. Maybe he'll just open his arms and make everything all right."

There was no bell, so she hammered on the wet rough wood with her fist, waiting a few moments and then hammering again. The rain seemed to be coming at her horizontally, whipped into needles by the merciless wind. Gasping in a breath of warm air, Rose glanced back at Ted, watching her from his truck, and wondered about going back to the B & B with nothing changed, no grand reunion, no lost love restored. Something had to happen, she knew that. Richard was coming, either to claw her back into her old life, or . . . or God only knew what else. Whatever happened, it had to be something; she couldn't just sit here and wait for her husband to find her.

Still there was no reply and, deciding she had no option,

Rose prepared to leave the meager shelter of the porch. Before she could take a step the door opened at last, and an elongated rectangle of electric light snapped on, slicing through the rain.

"What the hell do you think you're doing?" an angry male voice said behind her. Rose steadied herself and turned round, lifting her chin to look the old man in the eye. He was barely recognizable as her father, and yet she knew instantly that it was him. He'd aged, of course. He was smaller, almost withered; the huge life force of a man she always envisioned when she thought of him looked shrunken and diminished. The strong, tall, dark-haired man she remembered so well was thin, his face gaunt and etched with deep lines. His hair was gray, but he still wore it long, over his collar. Rose observed him for a moment longer, unable to tear her eyes away from the face that she used to adore. And then she realized he was scrutinizing her in exactly the same way. Dropping her chin abruptly, she hid her face from him, not wanting him to see the same passing of time in her that she did in him, aware of what a foolish impulse that was. She had been just a little girl that last time he had seen her.

"This is private property," he said, his anger suddenly muffled and muted by shock.

"Don't you recognize me?" she asked him, searching his face for any trace of the man who had kissed her in the middle of the forehead and then walked out of the door. "It's me, it's Rose, your daughter."

John Jacobs opened the door a fraction of a centimeter more and stared at her in the poor light, as the rain began to increase in intensity, dribbling through the gaps in the porch roof. His brow furrowed as he studied her face, and for a moment Rose wondered if he remembered that he had once had a daughter at all.

"Of course I recognize you," he said after a moment, his voice flat, even.

"Hello, John," Rose said to the father she hadn't seen since she was nine years old. "I've found you."

It was such an odd thing to say, like they had just completed a long, long game of hide-and-seek, and yet it was the only thing Rose could think of to say. His jaw clenched tightly as he observed her from behind the safety of the door, and Rose knew he was debating whether or not to let her in.

And then, without another word, John Jacobs reached a decision and stood aside to let Rose pass over the threshold into his house. Glancing back briefly at the truck, Rose took a breath and went in.

At a loss as to how to behave, she looked around the single kitchen-cum–living room, paved with cold-looking flagstones, to find a battered old sofa covered in a dusty-looking throw positioned in front of a cold grate. Without looking at her father, she eased off her sodden coat, pushing the damp hair back from her face.

"Have you got a towel?"

John, who was still standing by the open front door, sighed heavily, pushed the door shut with a begrudging slam, shrugged, and looked around, crossing the ancient stone in two long strides to pick up a tea towel that had certainly seen better days and handing it to Rose. For want of anything better, Rose took the grubby paint-stained article and rubbed it over her hair until the worst of the moisture was absorbed.

"So then," Rose said, pulling her fingers through her long hair, unaltered in style and color since she'd last seen John, and struggling to know what to say, "I suppose this is a bit of a shock for you. For me too, as it happens."

John opened his mouth and then shut it again, turning his

back on her and staring at the white-painted brick wall behind the old ceramic sink for a moment, perhaps hoping that if he waited long enough, when he turned round she would be gone, and he'd be waking up from some fitful nightmare.

"How have you been?" Rose asked his back, gathering herself to be strong, to keep her tone even and audible, to somehow find a path through this impossible situation. John's shoulders remained tense and resolute, as if he could drive her out of his house with sheer force of will. Rose bit down on her bottom lip hard enough so the pinch would distract her from the tight band of anxiety that constricted her chest. He palpably wanted her to disappear from his life as quickly as she had reappeared. If hers had been a different life, if she hadn't been cramming in a lifetime of questions in the time she had before Richard came, Rose would have turned round and left, but if hers had been a different life then perhaps she would still have had her father and her mother, and would never have married the very first man who asked her when she was only eighteen years old. Whether he knew it or not, John had started the chain of events that had brought her to his doorstep on this stormy afternoon, and now it was time to deal with the consequences.

"Look," John began, his tone curt and stiff, his voice a little hoarse as if he wasn't used to talking, his gaze still fixed on the whitewashed wall. "What do we have to say to each other, really? We are strangers. And I'm sure you have feelings and anger that you want to talk about, but you see, Rose, it won't make any difference to you or me, or the way things have been, if you do. I do not wish for either a reunion or a heart-to-heart. I have no place in my life for a long-lost daughter, and I don't want to make one. There is simply no point, don't you see?"

"I didn't come to find you, you know," Rose said after a moment, feeling it was important he knew that, and surprised by the lack of emotion in her own voice, which came out flat and even, the tidal wave of feelings that she had feared suddenly utterly gone. "I came here, to Millthwaite, because of you, sort of. Because of this." She held out the postcard of John's painting, which he squinted at but did not take. "I left my husband, you see. I needed a place to go and this place was the only one I could think of. I had no idea that you were here until I arrived. And it's taken me two days to decide to come up here to the cottage. And now I'm here, now I'm looking at you . . ." She paused, examining his aged face, looking for any trace of the man she'd once worshipped. "I agree, I don't know you. And you certainly don't know me. And perhaps talking wouldn't make any difference to you, but I think I found you here for a reason, and I think it would help *me.* And after all is said and done, I think you owe me, don't you, John? More than you know."

John looked at her for a moment, a deep furrow carved between his brows, and then he bowed his head, standing where Rose had cornered him. In the weak light it was hard to see him properly, but he seemed to be wearing the same pair of round wire-framed glasses as he had when she'd seen him last. Rose wouldn't put it past him. He always was a man who liked objects, who kept them around him like talismans. Those glasses had once been his father's too, her grandfather, whose knee she had once sat on, she dimly recalled from a far-removed childhood memory, in a summer garden full of flowers. Typical that her father would treasure so carefully such an object and yet cast away his family without a second thought.

"You can't stay here," he said finally.

"I don't want to stay here," Rose said. "And I don't expect

anything. I might have, perhaps, until I saw you. But now, not only do I know that there isn't going to be a grand reunion, or hugs and tears and love, I'm not at all sure that is what I want either. The only thing I want from you, John, is answers. When you left, you changed my life forever and I want to know why, and I want you to meet your granddaughter, and find out about me, about the life you left behind. You don't have to care, you don't have to love me. I just want you to listen and answer my questions. Which, quite honestly, is the very least you can do."

Rose wondered at her own coolness, her control. Perhaps Richard had taught her this also; when faced with unbearable pain to simply cut off all emotion, to numb every nerve ending so that no matter what might happen next, nothing could hurt her.

After several seconds, during which John did not respond, Rose spoke into the void, emboldened by her self-possession and immunity to his cruelty.

"Do you mind if I make a cup of tea?" she said, crossing to the stove, where a battered old kettle sat squat on the hob. "Do you want one?"

"Rose," John said quietly, "you can't just turn up here like this. You can't just foist yourself on me. I've told you, I do not want it."

"Well, I do." Rose stopped, clenching the handle of the kettle, forcing herself to keep her voice low and quiet as decades of angry words she had never had a chance to voice began to boil away quietly in the pit of her stomach. "Dad, you left me when I was nine years old and I've never asked you for a single thing from that moment until this. All I want is a cup of tea."

John took the kettle out of her stiff hands, filling it himself from the clanking, creaking tap.

"Why?" he said wearily. "What do you think that talking to me will change?"

"It will help me understand," she said quietly, firmly. "I don't think I realized until now that I need to understand everything that's happened to me since you left. I thought I could perhaps ignore it, sweep it under the carpet, get on with things. But I can't. My marriage is over, my daughter is . . . unusual. I somehow got this life that doesn't feel like it's got anything to do with me and—"

"You blame me," he said, not as an accusation but as a statement of fact.

"I don't know," Rose said. "I don't think I blame anyone. I just . . . I need to know now, soon, why my life turned out like it did, because I think I only have one chance to change it. I ran away here because . . . I was chasing a silly daydream, and I found you. I have no idea what is going to happen next, but I do know that that has to mean something, or if it doesn't then I have to *make* it mean something."

John shook his head, putting the kettle on the hob and lighting it with a match, the gas flaring in a brief roar before settling into a steady blue flame.

"I live alone, I work alone, I don't make conversation. I don't play with small children. I don't drink anymore. I haven't had a drop for nearly three years. If I keep myself to myself, then I know I can stay sober and work. And I can't let anything get in the way of that."

"Not even me," Rose said, her voice unintentionally small at the thought of that last kiss that her father had planted on her forehead.

John shook his head. "Not even you."

Rose drew in a sharp breath, as if he'd slapped her physically in the face with his words. Maybe that touched him, somehow, more than everything she'd said, because there was the smallest shift in his expression, something barely visible, as if in that second he truly recognized her for the first time.

"Very well. Come back tomorrow, then," he said wearily. "If that's what it takes to go back to your life and get out of mine, then I will try and answer your questions, but I must warn you, it is very unlikely that you will like what you hear. And now I need to work. Shut the door behind you when you've finished your tea."

Rose stood stock-still in the small, dingy living room for several moments longer after John left the cottage, presumably making his way to the barn across the yard, waiting for the wave of tears, of emotion, bitterness, and hurt to hit her, but nothing came. Nothing at all, though she was rooted to the spot, caught in a moment that didn't seem real to her.

The spell was broken and Rose jumped when the door creaked open and an uncertain-looking Ted appeared around it.

"I was just checking he hadn't axe-murdered you or something," Ted said a little anxiously, advancing farther into the room. "Are you OK? You're as white as a sheet. You look like you've just seen a ghost."

"Perhaps I have, in a way." Rose shook her head. "I have no idea what just happened, but it wasn't exactly a conventional reunion."

"Do you need a stiff drink?" Ted asked her. "I'll pop you back to the pub and sort you out a single malt."

Rose had been about to trot out her usual line when anyone offered her alcohol—"No, thank you, I don't drink"—until it occurred to her that she had no idea why she didn't drink. She'd always thought it was because of her father's recklessness, her husband's disapproval, her own distaste. But in actual fact she'd never taken the time to decide for herself if she liked drinking or not. And now, this very strange and difficult day seemed like as good a time as any.

"Yes, please." She nodded, allowing Ted to escort her back to the truck.

"You knew that wasn't going to be easy," Ted said as the truck bumped and bounced its way down the track and turned back towards Millthwaite, via the petrol station. "I mean, I suppose it's never easy, but when your dad is famous for being horrible, it's bound to be a bit tricky."

Rose smiled faintly, enjoying the simple spin he put on the impossible to understand.

"Yes, I suppose it is," she said.

It wasn't until they were seated in the pub, with Albie regarding them from the other end of the bar, that Ted spoke again.

"So you left your husband, then?" he asked her, leaning his chin on his folded arms, so that his dark eyes could find hers under her curtain of hair. "Ran out on him?"

"Yes." Rose looked up. "I suppose you would call it a midlife crisis."

"I wouldn't call it anything, I have no idea what happened, only that . . ." Ted hesitated, "you look like you need that drink."

"I do," Rose replied simply. "Maybe a little too much. Dad drank, Mum drank. I must be a shoo-in for alcoholism."

"I don't reckon you are," Ted said, scrutinizing her with a sideways tilt of his head. "One thing about working in a pub is that you get to see the real drinkers, the ones who can't get through the day without taking the edge off, firsthand. They've got a particular look, a way about them. Even the ones that look respectable and in control. You don't have that.

And besides, you're obviously going through a bad patch. I feel for you."

Rose shook her head. "Don't pity me. I don't need to be pitied. I've escaped, you see, I've made it this far. I might look like a waif lost in the storm but, I promise you, right now is the strongest that I have ever been in my life."

"Is that right?" Ted smiled at her, as if he somehow knew different.

Rose found herself returning his smile, as each consecutive sip of whiskey seemed to thaw her out.

"How unchivalrous you are to doubt me," she said. "So are you saying I look old and tired and worn out from fighting?"

"Not at all," Ted said, slipping just a little closer to her. "You look great, as it goes."

Rose snorted with laughter, inhaling the whiskey the wrong way, so it burnt her tubes as she coughed and sputtered.

"Oh, Ted," she said, smiling at him, "you are young and naïve, and oddly interested in me for reasons I still don't really understand. But you make me laugh, and that's rare, so thank you."

"Happy to oblige," Ted said, smiling as he took a sip of his own drink. "And you are interesting, that's why I'm interested in you. We don't get many interesting women round here. You're like one of those femmes fatales out of a film, dangerous and mysterious!"

"Oh my God, you really know how to spin a line, don't you?" Rose laughed, wondering what her life would have been like if she'd met a boy like Ted when she was the right age, before Richard had ever come into her life. How different would she, her life, have been if she'd met a man with whom she could simply laugh, whose eyes she could look into without hesitation, a man who'd made her feel . . . simply normal? "Luckily for you I'm far too old and experienced to fall for it."

"So far." Ted nodded with a slow smile. "So far. That will all change when you come to my gig."

"I'm not coming to your gig," Rose said firmly.

"Oh, you are," Ted said. "I guarantee it. It's either a night in the pub or another night with my mum."

"You make a compelling case," Rose said, smiling.

"Good." Ted seemed genuinely pleased.

"But now I have to get back to Maddie." Rose pushed her empty glass across the counter towards him, glad that she didn't feel the need to have another. "Thanks, Ted, for the lift."

"Anytime," Ted said. "I'll drop that petrol can off for you." Rose could feel his eyes on her back as she walked out of the pub. When was the last time a man had looked at her at all, let alone that way? Rose knew exactly, down to the very last second.

Rose remembered vividly what it had first been like to be noticed by Richard.

Almost eighteen years old, she hadn't realized until she saw that flash of recognition in his eyes that she'd been living for months, since even before Mum died, out of sight. She had made herself invisible, keeping her head down, doing her work without soliciting any attention, happy just to be Rose, the girl who always tagged along, sort of funny, not too pretty, quiet, nothing-special Rose. The one Shona always made come out on a Saturday night with the rest of the gang, even though the rest of the gang could take or leave the Goth girl. In a funny sort of way, those few months after her mother died and before Richard had been some of the happiest in her life. She had been no one special, but she had been free, and it was a freedom that, at the age of seventeen, Rose was just blossoming into. And then Richard looked at her, noticed her, and she realized in that exact second how much she longed to be looked at, talked to, touched by him. How much she wanted him to think she was special.

When Rose left work that evening he was waiting for her outside the café. Momentarily halted by the sight of him, Rose thought about ignoring him, hurrying past as if she had no idea who he was. But she found it impossible.

"Hello," he said. "I suppose it would be wrong to ask you if I could buy you an ice cream?"

Now Rose remembered how warm his smile made her feel, almost like the whiskey.

"I'd be very happy if I never saw another ice cream again," she said, brushing her loose hair off her face, making herself look him in the eye. He looked quite a bit older than she was, in his late twenties, with a business suit on and his neat haircut, completely different from any of the people she had ever known. The boys that Shona and her other friends hung out with, the ones that Rose observed once removed, were just that: boys, still. Here was a grown-up.

"I'm a doctor. I've just been for a job interview, for a GP, down the road. I don't know Broadstairs very well, and as I might be moving here it would be nice if a local might show me a good place to get a cup of tea."

Rose hesitated, glancing over her shoulder as if someone might be waiting for her. It wasn't that she didn't want to go with him, it was just that she had no idea what to say, or how.

"I mean, don't worry if you have to be somewhere," Richard said, sweetly nervous. "You're probably just about to go and meet your tall boxer boyfriend, aren't you?"

"No!" Rose found herself laughing; it was an unfamiliar sound. "I don't have a boyfriend."

“I can’t think why not,” Richard said, his gaze focused on her. “You are very lovely.”

“There’s this place, more up in the town,” she said, feeling heat flare under her skin. “Where the cabbies go for breakfast. They do a good cup of tea.”

“Will you show me?” Richard asked, holding out a hand. “I’m Richard, by the way.”

“I will show you.” Rose took it, feeling his warm, strong fingers encircle hers and suddenly discovering that she was reconnected with the world. “My name is Rose.”

A long time later, as the moon rose in the sky and they talked and talked and talked, Richard walked her home.

“House share?” he asked her, looking up at the large, looming house.

“No, it was my mum’s house. Both my parents are dead,” Rose told him apologetically, as if her unconventional life, lived alone, might put him off her.

“You poor thing,” Richard said. “Having to live in this great big pile alone. You should sell it, buy somewhere new—a fresh start.”

Rose shook her head and half smiled. “I don’t actually know how to,” she said. “And besides I don’t think I can until I’m eighteen.”

Richard’s eyebrows had raised, and Rose realized they hadn’t discussed the matter of their respective ages; it hadn’t seemed important.

“I’m seventeen,” Rose told him, adding, “eighteen in October, though.”

“I’m twenty-eight,” Richard told her. “Does it matter?”

“Not to me,” Rose whispered.

“Can I kiss you, Rose?” Richard asked, so softly it was almost a whisper.

Rose took a deep sharp breath, full of the scent of the roses her mother loved to grow, which were just coming into bloom in the garden.

"I've never . . . I don't know how," she said. "I don't know what to do."

"You don't have to do anything," he whispered.

Rose stood perfectly still on the pavement outside her house, the scent of roses in the air, as Richard kissed her, so sweetly, so gently and tenderly. Her hands remained dormant at her sides, she daren't even breathe, and yet for every second his lips were on hers she was pulsating with life.

Chapter Six

"Fuck me, don't they have summer up here?" was the first thing that Shona said to Rose as she clambered out of her mother's pride and joy, a ten-year-old lilac Nissan Micra. "You better tell someone it's August."

Rose grinned, relief flooding through her to see her friend in the flesh. It felt like a lifetime since they'd seen each other, and just having her friend here lifted Rose's spirits immeasurably. The two women hugged each other tightly.

"Hello, Shona," Maddie greeted her. "Where are your children?"

"With their gran," Shona told Maddie, cheering silently at Rose the second the small girl looked away, disappointed. "When I finally tracked her down she offered to have them for a bit."

"I wanted to see Tyler. I like Tyler if he plays what I want to play. Still, I don't like Aaron at all, so I shan't miss him."

"He sends you his love too," Shona said, amused. She was one of the few people that Rose was able to relax with around Maddie. Either she didn't care about Maddie's lack of social niceties or didn't notice them the way most adults did, with sniffy disapproval as if Rose had deliberately done all she could to bring her daughter up with an unerring ability to offend and annoy. "Mum didn't think a trip up north would be good for them, mainly because she thinks the north is full of cannibals and trolls, so they're having a few days with her. Which means, I'm off the leash! Where's the talent round here? I'm gagging."

"Very nice, I must say," Jenny, who emerged from behind the front door, muttered quite decidedly over her breath.

"Who's this, babe?" Shona asked Rose, as she dumped a couple of carrier bags full of her stuff on the pavement and hugged her with one arm whilst taking a packet of cigarettes out of the pocket in her denim jacket and expertly inserting one into her mouth. "Tourist information?"

"This is Jenny. She's my . . . our landlady." Rose glanced at Jenny, who wasn't taking much trouble to hide her disapproval of Shona, which to be fair, in Shona's case was usually justified. It didn't help that she had rocked up in the tightest pair of white jeans that Rose had ever seen, with a full three inches of fake-tanned tummy blossoming over the waistband before being barely covered by a flesh-pink top that plunged in a deep V, leaving very little to the imagination. Which was exactly how Shona liked it. It was funny, odd even, because Rose knew that despite her promiscuous dress sense and feisty man-eating attitude, Shona's actual sexual experience hadn't been that much more comprehensive than her own. There had been that ill-advised encounter with the neighbor's oldest son when she was fifteen, a boy she used to knock around with when the girls had waitressed together and who had been much more into Shona than she had been into him, and then there had been Ryan. And despite his constant philandering and serial betrayals, Shona had never seriously looked at another man since she'd first set eyes on him, not even after he had a baby with another woman. And yet, when you met her for the first time, it was a little like meeting Mae

West, updated for the twenty-first century in her cutoff tops, her huge hooped earrings swaying back and forth.

"No smoking on the premises," Jenny said, nodding at the lit cigarette in Shona's mouth. "Or drinking, or funny business."

"Funny business?" Shona took a deep drag of her cigarette before flicking it onto the pavement and letting it smoke quietly away in the gutter. "Nothing funny about it, darling, not when I'm doing it."

"Sooooo!" Rose said cheerfully, picking up Shona's bags, quietly stubbing the errant cigarette out with the toe of her shoe. "Let's get you to your room, shall we?"

"I've never driven so far in my life," Shona said as she followed Rose up the stairs, Maddie and Jenny in hot pursuit. "I had to borrow a ton off Mum and that barely covered the petrol, so I'll probably be doing a midnight flit from here."

"I want payment up front!" Jenny said, immediately rising to the bait that Shona had dangled so cruelly in front of her, much to Shona's amusement.

"It's OK, Jenny," Rose said, as she opened the door to the room next to hers, which she had requested specifically for her friend. "Shona's only joking. Aren't you, Shona?"

"Yep." Shona smiled briefly at Jenny, which was about as warm as Rose ever saw her get with someone before she knew them. Why she had singled Rose out to befriend from the very beginning, even back in the café days, Rose had yet to work out. It wasn't as if they were ever obvious soul mates, even after they realized that their relationships had more in common than either one was comfortable admitting. Perhaps for all of Shona's bravado, her leader-of-the-pack attitude, and the sense of humor that always made her so popular, she'd looked back then at that skinny little orphaned teen selling ice cream because she didn't know what else to do and seen a true reflection of herself, the way she really was behind all the cut-price glamour. In any case, Rose was reluctant to ask; her dependence on Shona, to be the one person to reassure her that for all her faults she wasn't completely mad, made her reluctant to do anything that might jinx her only adult friendship.

"When you first arrived, Jenny saw you out the window and said you looked like a hussy," Maddie told Shona cheerfully, sitting demurely on the bed as Shona tipped the contents of one of her carrier bags into a drawer.

"Maddie," Rose grumbled, cursing her daughter's uncanny ability to report verbatim adult conversations that she wasn't suppose to have listened to.

Shona raised a plucked brow at Jenny.

"Breakfast is between eight and eight thirty, I don't take orders, I don't do coffee." Jenny was clearly determined not to be intimidated by Shona. "I take as I find and speak my mind. That's the way I am. If you don't like it, you know what you can do."

"Or," Rose said, raising her palms, "or I could just make us all a nice cup of tea."

"I've got to go out," Jenny said uncertainly, looking as if she was unwilling to leave Shona unsupervised or, indeed, without an armed guard. "Would you like to join us for dinner tonight, Rose? And her too, I suppose."

"Cheers, thanks," Shona said. "I will, as I don't suppose there's a KFC round here. What is it, haggis or some shit?"

"OK, thank you, see you later!" Rose said, shutting the door on Jenny before a full-blown fight could break out.

"Why do you do it?" Rose asked Shona as soon as she heard Jenny stomping down the stairs, muttering furiously to herself. "You're not like that, like some cartoon psycho, why do you let people think you are?"

"Dunno." Shona shrugged at Maddie, who was sorting through her make-up bag, a rare treat, as Rose rarely wore any. She was having a wonderful time not because she was a little girl who liked to play dress-up, but because she liked to sort things. Within a few minutes, Shona's extensive collection of lipsticks would be lined up, organized by color gradient, and her eye shadows the same. "It's easier, I suppose, if that's how people expect me to be. It's too much effort to make them see different."

"I see you." Rose shook her head. "It doesn't take any effort at all."

"Ah, no, I think you'll find that's you. You're mental, it's practically official." Shona glanced at Maddie and, picking up a bright pink lipstick, pointed her in the direction of the bathroom next door. "Go and try it on. I bet it'll look lovely."

"Really?" Maddie eyed the lipstick suspiciously. "I'm only a child, you know. I don't want to look tarty."

"Oh, go on, you old stick-in-the-mud. If you're a child, act like one! Smear it on good and thick!" Still looking uncertain, Maddie obediently trotted off to experiment with make-up, Shona careful to close the door after her.

"Dickhead's telling anyone who'll listen that you've had a breakdown," Shona said, suddenly serious. "That you've run off with Maddie and that he's worried for your mental health, that you've been talking a lot about your mother's suicide recently."

"What?" Rose exclaimed, her eyes widening. "He's saying I want to kill myself?"

"He's not saying exactly, he's saying everything but, and then letting people fill in the gaps. My mum heard it off Yvette Patel, who heard it off that nurse, Margaret. Apparently he 'confided' in her about what a terrible burden it's been, keeping your problems hidden from view all this time, and how he's worried sick about Maddie's safety."

"But that's not true, that's not true at all." Rose was horrified. She knew Richard, she knew how very good he was at being believable. It was his speciality, getting people to trust him, to put their faith in him "The *last* thing I want to do is kill myself. If anything, I want to save my life, and Maddie's, by getting away from him! Has he called the police, social services?"

"I don't know," Shona apologized, seeing the anxiety wrought on Rose's face. "But I do know that even if he has, they're not going to start a nationwide search straightaway and do a reconstruction on *Crimewatch*. The police are used to couples threatening each other in the heat of an argument, trust me. The neighbors called them out on me and Ryan more times than I want to remember. Only a couple of times did they take us seriously, and even then they needed both of us to agree before they did anything. Anyway, I reckon it's the same for the social. They've got enough on their plates without being sent off on a wild-goose chase at a moment's notice, even if it is Dr. Dickhead making all the noise. I think you've got a little while yet before you have to really worry. Like I said, Rose is mental, chasing some bloody bloke across the country, just because he once sent her a postcard, but not in *that* way."

"Said to who?" Rose asked her, worried. "You didn't tell anyone I was here, did you?"

"No!" Shona said instantly. "Well. Yes, I told my mum. I had to. You don't just get lent a car, your kids taken care of, and given a load of cash to take off for no reason. But Mum won't say anything, I swear. You know how grateful she was for how you've helped me and the boys before; she's not going to land you in it."

"I hope not," Rose said anxiously, wondering what Richard

was up to even now to make sure that the whole world would believe him when he said it was she who was the danger. She who was unstable and couldn't be trusted. If anyone could do it, it was Richard.

"Look, don't worry," Shona said reassuringly, as she dropped an arm around Rose's shoulder, kissing her on the cheek, hugging her tightly, and lifting her chin in defiance. "We're miles from fucking anywhere here. The right arse end of the universe. What fuckwit would ever think of looking for us here? So, where are the local sex spots? I hear it's all about doing it outdoors in the country."

"Honestly, as if you would!" Rose said, shaking her head at her friend. "That's another thing I don't get about you, always playing the tart, when really we both know nothing could be farther from the truth. You're just a big old romantic at heart. Always believing in the happy ending."

"Well, you've got to believe, haven't you?" Shona said. "Otherwise what else have you got? Anyway, it's you who wants me to pack in Ryan for good, so maybe I need to start looking around." Shona was thoughtful. "Hey, maybe I'll marry a farmer, bake cakes and shit."

Rose laughed. "*That* I would like to see."

"Well, you never know what sort of romance a quickie in a car park might lead to." Shona chuckled, digging Rose in the ribs.

"What's a quickie in a car park?" Maddie asked, returning from the bathroom with a thick slick of pink gloss plastered around her mouth.

"Um, it's like a sort of parking ticket," Rose said.

"Aw, now don't you look pretty?" Shona said, holding a mirror up for Maddie to look in, making her giggle. "You stick with your Aunty Shona, I'll teach you the true meaning of style."

Rose looked at her barely dressed friend, a pumped-up invention of a tough, sexy woman that had nothing to do with the real person that lay beneath, and shook her head.

"Only over my dead body," she said.

"Tell us all about it, then," Jenny said as soon as Rose, Shona, and Maddie appeared in the dining room. "How did things go with your dad? I rang Ted to find out, but he wouldn't answer his phone, bloody boy."

Rose puffed out her cheeks, looking at Maddie, who hadn't been the least bit curious about how the meeting with her long-lost grandfather had gone. Nor had she looked like she missed Rose when she turned up after two large whiskeys and with a slightly fuzzy head. If anything, she'd looked mildly inconvenienced to have to stop playing with the doll's house and engage with her mother. Sometimes—often, actually—Rose would look at Maddie and wonder if the child loved her at all. Although more often than not Maddie's anxiety when separated from what she knew was acute, Rose didn't think that Maddie's source of comfort particularly had to be her mother or her father. A favorite jumper or Bear would do equally well. It was certainly true that Maddie had slotted happily alongside Jenny with the sort of ease of companionship that Rose found very rare herself. For her part, she loved Maddie with a passion that she never thought would be possible, and one day, she supposed, it would just be nice to know with certainty that the little girl loved her back.

"It went how I expected, I suppose," Rose said. "He was shocked to see me, and very unhappy that I'd come at all. He really just wanted me to leave."

"I feel like that when you make me play with Belinda Morris," Maddie said, carefully removing all the green beans from her plate, referring to the little girl that lived two doors down.

Richard was keen that his daughter appeared to be just like all the other little girls and had encouraged the friendship, only for Rose to have to make excuses once Maddie had called Belinda "an insufferable little fool" in front of her mother, claiming, "She's got a stupid face."

"Awful, how a man could turn his back on his own child that way," Jenny said, looking at Brian, who was quietly reading the paper. "You should do something about it, Brian."

"Me?" Brian said, affronted. "What the bloody hell should I do about it?"

"Go up there, talk to him. You wouldn't have anyone treat your Haleigh the way that man's treated Rose!"

"I know, that's 'cause I'm Haleigh's dad!" Brian said.

"And he's hers," Jenny declared, as if somehow that made her whole argument watertight.

"Really, no one has to go up there," Rose said, desperate to rescue Brian, who, she suspected, had been propelled into the middle of more than one of his wife's feuds on very tenuous grounds. "I'm going back up there tomorrow. He said he'd answer my questions, so really all I have to do is think about what I want to ask him. I mean, I want to ask him about so much, but then again, I'm not really sure I want to know the answers. I'm not even really sure if I want to go."

"Ask him if he's got a will," Jenny said.

"Ask him which leg he'd like me to break first," Shona added.

"Ask him why I've never met him," Maddie said casually, almost as if she wasn't really interested in the answer, but it was the question that struck home hardest with everyone else around the table.

"I'll come with you," Shona said. "Like your bodyguard."

"Really, I think it should be me who comes with you," Maddie said. "He's my granddad, after all."

At first the idea horrified Rose, but it took her only a moment to wonder if actually it was the best way of tackling John again. Bringing Maddie would take the tension out of the situation, defuse it from being confrontational into more simply a visit. And perhaps that way it would be easier for John to talk to her, knowing that she wasn't there simply to accuse him or to start a fight. Maddie wasn't the most relaxing child to introduce to new people, but Rose had a feeling that John would like that about her.

"I think that's a good idea." Rose nodded. "I think you should come, Maddie."

Maddie looked up as if she'd forgotten what she'd recently suggested. "Hmm?"

"That you come to meet John," Rose said.

"Should be interesting," Maddie said to Brian, with an air of curiosity. Was it nice, Rose wondered, to be as disconnected from the world as her daughter sometimes seemed to be? Life raged on around her, full of violent storms and upheaval, and yet most of it literally went over her head. Yes, the things inside Maddie's head could frighten her—she was often terrorized by various imaginary ghosts and goblins—but Rose had only ever seen her scared by real life once, the little bubble of her own world finally pierced, and that had been the night they had left Richard.

"And me." Shona helped herself to a second helping of chicken pie, much to Jenny's chagrin, which was only slightly softened by her adding, "Bloody lovely pie, mate."

"I think just us," Rose said. "Don't want to frighten him off completely."

"What are you saying?" Shona half accused, half laughed. "And what the bloody hell am I going to do in this dump while you're up there?"

Before Rose could answer, Ted appeared in the doorway,

his coppery hair damp from the drizzle, his battered leather jacket glittering with moisture.

"Thank you, God, for sending me to heaven," Shona said at the sight of him, not even wincing when Rose dug her elbow into her ribs.

"All right?" Ted nodded at Shona, his gaze dwelling for a moment more than was necessary on her ample and mostly on-display cleavage, before he smiled at Rose and then his mother. "Dropping you in a backstage pass for the gig tomorrow."

"Backstage pass?" Brian snorted. "I didn't know the pub had a backstage!"

"Yeah, well, it's got the snug, it's a VIP area." Ted smiled at Rose. "You're still coming, yeah?"

"Well, I haven't even asked about . . ." Rose had been too preoccupied with hoping that Shona wouldn't cause Jenny to spontaneously combust to ask her about babysitting.

"Mum, you'll look after the kid, won't you? So Rosie can come to the gig tomorrow?"

"Rosie?" Shona giggled. "Are you going to a gig, *Rosie*?"

"Course I will," Jenny said, smiling at Maddie, who was watching the whole thing unfold with minimal interest. "We get on, don't we, love? You can tell me all about the Egyptians again."

"OK, and I'll do you a test, say twenty questions, and then I'll grade you," Maddie offered, oblivious of the look of muted horror on Jenny's face.

"Or we could stay up late and watch a movie," Jenny offered.

"Or do a test," Maddie said. "Although I must say, I'd quite like to go to the gig if you are going to play that song."

"Which song, sweetheart?" Ted asked her.

"The one that's going to change the world. I'd like to see the world changing."

"I tell you what, I'll drop you off a CD," Ted said. He looked at Rose. "So you will come?"

"Course we will!" Shona said, taking the ticket out of Ted's hand and holding her hand out for another. Reluctantly, he handed one over. "Oh, and for the record, I like drummers."

As soon as Maddie's breathing became steady, signaling that she was finally asleep, Rose crept next door to Shona's room, where she found her pouring a glass of red wine into a tooth mug.

"Here," she said, holding it out to Rose. "You take this, I'll take the bottle. Don't worry, I'll fill you up!"

"Jenny doesn't allow drinking in bedrooms," Rose said nervously as she took the mug anyway and sipped the sour-tasting brew. "She barely allows sleeping."

"Fuck Jenny," Shona said cheerfully and without malice. "It was two for one at the service station on the way here and I thought you and me would need a couple of drinks while we catch up."

"Which means you're planning to interrogate me," Rose said.

"Yeah," Shona said. "So drink up."

Remembering the pleasant tingly feeling she had after her two whiskeys, Rose obliged, downing the mugful of cheap wine in one or two gulps and then holding it out for more.

"Fuck, where's Goody Two-shoes gone?" Shona asked her, amused.

"She ran away, didn't you hear?" Rose giggled. "So go on, ask me. Who the fuck is Ted, right?"

"That question is first on my list. Who the fuck is Ted, because he is fucking lush!" Shona's eyes sparkled as she spoke. "Although far too young for you."

"He's Jenny's son. He's been sort of flirting with me, but not in a serious way. More in a friendly, sweet sort of way, really. I think he's pretending to fancy me to cheer me up."

"Well, I don't know about that," Shona said, smiling to see that her friend was evidently cheered up by Ted's attentions. "But it was obvious that he really wanted you to go to his gig, bless him. Like a keen little puppy, all wet nose and waggy tail. Or waggy something, anyway!"

"Shona!" Rose's eyes widened, unable to suppress a chuckle at her friend's boldness. "Yeah, but he couldn't take his eyes off your boobs the second he walked in the room, and I don't exactly have much in the way of competition. So I expect his interest to wane now that you're here."

"He's a bloke, darling, they're all programmed to look at tits. If Jesus had walked in right then, he'd have been looking at my tits, because they are amazing. It wouldn't mean he wasn't the Son of God anymore."

"Oh my God." Rose clapped her hand over her mouth and giggled, the wine already beginning to take effect, which with Shona doing her utmost to take Rose's mind off things made quite a heady combination. "We'll get struck down by lightning."

"No, we won't. God loves my tits," Shona said, refilling Rose's glass.

"Anyway!" Rose said, glancing upward as if she were still expecting retribution. "Ted is just a lad who's been nice to me. And from what you've told me, I sort of feel like I'm on borrowed time here, so why not have a laugh while I can? After all, it will be the first time in my entire life. I never went to gigs when I was a teenager, or kissed a load of boys, or got drunk and had crazy hairstyles!"

"I agree." Shona nodded emphatically. "I think you should

go to the gig, I think you should have a laugh, let your hair down a bit, recapture your lost youth. And then I think you should fuck him."

"I couldn't do *that*!" Rose spluttered. "I don't want to do that. This isn't what this is about!"

"I'm just saying, if you're going to prison or the loony bin anyway . . ."

"I'm not, I'm not doing that," Rose said uneasily. Even though she knew Shona was joking, the idea that Richard could somehow manipulate her into either one of those situations wasn't entirely out of the question. He was very good at getting what he wanted, and if he no longer wanted her around, then Rose was very sure he'd find a way to make it happen.

"Anyway, I didn't come here to pick up a younger man for casual sex." Rose shuddered at the thought of it. "I don't even like sex."

"You freak," Shona muttered, before taking a swig from the bottle. "You don't like sex with Dickhead, and why would you? He's vile. Sex with a normal person, a warm-blooded one that doesn't bite the heads off bats in his spare time, that would be different."

Rose turned her face away from Shona, waiting for the moment of nausea to pass. How could she ever explain to Shona that the thought of anyone touching her that way, even Frasier, made her want to run to the hills and never come back?

"I came here for Frasier," Rose reminded Shona. "Not my father, and certainly not Ted. It's Frasier I'm waiting for."

"What if he never comes?" Shona asked, tipping her head to one side. "I mean, he'll come—it's only a matter of time until you see him again—but what if he's not at all how you remember him? What if he's fat and bald and mean?"

"He won't be," Rose said, smiling, her image of Frasier so firmly imprinted in her memory that she couldn't countenance him being any other way. "I'll find out soon enough, anyway. Albie said he's up here every week, checking up on my father. And if he doesn't come, I'll go to Edinburgh."

"What if he's blissfully happily married, got five kids and a dog? Or what if he's gay, blissfully happily married, got five dogs and an S and M dungeon? Both of those scenarios are much more likely than the one you are hoping for, you know."

"I know," Rose said, although she didn't know it at all. She was really very much more in denial about reality than she would ever let on. Because if she was wrong about Frasier, then she had no idea what to do next.

Rose combed her fingers through her long brown hair, looking at her sharp pale face peering back at her from the mirror. Always the same, timid, cowardly face. She was thirty-one years old and she still had the face of a little girl.

"I do know that, I do. It's just . . . oh, I don't know. I realize how stupid it sounds that ten minutes of talking with a man seven years ago were the most . . . exciting of my life. But then again, have you seen my life?"

"I have seen your life and it's because of your life, and your fucking shit dad and shit husband, that you think those ten minutes meant more than they did. That's all I'm saying. I just don't want you to get more hurt than you already are, darling. And the odds are that is exactly what will happen."

"So what about Ryan?" Rose asked, lying back on Shona's bed a little too quickly so that her curtain of hair covered her face.

"I told you," Shona said stubbornly. "He wants me back, I'm thinking about it."

"He wants you back and you're thinking about it? How is that any less crazy than me chasing Frasier across the country for a pipe dream?" Rose propelled herself upwards in her frustation and fury. "Shona, Ryan cheats on you! He can't stop himself. God knows what the other women see in him but then he's not that fussy."

"What are you saying?" Shona's hackles rose.

Rose struggled to find the right way to express herself, the exact words that meant that finally Shona would listen to her. "You're so bright, so clever and strong. Why can't you see this one blindingly obvious thing? If you take him back you will get hurt again and again. Ryan will never grow up."

Shona said nothing for a while as she cradled the bottle, her hair covering her face. Rose watched her, desperate for some sign that her friend was registering what she was saying.

"But this time he says he's changed . . ."

"Oh, give me strength." Rose flung her hands above her head, letting their weight carry her back onto the bed with a thud. "Shona, listen to yourself!"

"I am," Shona insisted, her eyes flashing in defiance. "I know him, I know him better than anyone. I'm not a fool, Rose. I know what I'd be taking on if I went back with him, I do. He has changed, and who else will give him a second chance if I don't?"

"Why does he deserve one?" Rose said angrily.

"Because Ryan's not like Dickhead," Shona flashed back. "*He's* not evil. He's just stupid."

"But you love him anyway!"

Rose could see that getting angry was just making Shona more determined. With some effort, she softened her voice, reaching out to touch her friend.

"Shona," she said gently, "my beautiful, brave, fierce, mad Shona, you aren't afraid of anything except being alone. But you don't have to be alone. There are a million better men out there!"

“Not for me,” Shona said quietly, a single tear tracking down her cheek. “Yes, I know how it sounds, I know how impossible it must be to understand, but I miss him. I miss his shelter, the way he used to protect me from the whole world. If . . . if I could just have that feeling, one more time, of being with Ryan, you know, when everything’s good between us and he’s trying extra hard to be sweet. And we’ll go to bed and it will be so special, the care and love he’ll show me, and then after, he’ll wrap his arms around me—his big strong arms—and hold on to me like I’m the most precious, loved thing in the world and that feeling . . . it’s . . . it’s . . .” Shona couldn’t find the words she wanted. “I don’t know if I can ever feel that again unless it’s with him.”

“You *can*,” Rose said carefully. “You will, with someone who doesn’t come and go out of your life, and the kids’ lives, like there’s a revolving door. Look, I’ve broken away from Richard, and I know it’s not really real yet, and that I’ve still got to face him and all the things I’m sure he’s planned for me, but . . . if I can, *you* can. You already have. You just need to stay strong.”

“I did think about dyeing my hair,” Shona said, swiftly turning the conversation to lighter things with a flippancy that Rose knew was more about self-defense than a blasé attitude. “This was on special at the garage too, but now I’m not so sure. What do you reckon?” Shona reached into her bag and pulled out a home dyeing kit, featuring a golden-haired blonde on the cover. “Is it me?”

Rose took the box from her and gazed at the photo of the woman glancing coquettishly back at her from over her naked shoulder, her luscious locks fanned out around her like she didn’t have a care in the world. Never once, Rose thought again, not since she was a little girl, had she had her hair different from the way she was wearing it now: long, perfectly straight chestnut hair, reaching down to the middle of her back.

"Do mine instead," she whispered, mostly to herself, half daring, half hiding from the impulsive thought.

"What?" Shona asked her, leaning dangerously forward on the dressing table stool to try to catch what she thought Rose had said.

"Do mine! Why not?" Rose said, feeling a little bolder, as both the idea and the wine took hold of her. "You did that hairdressing course, didn't you? Cut my hair! Cut it off and then dye it this color. I want to be Sun-Kissed Sizzle. I want to be blond."

"Fuck, you've gone all Britney Spears on my arse," Shona said. "I can't just hack off all that hair. That hair is you."

"Exactly." A little giddy, Rose stood up and dived for the dressing table, where Shona's hairdressing scissors, a remnant of two weeks' work experience in a salon, were poking out of her voluminous make-up bag. Before Shona could wrest them from her, she leapt up onto the bed, brandishing them like she'd just pulled Excalibur out of the rock, bouncing up and down on the creaky mattress. While Shona gazed on, half in horror, half in hilarity, Rose chopped off a length of hair right at the front of her head, stopping only a couple of inches short of her scalp.

"Go on," she all but shouted, waving the chunk of her hair at Shona. "Now you *have* to cut it!"

"Christ, Rose!" Shona gasped. "What have you done? Well, sit down, then. I'm certainly not cutting your hair whilst you're bouncing off the walls."

Taking the scissors from Rose's hand, Shona stared at her hatchet job.

"Well, you've sort of blown it for a nice bob or a feather cut, neither of which I know how to do anyway. I could have a go at making it really short and spiky, and I think that's pretty much it."

"Go on, then!" Rose urged her. "Do that, and then dye it!"

"Rose, are you sure? It might look shit."

"Yes, it might look shit, but it won't look like me, will it?" Rose said emphatically, reaching for the bottle of wine and draining the last of it. "Boring, meek, loser, pathetic old me. And I can't tell you how much I don't want to look like me anymore. I'm not her, I'm not that mousy trapped girl. I'm dangerous and cool and—"

"Clinically insane, Dickhead's right after all," Shona laughed. "Oh, go on, then, as it's you. I can always pick some more dye up at the service station on the way home."

Sitting Rose down on her dressing table stool and handing her the second bottle of wine to unscrew, Shona wielded her scissors. "Now, hold on to your knickers and pray for a miracle."

Chapter Seven

The first thing that Rose realized when she became conscious the following morning was that her head hurt. A lot. Her mouth was bone dry, her tongue felt like it had swollen up to triple its normal size and had developed scales to boot. And she felt sure that if she opened her eyes certain doom would follow. Belatedly, after wondering if she'd caught the flu, the plague, or worse, Rose realized that she had a hangover, her first ever proper one, a genuine bona fide hangover that meant even the slightest movement or noise made her want to throw herself off the edge of the universe, never to return. It was a sensation she felt curiously proud of.

The second thing she realized was that Maddie was screaming.

"Mummy! Mummy!" The child was shrieking over and over again somewhere inside the house, the sound conveying genuine terror, a scream like she had only ever heard once before from Maddie, the night that they left home. Automatically, Rose threw herself out of bed, stumbling and swaying, her feet and head seemingly utterly disconnected as she struggled to find her balance. Panicking, she looked around for her little girl, but Maddie, still shrieking out for her, was nowhere to be seen. It took Rose several pounding heartbeats to realize that

Shona's tattooed ankle was sticking out from under the bedspread on the other side of the bed and that she was not in her own room. Lunging toward the door, Rose flung it open and found Maddie standing in the hallway, clutching Bear and her book, tears streaming down her face, her mouth open wide as she screamed again.

"It's all right, it's fine, I'm here," Rose said, dropping painfully to her knees in front of Maddie. Gently she took her by the shoulder, gripping her firmly, trying to snap her out of her frenzy of fear. "Maddie, Maddie, it's fine. Open your eyes, look at me. I'm here, I just fell asleep next door, darling. I'm so sorry . . . Maddie look at me."

Her body still convulsed with sobs, Maddie calmed a little, unscrewing her eyes to look at Rose. But before Rose could scoop Maddie in a reassuring embrace, the poor child took one look at her and, her screams renewed, flung herself into the bedroom, slamming the door behind her.

"I wondered what all the fuss was about," Jenny said, arriving slightly breathless at the top of the stairs in yet another negligee from her extensive collection, black this time and disturbingly see-through. "Now I know. What's happened to all that lovely hair, lass? No wonder the poor child's beside herself. You look like a . . . a punk!"

Rose whipped her hand to the back of her neck and felt nothing but skin and the rough stubble of what had once been her long locks, dimly remembering, as she ran her fingers over the extremely short, velvety soft, and unfamiliar texture of her hair, what she had made Shona do last night. How she had cut lock after lock of her old hair, watching it float to the floor as if it were happening to someone else entirely, and then sat with her head bowed as Shona used her bikini-line razor to taper it into the back of her neck.

"This is fucking out there," Shona had told her.

"Good," was all that Rose had said, and after that she had a hazy recollection of shrieking with laughter in the bathroom, the smell of chemicals, a slight tingling burning on her scalp, and nothing else.

"Oh," was about all she could think to say as she realized that she no longer had her hair.

"Well, you'll be needing a hat," Jenny said with an expression of distaste. "But in the meantime you'd better go and reassure that poor child of yours that you haven't been abducted by evil hairdressers in the night. Although I'm not entirely sure you haven't."

Guiltily, Rose pushed open the bedroom door to find Maddie, or what she presumed to be Maddie, huddled under her bedspread, which she had pulled tightly over her head, wrapping it around herself to block the world out. It had been a long time since Rose had seen her like this. The last time was when Maddie was barely three and suddenly became terrified of the dark and all the things her imagination could picture lurking in the shadows. The cheap wine, the strange surroundings, even Maddie's apparent and uncharacteristic ease at settling into the B & B and getting on with Jenny had all contributed into lulling Rose into a false sense of security. Of all the things she had thought as Shona chopped off her hair, and Rose had seen glimpses in the mirror of the madwoman Richard told everyone she was, Rose hadn't for a moment thought about Maddie and how much her daughter would absolutely hate her to look so completely different. Rose had learnt over the seven years of being Maddie's mother that the child required certain fixed points, like north on a compass, to feel secure. Certainties that as long as they remained unchanged meant she was sure of her place in the world and what everything meant. Having wrenched Maddie from her home and her father, Rose had let herself start believing that perhaps Maddie was growing out of her difficult stage—this strange phase that set her apart from other children—and was becoming more adaptable and at ease with the world, but of course she had been naïvely mistaken. Maddie insulated herself from everything that was going on by doing her best to ignore it and focusing on the things that she liked. Rose's new hair, though, or rather lack of it, could not be ignored.

"Maddie," Rose said softly, sitting down on the edge of the bed. She reached out to touch what she assumed was Maddie's shrouded shoulder, which flinched. "I'm so sorry you woke up alone. I got talking to Shona and I suppose I just fell asleep next door. I'm sorry I scared you."

"I thought you'd left me," Maddie said, sounding quite calm under the covers, despite her refusal to show her face.

"I would never leave you," Rose said. "Don't you know I would never leave you?"

"You left Daddy," Maddie said.

Rose ran her fingers through her unfamiliar hair once more, catching sight of herself in the dressing table mirror. It was like looking into the eyes of a stranger. The cut had completely transformed her. Suddenly the angles of her face, so like her mother's, were clear to see. The sharp cheekbones and pointed chin, which had once seemed so demure, so girlish, now looked strong, bold, even. And her gray eyes, fringed with dark lashes and framed with dark brows, seemed huge in her pale face, capped off with bright blond hair. If Rose bumped into this person in the street she'd have been a little intimidated by her, by her self-assurance and seeming confidence. Only a woman very comfortable in her own skin would dare to assume she could carry off this look. The only clue Rose had that the reflection she was looking at was her own was that small ember of terror that was always present in her eyes, always knowing that before long, the spark would be lit to ignite it. Perhaps that's what she and Maddie had in common: They were both always battling back against the constant fear that plagued them. For Maddie it was fear of change; for Rose it was a terror that somehow she'd been sucked back into the prison of her old life, that nothing would change at all.

How on earth was she going to bring Maddie round to the way she looked? She couldn't blame her daughter for hating it. She wasn't at all sure she liked it herself.

"Maddie." Rose gently tugged at the cover that Maddie clung to. "Maddie, come on, come and look at my hair. I know it was a shock, I know it's really different, but if you look you will see it's still me, it's still Mummy." There was no movement. "If you don't look, you won't be able to see, will you?"

Maddie sighed deeply. "I'm not coming out. I don't like it out there. I don't like you like that."

"Look, Maddie . . . I haven't really been fair, I know that. I've changed everything around you and it's not that I haven't thought about how it will affect you, it's just that I didn't expect it to affect you so much."

"I am a very sensitive child." Maddie repeated what her father often told her, much to Rose's distress. Rose felt that if you told a child enough times that something was wrong with her, she'd start to believe it.

"You are a very brave child, who's coped very well with a lot . . . Look, do you want to talk about what happened the night we left Daddy? About why we had to go?"

There was a long silence under the covers and then, "No."

"OK, but come out and look at my hair? I know I look a bit different, but it is still me. If you look, you will see."

"I don't want to look. I saw it, it's disgusting."

"It's not, it's . . . modern," Rose said, although she wasn't sure she disagreed with Maddie's first assessment. "Look, come on, come out and look." Once again she pulled gently at the covers.

Finally Maddie emerged from beneath the bedspread, her face flushed, her dark hair tangled and damp.

"Now look," Rose said, smoothing Maddie's hair out of her eyes, picking up her hands and putting them on her face. "Still the same eyes, nose, mouth, ears that are a bit sticky out. Still the same Mummy, just with different hair."

Rose waited patiently while Maddie studied her, searching her face for a long time. Finally she dropped her hands from Rose's face and sat back a little. "It is you, I suppose."

"So do you like it?" Rose asked her, chancing a hopeful smile.

"No," Maddie said. "You look thin and old."

"Oh, well," Rose said, suddenly feeling rather deflated instead of energized and youthful. "Perhaps you'll get used to it. Perhaps I will, and if not I can always grow it back." Maddie stared at her for a few moments more, her brow furrowed as she tried to adapt to her mother's new look.

"Mummy, did you change your hair to stop Daddy from finding us?" Maddie asked her, the question unnerving Rose more than she had been prepared for. "Is it a disguise?"

"Why do you ask, sweetheart?" Rose said tentatively.

"Because if that is why, then I want yellow hair too."

Breakfast was something of an awkward affair, not least because no one made it down for the eight thirty deadline, and today, for some reason—perhaps to mark her disapproval of Rose's hair, or Shona, or both—was the first time that Jenny had decided to enforce her law. By the time Rose had showered and dressed in Haleigh's denim miniskirt over a pair of leggings, topped off with a red and white striped off-the-shoulder T-shirt, which Maddie chose, all that was left out for breakfast was miniboxes of cereal and a jug of lukewarm milk. Still immersed in her dressing gown, her hair matted and last night's make-up staining her face, Shona followed Rose and Maddie downstairs, cursing miserably under her breath and swearing off alcohol for life.

"Fuck's sake, I could murder a pig," Shona said, slouching into a chair and resting her head on the table.

"That wouldn't be very nice," Maddie said. "And besides, dead pigs are turned into bacon, so you don't need to."

"Not today they're not," Shona growled. "The bacon police have taken away our pig privileges."

Hearing Jenny bustling about, banging pots and clanging cutlery with ostentatious fury, Rose ventured into the kitchen.

"Sorry we are late for breakfast," she said gingerly as she watched Jenny scrubbing at her stovetop. "It took a long time to bring Maddie round."

"I'm not surprised," Jenny said primly, refusing to look at Rose herself. "That poor child needs a routine, parents she can count on, not some gadabout of a mother who decides to run away and dye her hair at a moment's notice."

Rose took a breath. Jenny hadn't disapproved of or commented on her motives until now. Was it really just her hair that annoyed the landlady so much, or was it something else? Watching Jenny bustle crossly gave Rose that familiar sense of discomfort that she would have with Richard so often, knowing she had done something to displease him, and that he'd toy with and torment her for as long as he pleased before he finally revealed, in a usually explosive burst of anger, exactly what crime she was guilty of that time. Day after day, hour after hour, year after year, Rose tiptoed around him, trying to second-guess his every move, his every thought, the sick feeling of knowing she was inevitably getting it wrong dogging her steps. She didn't want to feel that way now, not here, not like this. This was her new start, and as short-lived as it might be, she was determined to be the person, here in this place and this moment, that she had always wanted to be.

"Look, Jenny," Rose said, "I know we were up late, that maybe we were noisy last night, and that you don't like my hair, but . . . this isn't like you. What's really going on?"

Jenny slammed down a breadboard, making Rose jump a little.

"How long are you staying for?" she asked.

"I don't know," Rose said. "Until I've spoken to John a bit more, until I've talked to all the people I want to, until . . ." Until my husband catches up with me and all of this is over. "Why are you so keen to get rid of me? Is it Shona?"

Jenny pursed her lips. "I don't want you getting involved with my Ted."

"I beg your pardon?" Rose asked her. "Is this about going to his gig? I'm only going to be friendly. Do you think I'm chasing your son? He's half my age!"

"He isn't," Jenny said. "He's a few years younger than you, not much. My Brian is three years younger than me; you wouldn't think it to look at him, I know. It's not your age I'm worried about, it's Ted."

"Ted!" Rose couldn't help but laugh. "Ted's not really interested in me. I'm a novelty to him, that's all! He's a nice young man, you've brought him up well. And he's funny and a laugh, but I think if I'm anything to him, it is a project, something new to think about for a bit."

"Well," Jenny said awkwardly, obviously finding it quite hard to be cross anymore and struggling to climb down, "he's not normally so keen on a girl as to get her to go to his gig. Normally they are the keen ones." She looked sideways at

Rose. “Maybe you’re not quite such a risk, now that you’ve butchered that lovely hair of yours.”

“I wasn’t ever!” Rose exclaimed.

“It’s just . . .” Jenny paused, as if weighing whether or not to say more. “He makes out he’s some gigolo type, but deep down he goes soft on a girl far too easily. I don’t want him to go soft on you.”

“There really isn’t any chance of that happening,” Rose assured her. “Nothing is going to happen between me and Ted. That’s the last thing on my mind.”

“Hey,” Shona called out from the dining room, “where’s the nearest town? I can’t stand seeing this poor kid dressed in hand-me-downs anymore, or you dressed up like mutton.”

“That’s rich, coming from you!” Rose called back. “I guess Carlisle is the nearest town.”

“Right, then, before we do anything else we’re going to buy you two some clothes,” Shona said, and Rose turned to watch her grinning at Maddie and ruffling her hair. “Maybe we can stretch to a bacon sandwich while we’re there.”

“Well, I suppose you do look like a refugee from a prison camp,” Jenny said, scrutinizing Rose’s hair once more, “and my Haleigh’s clothes are a bit young for you.” She held out a newly washed frying pan. “Here you are, if you want to do yourself some bacon, you can. Make sure you clean up after, though.”

“Thank you,” Rose said. “I will. Not that I’ll eat anything. I’m too nervous.”

“About talking to your dad?” Jenny asked.

“Yes,” Rose admitted. “I didn’t think I cared anymore. I honestly believed that I’d given up minding about him not being around at all, and God knows I shouldn’t. I didn’t even come here to find him. But I have, and the thing is, I think that maybe I *do* care. That I really, really do mind. That it turns out that I've been missing my dad for a long time. And that makes me nervous, because if I feel one thing for him, then the anger and hurt and pain will be bound to follow. And he's already made it pretty clear that he doesn't feel anything about me."

"Now then," Jenny said, her voice softening, "who's to say he doesn't feel the same?"

"Him," Rose said simply. "He couldn't have been more blunt."

"When the kids were little," Jenny said, "we had this old collie. Got her off a farmer who couldn't use her anymore as a working animal. She'd got arthritis, you see, wasn't quick enough on her toes. She was an old girl, Ginnie, but had plenty of years left in her so Brian brought her home for the kids. And they loved her. Fussed over her like nothing I've ever seen. We all did." Jenny smiled fondly as the memory played out in her mind's eye. "And then one day Ginnie got out, which normally wouldn't matter round here, but she got out on the one day this big old lorry was hurtling through the village. I could hear her cries from upstairs. I had to take her to the vet, and there was nothing for it, she had to be put down. It was my fault, you see. I left the back gate open. And I was heartbroken—not that you'd ever know it. I acted as if for all the world I didn't give two hoots that Ginnie had passed on. The kids were howling, Brian was distraught, and I was as hard as nails, tough as old boots. It's just a dog, I'd say."

"Your point is?" Rose asked her uncertainly.

"Guilt," Jenny said. "It makes you act in very strange ways."

A morning of shopping in Carlisle was not quite enough to take Rose's mind off everything, but it went some way to establishing her fledgling sense of self a little more. Shona picked stuff for her to try on that she never would have dreamt of wearing before: skinny jeans, bright summer dresses, and tops that Rose almost couldn't bear to look at, at first, just as she almost couldn't bear to look at her radically altered reflection when she tried them on. Then after a while she stopped thinking of the slender blonde in the mirror as herself, and it was almost like she was dressing up a stranger, picking and choosing for another person entirely. As soon as Rose saw it that way, she stopped letting Shona choose for her and began to make her own careful selection of the few things she decided she could afford until, when she picked her final shopping bag up off the counter, Rose at least knew what the new her looked like, even if she still wasn't at all sure what it felt like to be her. It brightened Maddie too, as she led her mother around the shops, doing her best to replace her absent wardrobe with items identical to those left at home, insisting on ditching her boy's jeans for good in the changing room and wearing her new Hello Kitty ones from that moment on.

They were in good spirits when they got back to the B & B in the early afternoon, and for a few fleeting hours it had felt to Rose like she really was on holiday. And then she remembered she was due to visit her father again. Even in her new handpicked jeans and dark green scooped-back T-shirt, Rose was sure she wasn't completely prepared for that.

Shona looked pale and sickly as Rose prepared, with a definite air of doom, to go and see her father. She wasn't sure how much she'd drunk last night, but Shona must have had more. Her brightness of the morning was fading rapidly and her normally tanned complexion was decidedly sallow.

"I like your hair," Shona said as Rose collected her bag and waited for Maddie, who was fetching Bear and her Egyptians book. "It suits you. Which is really lucky, because I didn't have a clue what I was doing. Who knew that sensible little Rose could be so wild? Next time you get drunk, let's not hang around any tattoo parlors . . ."

"I'm thinking maybe a double nipple piercing next time," Rose said, smiling weakly, preoccupied with what was about to come.

"Look, babe," Shona said, holding the car door open for Maddie to scramble into the backseat. "Don't let the fucker see you're upset. Don't let him have the power. You and me both know it's the tears that give them the power."

Rose hesitated as she opened the driver's door. "That's our men, Shona. Not all men are like that."

Shona shrugged. "If you say so. Just don't let him see you cry."

"OK," Rose said, reaching out to touch her friend's arm, suddenly reluctant to leave her. Every now and then she'd get glimpses of what life was really like for Shona, lonely, difficult, a constant struggle to keep her head above water, and all she wants is someone to make everything all right, even if it's only temporary. It was a yearning that Rose understood. "Should I stay?"

"Stay? Why?" Shona looked puzzled. "Go on, sod off. I'm going to spend the afternoon tormenting the old bag; I'm cool. Stop trying to get out of it and fuck off."

"Right." Rose nodded. "Wish me luck and I'll tell you all about it at the gig later," she said. "Over a lemonade."

"Don't be so fucking ridiculous," Shona said, rolling her eyes at Maddie. "The only thing that's going to cure this hangover is vodka."

Rose found that her stomach was in knots as she pulled the car into the muddy yard. It was a brighter day today. A certain golden light reflected off the relentless steel-gray clouds, bringing sharp contrast to the early August day. In this oddly surreal light Storm Cottage sat like a bright white jewel in the crook of the mountain, looking much less grim and cold than it had the previous day. Rose turned off the engine and sat for a while, watching the dark, empty windows of the cottage as Maddie climbed into the front passenger seat to sit alongside her, offering her own particular brand of solidarity.

"It looks like a troll's house," she said after several moments of observation. This wasn't a good thing. Maddie had developed a genuine fear of trolls after a particularly graphic storytelling session at the local library with some wannabe actress who seemed to think that Storytelling Saturday was a chance of impressing the Royal Shakespeare Company. For months Maddie's debilitating fear of trolls and where they might be lurking had prevented Rose from doing anything with her that didn't involve school and home, and home only after every nook and cranny had been proved to be free of any child- and goat-eating troll.

"Trolls only live under bridges, remember?" Rose said, referring to their second visit to the library, where a very kind librarian put on her serious-looking glasses especially in order to assure Maddie that it was a fact that trolls only live under bridges in Scandinavia and aren't indigenous to the UK at all, even producing a book to that effect. It had seemed to work in quelling fact-hungry Maddie's concerns up until now, and Rose hoped it would hold a little longer. The last thing she needed was to be managing her daughter's irrationalities when she had so many of her own to contend with.

"And besides," Rose continued, looking across the yard to where an arc of bright electric light was escaping from the barn, its door slightly ajar, "we're not going into the cottage. We're going to the barn. Only nice things can be found in barns."

"Mum, I'm scared," Maddie said, staring at the barn, which imposed itself starkly against the mountain that rose behind it.

"Me too," Rose said.

"Are you?" Maddie twisted in her seat to look at Rose, suddenly fascinated. "But you are a grown-up."

"I know," Rose said. "Will you look after me?"

"OK, then," Maddie said, the sudden novelty of responsibility banishing her own worries in an instant.

Steeling herself, Rose got out of the car, Haleigh's slightly too large and downtrodden fake Uggs sinking immediately into the mud. Going round the car, she opened the door and took Maddie's hand, allowing her daughter to march her across the mire towards the barn, her heart beating furiously as she approached. Had John even remembered that she was coming back today?

With Maddie's hand in hers, Rose ventured into the barn.

John was standing with his back to them, his nose millimeters away from the surface of a huge canvas which covered almost an entire wall, his white-clad figure standing out like a bolt of lightning from the mass of color. Completely absorbed in what he was doing, he was unaware that he had visitors, and Rose was content to let it stay that way for a few minutes more as she watched him at work, instantly transported back in a vivid flash to her childhood: the scent of paint, the touch of it, oily and viscous beneath her fingers, breathing in the heady fumes of her father's secret world as she'd watched him working, feeling closer to him as he ignored her than she often did when she had his attention. Rose had always known, even when she was very small, that when her father was working, nothing else existed for him, and when he wasn't working he longed to be. Even when they were walking on the beach, or when he would swing her around and around so fast the world became a blur of color, she knew he would rather be at his easel. How he would hate this new distraction.

Forgetting her caretaking duties, Maddie wriggled her fingers free from Rose's tight grip, taking a few steps forward to watch what John was doing, clearly fascinated but making no attempt to approach him.

Caught in a paralysis of uncertainty as to what to do next, Rose looked at her surroundings, forcing herself into the present moment, determined to be the adult woman who'd broken away from her marriage, traveled hundreds of miles, and cut her hair, and not the little girl who'd do anything for a few seconds of her father's attention.

It came as no surprise to her that the building, as shabby as it had looked on the outside, had had more money spent on it than what she had seen of the ramshackle old cottage. It had been divided into two by the white plasterboard partition wall that the work in progress was leaning against, the farther room secured behind a white padlocked door. The plastered walls had also been whitewashed, and long skylights had been cut into the high ceiling to allow in the maximum amount of natural light. When, like today, this was in short supply, there were huge daylight lamps plugged in all around, bathing the room in artificial sunlight and giving it a dreamlike, surreal quality. To their left, a stack of huge blank canvases, some taller than her father, stretched and ready to be worked on, were leaning against the far wall, and one work, a curiously disjointed version of the landscape that enveloped them, completed with her father's signature, still glistening with the thick slick of fresh paint, rested against another.

"Your style has changed," Rose said, surprising herself and causing John to start.

He had been silently regarding his work, his long arms wrapped around his chest as if he were hugging himself. Still clutching himself, he half turned to look at her, and if he was shocked by her appearance his expression did not register it. Despite her best intentions, Rose felt acutely the same sense of trepidation and uncertainty she had had when, as a little girl, she'd crept into his studio, even though her mother used to warn her not to, crawling along the dusty floorboards of the converted garage where he was working, sitting at his feet, watching in contented silence as he created universes with his brushes. Sometimes he wouldn't notice she was there for hours, and then when he did, he'd pick her up and twirl her round until she was giddy with laughter. Then he'd throw down his brushes and take her to the beach to look for "interesting things" until well past teatime and bedtime, and any time a little girl should be out rooting around in sand and stones at all. Other times he'd see her creeping up on him and settle her at a table with her own little piece of board, brushes, and a palette full of fat blobs of color, telling her she could stay as long as she was quiet. And sometimes, just every now and then, the sight of her would make him furious. He'd pick her up, his grip pinching her arms, and march her back into the house to deposit her at her mother's feet, raging all the while at the useless mother and pointless wife who utterly failed to understand his need to work in peace. As he slammed the door shut, Rose would run to it, pressing her palms against the glass as he strode back down the garden to his studio, her sobs muffled behind the closed door. And yet she never blamed him for his taciturn fury, not once, no matter how precarious her place in his affections could be. It took Rose a very long time to blame him at all, to realize it was John who had taught her always to feel like an impostor. And now, when she had crept up on him in his studio again, would he throw her in the air and kiss her, or throw her out? This time she knew the answer.

"How has it changed?" John asked her, choosing not to acknowledge Maddie, who was inching closer to the painting, ignoring the man as she was seemingly fascinated with the image. Rose found it infinitely harder to think what to say next.

"It's friendlier than I remember. Less . . . like you. And you can tell what it is. I can only think of a few pieces like that from before." Two pieces, to be precise: his painting of Millthwaite, which she had kept all those years, and one of Tilda, the woman he'd left her for, a painting that Rose had happily let Richard throw into the trash with the rest of her father's things, soon after they were married. What paintings were there of her now? Rose wondered. What markers of their life together? Rose wasn't sure if she wanted Tilda to be part of John's life or not. It would seem like an awfully cruel twist if he no longer knew the woman he'd ripped her life apart for, if he'd discarded her as easily as he had his first family, and yet Rose was hoping that she wouldn't appear carrying tea and calling her "dear." John had yet to mention her, and Rose decided not to ask.

"It's more commercial, is what you mean," John conceded, untouched by the barbs in her comment. "This is the work that pays the bills. My real work I keep elsewhere."

"I think this is much easier to look at." Rose gestured at the work, finding it rather beautiful. "I like it."

The hint of a smiled played around John's mouth. "It's often the people with no taste who have all the money," he told her.

"I clearly have no taste or money," Rose said, his words stinging her pride, even though she was certain they weren't intended as an insult. "So, after everything you've done for the sake of your artistic integrity, all the lives you've ruined for your work, you've given up and started painting picture postcards?"

The words shot out of her mouth like a bullet from a gun, far more pointed than she had intended them to be, her desire to strike back at him greater than her restraint.

John shrugged, unconcerned by the barbs that flew his way. "Integrity is for young men."

"Funny, I didn't notice that you were too concerned with integrity when last I saw you." Rose walked a little nearer to him, searching his face for any trace of the father who used to take her beachcombing and, finding none, wondered if he even remembered the last time he'd left her sitting on the stairs as he cheerfully said goodbye. This would be a losing battle, Rose was sure of that. No matter how much she fought for him to care and remember, he would not let it happen, perhaps because he couldn't do either, and yet, even though she knew she should turn on her heel and walk away from what would certainly be a painful and disappointing experience, she could not.

"Well, anyway," she said, struggling to regain her composure, "this is Maddie. She is your granddaughter."

John said nothing and, without even glancing at the child, he returned his gaze to the canvas.

"Aren't you going to say hello at least?" Rose asked him tightly, much less able to bear the slighting of her daughter than she was when it came to herself.

"I recall agreeing to answer your questions," John said coolly, "and I emphatically remember saying that I do not wish for a family reunion of any description. I told you, Rose, you will not find that here."

"I do not wish for a family reunion of any description either," Maddie said with such calm certainty that John glanced down at her for a moment. "I just wanted to look at you. You look old and quite dirty. I'm not really interested in you. But I do want to know what that paint feels like between your fingers. It looks much more slimy than poster paint. I like how it stands up, like icing from the cardboard. And sort of swirls together instead of mixing. Tell me how you mix it up but can still see the separate colors."

John took a step back, his brows raised as he observed his granddaughter.

"It's called canvas, not cardboard," he told her. "Here."

He held out his palette, heavily laden with paint, and watched as Maddie took a finger full of deep crimson oil paint and rubbed it between her thumb and fingers, bringing the paint up to her nose and inhaling deeply.

"It's sticky," she told Rose, who watched from a distance, "and greasy."

Cheerfully, she smeared it on the back of her hand and then impressed that smear against her cheek, smiling at the cool sensation and acrid scent that accompanied it. "I want to paint with it too."

"Come on, Maddie." Rose held out her hand, keen that Maddie should not be disappointed. "John is too busy for us."

"No," John said. "No, I said I will talk to you and I will. The child can paint while we talk, if that is what she wants."

He rooted around in what looked like a pile of rubbish for a while and then brought out a small piece of board. Taking an old china plate from a shelf, he picked up four or five lifeless-looking tubes of paint, squeezing fat slugs of color onto the plate and placing it on the floor, leaning the board against the back wall of the barn, and throwing down a couple of balding brushes.

Without needing to be told, Maddie knelt in the dust on the floor in front of the board and picked up a brush. "What shall I paint?" she asked him.

"Paint what you see," John said, returning to his work. "The only way to begin as an artist is to paint what you see, because it's not what you see that matters, it's how you see it."

Disconcerted by her father's sudden almost grandfatherly gesture, not to mention his unexpectedly good-natured exchange with Maddie, Rose was at a loss again to know what to expect, how to be. Cool and aloof had been her plan, and his too, it seemed, but five minutes with him had made her angry and resentful, ready to leave until suddenly he was fairly kind and conversational. At no point had bringing Maddie to Storm Cottage been about getting to know the man he was today, or building bridges, but if he was to become a memory of Maddie's, if only for a few hours, then it seemed sensible to try at least to get a better sense of him so that she and Maddie would be able to talk about the time they met John Jacobs, whoever he was. Rose only knew that the father she had known as a child, the bright, shining giant of a man she had been dazzled by, seemed entirely disconnected from this gaunt, gray man, who had turned back to his canvas and was doggedly moving waves of paint around with a palette knife.

"Talk," he instructed Rose, putting her at an instant loss to know what to say.

"Millthwaite seems like a nice place to live," Rose said awkwardly, finding it impossible to make small talk with him.

"It's a place," John said evenly. "The place that I happened to end up, though I must admit the landscape is very useful for my work. People in boxes in cities like to look at mountains and imagine they have a life outside their dull, pointless existence."

"So you don't mix much with the villagers, you haven't any friends here?" Rose hesitated. "You live alone now?"

"I live alone now. Look, I haven't seen you for twenty-odd years. Do you think that if I can live without my daughter I'd need the reassurance of strangers to get by?" John asked, pausing to look at her for a second, clearly irritated. "The whole point of my life, of the person that I am, is that I don't need or want people in it. I want seclusion, I want to be left alone. For the most part, I get it."

Rose took a breath, looking towards the partially open barn door, fighting the sudden urge to run out of it, and run and run up the nearest slope without stopping until her lungs threatened to burst and she could suck in mouthfuls of air that had not also been inhaled by this man, this cold stranger. Was this what her father had always been like, or were her sun-drenched memories of the man that she had once believed loved her figments of her imagination?

"Is that what happened to Tilda?" Rose said, tasting the metallic taint of lips too often bitten of late, as she searched for some word or memory that would make him feel *something*. "Did you use her up and throw her away too? After leaving Mum, devastating our lives without a backward glance, did you do the same to her?"

"What happened between Tilda and me is none of your business," John said curtly. "You are two separate chapters of my life. And both are now closed."

"*That's* your logic?" Rose asked him, incredulous, her determination to remain as detached as he was crumbling easily away. "You decided to leave one life behind and start—or rather, wreck—another, and never the twain shall meet? Children don't have an expiration date, you know."

"Apparently not." John sighed, wiping his knife on the hem of his shirt and turning back to his tubes of paint, his fingers hovering over the colors until eventually he selected burnt umber. Glancing up at Rose, who was still rooted by the door, he asked, "Have you thought about talking to your husband, trying to work things out? It might not be too late if you go back now."

"If I go back?" Rose shook her head, forcing herself to keep her voice low. "You really will do anything to get me out of here, even try your hand at matchmaking. Even though you have no idea what hell you'd be sending me back to."

"You are not me," John said. "You need people. And as you have so vociferously reminded me, a child needs a father. It is worth talking, surely. At least attempt to work things out."

"Like you talked to Mum and tried to work things out?" Rose snapped before she could help herself, unable to maintain this distant impartiality, tipping her head sharply to one side. "Oh, except that you disappeared one morning, leaving without even having the courage to wake her up and tell her you were going, leaving only your daughter to tell her, once she'd sobered up, that you'd said goodbye."

Rose remembered all too clearly that morning, those moments of confused quiet after John shut the door. She had remained sitting on the bottom stair, wondering exactly what had just happened, torn between this pain that seemed intent on rending her chest in two, and a child's desire just to be normal. To pretend it hadn't happened, that her father hadn't just left, and that if he had, he would be back again soon. Glancing up the stairs to where Marian was still sleeping off the bottle of wine she had drunk the night before, sitting at the kitchen table, weeping quietly as Rose made them sandwiches for tea, Rose had wondered if she should wake her mother. Maybe Marian would hold her, stroke her hair and comfort her, like she had when she was very little, or maybe she'd start crying again, bury her head in the pillow, and ignore Rose, who'd sit uncertainly on the edge of the bed, tentatively rubbing her mother's shoulder, until it became clear that it didn't matter to Marian whether she was there or not.

But by the time Rose had reached the top of the stairs, her fairy-tale ending played out in her head, she realized the truth. Her mother was still in her bed, still sleeping through the deep debilitating misery that Rose would later understand as depression, but which then, as a little girl, hanging on the bedroom door, she saw only as a lack of care. No one cared about her anymore.

"Dad's gone," she'd told Marian, shaking her shoulder as hard as she could, until her eyes flickered open and focused on Rose. "He's gone with his fancy woman. He went hours ago. I've been on my own all day, not that you care."

Nine-year-old Rose had slammed her mother's bedroom door on the way out, running downstairs in her own sudden flood of tears. But it had been the sound of Marian's dry, rattling repeated sobs that had carried on as Rose had gone to sleep that night, still dressed in her day clothes, teeth and hair unbrushed, hoping against hope that everything would be OK in the morning. But the truth was that, really, nothing had ever been OK again.

"You know, I thought that when I saw you I'd remember how much I missed you and loved you," Rose said bitterly, and for a moment there it was almost like that. "But looking at you, listening to you now, all I can remember is how much I hate you."

"I don't blame you for hating me." John turned round to look at her directly for the first time. "I made mistakes, bad ones. I was wrapped up in the alcohol, I behaved . . . thoughtlessly. You won't find me denying that. I am what I am. But *you* are not me, so don't try to escape your own problems by laying them at my feet. You have a child. Perhaps you haven't reached the end of your relationship, perhaps there is more ground to cover. Maybe you can sort it out. He might take you back, for the girl's sake."

"Take me back!" Rose breathed, the fury that had bubbled

constantly under her skin since she arrived threatening to erupt. Desperately she tried to contain her voice to an urgent whisper, for fear that it would distract Maddie from her painting. "Do you know, Mum would have taken you back, even after everything, even after the humiliation, the years of silence from you? Even up until the point she walked into the sea and drowned herself she would have taken you back, John. All those years, wasted on loving you and she never got over it, never moved on. I know, because I was there every day from the age of nine to pick up the pieces. Every single day I had to put her back together as best I could, made sure she was washed, fed at least. Every day until the day she died I cleaned up the mess you made, the destruction you walked out on. Oh, I know my husband would have me back. I know he'd have me back like a shot, he'd be thrilled. But *I won't go.* I won't make the same mistake Mum did. I won't go back and no one can make me, not him and especially not you."

The tension crackled in the air between them. For the first time since she had arrived he studied her face closely, and Rose knew he was searching for traces of what had happened to make her so angry, so frightened. Something akin to concern showed in his expression, and the next time he spoke, his voice was more gentle, if still halted and stiff.

"It must have been hard for you," he conceded quietly. "All that business with your mother."

"All that business." Rose laughed mirthlessly. "Which part, becoming a carer for my clinically depressed mother, or discovering that just when I thought she was finally getting better she more than likely killed herself?"

"All of it, of course," John said. "Although I didn't realize the extent of how very ill she was. I knew she was upset, of course, but I didn't realize it became such a burden to you."

"It wasn't a burden," Rose snapped. "She was my mum. I loved her. Which doesn't mean to say that it was OK for you to leave a little girl to cope with all of that. It wasn't. When did you find out she was dead?"

The words still stuck in Rose's throat when she was forced to articulate them. Because although her mother had never again held her, or stroked her hair, or comforted her after John left, Rose still missed her keenly every day; she still wished for her mother over and over again.

"The week it happened, or thereabouts." John dropped his gaze from hers. "Tilda still had a friend down there. She phoned to let us know when she read about it in the local rag, I assume."

Detaching herself from the refuge of the door, Rose sat down hard on an ancient stool that stood in the middle of the studio for no apparent reason.

"You knew, and you didn't come for me?" Rose asked him. "You left me to deal with all that, alone? I can understand that perhaps you couldn't face Mum, but even when I was alone, you still didn't think enough of me to come?"

John bowed his head, pinching the bridge of his nose between his fingers. "I didn't think of you at all," he said simply, finally raising his head to meet her eyes. "What I thought of was the next drink, and the drink after that. And that was all. Rose, I'm tired, and you are upset. Perhaps it would be best if you left now. I need to work."

"Finished!" Maddie said, trotting cheerfully over to Rose and, taking her fingers, pulling her towards her painted board. Suddenly exhausted, Rose went with Maddie and looked at her painting. Taking John at his word, she had painted the rough wooden slats of the end of the barn, which was what she could see from her position on the floor, thick black lines delineating each plank, which she had built up with layer upon layer of colors, with a striking textured and pleasing result.

"Darling, that's lovely!" Rose breathed, seeing the rare flash of pride and pleasure on Maddie's face. "Really, really lovely."

"It is good," John said, standing some way behind them. "The girl's got an eye, that's for sure."

"I know," Maddie said happily. "I didn't even really try. It just came out. It's brilliant. Painting is brilliant." She looked John square in the eye, unflinching. "I want to come and paint again. Soon."

Rose felt her heart clench, unable to bear her daughter, who was so rarely and so purely happy, suffering rejection.

"Come tomorrow," John said, so quietly that Rose wasn't sure she'd heard him.

"I beg your pardon?" Rose asked him.

"Bring the child tomorrow. Shc can paint, I can work. We can talk more."

"You want to talk to me?" Rose was incredulous.

John looked pained by her skepticism, and suddenly very frail, as if contact with another person did genuinely drain him.

"Rose"—he said her name slowly, testing it on his tongue—"please understand, I am not a good man, or a kind one. I am not any sort of father or grandfather. I may well have ruined your life, and if I have . . . then I think the booze killed any part of me that would feel guilty about it years ago. But you are my daughter, and I do wish to do for you what little I can. I must be honest, I don't believe that talking to me will make your life any more tolerable, but it may help you see the way forward from here."

"If you are talking about going back to my husband . . . ?"

Rose said warily, very unsure of what, if anything, this remote man was offering her.

"No," John said, turning back to his work. "You should realize that I am not the sort of person to make another do a single thing she doesn't want to. Come back tomorrow if you want the girl to paint, and for us to talk some more. If not, then I shall carry on as before."

"I want to come back," Maddie said. "And paint. I want to paint that wood again."

"What time?" Rose asked him.

"Makes no odds to me," John said. "I'll be in here as long as the sun is up."

"That was good," Maddie said happily as she and Rose headed back across the yard, Rose caught up in a flurry of confused emotion. It would have been impossible to feel more anger or animosity towards her father than she had in the barn. It had been pure and visceral, pumping through her veins instead of blood. But somehow their meeting had resulted in a planned return visit. Rose wasn't entirely sure how that had happened, or what it meant, except that for some reason that she wasn't able to fathom yet, John wanted her to come back. He must, otherwise Rose was very certain that they wouldn't have been invited.

"I like John, actually," Maddie said. "He's very interesting."

"Good," Rose said, pausing and turning to gaze up at the mountains around them, finding their ancient enormity a comfort for her sore mind. "I think he liked you too, in his way."

"He liked how I painted," Maddie said proudly, certain that was more important than personal affection. "I am extremely good, after all."

"You are." Rose smiled, letting her hand rest briefly on Maddie's shoulder before she inevitably shrugged it off. Maddie had looked more at ease in the company of her strange grandfather, and with a paintbrush in her hand, than Rose had seen her for a long time. Naturally it was easy to blame Richard for Maddie's sense of unease, the tautness in her face and limbs, the underlying current of anxiety that Rose thought she could sometimes feel vibrating from her daughter. But perhaps she had to accept responsibility for at least some of what happened to make life with Richard so toxic. If she'd been more experienced with men, if she'd listened to the sense of disquiet that had always been there, even when they were first together and she had thought she was at her happiest . . . But she'd pushed it away, and pushed it away, ignored her own instincts for the chance of having the kind of normal happy life that she saw going on all around her. For the chance to be anything but like her parents.

Perhaps it was her anxious, frightened, overprotective, uncertain mother that was stifling Maddie the most, Rose thought as she remembered the sense of creeping dread that used to pervade her as she made the slow walk home from school to where her mother would be waiting for her, waiting to unleash all her unhappiness and sorrow onto her daughter's shoulders. Rose dreaded sliding the key into the lock, knowing a tidal wave of misery was waiting for her on the other side of it, and yet she always opened the door. She always went in. What if, even at this young age, Maddie's oddness, which set her so far apart from other children her own age, was really caused by Rose, by her failure to stop her unhappiness leaking out through every pore, no matter how much she tried to hide it? Being free of Richard, even if for only a little while, had seemed to breathe life into her. She felt like a wind-up toy, finally able to release all that pent-up energy after sitting on a shelf for so long. Rose had to acknowledge that she felt released, here in the wild country, and perhaps that was slowly starting to rub off onto Maddie too.

Rose had come here chasing a pipe dream, a fantasy, but the reality was that nothing else mattered but Maddie, because if it wasn't for her odd, awkward, strange, distant little girl and a battered and tatty old postcard with a few lines scrawled on the back, then Rose would have walked into the sea after her mother a long time ago and have been glad to feel the cool, soft waves closing over her head. And just as Rose didn't want Maddie to dread coming home to her, neither did she want to leave her with the legacy her mother had. It was time to thank Frasier, for keeping her heart beating when it was almost ready to give up hope. After that she could try her best to forget him.

Albie had told her that she was bound to bump into Frasier; that any day now, she'd turn a corner and he'd be here. It seemed strange that she'd found her way to this random, abstract corner of the world to find the converging threads of her past and future meeting head on. If she just stayed here and did nothing, then one day she would do the thing she'd dreamt of for a very long time. She'd see Frasier again. And even at her most rational and pragmatic, Rose could not imagine how the world might continue after that moment, even if it was, as Shona seemed certain, an epic anticlimax.

How childish of her to believe that somehow he would just walk into her life like a knight in shining armor and rescue her. It was time she stood on her own two feet, forgot her silly romantic notions and got on with the business of being a grown-up and a parent. Perhaps she had come here seeking something that didn't ever truly exist, but even if that was true, the look on Maddie's face when she'd been painting was reason enough to go back and see John again tomorrow; it was reason enough to stay for as long as she could.

"Do you know, I wouldn't mind going up one of those big hills," Maddie said, squinting at the horizon, where the sun was doing its best to burn away the thick insulation of cloud.

"What, now?" Rose asked her. Walking up a hill was the very last thing that she had in mind right now, but it was so surprising for Maddie to want to do anything physical that she didn't like the thought of turning her down. And besides, Rose had a feeling that if there was ever a place to clear her head of all the cotton wool and confusion it was packed with, then halfway up a very big hill would be just that place. "Well, I don't suppose it will hurt to go a little way. Looks like the rain's going to hold off for a while. There's a footpath over there, I think."

Rose pointed towards a stile across the yard, bridging a fence that led into a field of sheep, a worn-away path snaking up the more gentle slope of the mountain.

"We are like archaeologists about to open the lost tomb of Tutankhamen!" Maddie said, charging off across the yard with a sudden burst of energy, just as a shiny, outsized 4×4 Audi rolled into the yard, missing squashing her by mere centimeters.

Maternal fury filling her instantly, Rose marched across the squelching mud to confront the driver, pulling open the heavy door before he could turn the engine off.

"What the hell do you think you're doing?" she shouted as he climbed out of the car. "You almost killed my daughter with your idiotic driving!"

"What do I think *I'm* doing? How about *you* controlling your child?" he said, hackles rising instantly, clearly shocked by his near miss. "I wasn't expecting a child in my path. I've been here many times and there have never been any small children before."

"You've never seen any small children before—that's your excuse, really . . ." Rose faltered to a stop, her mouth freezing before it could form another syllable as she realized whom she was looking at. The man who had almost run her daughter over was Frasier McCleod. The moment she'd just been anticipating had arrived without any fanfare or warning, and standing there, looking slightly flushed and furious, was her pipe dream in the flesh. He hadn't changed, not a single bit, since the moment she had first set eyes on him standing on her doorstep, although everything about him—his clothes, his car—indicated wealth and success. And yet she had changed almost completely, and most radically in the last few hours. With a freezing cold shock, Rose realized that Frasier McCleod was looking her right in the face, ready for a showdown, and completely oblivious of the fact that they had ever met before. He had forgotten her.

Unprepared for the tidal wave of emotion that raced through her body as she looked into his sea-green eyes, Rose struggled to steady herself, to reconcile how her heart leapt at the sight of a man who was, after all, a stranger. Rose felt like she was looking into the eyes of an old friend—more than that, of the love of her life.

Frasier, however, obviously felt like he was looking into the eyes of an irate mother, with a taste in clothes that were far too young for her and an edgy hairstyle that looked like she meant trouble and should probably not be messed with, as she stood frozen like a manic mannequin, her hands glued to her hips.

"If you don't mind, I'm running late," he said in his soft Scottish accent. "No harm is done."

"No harm?" Rose managed to say, barely raising her voice above a whisper, battling to blink away the tears that had suddenly sprung to her eyes.

"Are you OK?" Frasier sighed, looking around as if hoping to be rescued. Reaching out, he touched her on the forearm. "Shall I call someone?" His tone was so tense, so impatient that Rose could hardly believe this was the man she'd traveled so many miles to meet.

"I'm fine," Rose said, wiping away the tears with the edge of her thumb, as she dared to glance at him. He looked a little older, for sure, with crinkles around his eyes, and he carried himself differently, with a self-assurance that was new, to Rose at least, but in every other aspect Frasier McCleod was just as she remembered him—except for one thing: he didn't seem very nice.

"Why aren't we venturing into the Valley of the Kings?" Maddie asked, eventually making her journey back from the stile where she had been sitting for some time staring up at the sky, waiting for Rose to finish whatever it was she was doing. She glowered at Frasier, clearly blaming him for her plans not coming to fruition.

"I was just talking to this gentleman," Rose said, barely able to contain her disappointment.

"Valley of the Kings, hey?" Frasier grinned at Maddie, who scowled at him. "Off to unwrap a few mummies, are you?"

"No, that would be a desecration." Maddie scowled at him. "We are archaeologists, not grave robbers, and besides, this isn't really the Valley of the Kings, that is in Egypt. This is the Lake District, although I haven't seen a lake yet, so I don't know why they call it that. It should be called the mountain district."

"Right." Frasier raised an amused eyebrow, his confrontational stance easing a little. "Look, I'm sorry. I should have been paying better attention."

"Yes," Rose agreed. "You should."

"I haven't introduced myself. I'm Frasier McCleod, Art Dealer and Agent, John Jacobs's art dealer and agent, to be precise. This is his land you are crossing, which strictly speaking is fine, it is a public right of way, but that doesn't make him any more happy about it, just so you know. He's not completely averse to throwing things at ramblers."

"We know who John Jacobs is," Maddie began. "He's my—"

"John knows we are here," Rose said, interrupting her daughter.

"Oh, really?" Frasier looked interested. "It's so unusual for him to have visitors. How do you know John?"

"She's his—" Maddie began.

"Oh, um, I've known him for a long time," Rose hedged, wiggling her eyebrows at her thwarted daughter, hoping she'd get the message, feeling suddenly utterly foolish. But Maddie, who wasn't the greatest at picking up subtle signals at the best of times, seemed to be bursting at the seams to tell Frasier who they were. And fair enough, really—how could Maddie know that Rose didn't want him to find out who she was that way? She didn't want to see him struggle to recall their meeting and shrug it off, an incident that had passed fleetingly and without consequence for him, vanishing into the past without significance.

"Really? How odd. I've known him for a long time too, and yet we've never met . . . ?" Frasier looked puzzled and Rose focused on the toes of her boots. "Anyway, is he in the barn?"

Rose nodded.

"We'll take you," Maddie said. "You can see my painting. It is very, very good. And it only took me twenty minutes. I don't know why John takes so long to do his."

"I frequently wonder the same thing," Frasier said, smiling at Rose, who continued studiously to avoid his eye. Maddie loped off ahead of them, clearly delighted to have an excuse to return to the barn, and Rose trailed along beside Frasier, wondering if he would even remember meeting her at all, once it all came out that she was John Jacobs's daughter. Now, after coming all this way, searching for this man, she discovered that she wanted nothing more than to keep things as they were, after all. To keep Frasier as that happy memory that had meant so much to her. She would rather that these last few moments as strangers could stretch on forever than face the awkwardness and embarrassment that was sure to follow. As they reached the barn, Rose was not aware that Frasier had stopped a few paces behind her until he said her name.

"Rose . . ." He said it so quietly that it was almost like a whisper, uncertain. Rose paused, turning round to look at him as a look of recognition slowly spread over his face. "You are Rose," he said. "Well, well. Dearest Rose has arrived."

It was a difficult moment for Rose, standing there as Frasier observed her, seemingly so matter-of-factly.

"I'm so sorry. I never thought I'd see you again," he said, a little as if he'd rather hoped not to, as his expression was one of pure incredulity. "So you made the journey to see your father at last. I thought I'd hear from you, after I wrote to you with his address a few years back, after I'd got him sober. When I didn't, I assumed you moved, or decided not to contact him."

"You wrote to me?" Rose said, her mind struggling to keep up with the words tumbling out of Frasier's mouth. "Another letter, apart from the postcard, you mean?"

"Yes. You didn't get it?" Frasier shook his head, as if the sight of her irritated him. "How Shakespearean. It must have got lost in the post. I could have phoned you, of course, but . . . I don't know, it never occurred to me. I suppose I thought you'd made your choice and you were sticking to it."

"You wrote to me?" Rose said. "I didn't get it."

"Well, it doesn't matter now," Frasier said with a dismissive gesture. "You are here now. So how did you find the old bugger, anyway? It's not easy, he's an official recluse. I've known journalists who say finding the Holy Grail is a cinch compared to Mr. Jacobs."

"I . . ." Rose almost told Frasier she had been following the clues to him, not to John, and then thought better of it, remembering the crushing disappointment she had felt only a few seconds before. It would have to be enough that Frasier remembered her at all. The very last thing she must do was reveal any more of her stupid heart to this remote, if pleasant, man. And, as Shona had brutally reminded her, his life probably contained a wife, children, lovers, dogs, and a hundred more reasons why he wouldn't want to know that she'd come here to tell him she thought she very well might love him. But it was the way he looked at her now, so detached and disinterested, that made her realize she must never let her years of pent-up feelings for him show themselves. "Actually, it was you that led me to him in the end. The postcard you sent, it was the only link I had to . . . to him. That's why I came to Millthwaite. I didn't know what I would find here when I came, if anything. I just . . . I felt like I had to come. And here he was—a miracle, really."

"You followed your instinct." Frasier studied her face for a moment longer. "You've changed. Barely recognizable with that hair."

Self-consciously, Rose touched her still unfamiliar hair. "I'd forgotten my hair . . . this is all new to me too. Bit of an impulse decision last night."

"It suits you." Frasier smiled briefly. "You're obviously fearless."

Before Rose could correct his assumption, John appeared in the doorway.

"This child will not stop talking at me about Ancient Egypt. I told her, I don't care about Ancient Egypt. She does not seem deterred." He looked Frasier up and down disparagingly. "Oh, you are here."

"John!" Warmly, Frasier greeted John, who sighed at the sight of the man before ignoring him by turning round and going back into the barn, returning to his canvas. Taking a breath, Frasier followed Maddie in, Rose close behind him.

"This is my painting," Maddie said very seriously, pointing at her work, which was still propped up against the back wall. "He's given me more board to shut me up, so I am also working. I shall also not talk to you."

"Fair enough," Frasier said amiably. "Very good work in progress, excellent use of texture and depth of color."

"That's what I thought," Maddie said. "I thought that about the texture. If you like, you can sell it in your gallery and give me the money."

"The thing is, John," Frasier said, taking a couple of tentative steps closer to him, "the clients are chasing me for their commissions. I need to send the van. I keep leaving you message after message, asking when I can send the van and pick up the latest pieces, and you never reply or call back. Three clients are waiting, John. Three. They're ready to pay the big bucks, and the long and the short of it is if it's not your painting on their walls, they'll take someone else's. They're idiots, but that's how it is."

"Good," John muttered. "Three corporate bastards who care more about color coordination than art—why should I do their bidding?"

"John!" Rose was amused and surprised that previously cool and calm Frasier was flustered by John's disdain. Something about her father clearly set him on edge. Odd, as after all, Frasier had known him in person for almost as many years as she had. "You do realize this isn't just about you, painting in a shed, don't you? It's my reputation at stake here too. The years I've put into getting you fit, building your profile, making you a success. Why do we always have to have this conversation every single time I win you a commission? You know why you do it: we all have to pay the bills, John. Even you."

John withdrew his brush from the canvas for a moment.

"Believe me, if I could live for free, I would. This whole cesspit of art dealership is repugnant. It's prostitution by any other name."

Frasier sighed, and Rose could see him wrestling with what seemed like a familiar struggle: deal with John and all his angry tics to get what you ultimately wanted. Rose was intrigued that her father had let anyone so far into his life, let alone have any sort of contact with a dealer or agent, especially one that made him and Frasier seem like an old married couple, destined to bicker away about the same old thing for all eternity.

In the old days, John had seemed to paint almost *because* nobody wanted to look at or buy his work. But then again, in the old days he hadn't painted these huge, looming, beautiful canvases of the landscapes that surrounded him. At some point John would have either decided or have been encouraged to become commercial, Rose realized, as she watched Frasier search for the right way to talk to her father. What on earth had happened to make him do exactly what he always swore he never would?

"All I'm asking," Frasier said eventually, his tone carefully neutral, "is that you sometimes switch your phone on, or look at your emails on the laptop I bought you."

"Bloody contraptions, they poison your mind. Rose!" The sound of John speaking her name out loud was so unexpected that it made Rose start a little and have to stop herself from looking over her shoulder.

"Yes?" she said.

"Take McCleod here to the storeroom." John held out a bunch of keys, one of which was presumably to the padlock on the partition wall. "Two of his canvases are there, should be dry by now. This one will be ready early next week. The city folk will have their pretty art after all, and Mr. McCleod will get his fifteen percent."

"And you will get your money in the bank," Frasier chided him softly. "Thank you, John. You know, if you'd just taken the time to tell me that when I asked you, ours would be a much smoother friendship."

"No one said anything about friendship," John said, raising a brow at Maddie, who treated Frasier to a very haughty look, cloned exactly from her grandfather.

"And this is the one destined for the Berlin bank? May I take a closer look?" Frasier asked.

"No, you may not." John presented his back to Frasier, blocking what he could of his view with his thin shoulders. "Rose, the storeroom."

Rose wasn't entirely sure of this unexpected dynamic between her and her father, where he asked her to do things, and she did them, but given the disappointment of her reunion with Frasier, she didn't dislike it. As dreadful as he found talking to her, he must hate dealing with Frasier even more, and so was glad at least that she was there to pass the buck to. She was useful for something.

When Rose eventually found the right key and opened the locked door, they discovered that the two canvases were ready and waiting. The air was heavy with the sweet smell of oil paint. This room also was lit by two skylights high in the roof, which gave the room an almost churchlike air of mystery, two heavenly beams of sun cutting squares of gold into the dirty floor. Frasier McCleod was noticeably more relaxed now that he wasn't in John's immediate presence, his neatly manicured hands resting loosely on his hips, an expensive-looking gold watch circling a wrist.

"Beautiful," he said, more to himself than Rose, as he took in the two huge paintings. "What amazing color and light. This is why people love his work. John is the only modern painter I know who can paint something on this scale which still manages to feel like an intimate, private experience."

Standing next to him, Rose also observed the paintings. They were so vastly different from what she remembered of her father's brash, abstract, confrontational work. Instead, these were breathtaking landscapes that felt almost as if he were painting the Cumbrian Lake District in its actual size, as if you could step into the landscape and slog through the thick layers of paint, slash upon slash of color that somehow, when you stood back and looked at the work as a whole, made perfect sense. The paintings were beautiful, easy to look at, restful almost. They were everything that John had once abhorred.

Perplexed by what had happened to change her father so radically, Rose looked around the quiet room for more clues. The rest of the room was bare, but at its rear, in what must be the very end of the barn, there was another wall, with another door cut into it, secured with another heavy-looking padlock, the key to which might be on the key ring he'd given her.

What did he keep in there, Rose wondered darkly, the heads of his previous wives on sticks?

"So you sell these?" Rose asked Frasier, who, she became aware, was scrutinizing her rather more closely than the paintings. "To whom?"

"To corporate clients, mainly," Frasier said, returning his gaze to the paintings. "They work really well in big spaces—reception halls, boardrooms, that sort of thing. John Jacobs's work is in demand all over; we do particularly well in China and Russia. Can't get enough of it over there."

"Really?" Rose was impressed. She'd never thought of her father's work hanging all around the world. Looking at him, at where and how he lived, it seemed impossible that he had such reach.

"Did you ever feel the need to paint?" Frasier asked her, breaking her train of thought. "Like your daughter?"

"Me? No!" Rose shook her head, genuinely surprised by the question. "I never wanted to, not even as a child. I had no idea that Maddie was artistic until literally just now. I'm afraid I haven't done much to encourage her . . ."

"It's no surprise, really. Art hurt you; you are hardly likely to want to embrace it. I wonder, though . . . perhaps you should pick up a brush one day and see what happens. You never know, with your parentage you might be an undiscovered talent. You can certainly see glimpses of creativity in the way you . . ."

"The way I look?" Rose questioned him.

"Well, it's very different," Frasier said, his exact opinion of her look unreadable.

"Thank you," Rose said for want of anything else to say.

"Sorry," Frasier said, smiling unexpectedly. "I didn't mean to make you uncomfortable. I can never stop saying what I'm thinking. It's been the bane of my life. I'm sure I would have a much more standard and conventional life by now if only I had kept my mouth shut at the appropriate times, but then again, who wants a conventional life?"

"Are you gay?" Rose blurted, quite out of nowhere.

"So you're one of those say-what-you-think people too!" Frasier laughed so loud that Rose felt somehow the sanctity of the storeroom had been broken, and yet she found she was giggling too.

"I never say what I think." Rose shook her head, smiling. "I never say anything. I have no idea why I just said that. I'm sorry."

"Don't be," Frasier said. "No, I am not gay. I'm just really terrible at meeting suitable women—well, until recently, anyway. I do have a decidedly female and very wonderful girlfriend, though."

Rose felt the smile freeze on her face and threaten to fade as the last fragments of her foolish dream crumbled away.

"And you?" Frasier asked. "Your daughter's, what, seven? What's your secret to a happy marriage?"

"Oh, I don't have one," Rose said, suddenly keen to be free of that room. "I really don't think I've ever made any true choices in life, I've just sort of let it sweep me along."

"And now it's swept you here." The two of them looked at each other for a moment in the half-light, sharing a smile, a memory that was the same but also very different. To Rose, their first meeting had meant everything. To Frasier, it was inconsequential. Almost entirely forgotten.

"Well, it's nice to see you, Rose," Frasier said.

"Yes," Rose said, wishing she had the courage to say much more but supposing she always knew it would end up like this between them, a friendly, if distant, familiarity. "I have often wanted to thank you, for how kind you were to me that day."

Frasier brushed aside the significance that Rose had

placed on that meeting in one well-meant gesture. "I don't really remember."

"Oh . . . well," Rose said, uncertain where to look, or how not to betray the feelings that were unraveling so rapidly inside her.

"Look," Frasier said amicably, "I always stop at the pub on the way back, have a drink to get over your father. How about you have one with me? We can have a proper catch-up?" Frasier said, lowering his voice as Rose escorted him past an oblivious John and an intent-looking Maddie.

"I can't," Rose said, suddenly very keen not to be near him. "I promised Maddie a walk, and I have a friend staying with me." The truth was she knew that if she spent even a few more minutes with Frasier she wouldn't be able to stop herself from telling the truth and ruining everything and humiliating herself even further. Of course he had a girlfriend. Shona had been right, and secretly Rose had expected that. No, what she needed now was time to go away and collect her thoughts about everything that had happened at Storm Cottage that day.

"Probably just as well," Frasier said amiably, not overtly disappointed. "I've got an opening tonight, this bloody awful woman, paints with found pigment. You know, ketchup, egg whites, and bodily fluids. Utter rubbish, but Edinburgh's glitterati seem to love her. But I'll be back in a couple of days with the van to pick up the paintings, so perhaps then?" Frasier looked thoughtful for a moment. "Let's have dinner. Although to be fair, dinner round here means a packet of peanuts in the pub."

"Perhaps. I'm not sure if I will still be here," Rose said, looking at Storm Cottage sitting so small and silently squat in the crook of the mountain. In that moment, she felt just like that broken-down little building, dwarfed by everything that was happening around her. It was still standing, though.

"Well, here's my card, anyway." Frasier handed it to her. "Let me know if you are. Least I can do is entertain my most profitable artist's daughter for an hour or two."

Rose took the card and looked at it, sitting nonchalantly in her hand. For so long she dreamt of knowing where he was in the world, and now that she did, she was dismayed to realize that it changed nothing.

"Hope to see you again," he said, catching her hand for a moment before letting it go. "Don't go and disappear again!"

Rose watched as his car pulled away.

"I never went anywhere," she said.

Chapter Eight

"What, he didn't know who you were?" Shona asked her, liberally applying liquid eyeliner under her pale blue eyes, giving her something of a warrior princess look, particularly as she swept it up at the corners into cat-like points.

"No, not at first, but then why would he?" Rose looked at her reflection in the mirror and ruffled her hair again. She wasn't used to this ritual preparation-to-go-out thing that Shona was so excited by, insisting that they lock themselves in her room at least an hour before they were due to arrive at the pub for Ted's gig to "get ready."

Rose had left a very serene and calm Maddie telling a long-suffering Jenny about the intricacies of color, which she had read about in an old book called *The Theory of Art* she'd picked up from the dusty floor in John's barn, and which he'd said, with a wave of a disinterested hand, she could take home. It wasn't until Rose had been helping Jenny clear up the kitchen after dinner that she noticed that the battered book's author was "J. Jacobs." Unable to wrest the book, which looked like a very dry and difficult read, from an apparently engrossed Maddie, Rose couldn't investigate further to see if it was true, if during the life—the *lifetime*—he'd had apart from her, her father had at some point written a book. Rose tried to imagine John sitting for even one moment at a desk to write about how to do the things he'd always claimed were instinctive and could not be taught. It seemed impossible, but then again she was still measuring him against the man she'd once known, a man who might very well have been a figment of her imagination even then. The lonely, cross old man who was probably still at work in his barn, in the middle of nowhere, had nothing to do with the father she had thought she'd known, just as really he had nothing to do with her. What else had he done in that lifetime, Rose wondered, while all the time she had been standing perfectly still, almost exactly as he'd left her?

"What, and then he snogged you?" Shona said, unscrewing a pearlized lipstick, which she slicked on with gusto, pressing her lips together and then kissing the dressing room mirror in lieu of a piece of tissue.

"No! Far from it," Rose said thoughtfully. "I seemed to make him . . . quite annoyed. But he was perfectly polite. Told me about his girlfriend, asked me out for a client dinner, even. But there was nothing there between us. Nothing at all." That wasn't quite true; there had been plenty there for Rose, but she chose to not mention it.

"You knew that might happen, you knew that his life wouldn't just stand still. Life doesn't do that. Well, other people's lives don't." Shona examined herself in the mirror and then, dissatisfied with her look, peeled off her skin-tight white top and replaced it with a black one, with an even deeper plunging neckline. "Christ, I look fit tonight. You are going to have to fight blokes off me." She grinned at Rose over her shoulder, arming herself with her cast-iron confidence, the defense she needed to face the outside world. "You did what you came here to do: you left Dickhead, which matters more than anything, and you found your dream man. OK, so he's taken and it's not the dream ending you'd planned, but does that matter? Really? The last thing you need is another boyfriend to let you down now anyway, and I bet you he wouldn't live up to your expectations, even if he was into you. He'd be farting in bed and picking his nose before you knew it."

"Should I go out to dinner with him?" Rose asked uncertainly. "He made it sound like he was obliged to offer."

"No," Shona said categorically. "It will only confuse you, and you need to get your head straight now, work out what you're going to do next, how you're going to get Richard off your back, how you are really going to be you, for once in your life. Not pine after someone who's already moved on."

"Really? You really think that?" Rose said, feeling her high spirits at seeing Frasier again rapidly deflate.

"All I'm saying is, be careful with your heart. The happy ending you were looking for wasn't *really* here, not the way you imagined it, at least. Life just isn't like that. Trust me, I know. But it doesn't matter, because some poncy art bloke isn't the ending you need, anyway. In fact, it's not an ending you need at all; you need a beginning. And the way you look, the way you talk, the sound of your voice, your smile, your laugh, that's it, that's your beginning, because it's you, Rose. The real you. It's like now that you're out of Richard's shadow you're blossoming into the woman you were meant to be, and I'm finally getting to know you properly, and you know what, you are actually quite a laugh. Now before I sound even more gay, tell me, *when* do you plan to start getting ready?"

"I am ready," Rose said, glancing down at herself in the outfit she'd been wearing all day.

"For a funeral maybe," Shona said.

• • •

Rose stopped outside the pub and chewed her lip. It tasted slightly soapy and slightly fruity, the combination of the several layers of lipstick and lip gloss that Shona had put on her, after pouring her into one of her new dresses, a simple enough black jersey number, slashed across the shoulder, about midthigh length, which had looked not bad in the safe confines of the changing room but now Rose found uncomfortably racy. Shona had tried her level best to get Rose to wear it without a bra ("You ain't got nothing there, so what's the difference?") and with some lacy tights, but Rose had point-blank refused, stating that she wasn't going to traumatize her daughter any more for one day by dressing up like a hooker. Eventually they had settled on allowing Rose to wear the dress over some skinny jeans and with a bra, as long as she pulled it off both shoulders.

"Come on, New You," Shona said. "You got to sexify it up a bit if you want to keep Ted interested."

"I do not," Rose said. "I do not wish to be sexified, whatever that is. Ted is not interested in me and I am not interested in him."

"I am the definition of sexification, and I'm on a mission to spread the love," Shona said, pulling her own top down so that her bosom spilt over the top of it. "And you know what, it's all your fault. You've inspired me to let myself go a bit. Maybe I will pull another bloke tonight; maybe I'll start again, just like you."

"I'm not really starting again," Rose reminded her. "I'm more sort of hiding. Being sexy, that's not really me. Not the old me, not the new me. I'm not . . . well, it's just not me."

"It should be you," Shona said determinedly. "Just because you've spent too long being married to the world's most unattractive creep doesn't mean you have to spend the rest of your life as a dried-up old maid. You did your mental stalking-Frasier thing and I admire you for it. You came all this way on a wing and a prayer and you got closer than anyone thought you would. Now it's done, it's time to move on to the next thing, and I've decided that the next thing on your list is to shag Ted."

"Shona!" Rose hissed, worried there was a very real possibility that Jenny had a glass to the bedroom door. "Just stop it, will you? The very last thing I want is . . . *that.* I don't want to talk about it, I don't want to joke about, so just, please . . . leave it, OK?"

"OK," Shona said slowly, frowning. "I was only joking, mate. Didn't think it'd get you so rattled. Anyway, all you need to worry about is finally telling Dickhead where to get off."

"Why are you always so good at giving advice and not taking it?" Rose said, still a little shaken by Shona's insinuations.

"I could say the same for you," Shona said. "But you're right, I know. And I'm just wondering, if you can do it, if you can finally get Dickhead out of your life for good . . . then maybe I can do the same with Ryan too."

"Really?" Rose asked her, touched that her friend had so much faith in her that it made her see her own life differently. "Really, you'd thinking about ending it with Ryan for good?"

"Yes," Shona said, with about as much determination as she had ever mustered over this point. "Well. Maybe, anyway. Now let's go and find ourselves some country totty."

Maddie had pretty much ignored her as Rose kissed her good night on the way out, and Shona's ensemble was quite enough to distract Jenny from any further thoughts of her son's interest, real or imagined, in Rose.

"There's no red-light district in Millthwaite!" she called out as they finally escaped out the front door, giggling like a pair of teenagers trying to sneak their short skirts and eye-liner past Mum.

"I've never done this," Rose said, the realization hitting her hard.

"What, gone to a pub?" Shona replied, as if she wouldn't be in the least bit surprised.

"No, I mean gone out, dressed up, done the stuff young women normally do. Before Mum died it never felt like I could go out and have fun, knowing that she would be back at home sitting on her own in the dark with a bottle of gin. And then after, even when we were first working together, I know you took me under your wing, but I never really did *this*. I never really had a proper laugh, like you and the other girls did. There I would be, sitting meekly in the corner, dressed in black, just watching everyone else. And then—"

"And then there was Dickhead," Shona said. "Well, now you are off the leash, we are in the middle of nowhere, no one knows us, and babe, what happens in Millthwaite stays in Millthwaite! Let's be outrageous!"

Which was when Rose stopped outside the pub, filled with sudden apprehension.

"I don't know if I can be outrageous," she said. "I don't know that I've got fun and outrageousness in me."

"Mate, you've run away from home, cut off all your hair, and your dad is a legendary party animal. It's in your genes! Just relax, just for tonight. Let's celebrate one night of getting to be us for a change."

The pub was crowded, packed full of people of all ages but mostly on the younger side, the majority of them girls. Gig night had to be a big deal locally, because Rose was sure that most of the people crammed into the bar weren't from the tiny village. She hadn't seen more than three of them before as she walked around the frequently deserted green. There was a small platform, made of what looked like upturned beer crates, where the pool table usually stood, stacked with a battered-looking PA, a microphone, and a drum kit crammed up against the wall, on which someone had tacked a hand-painted banner reading "The Cult of Creation."

"Fuck this bar queue, we'll be waiting all night for a drink," Shona said, grabbing Rose's hand and heading towards the snug. "Let's go backstage and be proper groupies."

"I'm not really sure if we should." Rose attempted to make herself heard over the din. "I mean, do you think the band is really going to want a couple of mums gate-crashing?"

"We've got VIP passes, haven't we?"

"Not completely sure that beer mats strictly count," Rose muttered under her breath, but it was too late. Shona had already shoved open the door to the band's inner sanctum, or as Ted usually referred to it, "the old man's bar."

"All right?" Shona said, swinging in through the door and immediately picking up two bottles of lager, one of which she handed to Rose. "Got anything stronger?"

"Shona, Rose . . . Rose!" Ted stopped short when he caught sight of Rose lurking behind Shona. "Bloody hell, your hair! It looks amazing!"

Ted stepped over a beer-bottle-strewn table to greet her. "Wow, man. Radical! I love it!" Rose couldn't help smiling as he took her hand and led her in front of his band mates, one of whom was far too engaged in some athletic kissing with a girl of about nineteen to be bothered to look at her.

"This is my friend Rose, you know, who I was telling you about," Ted said, without letting go of her fingers. "Oh, and this is her friend Shona."

"What, I'm not your friend too?" Shona said, striding around the table and sliding into the vacant seat that Ted had left, grinning at a rather alarmed-looking young man who turned out to be Andy the drummer. "So, handsome, who are you? Ever done it with a MILF?"

"Want something stronger?" Ted asked Rose, leading her out of the bar and into a small liquor storeroom a little way down the corridor before she could answer. "I got my secret stash of vodka in here. I try not to get too loaded before a gig, and anyway, I'm driving later, so you have one."

Rose's eyes widened as he took her beer bottle and topped it up with a slug of vodka, but she took the bottle back anyway, taking a tentative sip.

"God, I can't stop looking at you. The hair, wow! Brave move, Rosie. Most girls think long hair makes them pretty, and for some of them it does, but you were born to have hair like this. It's wild. You look like a proper rock chick!"

"Are you sure you're not drunk?" Rose said, unable to resist being flattered by his enthusiasm.

"Not on booze, anyway . . ." Ted moved a fraction closer to her and Rose was sure that he was intent on kissing her. Just as she was frantically working out a way to outmaneuver his lips, Andy stuck his head in through the door, eliciting a dirty look from Ted for his troubles.

"Where's the voddy? This Shona chick wants it and we're on!"

"Right, OK, well, I'll see you out the front, yeah? Right by the stage."

"I'll try," Rose said. "But you know at my age, married, a mother, and everything, moshing isn't exactly up my street."

"Moshing." Ted grinned fondly. "You are *so* cute."

Rose couldn't exactly say that she was a fan of the Cult of Creation. Their music was very loud, and she had no idea what the lyrics were, although she had to concede that Ted had a great voice and real stage presence—or upturned-beer-crate presence, anyway. Although she remained at the bar for the set, Shona, who had had rather more vodka than Rose, gyrated in amongst the throng of mainly young women who seemed to be devoted to the band, pouting menacingly at Andy. Throughout, it was impossible not to notice that Ted didn't take his eyes off Rose, singing directly to her the whole time, which might have been exciting if she'd had any idea what he was singing about. And it was impossible not to concede that Ted really was very attractive, from any point of view, even hers. It was more than a little curious that Jenny was right, Ted did seem to be setting his cap at her—because she was different, new, perhaps, or because she was older. Rose genuinely couldn't fathom the reason, but for someone like him to give someone like her any attention at all was more than a little flattering and exhilarating, not to mention apparently enviable, as a young woman in her twenties elbowed her way past Rose after several minutes of failing to get Ted to notice her, muttering viciously, "What the fuck have you got that I haven't, you old bag?"

And apart from anything else, it was soothing salve to her pride that had been damaged so badly when she'd realized Frasier's kind indifference was simply that, and the hour that had meant so much to her was, for him, simply another hour lived and let go of.

"Having a good time?" Shona appeared at her side, her T-shirt clinging to her damp skin. "This lot are bloody brilliant, that Andy thinks I'm hot, I can tell, and young Ted's been giving you the eye all night!"

"I noticed," Rose conceded uncomfortably.

"Did you? That's a bloody first!" Shona exclaimed. "Well, then, what about it, you, me, Andy, and Ted after the show? We can snog in a bale of hay or some shit."

"No, no, I've got to tell Ted to back off," Rose said, her seriousness lost on her sparkling-eyed friend. "Would you really kiss Andy, even though you've only just met, even though . . ." She refrained from mentioning Ryan's name out loud, as if it might somehow evoke him.

Shona bit her lip, her eyes widening. "I think I bloody might! What about you? You sure you don't want to kiss Ted?"

"Yes!" Rose was adamant, shaking her head firmly, looking up at Ted just as the band finished the set, being swamped by a crowd of girls at least ten years younger than her as he made his way back to the snug, infuriating most of his fans by gesturing to her to follow him. He was obviously used to girls falling at his feet; he could have his pick. Why would he want to pick her unless . . . unless he could see something in her that made him think she would be a pushover? Rose shuddered.

"It wouldn't be right," she said, meeting Ted's eye. "It would be terribly irresponsible."

"Why?" Shona pressed her, sensing something that was remaining unspoken. "And don't tell me it's because of Dickhead?"

"No, not really. I'm a mother, he's Jenny's son. I'm still in love with Frasier—that will take awhile to wear off—and Ted is, well, he's Ted. We are the last two people who should be gallivanting."

"Gallifuckingwhat?" Shona laughed. "Maddie's safely tucked up in bed, Jenny is safely watching telly before indulging in some sort of kinky sex with Brian in one of her porn nighties, and Frasier is out on the town with his girlfriend. These are all the reasons why you *should* be getting off with Ted. And besides, what happens in Millthwaite, stays in Millthwaite, remember?"

"You don't understand," Rose said.

"Only because you aren't telling me what's really going on," Shona said.

But before Rose could reply, Shona was swept up in the crowd of girls, elbowing her way towards the snug, beckoning for Rose to follow.

"So what did you think?" Ted asked her the moment she came in through the door. He was glowing with sweat and adrenaline. "Impressed?"

"Very," Rose said. "The crowd loved you!"

"Yeah, to be honest they love anything round here. The real test will be when we go down to London, you know, to try and get a deal."

"London! When are you going?" Rose asked him, reassuring herself that no man could be more different from Richard than Ted.

"Don't know, when we're ready," Ted said, noncommittal. "Anyway, come on, I've something to show you."

"Oh, yeah, I've heard that before," Shona said, as Ted took Rose's hand, pulling her out of the room, through the pub kitchen, and into the warmth of a thankfully dry night.

"What, where are we going?" Rose asked him, alarmed. "Ted, I don't want to go. Where are you taking me? What do you think is going to happen?"

Ted stopped, brought up short by the note of fear in her voice. "What's wrong?"

"I don't, I'm not . . . Is this about sex?"

"Sex?" Ted's eyes widened. "Yeah, sure, if you want it to be."

"No! No, I don't want it to be. I want it to be completely clear that that is not going to happen. Do you understand that? I don't want to be kissed, or touched or . . . or . . . I just don't, I really, really—"

"Hey, it's OK," Ted said, raising the palms of his hands to her. "I'm not Jack the Ripper, you know. If you're not up for it, I get that. It's cool. Doesn't mean we can't hang out, though, does it? I want to take you somewhere," Ted said, opening the passenger door of his truck for her.

Rose hesitated, eyeing the truck warily.

"It's OK, I haven't been drinking, like I said. My mum would properly kill me if I drank and drove."

"I'm not sure . . ." Rose looked at the open door, seeing a corner she wouldn't be able to escape from.

"You're really frightened of me, aren't you?" Ted took her hand, clearly perplexed by her reaction. "You're trembling!"

"It's just . . . I've led quite a sheltered life," Rose said. "I don't want to lead you on, I want to be clear."

"And you have been," he said. "Look, Rose, you don't have to be scared of me. I'm just Ted from the pub. I'm not going to whisk you away to the middle of nowhere and force you to do anything you don't want to, because frankly I'm not the sort of bloke who has to force women to do anything. Normally I'm fighting them off me. I just want to show you this place, it's my place. That's all."

"As long as you understand . . ."

"I understand," Ted said gently. "I repulse you. It's OK, I can take it. You are safe with me."

"Very well, then," Rose said, battling down her irrationality, aware that it was Richard, his shadow, his years of controlling her, that were scaring her just as much as the prospect of being alone with Ted. Whatever happened next, she would not let it be because of anything Richard had done to crush her. "Just don't try anything."

"Weren't you listening? I never have to try." Ted grinned as they pulled out of the pub car park.

• • •

They drove in near silence for what must have been almost twenty minutes, Rose too self-conscious and uncertain of what was really going on to even look at Ted, and him seemingly intent on the twist of country road that revealed itself in the headlights, inch by inch. Instead she gazed out of the window at the alien landscape that unfolded around her, the silhouette of the mountains standing out sharply against the still faintly glowing summer sky. After a while Ted pulled up a track that Rose would never have noticed if she were on her own, and after juddering over its rough surface for a few hundred yards, turned off the ignition, got out of the car and came round to help her out of the truck, lifting her down with his hands on her narrow waist.

He took her hand and led her towards what looked like a copse of trees, which were surprisingly well lit by the moon and starlight. Before long Rose could hear the trickle of water and, watching her feet, she followed Ted up a rough staircase of rocks that tumbled alongside the stream, until they came to a kind of plateau cut into the hillside. There, amongst the gilt-edged trees glittering in the moonlight, Rose could see a tiny waterfall, chiming rhythmically as it cascaded down into the stream below.

"Wow," Rose said, as Ted spread a blanket out on a rock for her to sit on. "This place is beautiful!"

"I know," Ted said softly. "When I was a little kid, me and Haleigh used to come here on the holidays. Mum'd pack us a lunch and then send us off for the day. We'd walk here, take us a good hour, stay here all day, just mucking about. Haleigh reckoned there were fairies living in the trees, and I used to play commando. Later, when Haleigh got too cool to hang out with me and started getting into lads, I came here on my own, and you know what the funny thing is, it does feel a little bit magical. I mean, I wouldn't say that to just anyone, sounds a bit mental, but it does, doesn't it?"

Rose smiled as she watched Ted's profile, as he leant back on his hands and gazed at the night sky studded with stars, through the canopy of thin, windswept trees.

"You're quite a sweet lad really, aren't you, under all that front and rock-star bluster?" she asked him softly.

"Me? Sweet? Never," Ted said, directing his gaze to her. "I've never brought anyone here until now. I don't know why I've brought you, really. I just wanted to see your face when you saw it. I knew it would make you smile. And I don't know why, but I get the feeling you don't smile nearly enough."

"I've smiled a lot more since arriving here," Rose told him.

"That'll be down to meeting me," Ted said, his expression hard to read in the darkness, but the sound of his voice light and playful. He was flirting, that was what flirting was, Rose thought, relieved that being alone with Ted out here, with no one around for miles and miles, didn't make her as frightened as she'd feared, or indeed frightened at all.

"Rose, can I ask you something?" Ted said. "Not about kissing or anything."

"I suppose," Rose said.

"Were things really bad with your husband?"

Rose was surprised by the question, surprised that Ted cared how things were with Richard, assuming that whatever problems Rose had at home, they would be low down on his list of interests.

"Yes," she said bluntly, feeling that here, in the middle of all this beauty, it would be pointless and wrong to lie. "Yes, things were very bad. Still are, I suppose, although I haven't spoken to him since I left."

"Do you want to talk about it?" Ted asked her.

Slowly, Rose shook her head. "Not here, not in this lovely place. It's too . . . special."

"Fair enough," Ted said with a simple shrug.

"Do you know what?" Rose said, touched by his frank concern. "You're OK."

They sat quietly for a few minutes more, Rose finding that the more she listened to the cascade of the waterfall, the more relaxed she was becoming, approaching something as close to peace as she'd felt in . . . forever. Suddenly it wasn't just miles that separated her from Richard, from the life that had imprisoned her, but it seemed like universes too, as though somehow she'd traveled light-years through the stars that spun overhead. Perhaps it was possible, her new beginning, her fresh start. It felt possible in that moment, as if really she could wash away the pain and the hurt of the past until she was clean and smooth, like the pebbles in the stream, soothed by the neverending flow of water. Even with her dreams of Frasier becoming a different reality than she'd hoped for, maybe she could still be happy.

Rose was taken by surprise when Ted suddenly lunged forward and attempted to kiss her, shattering her serenity in a second. Squealing, she scrabbled backward, away from him.

"Ted!" she exclaimed. "I thought you—"

"I know, and I do, I just . . . I really want to kiss you."

Rose stared at what she could make out of his expression in the darkness.

"You don't just lunge at someone," she protested, the fear that had temporarily surged through her dissipating as quickly as it had built up.

"I know!" Ted said, rolling his eyes like a teenager. "I just . . . It's such a pretty night . . . and . . . I was just checking that you were completely sure you didn't want to kiss me."

"I'm such a mess, kissing anyone now would be a mistake," Rose said. "It's not you, it's me."

"Oh, God." Ted looked so despondent that Rose almost wanted to reach out to touch him. Almost. They sat there for several moments in the moonlight, in silence, Rose thinking of the look on Richard's face when she'd last seen him. Of the way her father did his best not to look at her, of how Frasier had so politely shaken her hand and said goodbye, and it was as if, for just that moment, none of it, not a single second of what had come before or what would come afterwards, mattered at all.

"Kiss me, Ted," Rose heard herself saying.

"What?" Ted looked sharply at her.

"Just kiss me, I'm ready," Rose said anxiously, before clamping both hands over her mouth. "Wait . . . OK. Ready. Now I'm ready."

Rose watched warily as Ted took her hand in his and ever so gently tugged her towards him; their eyes met, his shining blackly in the moonlight, at the same moment their lips met. Rose closed her eyes then, feeling the warmth of his lips gently pressing against hers, his fingers sliding up from her wrist to her forearm. After a few seconds more with no obvious signs of protest, he gently opened her mouth with his tongue and Rose felt his fingers tighten around her arm, his other hand resting on her waist as he kissed her properly.

"OK," Rose said, breaking contact as soon as she felt that she might get a little too lost in the moment. "OK, great. Thank you."

"Thank you?" Ted said, his face still close to hers, his lips still moist. "So how was it so far for you?"

"Nice, thank you," Rose whispered back, caught between wanting to experience that altogether pleasant sensation again and wanting very much to run in the opposite direction.

"Same for me. You are a very good kisser," Ted said sweetly, and Rose couldn't be sure in the half dark, but she thought he might actually be blushing.

"Really?" she asked him. "Only . . . really?"

"Yeah, a lot of girls are very, you know, full on. Sometimes kissing can be like fighting off a man-eating tiger. But not with you. Kissing you is very lovely."

"Lovely," Rose said, testing the word on her lips, just as much as she'd tested Ted's lips. For so very long kissing had been a thing to be endured, a hated thing, an expression quite often of contempt and control. Never, not once, not even at the very beginning, had Rose ever kissed Richard and thought it was lovely. But that is exactly what it was like with Ted. It was soft, sweet, innocent, and . . . lovely.

"Could we kiss again?" Rose asked Ted. "I mean just kissing. Nothing else, no touching or getting heated. Just like we were before. Just like that. Can we kiss like that, but for longer?"

"How long?" Ted asked her, sweetly amused by her list of kissing criteria. "Should I set a clock?"

"Until I want to stop," Rose said, suddenly burying her head in her hands. "Oh God, I know what I sound like, I sound like a nutter. A grown woman wanting to kiss like a twelve-year-old, but if you knew—"

"I don't need to know," Ted interrupted her. "I'm just ridiculously happy that kissing me makes you feel nice. And I'm very, very happy to keep on kissing you until the sun comes up, if that's what you want."

Before Rose could think of anything else to say, Ted was kissing her again, this time pressing her very gently backwards until she found herself half lying on his blanket. Rose closed her eyes against the starry sky and felt her skin tingle and fizz with pleasure, her hands lying chastely at her sides, and Ted's hands holding her ever so lightly. Kissing Richard had never been like this, she thought dimly, and without knowing it would happen she heard a sigh become a tiny moan and realized that noise had come from her throat.

"I have to say," Ted breathed into her ear, "I'm finding kissing you very nice indeed. Say if it gets too nice."

"I will," Rose whispered back. "I think I'm fine for now, though."

Rose wasn't sure how long they went on that way, simply kissing as the stars wheeled above them, the water splashing by, the world as oblivious of them as they were of it, but suddenly, from nowhere, she felt something shift inside her, a rush of longing or desire that she was completely unfamiliar with bubbling up, and for one moment, without her even realizing it, her arms had wound themselves around Ted, and she was pulling his body tightly against hers. Panicking as she came to her senses, Rose pushed him away and sat up, catching her breath.

"Oh," Rose said as his lips were about to close over hers again. "Oh goodness."

"I'm sorry," Ted said anxiously. "I didn't mean for that to happen. Have I scared you?"

"No." Rose caught her breath as she looked at him, feeling the heat in her cheeks. "I scared myself. I'm sorry, Ted. But I think I need to stop kissing you now."

"But not because I've done something wrong?" Ted asked her, genuinely worried. "Because, honestly, there's something about you that makes me feel . . . stuff I'm not used to. I don't know what it is, or why, and at this moment I don't care about much, except that . . . I really, *really* liked kissing you, Rose."

Rose shook her head, unable to believe what he was saying, scared that kissing Ted had stirred her own embers of desire, a feeling that she wasn't ready to confront yet, not for anyone.

"That's so sweet," she told him again, a little unsteadily. "But now I think I need to go home."

"I know," Ted said, holding out a hand. "And although you

are killing me, I can accept that. But, well, if the mood ever strikes you again, if you ever need some more therapeutic kissing, then I'm available."

Rose looked at him, biting her swollen lip, and wondered what on earth she had done.

Chapter Nine

Rose woke up early the next morning, along with the first of the dawn light to filter through the thin curtains, with a terribly uneasy feeling in the pit of her stomach, as if she had done something really badly wrong. Then the slight tingle in her aching lips, and the sore skin around her chin, made her remember. She'd spent quite a large portion of last night kissing Ted. Catching her lip between her teeth, Rose darted under the covers, fearful that if Maddie caught the expression on her face she would be able to tell instantly that her mother had been kissing inappropriately. Now it seemed like a dream, the long languorous minutes that almost made up an entire night she had spent under the warm night sky, with the sound of the water in the background and Ted's lips on hers. Ted, it turned out, was an exceptionally good kisser, not that Rose had much to compare him to, but that didn't matter. What mattered was that between them they'd created a part of her past that had never been. Her teenage kisses under the stars, the ones she had never had until the age of thirty-one.

Ted had held her hand all the way down the mountainside and even on the drive back, steering with one hand at speed through the twist of country roads. As they'd pulled up outside the pub, which was still thriving from a late license, Ted had turned to her, bending over to kiss her again.

"I don't think we should tell anyone about this," Rose said, backing away. "I just . . . not because . . . only because I've got Maddie to think of, and your mum."

"OK," Ted said. "I'll hold off bragging about how I had you in the palm of my hand until after you've gone. Look, lighten up, it was a bit of kissing, not the opening scenes to *Romeo and Juliet*!"

"Your mum thinks you are secretly vulnerable and likely to get hurt over 'a bit of kissing,'" Rose told him, feeling guilty that she'd forgotten her assurances to Jenny so easily in a moment of madness.

"My mum still thinks I'm six," Ted said, shaking his head. "Did she warn you off me, really? That woman . . ." He chuckled.

"Still, we won't tell anyone and"—Rose cringed at what she was about to say—"we won't do it again, will we?"

"You sound uncertain about that?" Ted raised an eyebrow.

"I'm not," Rose said determinedly.

"We'll see," Ted had said. "Now come on, let's go and see if your friend Shona's scared Andy into snogging her."

Under her covers, Rose decided she would have felt a lot better about letting Ted kiss her if Shona had indeed been doing the same—or more—with Andy, but although her friend was very drunk, and full of fun, the life and soul of the after-show party, she was nowhere near Andy, or any other man, for that matter.

"Oh!" she said when she clapped eyes on Rose. "Where have you been?"

"Out for some fresh air," Rose said, expecting one of

Shona's typical sarcastic comebacks. Instead her friend grabbed her by the arm.

"Take me home," Shona said. "I've lost the bleeding key the old witch gave me, and I think I pissed that Andy bloke off by not wanting to fuck him. Besides, I need to go to sleep in a bed."

"You didn't want to after all?" Rose asked her.

"I did, but then I didn't, and then I thought of Ryan and just couldn't . . . Very, very pissed."

Putting her arm around Shona, Rose guided her through the crowd.

"Bye, everyone," Rose had said, meeting Ted's eyes briefly as she headed for the door. "Thanks for everything."

The thing was, Rose wondered, touching the slightly inflamed skin around her mouth, what would she do now? How would she look Ted in the eye, or Jenny, or Frasier, or Maddie, or anyone now? How would she know how to act the next time she saw Ted, what to do if they were alone together and, most important, what not to do? It would be very hard to resist the chance to feel the way he'd made her feel last night again, and if she did, did that mean that she wasn't in love with Frasier after all and that everything she had believed in for the last seven years had been swept away with a single kiss, or many kisses and some heavy petting? Rose squirmed farther under the cover, screwing up her eyes against the invading sunlight, before she realized that she was smiling. For once Rose was rather enjoying having a complicated life.

"Good gig, was it?" Jenny asked her suspiciously when she arrived at eight thirty prompt for breakfast, or at least it seemed suspicious in Rose's heightened state of awareness.

"It was great, thank you," Rose said, smiling at Maddie, who'd collected together a ramshackle collection of felt pens, ballpoints, and colored pencils from Jenny's rainy-day box and was carefully copying a color wheel out of her battered book, in between bites of toast. "The band was really good. Your son is a talented young man."

Rose winced at the matronly expression, especially the "young man" bit.

"I suppose Ted was surrounded by girls," Jenny said, her face hovering between pride and disapproval. "He always is. I don't know what they see in him, myself."

"There were hundreds of them," Rose assured her, "all vying for his attention."

"If you ask me, he only had eyes for one," Shona, who had lumbered down the stairs, despite looking ashen, began.

"In particular," Rose said, "some young thing really caught his eye. Some slip of a girl."

"Sounds like my Ted," Jenny said with some satisfaction. As she returned to the kitchen, Shona's eyebrows shot sky high and Rose shook her head in warning, nodding at Maddie.

"Mum, did you know that red and green are complementary colors, which doesn't mean that they go well together, it means green makes red look as red as it can be, and red does the same for green. Did you know that?"

"I did not," Rose said, smiling at her.

"It really is very interesting," Maddie said, returning to the book.

"Tell me!" Shona hissed at Rose, but before she could say more the front doorbell sounded. Rose felt her stomach clench, certain that it was Ted, that he wouldn't be able to keep their liaison to himself after all, and that he was about to waltz in and announce plans for seminakedness with her all over again.

But it wasn't Ted who walked into the dining room, it was John.

"Oh," Rose said, standing up for no apparent reason. "What is it?"

"Nothing," John said. He looked supremely awkward, filling the room with his height, all too aware of the burning look of disapproval that Jenny was boring into his back. "I thought rather than wait for you to appear, I might come and collect you and the child."

Rose stared at him, this version of the man who had once been her father standing in front of her, actually seeking her out. He looked strange in the neat homey room, as if he brought the wildness of the landscape in with him, what was left of his hair standing on end, his clothes ingrained with paint.

"Really?" she said, unsure what to make of the invitation. This was the man who only yesterday had told her there was nothing for her, at least not from him. He'd been so clear about it, and nothing very much could have changed in the last few hours. Why was he here, really?

"I looked at her work again this morning," John said, as if it were something he did every day—meet a grandchild, give her a paintbrush. "Really quite impressive, intuitive, interesting. I wondered if it was a fluke or if she has some talent. I'd like to see more. The more time the better, and so . . . I came."

"Oh, I see," Rose said, feeling a flare of jealousy. John had always been very appreciative of her efforts as a child, but only in the way that any adult will nod and smile and tell his child how wonderful her drawing was; he had never been this keen with her. Still, she reminded herself, that was not the point. The point wasn't why he was here, it was merely that he was here.

"It's talent," Maddie told him, with self-assurance. "I've already read the whole of this book and now I know everything about color theory."

"All that theory is rubbish," John told her. "Nothing can teach true talent. That book was written by some old soak who'd do anything to pay for his next drink. Take it from me, I know."

"Oh, well, anyway I am very talented," Maddie said. She pushed her half-completed reproduction of a color wheel across the table towards him. "Look. And yes, I do want to come and paint. I want to come now. I'm ready."

Maddie stood up, still in her pajamas, and went to John, taking his hand, which he looked at as if it were an alien object but he did not let it go.

"Maddie, you're not even dressed," Rose protested, feeling somehow swept aside by this new, unexpected bond.

"She doesn't need to be dressed to paint," John said. "Old clothes are all the better."

"You see," Maddie said.

"All the same, go upstairs and find clothes. Five more minutes won't make a difference."

"I'll go with her," Shona said. "Give her a hand." She paused by Jenny, who was still standing resolutely in the doorway. "Come on, Jenny, you can help too."

"Hmph," Jenny said, reluctantly leaving with Shona.

Rose and John regarded each other across the room for a moment.

"You came here to find us," Rose said, emphasizing the last word.

"I'm interested in her ability," John replied, looking out the window.

"You came *here*," Rose repeated. "What does that mean? Does it mean anything? I wouldn't ask, only I'm tired of not knowing where I stand in life. I'm exhausted by it, actually, second guessing, trying always to do the right thing. So just tell me, does it mean anything that you came to get us?"

John shook his head, shrugging apologetically. "I don't know . . ." He hesitated, as if debating what to tell her. "Frasier and I argue all the time, but he has been, he is, a friend, perhaps my only one. He phoned me last night, on the proper telephone, the one he knows I will answer. He was at some sort of party, all sorts of nonsense and noise going on. He told me he couldn't concentrate until he'd told me I would be an old and stupid fool to pass up the chance of making peace with you. I do not know that there is a chance for us to make peace, but nevertheless I do respect the man. If it weren't for him I would certainly be dead now. I feel that there are things you will want me to say, to do, to feel, for you to be . . . satisfied. And I suspect that I am capable of none of the things you want. So on that basis I have come to collect you, to see what, if any, sort of peace we can salvage. And also because I am interested in the child."

"Frasier said that?" Rose struggled to reconcile the man who would go to all that trouble to help with the one she'd met yesterday. John's description made him sound much more like the Frasier she'd dreamt of for so long.

"My name is Maddie," Maddie reminded John, appearing in Jenny's grandson's bright green Spider-Man T-shirt and red pajama bottoms, picking John's hand up again instantly. "Did you know red and green are complementary colors, that means . . ."

"So you will come?"

"Yes," Rose said. "Of course."

Shona stopped Rose just as she was going to the door

to where John was helping Maddie into a battered old Citroën.

"You sure you're OK?" she asked. "This all seems a bit dramatic."

"What part of my life hasn't been dramatic?" Rose said, as if the revelation was news to her. "I have literally no idea what it will be like, or if it will work out, if it even can. But it's better than wondering, I know that much. I'm sorry to leave you here all day at a loose end."

"She won't be at a loose end," Jenny said. "I've been meaning to clear out the annex where Brian's mum lived before she passed away, for a year, see if I can't do something with it. Shona, you can help me do that and I'll knock a night off your bill, agreed?"

"Agreed, I suppose," Shona said. "Although I don't have any problem at all with being at a loose end." She turned to Rose. "See you later, quick one in the pub?"

Rose knew that her cheeks had instantly burst into two spots of color, from the way Shona's eyes widened in mischievous delight.

"We'll catch up later and you can tell me everything that happened," she whispered. "That's if Mrs. Hitler here doesn't kill me first."

For most of that morning, Maddie painted on anything that John could find her—pieces of boards, scraps of cardboard—filling them with swathes of color. Sometimes she painted things, but mostly just colors, jostling with each other for supremacy. When scrap material ran out, she begged him for a canvas, and after a good deal of grimacing he deigned to part with a small square one that he had already stretched, warning her to take her time over her next creation as she'd have to wait a few days for there to be any more canvases.

"Oh, well, in that case I will paint tiny things," Maddie said, selecting a fine brush from John's collection without a second thought before she settled down at the small easel he'd set up and stared contemplatively at the blank expanse of white.

"That doesn't look like it was going to be one of your usual works," Rose said to John, searching for a conversation opener. For the most part she had been watching John and Maddie in silence since they'd arrived, although at one point John had offered her a cup of tea and then told her where everything was in the kitchen so that she could make it, but beyond that they had barely conversed at all. It was probably best that they start slow, Rose supposed, as she sat on a stool in the corner, trying to take in the fact that she was in the same room as her father. For so long he'd been like a fairy-tale figure; now it seemed almost impossible to believe that he was real.

"I don't have a usual work," John said a touch snippily.

"I only mean, well, compared to the other work I've seen, it's very . . . small."

"It was for my own work, my private work," John said. "Not the stuff I do for McCleod."

"Can I ask you something?" Rose said carefully.

John dropped his head, his shoulders slumping. "If you must."

"If you hate these paintings, which by the way I think are beautiful, why do you keep on doing them?"

John sighed, stepping back to observe his latest touches of paint. "Money."

"Really?" Rose asked him. "Are you very hard up?"

"I have what I need, I am comfortable. And at my age, with my . . . life, that is very important to me. I'm not proud of it, but it's a means to an end. An end that has become vital to me. I still do my own work, my true work, that's what keeps me sane. And that's why it's not for sale. I don't want that part of me to be tainted by this part of me, the part that makes money."

"It strikes me that out here on your own, you live quite a frugal life. Frasier looks like the kind of man who moves in rich circles. What do you need all that money for? Are you in a lot of debt or something, because it's not exactly like you live in the lap of luxury?"

John's expression became stony and solid, and Rose sensed she'd touched a nerve. Who knows what sort of debts he had racked up during his drinking years? Perhaps it was a part of his life he now had to pay dearly for, and the fact that he was doing that, although it cost his pride dear, impressed her.

"May I see it?" Rose asked him, swiftly changing the subject. "May I see your private work?"

"No." John was not cruel or unkind in his refusal, just matter-of-fact. "My private work is like my diary, it is too personal to show anyone, even . . . especially you. I'm sorry, I expect that seems cruel, given the circumstances."

"Don't be," Rose said, but nevertheless she did feel deflated, uncertain what to do next. How would it be possible to know, to forgive and love a man who kept himself locked so tightly away, in every sense? Rose sat and watched John and Maddie for a few moments more, feeling very much surplus to requirements, a spare wheel in her own reconciliation.

"I might just . . . I'll probably just pop over and use the loo, if that's all right?" she said, feeling the need to put some space between her and John for a few minutes at least, but he did not acknowledge having heard her. After a few seconds more, Rose shrugged and left the two artists to their work.

Pushing the unlocked door of Storm Cottage open, Rose hurried across the large living area, which seemed eerily still to her, as if it were waiting for something to happen. Hoping to find a loo, she opened a stable door on the far side of the kitchen, but she was disappointed. There was only a large pantry, filled not with food but tins and tubes of oil paints, various old white spirit bottles filled with a rainbow of colored liquids that could be anything and might just be old bottles of white spirit that her father had kept for reasons known only to him. Also there were pots and pots of brushes, in various states of disrepair, some all but naked of bristles, but still he kept each one of them, perhaps every brush he'd ever worked with, lined up in old mugs and jars like comrades-in-arms.

"There's nothing in there for you," John said behind her, making Rose jump. She turned round, running her fingers through her short hair, which she knew stood up in rebellious spikes.

"I was looking for a loo," she said. "Is Maddie OK on her own in the barn?"

"Yes, very dedicated. I said I was coming in for a sandwich, and she said to make her one, cheese, no butter, no salad, she'd come across in a little while." John seemed mildly amused by his granddaughter's pickiness. It was a good thing, Rose thought, that he was the sort of person to admire eccentricity rather than be irritated by it. It boded well for his and Maddie's relationship. Still, she couldn't believe Maddie was happy alone in the barn.

"It's not like Maddie to want to be on her own," Rose said, raising an eyebrow. "Normally she'd be running in here after a few seconds, convinced there is a child-eating gnome hiding in the attic. I suppose there must be something about this place that makes her feel . . . confident."

"It's probably that she can be who she is here, without anyone expecting anything of her," John said, implying very much that that was what he most enjoyed about life in Storm

Cottage. "She is a little different from most children, in some ways more mature and in others she seems very young. Quite fascinating."

"I know," Rose said uneasily. "I'm not really sure what to do about it, if anything. I love her the way she is, but other people . . . other children find her hard to tolerate a lot of the time. I worry about her, growing up in her own little world. How will she ever fit in, meet a boy, get a job? I keep hoping it's just a phase, but I don't know. Was I like her when I was little?"

John shook his head. In the August sunshine, he looked even older than he had yesterday, his skin sallow and thin, sunken around the contours of his skull. Once he'd been an immensely handsome man, and Rose supposed that hadn't entirely gone. There was still something about that Roman nose and jawline, a little of which was echoed in her own face, although she was much more her mother's daughter when it came to looks, small, slight, with a delicate heart-shaped face. Rose looked at John, the deep shadows engraved under his eyes, the silver bristle of stubble that covered his jaw and neck, the slight stoop in his broad shoulders, and she discovered she was glad that all the years of alcoholism had taken their toll. It didn't seem right that a man could live as badly as her father had and not pay some price for it. And yet, looking at him like that, so frail and fragile, made her want to hold him. Something she was certain he would be horrified by.

"You were a little ray of sunshine," he said. "Always so eager to please, always so happy to get any scrap of attention, never angry with me, even after I'd been angry with you. Perhaps that's why . . ."

"Why what?" Rose asked him.

"Why I was able to leave you so easily, because I was certain you'd forgive me, just like you always did."

Rose swallowed, for a moment taken back to the bottom step, her father cheerfully kissing her goodbye.

"It's not easy to forgive someone who isn't there," she said simply.

"I don't imagine that it is," John replied.

"I just can't understand it," Rose said, shaking her head, forcing him to hold her gaze. "That's what I can't get past. That you walked out and then nothing, nothing. Not a phone call, a letter, nothing. Not when Mum died . . . not ever. Not ever, Dad. It's nice being here with you, watching you work, watching you with Maddie. I like it. It's strange but I like it, and then I remember . . . and I can't get past that. I can't get over the fact that you just left me, completely and utterly. Why?"

John stared at her for a long moment, and then Rose watched as his whole body seemed to crumple and fold in on itself and he sank wearily into a chair.

"I didn't care about you, Rose," he said, his face ashen, scratched deeply with emotion. "I didn't feel a thing for you, or Marian. Or even Tilda, really; she was more just a reason, a better reason than the real one."

"Which was?" Rose asked him, forcing herself to hold her ground in the face of his brutal words.

"I wanted to be somewhere else. I wanted to be on my own, to be free, to drink. Really, all I wanted was to drink. Not even the work mattered at that point." John closed his eyes, and for a moment Rose wondered if he would ever open them again, he looked so drained, so finished. "It is very hard to live with, the knowledge of the person that I have been, the man I am. The hate I have for myself, which is eating me away inside, even now, is a thousand times whatever you might feel for me." He looked at her, his face like granite. "For you to come here, to be here, it's almost too much. It's much more than I can cope with. And in truth that's why I wanted you to go so badly. To look at you, Rose, is to face what I have done. And to accept that a very large part of me doesn't want your forgiveness because I don't deserve it. Redemption now would be too easy. Too neat. I need to suffer, Rose. I need to suffer more than I have. And this, you and Maddie here now, it's too much. It's more than I can take."

Rose stared at him, unable to comprehend what he was saying, or even to accept that he was saying it, that he was talking to her like this at all. Was he telling her to go, or to stay? She couldn't be sure.

"I don't forgive you," she said, "if that helps. I don't forgive you, I never will. Not for what you did to me and to Mum. And if you're worried about not deserving us, then forget it, because this isn't about what you deserve. It's about what Maddie and I deserve. That's why we're here, why we are still here. To know you, to be part of your life, whether you want it or not. John, open your eyes, this isn't about you. It's about me, for once; for the first time in my life, it's about me. You owe me that at least and that's why Maddie and I are going to stick around and see what happens. Not because I forgive you. Because I don't."

John leant his head back on the chair and simply nodded.

"There's only one toilet," he said, gesturing behind him. "You'll find it upstairs. It used to be outside. I was quite happy with it where it was, but then Frasier made me move it—something about my age, no doubt. Whole load of fuss and nonsense, if you ask me. People in and out for days, messing the place up. But everyone seemed to think it was important."

"Everyone? I thought you didn't talk to other people, let alone worried about what they thought," Rose said, shutting the pantry door behind her.

"I don't. But what I have learnt over the years is that sometimes giving in is the only way to get a quiet life," John said. He drew his closed fist from his pocket and opened it, revealing four or five twenty-pound notes unfurling in his palm. "I didn't want to say this in front of Maddie, but I thought, what with things being the way they are, you might need some money, for the B and B."

"No, thank you," Rose said, feeling a little uncomfortable at the gesture. "I have enough for now. I had a savings account. I emptied it on my way up here, so I'm OK. I really don't want to take your money. It doesn't feel right."

John said nothing, but he looked a little hurt, as if he felt rejected. His offer of money was his only demonstrable way of trying to show her that he cared for her.

"Well, then," he said, stuffing the notes back into his pocket. "I'll put the kettle on."

Upstairs, Storm Cottage was much smaller than its large, long ground-floor footprint. The first floor was probably an afterthought, added much later to the original cottage. There was a small square hallway with three doors leading from it. The first door, left slightly ajar, was obviously her father's bedroom, consisting of nothing more than a bed, with stacks of books and piles of magazines all around it and a single naked bulb hanging from the ceiling. The only other ornament was an assortment of amber plastic pill bottles lined up along the thick windowsill, probably collected over the years, another relic of his life, carefully cataloged.

The second door was the boxroom, barely more than two meters square, and filled with clutter, so much so that she could open the door only enough to be able to glimpse its hoard of hidden treasures. Rose peered through the gap, intrigued by the things that John kept, longing to be able to climb into the tiny space and explore it, like a genuine Egyptian tomb, filled to the brim with relics that meant something only to him. God only knew what was in there, what oddities he had collected on his haphazard journey through life. What if she found something, some small thing saved from his life with her and Mum, a photograph or object, some small pointless token to sum up an entire life? Or worse, what if she found nothing at all to show that Rose and her mother had ever been a part of John Jacobs's life? Suddenly overcome by a confusion of motives, Rose drew the door firmly closed, afraid of what demons might lurk in the tiny room. John was right, they couldn't just be close again. If they were to achieve any kind of affection for each other at all, it would be a long process, full of pain, blame, and recrimination, and one that either one of them might not be willing or able to complete.

The bathroom was basic although modern. Rose was shocked to see an old man's seat, positioned above the toilet, to save her father from having to bend his knees too much when he sat on it. He was only sixty-four, which seemed very young to have to have a handle screwed into the side of the wall to help his knees. Perhaps it was the same mysterious "everyone" who'd influenced him to get the bathroom moved inside at all, who was also future-proofing him against his advancing years. Was Frasier really the only person in his life? Rose wasn't so sure. Despite being ramshackle and full of clutter, Storm Cottage was very clean and well stocked. Rose couldn't imagine that John either cleaned or went to the supermarket for his weekly shop. She certainly couldn't picture Frasier in a pair of rubber gloves, on his hands and knees scrubbing out the loo. So who was it, then? Rose wasn't entirely sure she wanted to know.

Coming down the stairs, Rose found her father sitting with his mug of tea in hand, another waiting for her on a small, hand-carved table in front of the cold grate of the fireplace, a plate of roughly cut sandwiches balanced on the arm of his chair.

"What are you doing?" Rose asked him. He was sitting with his legs outstretched, staring at the rough stone wall opposite.

"Looking," John said, adding after a moment, "Seeing. Trying to think of a way to make you see why I did what I did."

"I don't think I will ever understand," Rose replied.

"I don't think you have to," John said. "You just have to see."

He paused for a moment, his body contracting as if he were physically fighting to get the words out of his mouth. Glancing in the direction of the barn, where Maddie was all alone, Rose hesitated, and sensing a now-or-never moment, sat down opposite him.

"Soon after I . . . soon after I left . . . Broadstairs, I felt disconnected from not only what I had left behind but also from myself." John spoke haltingly, as if the sound of his own voice was uncomfortable to listen to. "The vodka made me numb inside and out. I started drinking to kill the pain in my gut, but in the end I killed everything that was there. I couldn't remember anything—how to feel, how to love, how to miss you, how to care. Not even for Tilda, who must have woken up one day kilometers from anywhere or anyone she'd ever known, and wondered what on earth she'd got herself into. The worst of it was I couldn't even paint. I didn't feel enough of anything to work. So I began to drink even more. There would be weeks when I was never sober."

His tone was so matter-of-fact, so flat almost, that it made it all the harder for Rose to hear him admit that he didn't, couldn't care. That the drink had chipped away at every nerve ending until there was nothing left, only his passion for painting and collection of other people's defunct hopes and dreams.

"And now?" Rose asked him carefully. "Now you're sober, do you feel again?"

John sat back in his chair, staring into the cold grate, so still and silent that Rose wondered if he'd simply shut off from her question. But then, after a moment, he spoke.

"I think I have forgotten how to feel," he said, turning his gray eyes on her. "Perhaps it's too late now to do any more than acknowledge the people I have hurt and admit responsibility. There is very little else I can do."

A flood of words flew into Rose's mouth, but she kept her lips very firmly shut. This was the most meaningful, important thing that he'd said to her since she'd found him.

"The work that you do, the paintings for Frasier, I mean—they aren't inspired by what you've done, what you've been through. I don't see the connection."

"Because there is no connection," John said, sitting suddenly forward in his chair. "Those . . . those *posters* are nothing more than a lifetime of not giving a damn, which now I find compelled to pay interest on." He paused, twisting his fingers into a knot. "I could help you and Maddie, financially, I mean. Give you something for a fresh start. Find you a new home. Help you with the rent, or a car until you get on your feet. I could do that, I have enough."

"So we would leave Millthwaite, you mean?" Rose asked him quietly, without anger, because she could see he was trying to be something that he understood very little about. He was trying to be kind. "Buy back your solitude?"

John shook his head. "No, no, not at all. If you want to stay in Millthwaite, stay. I'm getting reasonably used to it and Madeline is a tolerable child, as far as children go."

Rose took in a sharp breath, deciding that now it was her turn to be frank.

"Can I be honest?" she said. "I didn't come here to find

you. You were just *here*. When I came to Millthwaite it was because there was nowhere else for me to go. After a life of staying in one place, it was the only other place I'd ever thought about going. And I had some silly notion that this was one way of finding something that would make me understand my life, make me happy. When I found out that you lived here, I almost didn't come to see you, I wasn't sure I wanted to. That's a terrible feeling, to not know if you even want to see your own father. What I'm trying to say is that I didn't come for a reunion, or a final scene. I came because I had to, and you happened to be here, but now that I am here I realize that knowing you, in any way at all, is better than the alternative. Perhaps we might even be friends one day."

John said nothing for a while and then eventually, "You could stay here. There is a small room. It's full of junk, it would need clearing out, but if you wanted to . . ."

Rose held her breath, listening to the house creak and breathe around her as he waited for the answer.

"I . . . I don't think that is quite the right thing to do yet, do you? You need your space, not me under your feet and Maddie constantly questioning you."

"You're right," John said, his expression hidden as he turned his face away from her. "Of course. I . . . I was trying too hard again. I admire you for not being taken in by it. Let me ask you something now." Rose waited. "What happened to make you run away to a place on the front of a postcard?"

Rose's face crumpled, and she turned away from him. "It's too soon, it's too soon to talk about that too," she said. "Just that I had a line that I promised myself I would not let be crossed again. And it was."

John's expression was immobile as he processed the information.

"Well, whatever I can do," he said, "even if it might be very small, I will try to do it. I shall try to be some kind of father to you while I can."

"Oh, here you are, hello!" Maddie pushed open the kitchen door, completely unaware of the tension and emotion that washed through the room, flooding out into the August sunshine. "I finished that canvas—what else is there to paint? Those sandwiches haven't got butter in them, have they?"

When Rose returned to the B & B, it was on her own. Feeling that there really wasn't very much else she and John could talk about for now, she'd tried to get Maddie to leave with her for lunch. But Maddie had not wanted to. Her particular style of persistence, which Rose had often felt was based on Chinese water torture, meant that John had abandoned his painting to make her her own canvas, which was exactly her height squared, with the specific instruction that she was to paint something that would take at least a week. Maddie had been fascinated as she watched John measure her against a length of wood, sawing it into mitered corners, quickly assembling the basic frame, questioning him constantly about what he was doing next and how long it would take. For someone who didn't much like conversation, John was remarkably tolerant of Maddie's relentless curiosity, even her habit of repeating questions a few minutes apart. He liked this, Rose had realized slowly, he liked talking about what he knew, and he particularly liked the fact that he had a granddaughter to impart his knowledge to. Perhaps it was a primeval thing: after all these years in the wilderness, John now had someone to keep his memory, his existence alive a little longer, just as he kept the relics of others who would otherwise now be long forgotten. As he stood the completed canvas against the back wall of the barn, next to Maddie's other prolific offerings, Rose suggested that now might be a good time to leave.

"But look!" Maddie said, her face wrought with anxiety as she pointed at the tantalizingly blank canvas. "Look!"

"You can't paint on it yet," John said. "I have to prime it. It will take an afternoon to dry."

"I don't want to wait an afternoon, I want to do it now!" Maddie demanded furiously. Rose sighed; it was these outbursts that other people found so hard to understand, seeing her daughter as a spoilt brat. The truth was that Maddie really did need to paint *now*, at least in her world.

"Maddie . . ." Rose began, feeling that familiar sense of awkwardness and ineffectuality creep up her spine.

"You need to draw first, anyway," John told Maddie with a shrug. "All the great artists draw and draw for weeks before they start to paint. You haven't drawn a stroke so far, very amateurish."

"Drawing is boring. I don't draw, I paint," Maddie told him emphatically. John did not know that Maddie was not one to be swayed by reverse psychology if it conflicted with her idea about how things should be, either.

"Here." John opened a drawing chest, pulled out a large sketchbook, and waved it at his work in progress. "These are my drawings for this painting. This is what you do if you are a real artist. Just painting splodges of color, as lovely as they are, is actually very childish, but then again I suppose you are a child."

Rose's eyebrows shot skywards as she expected Maddie to be infuriated by what her daughter would certainly see as an insult, but instead Maddie seemed to consider what he said.

"I'm not like other children," she said after a moment, with something like a touch of sadness.

"Good," John said emphatically. "I don't like other children."

"What should I draw, then?" Maddie asked him, climbing down from her position with unusual grace and ease.

"Well, if your mother would let you, you could come out and do some drawing with me now. We'll find a nice spot on the hillside and pick a view. You will be amazed how much movement, depth, and texture you can get with one of these." John held up a pencil. "As long as you explain yourself to my wretched agent why I've wasted most of today on a demanding little girl, that is."

"Can I?" Maddie asked Rose, who looked uncertain.

"I'm not sure I should just leave you here . . ." she said.

"She'll be perfectly safe," John said, a little affronted.

"No, it's not that, it's just . . . do you really want to do this?" She stared at John pointedly, giving him time to consider exactly what he'd just proposed.

"I find that I do," John said. "It puts me in mind of late afternoons on the beach with you as a child. We would make drawings in the wet sand and then wait and watch as the tide washed them away."

Rose found that she was unable to respond; that memory, long forgotten until that moment, was now suddenly so vividly present it took her breath away.

"Let me take her out to draw. I'll bring her to you in time for tea."

"I want to draw," Maddie said, in her usual forthright way.

"OK," Rose said. "But will you indulge me and take that mobile phone you hate so much, just in case? Maddie knows my number."

"Very well." John sighed, going to his drawer, finding the phone, and putting it in his pocket.

"Right, well. So." Rose looked at Maddie, who was sitting on the floor poring over John's sketchbook. "See you in a bit, then?"

She did not reply, of course.

Rose could not find Shona in her room, or Jenny in any of the places she usually frequented, but the sound of banging and bashing about, and the background fuzz of a distant radio playing told her they had to be somewhere in the building. After a little further investigation Rose found a sofa in the living room that normally sat across an unused doorway, pulled away, and the door swinging wide open. Stepping through a small, dingy hallway and feeling a little bit like she was crossing into Narnia, Rose opened a second door to find Shona and Jenny cheerfully stuffing garbage bags with what looked like old clothes, books, and more.

"Hello?" Rose said. "What are you doing and where am I?"

"This was Brian's mum's annex," Jenny told her. "She died a couple of years back, and since then it's been a junk room. Anything Brian's not sure what to do with he's put it in here. But I was thinking it's a waste, all this space. Maybe it could be more rooms."

"Not that you are exactly fully booked as it is," Shona said mildly, winking at Rose as she stuffed some aged-looking curtains into a bag. But instead of her usual sharp-tongued reply, Jenny stopped what she was doing and nodded.

"You're right there," she said sadly, looking around. "This place is on its uppers. When Eve used to be in here, we were a real busy little place. Not always fully booked, but almost always. I loved it, doing all those breakfasts, meeting all those people. Now, though, last couple of years it's like the world's forgotten us. If you haven't got a flat-screen TV on every wall, velvet wallpaper, and the word 'boutique' attached to your name, no one wants to know."

"You could try updating a bit, perhaps?" Rose suggested tentatively, thinking about the candlewick bedspreads.

"I don't know. I think I'm too old for all that modern nonsense, offering a choice of eggs at breakfast, herbal tea," Jenny said, wrinkling her nose, clearly horrified by the notion that the customer might even sometimes be right. "Eve was a terrible old cow, don't get me wrong, she was the mother-in-law from hell, always making me run around like a blue-arsed fly, and whenever Brian was stood in front of her he turned into a blithering ten-year-old lad again, but she must have brought us some luck—or cursed us on her deathbed—because after she went, that's when it all started to go wrong."

"Maybe she still could bring you luck," Shona said, picking up a framed photo that had been lying on its back, its glass filmed in dust. She cleaned it with the palm of her hand before showing it to Rose. It revealed a sepia print of a wedding photo, from around the 1930s, Rose guessed. A chubby-faced smiling young woman, in a long cream dress that trailed down the steps of the church, stood arm in arm with an equally well-built young man, who looked the spitting image of Brian.

"I don't see how," Jenny said. "We've got maybe another six months here, then we'll have to sell up and live on what Brian brings in. It's not that I mind living carefully, it's just I like to be busy, and I had all the kids here. Oh, sod it, it's just bricks and mortar, when all's said and done."

Rose looked around the annex. It was a large single living room–cum-kitchen with a bedroom off it, and what she guessed must be a bathroom.

"The pub was packed on gig night," she said thoughtfully.

"What are you saying, that I should start a nightclub? I don't think so!" Jenny snorted.

"No, I'm just saying, if you could think of something the

local people would use as well as tourists . . . I bet gig night is what pays most of Albie's bills."

"A lap-dancing club," Shona offered, shimmying her shoulders. "I could be the star attraction."

"I did think of a café," Jenny said, "but the start-up cost is too much and there are ten a penny around here."

"What about a community space?" Rose said. "I mean, do you have a village hall?"

"Not anymore," Jenny said. "They pulled it down a few years back. It was dangerous, apparently. Some old prefab that was meant to be temporary and then lasted fifty years. There was talk of rebuilding but nothing's ever happened."

"Well, what if you just made it a place where . . . I don't know, people could have parties, or knitting circles could meet, or my dad could give drawing and painting classes."

"Your dad teach a class? Never!" Jenny snorted.

"Never say never. He's just elected to spend the afternoon with Maddie. Anything is possible," Rose said, pleased to see that she had surprised both the other women with her news. In truth, she'd been rather anxious about leaving Maddie with John, despite the girl's keenness. He looked so . . . faint sometimes, as if he were barely there. Rose was worried that Maddie's strident determination might be too much for him.

"I saw this thing on the telly. Well, half of this thing, because it was quite boring," Shona said. "But anyway, it was some village stuck out in the middle of nowhere, bit like this. They brought in a hairdresser once a week, a beauty salon too, other things, services that you don't get local anymore, because there's not enough demand for them to be permanent. Did a storm, it did. This space would be great for that."

"You could have local crafts displayed, charge a commission for anything that sells," Rose said excitedly.

"How am I going to fit all this into here?" Jenny asked her. "Craft and hairdressers and the like?"

"I have no idea." Rose laughed. "I tell you what, you make us a cup of tea and I'll help you clear the rest of this stuff out, and we can think about it."

"So," Shona said as soon as Jenny had safely left the room.

"So what?" Rose asked demurely. "You and Jenny are getting on OK now, aren't you? I thought you two had more in common than you realized."

"She's not as bad as she seems, but if you ever say that again I will kill you. Anyway, did you fuck Ted?"

"Shona!" Rose gasped, looking back at the open door, expecting to find Jenny lurking there. "No, I did not!"

"Look at me." Shona attempted and failed to secure eye contact with Rose. "Look at me! You did something, you dirty cow. What did you do?"

"Oh, OK, we did some kissing, but that really is all," Rose said, unable to stop her mouth curling into a tiny smile at the thought. "I didn't think I wanted to kiss him, and then, well, then I thought, why not? Why not do something crazy and stupid for once in my life? I'm never the crazy one, I'm never the stupid one . . ."

"I wouldn't say that," Shona said.

"So we kissed and it was nice—kissing was nice—and I didn't think about anything else, not Richard or Frasier or Maddie or Jenny, just about kissing. And now I feel sort of terrible about it and I don't know what to do next."

"Nice?" Shona screeched in an excited whisper. "Kissing Ted was *nice*? So he didn't exactly make the earth move, then?"

"I'm pretty sure I didn't want him to do that," Rose said. "The kissing was nice. Sweet. It felt innocent and clean. At the time. Now I feel all stupid and confused. I mean, I *know* it was wrong, I'm still married, I'm still hopelessly in love with Frasier, and there's Maddie, but . . ."

"But?" Shona asked her expectantly.

"It didn't feel that way." Rose giggled unexpectedly, covering her mouth with both her hands. "I was so worried I'd feel scared of feeling guilty, or worse, dirty, but I didn't. I just felt like a girl kissing a boy because it's nice. And that was *lovely*."

"Why would a bit of kissing make you feel any of those things?" Shona asked, perplexed.

"What would make you feel what things?" Jenny asked as she came in carrying a tray of tea and cake.

"Seeing her . . . dad?" Shona said.

"Clearing out this place," Rose said at the same time, and equally inappropriately.

"I wasn't born yesterday, you know," Jenny said, pursing her lips. "Whatever it is, I've a distinct feeling that I don't want to know."

Chapter Ten

Rose was attempting to get oil paint off Maddie in the shower when her phone rang. Normally the bleep of the ancient ringtone would send shivers down her spine, as almost the only person who ever tried to ring her, who even had her number, was Richard. But just before dinner she had texted her number, having made herself delay for what seemed like an agonizing period of time in order not to seem too keen, to Frasier, and he had texted straight back saying he would call later. Without having to look at her phone she knew this would be him. Was it wrong to want to see him again?

"Be OK for a second?" Rose asked Maddie, who nodded, sitting cross-legged on the floor of the shower, as the water cascaded over her shoulders, rather enjoying peeling the flakes of paint, which she had somehow got everywhere, off her skin.

Rose took a breath when she saw Frasier's name on the display, attempting her best casual you-could-be-anyone-my-phone-never-stops-ringing hello.

"Hello?"

"Rose, hello, it's Frasier. Now a good time?" he said softly into her ear. Rose felt her heart rate quicken and her knees buckle as she sat down on the bed. Not even Ted, with all his good looks and charm, and definitely skillful lips, had cured her of the feeling that Frasier gave her.

"Now's fine," she said, careful to sound noncommittal and casual.

"So I hear you were with your dad today? I couldn't believe it, he actually answered his mobile! How was it?"

"Odd," Rose said thoughtfully. "Confusing, interesting. Nice."

"So mainly good, then?" Frasier spoke with a smile in his tone.

"I think so," Rose said. "Maddie thinks he is the most interesting person she has ever met."

"Ha, I bet he likes that," Frasier said. "The thing your father forgot when he decided to hide himself away for good is that he really does rather like being admired. If only I could get him to lecture, teach, make appearances. I think I could make him quite the celebrity of the art world. Still, he has his reasons and I respect them."

"That he is a miserable old git?" Rose said, smiling.

"That is one of them," Frasier admitted.

"Thank you. I know you spoke to him."

"Oh." Frasier sounded embarrassed, as if he'd been caught out. "It was nothing."

"Anyway, dinner. I'm coming down tomorrow. The van will be going back to Edinburgh, but I could stay. Take you out? There's this incredible place near Ullswater where they actually invented sticky toffee pudding."

"Please don't feel obliged . . ." Rose said.

"Don't be silly," Frasier said pleasantly.

"I'd need a babysitter," Rose said, not so sure if now was the right time to break down that dam of emotion after all.

"Surely your friend would oblige? And if not, I know—"

Frasier began, but before he could finish, a screech and a thump came from the bathroom, followed by a rising cry.

"Got to go," Rose said, hanging up and rushing into the bathroom, where she found Maddie splayed out on her back, her legs in the air, the water still pelting her.

"Oh, no, did you slip?" Rose asked her as she climbed into the shower, fully clothed, and switched off the showerhead. Maddie nodded, sobbing noisily as Rose pulled her up and bundled her into a soft warm towel that was waiting on the heated towel rail outside. "Oh, baby, I'm sorry. What hurts?"

Maddie pointed to the small of her back, which Rose rubbed, as she hugged the girl until she eventually stopped crying.

"Will I have a bruise?" Maddie asked her, attempting to look over her shoulder at the sore spot.

"Shouldn't think so," Rose said. "Maybe just a small one. I think it was more the shock that upset you."

"This bruise has nearly gone now," Maddie said, slipping the towel off her shoulder and looking at the now gray and yellowish bruise that covered most of her shoulder and extended down her back. "Purple and yellow are complementary colors. See how that yellow looks really yellow?"

Rose bit her lip as she looked at the bruise, her heart clenching as she remembered how Maddie had got it.

"Why did Daddy do it?" Maddie asked Rose, as she continued to examine herself. "It hurt a lot. That shocked me too, but mainly it hurt a lot."

"He was angry," Rose said. "He was completely, completely wrong. And bad. He was angry and he lashed out at me, and you got in the way. I'm so sorry, darling. I'm so, so sorry."

"So he didn't mean to hurt me, he meant to hurt you?" Maddie asked her, putting her hands on Rose's face, so that she had to look the child in the eye.

"Yes," Rose said, silent tears sliding down her face. She hadn't expected Maddie to choose a moment like this to face up to what had happened on the night they had left. She hardly wanted to do it herself. But Maddie was talking about it, she wanted to try and understand what was impossible for a little girl to grasp—the reason why her daddy had hurt her—and Rose could not let that moment pass to help her. "I'm so, so sorry. You were never meant to be hurt."

Maddie looked pained and confused, uncertain again, all of the things that so often characterized her when they were at home, that strange little girl, the odd one out, the one that no one understood and who never fitted in, her shoulders hunched against the memory, the truth.

"That night," Rose said, struggling to contain her sobs, "you were in bed, Dad and I were . . . talking. Fighting. I made him very, very angry, so angry he wanted to hit me. I didn't know you were coming down, I didn't know you were there until . . ." Rose stopped, picturing the moment Richard grabbed his seven-year-old daughter by the shoulder and slammed her into the door so hard it banged shut, as he made his way towards Rose, who was already sprawled on the floor, put there by a slap that numbed the side of her head and made her ears ring.

"Maddie," Rose had shrieked, seeing her daughter's stunned face, too frightened, in too much pain to cry. Richard had seen her too, then, her cries snapping him back into the room. He'd turned and looked at Maddie, horror sweeping over his blanched face. And that was when Rose knew what she had to do. Scrambling to her feet, she picked up Maddie, who clung to her, barged past Richard while he was still too shocked to react. She grabbed her secret bundle from where she kept it hidden at the back of the broom cupboard and a few still damp things from the wash basket. Then she picked up her bag and the car keys.

"Where are you going?" Richard asked. "What are you going to do? You can't say anything, you know . . . my job, my reputation . . . I didn't mean it!"

But Rose had ignored him, tearing into the night, knowing she had only a few minutes before his rage supplanted his shock and he came after her. She stuffed Maddie into the back of the car, slammed the driver's door shut behind her, and banged down the central locks. Richard did not attempt to follow her, though; he did not try to stop her taking his daughter, probably because he never imagined that his mousy wife would have the courage to go farther than once round the block. Rose had taken one last look at him standing in the doorway of her mother's house, leaning against the post, his arms crossed as he watched her, now utterly calm.

He doesn't think I can do it, Rose realized. He doesn't think I'm capable of leaving him. And for a moment, as her white-knuckled fingers gripped the steering wheel, she wasn't sure that he was wrong.

"Mummy, go," Maddie pleaded in a whisper from the backseat, her voice trembling with fear. "Mummy, drive."

It was at her daughter's bidding that Rose had switched on the ignition and pulled away.

"When we *will* see Daddy again," Maddie asked her now, quietly unable to make eye contact, "will he still be angry?"

"Not with you," Rose said. "Only me."

"He wasn't angry with me before. I still got this," Maddie pointed out, gingerly reaching over her shoulder to touch the bruise.

"I know," Rose said wearily. She was so tired, so desperate just to be able to close her eyes and sleep, but there was one more thing she had to say to Maddie while she had the chance. "I . . . Maddie, I don't think I can be married to Daddy anymore."

"I know." Maddie nodded as if she'd already worked that out for herself. "That's OK. We can stay here. I will become an artist with John."

"Wouldn't you miss home, school, Daddy?" Rose asked her as she escorted her into the bedroom, pulling her pajama top over her head. Maddie might feel this way about Richard now, but how long would it last? The last thing Rose wanted to do was impose an estrangement between daughter and father, even if she knew Richard was by no means the best of fathers. The damage done by ripping him completely out of her life could be worse even than the bruise he'd given her, which would heal, at least.

"No," Maddie said with certainty. "I don't like school there, and I like you better here. You are much more interesting to look at and listen to. You are kinder and funnier and . . . you smile more. Here is better for you, this is where you are happy. And you like me better here too."

"What do you mean?" Rose asked her, horrified at what Maddie thought she knew.

"I mean," Maddie said, with some emphasis, speaking slowly and carefully, "that you like me better here than you do at home. Because you aren't frightened or sad."

"I think not being at school, not being in the middle of all the worries that me and Daddy had, even though we tried our best to keep them from you, has helped you not to be so uncomfortable and anxious," Rose said, trying to work out what Maddie was feeling herself, and if being away from Richard gave the child the same sense of relief and being able to breathe that it gave her. "And so I am less worried about you, less worried about how you will fit in. But it's not that I like you better; I can't like you better than I do. I love you, Maddie, more than anything."

Maddie looked at her for a long moment, studying her face as if she were trying to decipher exactly what it was that Rose was saying, and then out of the blue she launched herself into Rose's arms, nestling her head into the curve of her neck, a rare gesture of affection that Rose embraced happily.

"I don't want to see Daddy," Maddie said after a while in her mother's arms. "And I don't want to go to school ever again."

"I think you will change your mind about Daddy," Rose said. "And you will have to go to school, as soon as we've decided where to live. It's the law, darling."

"Let's live here, then," Maddie said. "We've got a bedroom and our own bathroom, and Jenny cooks."

"We can't stay here forever," Rose said, as much as she would like to.

"John's house, then, although John doesn't cook, he told me. I do like Jenny's cooking."

Rose sighed and smiled all at once. "You are a funny girl, Miss Maddie."

"Can I go and see Shona and Jenny to say good night?" Maddie asked her. She liked tiptoeing up and down the carpeted stairs in her bare feet.

"Yes," Rose said, picking up a hairbrush and running it through Maddie's damp hair. "But don't hang around too long. Back in ten minutes."

Her phone started ringing again almost as soon as Maddie closed the door behind her, and absently Rose picked it up, looking forward to speaking to Frasier again, hopeful that the sound of his voice would calm her nerves from trying to talk to Maddie about the way things were, which had gone much better than she could have hoped for, all things considered. It had been such a difficult day, a day fraught with so much emotion, as her worries had come crashing home. Rose felt wrung out, every last little drop of her strength squeezed out of her. It would be nice to hear Frasier's soothing voice.

"Sorry about that," she said as she answered.

"You should be." It was Richard's voice that replied, calm and cold. "Where have you taken my daughter, Rose?"

"Richard, look." Rose panicked, uncertain what to say or how, her mind scrambling to know what to do. Her first instinct was to hang up, but if she never talked to him, then this constant nagging fear of what he would do if he caught up with her would never go away. She had to face him, confront him, make him see the way things were now. "I know we need to talk, I just needed time—"

"Time? Time?" Richard's fury was not tempered by the quiet control with which he spoke. "You abducted Maddie, and now you have to bring her back. Immediately."

Just the sound of his voice was enough to drag Rose right back to where she had been in those seconds, sitting in the car outside her house, before she had found the courage to switch on the car engine. Life without Richard's voice always in her ear, his demands, his wants and needs, seemed impossible in those seconds. How would she know what to do, where to go, what to say if he didn't tell her? Richard always knew what was best for her, he protected her, cushioned her from the world. And yet—Rose fought with her own habitual need to give in—and yet she was here because of the things he did to her that she couldn't bear to remember. She was a different person without him. Now was not the time to be weak.

"I'm not coming back," Rose told him, finding unexpected courage waiting for her in her words. She sounded strong, determined. Now all she had to do was to find the physical strength to carry it through. "I don't have to do anything you want. I'm free of you and so is Maddie, and she's glad. She *hates* you, Richard." Rose knew that not only was that last statement untrue, it was also unfair, the wrong thing to say, but still she said it because she knew it would hurt him the most, and because just once she wanted to wound him as badly as he'd injured her time and time again. Rose had had a lifetime of doing what was right, and what was expected of her. Not anymore.

"I knew it," Richard spat. "I knew you were unstable. This breakdown's been brewing for months, Rose. You can't see it because you are in it. You're deluded, caught up in this little fantasy of yours, the poor abused wife who has to escape her villainous husband. That's not how it is, Rose, and if you stop to think for one second you'll see that. *I* love you. *I* am the only person in the world who has always stood by you, *I* am the only one who can put up with your problems."

"Was it my problems that made you hit me, and hurt Maddie?" Rose asked him, the sudden rush of years of pent-up emotion, words, feelings, and questions, which she had been forced to clamp behind closed lips to safeguard herself as best she could, pouring out. "Or was it just that for once I wouldn't give in to your bullying, Richard, that for once you couldn't get control over me any other way?"

There was a long silence on the other end of the line, crackling with frustrated, impotent fury.

"That didn't happen, Rose," Richard said finally, his voice taut and strained. "Not the way you remember it. I only wanted what any normal man wants from his wife. You overreacted, went crazy! You are the one who hurt Maddie."

Rose was so shocked, so completely flattened by his incredible statement, delivered as if it was utterly incontrovertible, that it took her several seconds to be able to gasp in enough air to be able to reply. What was he planning, what was he trying to do?

"She still has the bruise, Richard!" Rose said, her voice rising in panic as the realization slowly dawned on her.

"You gave it to her," Richard said calmly, regaining his composure and the sense that he was regaining control.

"She's old enough to know what happened herself. She will tell anyone who asks her," Rose countered.

"She's a confused child, with problems of her own, probably brought about by her unstable and unaffectionate mother," Richard said. "No little girl wants to make her mother angry. She'll say anything to try and stop being hurt again."

"You . . . you . . . *liar*!" Rose cried, tears springing into her eyes, as yet again Richard twisted out of shape everything that was good in her life.

"Who do you think they will believe, Rose?" Richard inevitably said. "The family doctor, the loving, patient husband and father? Or the crazy woman who ran away without even stopping to pack her child a change of clothes? Come home now and we'll say no more about it. It's been a long time, I miss my wife. You belong at my side."

Rose closed her eyes, the room spinning around her.

"Why?" she said quietly. "Why do you want me, when you hate me so much?"

"Because you are mine," Richard said simply, almost tenderly.

Despite all her fear, her anger and resolve, Rose found herself wavering. She could almost feel the weakness spreading through her, as if Richard's words were sapping her strength. Perhaps she should just go back, go back to the life that she knew so well, that she knew how to endure, to survive. Perhaps that would be easier than trying to exist alone in a world where she had never fitted in. And then Rose remembered the bruise still flowering on Maddie's shoulder, and she knew she could never go back. No matter what Richard threatened to do to her, she could never, ever go back.

"No." Rose's voice was trembling but also strengthening with every syllable she found the strength to utter. "I'm not yours. I'm not anyone's, and I am not coming back. Say what you want, do what you want, Richard, but you can't frighten or bully me anymore. I am finished with you."

"You will regret this, Rose," Richard said, his voice icy cold, laden with menace. "The next time I see you, which will be very soon, you will regret ever speaking to your husband that way."

Once she was certain that he had hung up, Rose threw the phone across the room, where it skittered along the carpet and shot under the dressing table. Flinging her arms around herself, she held on tightly until her breathing regulated and she could remember that Richard was not there, not in the room with her. His threats, as menacing as they might be, could not reach her here. He still did not know where she was, and even if he did, she wasn't alone now. There were people here for her. People to stand between her and him.

"No, for the last time I am not going to let you paint my portrait," Shona was saying as she guided a very talkative Maddie into the room. Instantly, she saw the look on Rose's blanched face, sensed the tension in her clenched body.

"I've forgotten my . . . um, shoes," Shona said to Maddie, putting a hand on her shoulder to stop her advancing any farther into the room. "They're downstairs in the living room. Will you get them for me?"

"What do you need shoes for?" Maddie asked her. "It's bedtime."

"Bedtime for children, not for grown-ups. I want to go for a walk."

"Where?"

"Maddie, just get my shoes?" Shona told her in such an authoritative way that Maddie turned on her heel and went.

"What?" Shona said, crossing to sit beside Rose on the bed and hooking a protective arm around her. "What's happened?"

"Richard called. I spoke to him. He . . . he's saying terrible things, things he'll tell people if I don't go back—that I hurt Maddie, that I'm unstable, a bad mother. But I can't go back to him, Shona. I just can't."

"Rose, you're trembling," Shona murmured, the way a mother might comfort a frightened child, pulling Rose tight into her body as if she could physically stay her shaking. "What did he do to you the night you left? What was it that's frightened you so badly, made you leave after all these years of his bullying and put-downs? Did he . . . did he hit you? Did he?"

Rose nodded. "Yes, I made him so angry, he knocked me across the room. And Maddie too when she came down to see what the noise was. But that's not the worst of it," she whispered, the terrible scenes that had preceded Maddie entering the room flashing through her head in a series of dreadful tableaux.

"What, then?" Shona asked her in barely more than a whisper.

"He tried to rape me," Rose whispered, the words making her want to gag as she spoke them. "When I fought back, when I refused him, that's when he hit me. I made him so mad. That was the first time, you see."

"The first time he tried to rape you?" Shona asked her, appalled.

"No, the first time I fought back."

• • •

By the time Maddie returned with Shona's shoes, Rose was in the shower, the hot water riveting into her, scalding her white skin and imprinting it with red welts. Shona was standing by the bed, her mouth set in a thin grim line, her fists still clenched. As Maddie approached, she literally forced herself to unclasp her fingers, prising a smile onto her face as she took the shoes and slipped them on.

"Jenny doesn't like you wearing shoes inside," Maddie reminded her. "Where's Mummy gone?"

"Mum's just jumped in the shower," Shona said. "So I said I'd tuck you in and put the telly on for you for a bit."

"Can I do drawing?" Maddie said, wielding the outsize sketchbook that John had given her that afternoon. As soon as she had caught on to the idea of drawing what she saw around her, she had become obsessed with it, and the book was already filling rapidly with really quite accurately executed sketches of the countryside, sheep, trees, rocks, teapots, shoes, books, and even John. It was the first time in her life Maddie had discovered something she was naturally good at, and she was loath to give it up for something as mundane as sleep or even the treat of television in bed.

"Go on, then," Shona said with a shrug.

"Can I draw you?" Maddie persisted.

Shona sighed, glancing anxiously at the closed bathroom door and sitting down heavily on the bed. "OK."

Just then Rose's mobile phone sounded from underneath the dressing table. Maddie and Shona both stared at where the noise was coming from, neither making a move to retrieve it.

"Should we . . . ?"

"Just leave it," Shona said. "If it's important they'll leave a message."

• • •

Rose had no idea why she couldn't cry. She wanted to, she could feel it there like a heavy stone embedded in her chest, the grief over what she had endured for so many of her married years, but it would not be dissolved by tears. Richard's abuse of her had not been constant, nor daily, nothing like the grueling regime of violence some women lived under for so long.

There had been rare, sporadic attacks, if that was what they could be called, that came months apart, a year apart once. For the most part, after Maddie was born Richard showed no sexual interest in her at all, as if once she had borne him a child Rose had become less than the perfect flawless girl he'd first admired, and she had been secretly relieved. Their adult married life had been less than passionate, to say the least, first making love a week or so before the wedding. Inexperienced and clumsy, Rose had been tense and uncertain, and Richard had done his best to be kind. Although he was so much older than her, he didn't seem to know enough to put her at her ease, or ignite any more emotion in her than sheer nerves and uncertainty. And yet it had been a sweet union, the first time, and one that Rose remembered feeling was full of love. Richard so wanted her to be his alone, his wife, his lover, and she had felt cherished and safe for the first time in a very long while. How ready she had been to marry him, how gladly she went down the aisle, alone, without anyone to give her away and not a single relative on her side of the church. And that was how those first almost featureless years of their marriage had passed, Rose unaware of how Richard gradually controlled more and more of what she did, whom she knew, where she went, or even how she thought or felt, so willing was she to trust in him. And their sex life wasn't ever earth-shattering, but neither was it unkind or cruel. After years of marriage, it petered away to once or twice a month, and Rose, who never felt any kind of desire other than to please her husband, was content with that, letting him always take the lead. And then she became pregnant.

Richard was furious with her, more angry than Rose could have imagined, even if she had suspected that this was how he would react, which she hadn't. Happily, she went to him one evening with her news, sitting at his feet as he watched the ten o'clock news in his favorite armchair, and told him, with a small quiet smile, that they were to become parents.

His anger was shocking and disorienting. How had it happened? he demanded. Why wasn't she taking her pills? Did she think she could trick him into something she knew he never wanted? Bewildered, Rose said she wasn't sure how it happened, there had been that time she'd had food poisoning a month or so ago, perhaps then, but anyway, did it really matter?

Pushing her away from him, Richard got up and paced the floor furiously, telling her that now nothing would be the same. It wouldn't be just the two of them anymore; she would not be his perfect unspoilt girl anymore. There would be a mewling brat constantly demanding attention from her. A child would change everything and force them apart. He did not want to be a father; he'd made it clear from the start that he never wanted children.

Rose sat on the floor watching him, baffled and upset, her idea of what this moment would be like utterly shattered. Unable to recall the moment Richard had told her his opinions on parenthood, she asked him to remind her.

"If I'd wanted you to become pregnant," he told her, "I would have told you. That should be enough."

And then he picked up a bottle of port from the drinks cabinet and took it upstairs to the bedroom. Rose curled up on the sofa for a long time after that, uncertain what to do next, shocked by his last words. Gradually it dawned on her that the man she married was more than merely protective, adoring, concerned. Until that moment she'd always rather enjoyed knowing that she belonged to him, like some precious possession, that was until she realized that was exactly how he saw her: his possession, his to direct in all things—what she should wear, do, eat, cook, think, and now whether or not she should get pregnant—and she had been complicit in allowing him to treat her this way. She'd willingly let him take complete control of her without even realizing it.

Shuddering with icy cold as the truth of her life dawned on her in one moment of awful clarity, Rose realized she felt like an interloper in her own home, her house of which she had happily signed half over to her husband on their wedding day. At least he hadn't mentioned abortion, not yet, and Rose didn't think that he would. The local medical network was too small and too insular for him to want to force her to a clinic locally. It came as something of a shock to Rose to realize that the idea of Richard forcing her to abort their baby was horrifying, frightening, but not altogether surprising. He was utterly capable of doing just that. The question was, would he?

The very last scales dropping from her eyes, Rose sat upright on the sofa, wrapping her thin arms around herself and wondered how to adjust to living in this new world, this birdcage, that Richard had created for her, now that she was aware of the bars. At least now she had a focus, a purpose that was her own. She must think of what she could do to protect the baby, protect herself, to keep Richard happy and at arm's length. She had to find ways to placate him, please him, make him see that a baby would be an asset, not a disadvantage. She stared up at the ceiling, where she could hear Richard shifting in bed. Should she go to bed now, be meek and apologetic, deferential and willing? Would he even want her there? Perhaps it would be better to stay out of his way until he called down for her? Rose sat on the edge of the sofa, watching the ceiling and listening for sounds of movement until eventually the house fell quiet and she was almost certain that Richard was asleep. Her heart in her mouth, she tiptoed into the bedroom and undressed in the dark, slipping into bed beside him with the minimum of disturbance. Only the sheer exhaustion of early pregnancy dragged her off to sleep, and even then she dreamt all night of what terrors the morning might bring.

What she had not expected was Richard's silence, his complete refusal to acknowledge her with a look, a touch, or a word, which was somehow worse than if he'd screamed and shouted at her.

Richard didn't speak to her for weeks after that night, unable to look at her changing body or forgive her for what she had done. And it was at the height of her isolation, her punishment for unwittingly disobeying him, that one morning a kind, softly spoken young man came to the door and asked her about her father. That hour with Frasier became her one bright spot, her beacon shining in impenetrable darkness, the memory that, whenever she recalled it, which was often, gave her another layer of resolve. Resolve that one day, life for Rose and her baby would not be like this.

For a while Rose wondered if Richard might leave her after all, leave her free to get on with life alone with her child, and the prospect didn't frighten her as much as she might have expected. Except that the moment Maddie was born, he fell in love with his new image of being a proud father, drunk on his own godlike powers of creation to bring this tiny, screaming, mostly angry little being into the world. Perhaps it would be a new beginning, Rose hoped, as Richard fussed over her and their baby. Perhaps it would be a clean slate and life could go on as it had before—better, perhaps, because Richard would pour all his love and attention onto their child and leave Rose herself alone. But that hope ended a few months after Maddie was born and Richard noticed his wife again.

Exhausted, Rose had just got Maddie off to sleep one evening. She was a difficult baby who seemed rarely to sleep, and when she did it was never deeply. She never fed for long, or seemed very satisfied, and she cried persistently, as if even at that age she was aware of the injustice of her situation. Resting her in the bassinet beside the bed, Rose breathed a quiet sigh of relief, looking forward to a much-needed half hour or so of rest. And then Richard came into the room and looked down at the sleeping baby.

"She gets in the way a lot, doesn't she?" he said, not unkindly. "It's been months since we've . . . you know." He sat next to Rose on the bed, putting his arm around her and kissing her neck.

"Richard . . . no," Rose said, taken off guard by his sudden interest in her. The months since Maddie had been born could in no way be described as restful, but Rose had grown used to Richard's lack of interest in her, allowing herself to believe that perhaps she had overreacted before, that perhaps his behavior at the news of her pregnancy was understandable if extreme, and that now life, while it might never be happy—happiness being an elusive dream that Rose had caught the merest glimpse of during her hour with Frasier McCleod—could at least be tolerable. Rose so wanted to believe her own scenario that she shrugged him off with utter disinterest. Later she realized that had been a mistake.

"I'm so tired, I thought I might get a little sleep now while I can," she told him with a weary smile.

"Come on," Richard said, pushing her back onto the bed.

"It's been so long, Rose. You don't want me to look elsewhere, do you?"

"It's just she's only just gone to sleep," Rose whispered anxiously. "And anyway, don't you think it might be too soon? The stitches, and . . . I'm just not sure I'm ready yet."

"It's been well over six weeks, there's no excuse," Richard said, his intention set like stone in his expression as he tugged her top up round her neck. "I want you now."

Pinning her to the bed, he did not let her move until he was done, not even when the baby started crying. And from that moment on, when he came to her, as rare and unpredictable as it was, it was always that way. It was always by force.

Rose did her best not to show him any sign of resistance because she knew that he preferred it if she did. The trouble was that Richard also knew she couldn't bear him to be near her, she couldn't stand him touching her. And knowing that was enough satisfaction for him. It wasn't about sex, Rose realized quite soon. His desire for her had not increased in the slightest; if anything it was less now than it had ever been. No, it was that he had found another way to control her, a way that she couldn't predict or escape, plan to avoid or put off. And it was then, with Maddie crying in her Moses basket, as Rose stared up at the ceiling waiting for him to be finished, that she realized somehow, one day, if she were to do the best she could for herself and her daughter, she would have to find the courage to leave him.

Chapter Eleven

"All I'm saying is, I know people," Shona said as soon as they managed to find a moment together alone to talk the next day, which was just after Jenny had tried her best to stuff them all with an enormous Sunday roast. Rose had come upstairs on the pretense of fetching something, and Shona had followed her, closing the door behind her as she entered the room. Maddie was downstairs, drawing Brian, who was asleep in an armchair, his mouth open, his snores rattling the rafters, which Maddie found highly amusing.

"Hired assassins, you mean?" Rose asked her, casting about for something to fetch and settling on a tube of lip salve, before sitting next to Shona on the bed.

"Faces, sorts," Shona said, adding to, rather than clearing up, any ambiguity. "Blokes who'll do what needs doing."

"So you're suggesting I get Richard killed?" Rose asked her, raising an eyebrow.

"Ssh." Shona looked around as if she thought that Rose's bedroom might be bugged. "I'm just saying, if that was what you wanted I could get it done. Fuck it, I'll do it myself if I get my hands on him."

"It's fine," Rose said, as if she herself was a little surprised by the news. "I'm OK, Shona."

"You're not." Shona shook her head adamantly. "How can you be after what the brute did to you?"

"Is it worse than what Ryan does to you?" Rose asked her.

"A million times!" Shona said. "Ryan is stupid, thoughtless, self-obsessed, and idiotic. But he'd never force himself on any woman. What Richard did to you . . ."

"At least he never physically hurt me, not really. Not until that last day. And before that, when he . . . he did it because he hates me. I think he's probably hated me for a long time, and knowing that . . . it doesn't make it better, but it makes it bearable. Because I'm starting to see that physical . . . you know . . . it's nothing like what Richard did to me. It's an entirely separate thing. I might never ever want to do it, but that doesn't matter. What matters is that now I understand why Richard did what he did, I can escape it, be free of his hold on me. He hates me, and knowing that is an incredible relief. It makes everything so much simpler."

"Simpler? The psycho is out to get you whatever way he can, and you know he won't stop until he has. How can you be so calm?" Shona asked, horror and disbelief showing on her face. "Why don't *you* hate *him* for what he did? Why aren't you a shivering wreck?"

"Oh, I do hate him," Rose said with grim assurance, as she passed the lip salve from one hand to the other. "But don't you get it? I've been a shivering, wailing wreck. I've done that. But this time he is not going to win. I'm not calm, Shona, I'm something like what I think happy is. I'm free. Yes, he frightened me last night, he made me feel for a second that he had enough power over me to pull me back, whether I wanted that or not. And talking to you about that night, the night I left, did bring it back, the disgust, the fear, the uncertainty. But when I woke up this morning I wasn't afraid." Rose smiled as she picked up Shona's hand. "The sun was coming in through the curtains, Maddie was already up, humming to herself as she drew. I thought of seeing my dad, and how he's willing to try and be some sort of father to me, and how much it must cost him to do that. I thought of Frasier calling me last night to arrange to take me out, and you and Jenny and, yes, Ted, and Ted's crazy kissing ability . . ." Rose dropped her gaze, blushing a little as she remembered how sweet it had been to kiss Ted. How pure and clean and one million miles away from anything that Richard had ever done to her. "And I thought *this* is what life is supposed to be like, *this* is how it's meant to be. Complicated, difficult, painful, and quite probably disappointing, but with the possibility that everything will be all right." Rose laughed, spontaneously leaning forward to kiss Shona on the cheek. "Don't you see? It's the first time I've felt that way in the longest, longest time, and *I* got myself here, I rescued myself. What he did to me was all about keeping me down. Well, nothing is going to do that anymore. Let him come and find me, I'll be ready. And in the meantime, I'm going to practice being happy and, well, live my life for once! And you know what, it actually feels pretty good."

"You are a fucking hero, you know that?" Shona said, hooking an arm around Rose's neck and pulling her in close for a kiss. Just at that moment, Rose's phone, which she had forgotten was still languishing under the dressing table, rang, and she tensed, feeling her heartbeat thunder in her chest. Taking a deep breath, and then another one, she let it ring until she had control of her habitual fear. It was only a phone, after all.

"Leave it," Shona said, but Rose shook her head, falling to her hands and knees to reach it where it pulsated with light, wedged up against the baseboard.

"Oh," Rose said as she saw the name on the display, hurrying to answer it before it went to messages. "Hello? Hello, Frasier!"

Shona rolled her eyes, smirking as Rose knelt on the pink carpet, biting down hard on her lip as she listened to him.

"I know, I'm sorry. Maddie slipped in the shower and got a fright, and then . . . I suppose my phone must have been on silent. Yes, yes, lovely. I look forward to it. Six at Storm Cottage. I'll be there. Brilliant. See you then!"

As she ended the call, Rose couldn't help hugging the phone to her, as if she were cradling a little lovebird between her hands.

"I'm not sure about this, you know," Shona said, looking worried. "I mean, you do know there's no chance for you with Frasier. You have got that, haven't you? That Frasier's got a girlfriend, he's got a life, and you aren't part of it. I don't care what you say, I've watched enough daytime television to know that after everything you've been through you are bound to be fragile, like in the head." Shona tapped her own forehead to illustrate her point. "I mean, all this kissing Ted, seeing Frasier—do you think you should?"

"Yes, I do," Rose said emphatically, standing up to make her point. "This is about taking chances, being free. Doing what I want, what I've always wanted. And I've always wanted to have dinner with Frasier McCleod. I *know* that Frasier and I aren't going to have our fairy-tale ending, but I've got so much to thank him for that he doesn't even know about. Because if it wasn't for him and his postcard and my silly little fantasy, then I don't know where I'd be today. So I think seeing him, getting to know him—even if it is only *as a friend*—in the real world, can only be a good thing."

"I want to believe that you know what you're doing, I do," Shona said, Rose's certainty doing nothing to clear away the deep furrows of concern on her brow. "It's just that you seem far too sane for my liking. I'm sure it must be that post-traumatic stress thing."

"No," Rose said, going to open her wardrobe to take a look at what her meager selection of new clothes might have to offer for dinner at a Michelin-starred country house hotel. "Nope, it's not that. It's the freedom. I find it goes quite to my head."

Maddie drummed her heels impatiently the whole way, as they drove over to Storm Cottage later that afternoon, her sketchbook tucked in her arms, replacing Bear and the book about Ancient Egypt. She'd already unhooked her belt before Rose fully came to a stop, and shot out of the car, leaving the door open and dashing into the barn before Rose could turn off the ignition. Rose steadied herself, checking her reflection in the rearview mirror.

Keen not to look like she was trying too hard, she'd settled in the end on a white cotton dress with a scoop neck and fullish fifties-style skirt that settled just above her knees. She teamed it with a pair of cherry-red pumps she found in the bottom of one of the bags of clothes that Jenny had given her, then rubbed a little moisturizer into her skin, put on a flick of mascara, ran her fingers through her hair, and she was done.

"You look like... you look like a professional virgin," Shona had told her as she left. "Still, it's a look that suits you."

Getting out of the car, Rose saw that the gallery van was already here, but she couldn't see Frasier's car. He'd said he'd pick her up here at six, which wasn't for almost an hour, but still Rose wondered if he'd come at all, if he'd forget or prefer to do something with his girlfriend, or just change his mind about the whole thing. Fortunately it had been a warm day, flooded with sunshine, and so Rose didn't look too out of place in her flimsy cotton dress as she ventured after Maddie skipping across the caked peaks and troughs of the thankfully dry muddy yard.

"I understand that I am babysitting?" John tested the phrase on his tongue as if it were rather distasteful to him.

Maddie was already situated in her corner of the barn, her face a picture of concentration as she began the process of transferring a sketch she'd made of a view from the hillside onto her precious canvas with a pencil.

"Is that what Maddie said?" Rose asked. "I wasn't expecting you to. It's just that she so wanted to come up here today, and I couldn't keep her at the B and B any longer. I just thought I would drop her off with my friend on the way back. I mean, if I'm being too presumptuous, if it's too much, I don't want to overstep—"

"I don't want to go back, I want to stay here with John," Maddie said. "He won't mind."

"Sorry," Rose said to John. "Look Maddie, you can't just invite yourself—"

"She can stay if she must." John sighed. "Although I must warn you," he said sternly to the young girl, "it gets rather boring up here after work, Maddie. There is no TV or radio, only some books. And I've not much food in—some bread, I think, and cheese that is only a little bit moldy."

"I like cheese on toast." Maddie shrugged, as if that problem was solved.

Rose hesitated, wondering if this was wise. It had been only a few days ago that John had been so determined to keep them at arm's length, to shut them out of his life. From what he'd told her, she understood a little of why he had been so determined to keep them away, but this new willingness to bring them so fully into his life was hard to understand, and although she hated herself for feeling it, it made Rose wary.

"I'll come and pick her up. It might be fairly late, though," she said. "This is too much for you, too soon. And for Maddie too. You barely know each other."

"I said she can stay the night," John said, adamant. "As long as she won't be scared of the creaking old house and the noise the wind makes when it rattles by—sounds like screaming ghosts." He was trying to be playful, Rose knew, but John had no idea how prone Maddie was to taking these things to heart and to becoming a screaming, sleep-avoiding, stay-up-all-night, trembling wreck in a matter of seconds. It was a symbol of how very little they knew each other.

"John," she said, ushering him to one side as Maddie stared at his work in progress, her nose almost touching it, "I'm just . . . this all seems a bit sudden. Don't get me wrong, I want it to be like this, but why? Why all this now?"

John said nothing for a moment, his expression unreadable as he seemed to consider what to say next. "I was keeping you at bay so I didn't have to face my own guilt," he said finally. "Because I didn't want to know what I had done to you, what I had missed. Someone said something that made me think . . ."

"Who?" Rose asked him. "Frasier?"

"It doesn't matter who," John said, waving her question aside with his hand. "What matters is, I've reached a point in my life where I've finally learnt to listen. I am old, Rose."

"Not really. Being in your sixties isn't old these days," Rose said, feeling her heart clench at the realization of how much time had passed by as her life had stood still.

"I'm old. And I've hated myself for long enough." John's face softened, and Rose realized that he was looking at her with something more than fondness; he was looking at her with love. "You said that you can't forgive me for how I left you, and I don't expect you to. I'm not even sure I want you to. But I do hope, perhaps unreasonably, to live out the rest of my days without hating myself. If you could see your way to letting me get to know you and Maddie, from this moment on, as the person I am now, the man that I have never been before, then there is a very small chance I might achieve that."

John held out his hand to her, and Rose stared at it, wavering in midair. Since she'd found him they had never once touched each other and she was all too aware of what it would mean if she took his fingers in hers. Her hesitation was excruciating, but then she remembered what she had said to Shona as they had sat on the bed in her room at the B & B. Her life began now, and so, it seemed, did John's. What reason could there be to stop them from making that step together, except to perpetuate anger, bitterness, and hate? And Rose had had enough of all of those things to last her a lifetime.

Reaching out, she took his fingers, warm and rough with calluses, in hers, and nodded, noticing the tears like the ones that stood in her own eyes also glistening in John's.

"Thank you," he said, his voice thick with emotion. "Thank you, Rose. It's more than I deserve."

"Are we holding hands?" Maddie asked, noticing the adults again and plonking her hand heavily on top of John and Rose's. "Does this mean I can stay the night?"

"I suppose it does." Rose smiled at her daughter.

"Besides," John told Maddie, "I did some clearing out of the boxroom last night, just in case. You can get to the bed now, and there are clean sheets on it."

"Exciting!" Maddie squealed, with a little hop.

"Thank you," Rose said, uncertain how to proceed now

that this fragile bridge had been made between them. "The thing about Maddie is, she does sometimes get a bit scared—"

"Not really," Maddie said, looking mortified at her mother's revelation. "I don't really get scared. I pretend, that's all. It will be fine, Mum. John is my granddad, after all. Children are always staying with their grandfathers and it's always fine. Don't worry, I won't miss you. There is painting, drawing and books, and John will tell me things and I can do him a test on color theory. All the things I like are here. This is definitely not a place that makes me scared. Or *pretend* to be scared."

Rose bit her lip, somehow finding her daughter's newfound confidence as hard to take as it was pleasing. She was used to Maddie depending utterly on her, and as much as she wanted her to have exactly this kind of independent spirit, she still found it hard to let go.

"If you say so, Maddie. As long as you promise not to be pretend scared of the wind."

"It will be the wind," Maddie said, waving away the concern with her pencil.

Maddie looked at John, who nodded once.

"Wind," she said, rolling her eyes. "Wind doesn't scare me. I actually *like* wind."

"Very well, then," Rose said, feeling another new beginning emerging. "You may stay."

Just then the storeroom door opened and two men emerged carrying a carefully wrapped canvas between them with some difficulty.

"Third one's still not dry, you say?" the older of the two men asked John.

"Not for a couple more days," John said, offhand.

"So another trip down here, then," the man said huffily.

"I presume you will get paid twice," John said, unrepentant. "A veritable godsend in these uncertain times."

Rose pretended not to hear the man swearing as they carefully maneuvered the valuable piece of art out of the studio.

"So what are you working on now?" she asked John, who had restretched and prepared a small canvas since she had last seen him, exactly like the one Maddie had co-opted before.

"Something for me," John said. "Whenever I finish a commission I take some time for *my* work. It keeps me sane."

"What will it be?" Rose asked him, intrigued as she took a step closer.

John shook his head. "I can't share that with you," he said. "This is just for me. Perhaps one day, but not yet."

Rose glanced over her shoulder to where Maddie was painstakingly re-creating her sketch on her canvas, the curve of her cheek, the sweep of her lashes making Rose's heart ache.

"John," Rose said tentatively, "can I ask you something? You may not like it, but when I look at Maddie I see Mum, and . . . I don't have anyone else to talk to about her except for you."

John nodded, visibly steeling himself for what he knew was coming.

"Do you ever think about Mum?" Rose asked him.

"Yes," John said simply, heavily, as if merely uttering the word was almost too burdened with regret. "I think of her often. The older I get the more I think of her. The way she used to be, the first time I saw her. So smart, so sensible, so . . . full of light, like a beacon. I tried to stay away from her—she wasn't really my type at all, a good girl, a girl next door—but I couldn't, like a moth to a flame."

"Except you were the flame," Rose said sadly, without recrimination. "It was Mum who got burnt."

"Can I go outside and sit on the fence and draw the mountain?" Maddie asked. "I won't move from the fence, I promise. I just want to remember what it looks like *exactly*, for my next work."

"OK," Rose said, mustering a smile. "But don't move from the fence. I mean it."

"I won't," Maddie called over her shoulder as she headed outside.

"She looked like fine bone china." John remembered Marian, smiling just a little. "Delicate and slim, like you, but she had this passion in her, this strength of appetite for living that made everyone around her want to live harder, better, faster." He glanced sideways at Rose as he sorted through assorted crumpled tubes of paint. "I've been thinking about her more recently. You remind me a lot of your mother."

"I'm not sure if that's a good thing," Rose said, unable to keep the bitterness out of her voice, which was still there, which would probably always be there when she thought of the life that her mother had wasted, through no fault of her own, on grief. Rose had known the woman that John described for only a few short years, and even then she was already beginning to fray at the edges, battling daily to make the man she'd given up so much for continue to show an interest in her. How hard she must have tried to be fascinating, beautiful enough for him. How painful it must have been when she realized that even if she was always all of those things, it would still never be enough to stop him from looking elsewhere.

"I did that to her," John admitted. "I ruined her, and I regret that, deeply. I wish I could have cared when it counted. I wish so many things."

"But you left with Tilda instead," Rose stated.

"I stopped feeling anything real long before Tilda, and long after," John admitted. "Tilda was not the first and not the last of the women I used. The only thing that set her apart was that she somehow pierced the fog of the alcohol to make me take notice of her for a little while. Tilda is a strong, ferocious woman. I think she thought she could change me."

Rose turned away from him, finding it difficult to control the ferocious feelings that surged through her: anger, hurt, and somehow relief that he was finally saying what she'd always believed to be true, that he was to blame. And yet Rose almost didn't want to know. She liked this quiet-mannered man who had a way with Maddie and a sort of strength that she felt secure around. More revelations would sweep that man away for good, and she would be left to face whatever harsh truth was left. But she couldn't make the mistake of letting herself pretend that John was not the kind of man he was; she'd done that for too long with Richard.

"The day before she died . . . it was the happiest day of my life," Rose said. "She was so happy, so light and loving. That's why none of it made sense."

"When I heard how she . . . passed," John said, uncharacteristically squeamish about the facts, "I was drunk. I thought perhaps it might have been a dream. I think for a long time I preferred to think that it was a dream."

The two of them searched each other's faces for a moment, each one full of sadness.

"And you didn't come for me," Rose said softly.

"No," John said. "I didn't come. I didn't care, Rose. I didn't feel anything. I'm so sorry, but I didn't."

Rose nodded, finding it difficult to hold back the threat of tears that constricted her throat.

"After Mum died," she said, in a tone so low it was almost a whisper, knowing that she had to tell John everything she could, unburden herself of all her secrets, if they were to have any chance of moving on together, and now was the first and perhaps the last moment to do it, "soon after, that's when I met my husband. When I met Richard. I think he saw me, and he saw exactly what he wanted. Someone young, inexperienced, someone completely on her own, without anyone to tell her what to do or advise her. Without anyone to protect her. He wanted a wife who would love him unreservedly, a wife he could own. That's what he saw in me. It must have been written all over my face: abandoned girl seeks refuge. I don't suppose he meant for things to end the way they did when we got married; I don't suppose for one minute he foresaw how he would become." Rose made herself look John in the eye so that he would see everything she saw, feel everything she felt. "Controlling, restricting every aspect of my life, slowly, slowly over years and years, until I was afraid to breathe if he was in the room, or to chew too loudly, or accidentally wear the wrong expression. I don't suppose it was his plan to take a girl, already weak and vulnerable, and wear her down, centimeter by centimeter, until she had just the tiniest scrap left of her own identity. I don't suppose he planned any of that, but that is what happened to me, after Mum died. And if you'd been there, or just been in my life, another person to turn to, perhaps it would have helped me see things clearly and perhaps . . . I wouldn't be hiding from Richard now."

John nodded, swallowing with difficulty. "This is hard for me to bear too," he said. "I let you down, and I can never make up for that."

"No," Rose said. "And whether you believe it or not, I really wish you could."

"You still had that tiny scrap, though," John said, looking her square in the eyes, placing his hands lightly on her shoulders. "That small part of you that you hung on to, that was from your mother. It was her strength that stopped you from disappearing completely and made you start to fight back. Your mother saved you."

"Did she?" Rose asked him. "I'd like to believe that, but Mum was the one that gave in. That gave up. You beat your addiction—doesn't that make you the strong one?"

John shook his head. "No," he said. "It makes me the coward, too afraid to die, even though . . . even though I get closer to it day by day. But not your mother, she was not afraid."

"Hello?" Frasier's voice sounded outside, as Rose and John kept looking at each other, trying to search out some answers in those last few seconds they had before Frasier came into the barn.

"I think it's the courageous who want to stay alive," Rose said finally. "And I think that it's a little bit of that, of you, that has to be in me. Mum's there too, of course, but you are my father, you are part of me too." She wrinkled her brow as a thought occurred to her. "It never crossed my mind before to be grateful for that."

Before John could respond, Frasier walked into the barn, with a curious Maddie at his side. He was wearing a sea-green shirt that matched the color of his eyes, open slightly at the neck, his blond hair looking ruffled as if he'd been driving with the window down.

"Hello, all!" he said cheerfully, stopping and smiling at Rose in her white cotton dress. "You look very refreshing," he said. "And Maddie, I see you are quite the protégée. Your work is coming on apace!"

Maddie stared at her drawing as if she very much doubted him. It was clear that she did not like this planning stage nearly as much as she liked throwing paint about or sketching, but she had persevered, which was unusual for her.

"John, Greg tells me I have to wait three more days for the third work," Frasier said, trying his best to look stern.

"This is an artist's studio," John said, "not a McDonald's drive-through."

Frasier laughed. "Nothing you can say will put me in a bad mood today," he said happily. "I've sold almost all of the awful woman's work. And the world's finest sticky toffee pudding awaits Rose and me!"

Neither Rose nor Frasier were prepared for John's disapproving expression.

"Make sure you take care of her," he said gruffly, obviously a little embarrassed himself by his belated paternal concern.

"This is Dearest Rose," Frasier said. "Of course I will take care of her."

Sharrow Bay House Hotel turned out to be set right on the shores of Ullswater, an elegant white-painted Victorian house that Rose felt altogether underdressed for after all, although she was not at all sure that any of Haleigh's going-out clothes would have served her any better. The warmth of the sun was thankfully still strong, and Rose was enchanted when they were seated at a table on the terrace, overlooking the lake, the mountains glowing golden in the evening light.

"Wow," Rose said as she looked out at the view.

"Stunning, isn't it?" Frasier said. "It's at times like this I wish I had the skill to create art, rather than just appreciate it, and sell it, and make quite a lot of money from it."

"But it's not all about the money for you, is it?" Rose asked him, curiously, grateful to have something to say. The drive over had been mostly silent, punctuated with stilted small talk that soon petered out. "If it was, you wouldn't have come to my house in Broadstairs, would you? You wouldn't have tracked my father down, you wouldn't have put so much effort, time, and probably money into getting him sober. You basically saved his life." And mine, she thought as she dared to look at him. His strong nose and sensitive mouth and jaw made her want to reach out and touch his face, despite herself. It seemed dreamlike that she was here with him, in this beautiful setting. All the darkness and dread that Richard brought with him seemed like another lifetime, another universe away. Rose realized that she was going to have to work very hard to keep her feet on the ground, to remember that Frasier saw her as pleasant company at best, the daughter of a valuable client, not his long-lost soul mate.

"I tracked your father down because of his work. His true work is remarkable. I wanted to be the one to discover him; I wanted the credit, if I'm honest," Frasier said, smiling. "But when I found him, he was a wreck. He had no one, he didn't care what happened next. I only had to look at him to see he didn't have much time left if he carried on the way he was. I took a risk, a gamble. I paid for him to get medical help and the support he needed to become clean, hoping that if he survived I'd get my chance at discovering him after all. So I'm not quite as noble as you might imagine."

"He respects you, though," Rose said. "I can see that, despite how he grumbles and moans around you. What you say and think mean a lot to him, although he'd never admit it."

"And I respect him too," Frasier answered. "I do finally think, under all the bluster, that we are friends now, after all these years. I care about the man. If it was up to me I wouldn't have him painting like there's no tomorrow for big business and greeting card companies. As much as he likes to imply that it's me who makes him do it, I never have. The truth is it's easier for him to pretend I'm the heartless commercial dealer cracking the whip. In reality he insists on doing the big-money work and refuses to let me see his 'real' work."

"But why?" Rose asked him, intrigued, forgetting for a moment whom she was talking to. "That doesn't sound like the man I knew at all. Although to be fair I barely know him at all now."

Although she knew him a good deal better today than ever before, Rose supposed, thinking of the way that John had quietly squeezed her shoulder as she had left with Frasier, a sign of what they both hoped would become a new bond between them, a connection that, despite everything, they could both now admit that they wanted.

"I . . ." Frasier hesitated as he considered Rose's question, and whatever he was thinking remained unsaid. "He has his reasons. Perhaps he's lost confidence in his private work; perhaps it's just too painful to show. I do hope that one day he will change his mind, because he really is an amazing man, not just an artist. Which I know must sound a little trite, considering what you've been through largely because of him."

"Not trite," Rose said. "I suppose it's not impossible to be amazing in some parts of your life and terrible in others. I hope he *is* an amazing man, I hope he *is* redeemable, because if he is then I will be able to forgive him." Rose looked out across the lake, her brow knitted briefly in concern. "I told him that I would never be able to forgive him—to hurt him, I think—and yet he accepted it as if that was the way it should be. And yet now I find I would like nothing more. Nothing more than to be free of all those years of anger."

A waitress arrived with their starters and refreshed their wine, as the sun began to sink slowly behind the crest of the mountain, setting fire to ripples in the almost still lake.

"So tell me about you, your life, your husband, Maddie, everything," Frasier said warmly, leaning forward a little, eager to hear all about her.

Rose sat back a little in her chair, unprepared for that

question and reluctant to answer it, to bring even the mention of Richard into this idyllic setting. And yet she couldn't pretend he didn't exist.

"Well . . . I've actually recently separated from my husband," Rose said a little awkwardly. "I've left him, I mean. For good."

It occurred to her that Frasier might well think that taking a married woman out to dinner was one thing, but to take out a recently separated, newly single woman was quite another. And besides, Rose was very afraid that at some point he would guess the real reason she came to Millthwaite was to find him. That was something he could never know.

"Oh, no." Frasier looked genuinely sorry. "That's awful."

"Actually," Rose said, lifting her chin in unconscious defiance, "it's a good thing." She struggled to sum up her marriage in a way that wouldn't frighten or shock Frasier. "We weren't . . . compatible anymore. He didn't cheat or anything, and neither did I. Just . . . he wasn't a person I could be with anymore."

"It must be hard, though, to start again after all those years, just you and Maddie?"

Rose said nothing for a while, toying with the stem of her wineglass. "Hard" wasn't the word. She hoped, believed, that the hardest times were behind her even though she knew there would be much worse to come before she could truly be free of her past.

"I think there will be rocky times ahead," she said eventually.

"It's not amicable, then?" Frasier asked her, seeing the concern in her furrowed brow.

"Far from it," Rose admitted, raising her gaze to meet his. "He hates me very much. And I . . . I have no idea what I feel about him. Nothing at the moment. The very thought of him makes me feel numb."

"Well, if there is anything I can do, while you are here . . ." Frasier made the offer without hesitation. "I know an excellent lawyer this side of the border who I'm sure could help out."

"Thank you," Rose said. "But for now I'm just concentrating on being here. I'll cross all of those bridges when I get to them. Being here, it feels strangely wonderful. And I suppose it is. After all, I've walked into the picture postcard that I've carried with me every single day for seven years."

"Carried with you every day?" Frasier asked her, picking up on the remark before Rose realized that she'd made it.

"Yes, well, it was my only link to John," she said, unable to look him in the eye, feeling the heat creep up her neck. "Silly, really."

"Not at all." Frasier's gaze became suddenly more intense, so much so that Rose felt caught like a deer in headlights. "It's your talisman," he said. "Your link to another life that might have been, that perhaps still could be. I understand that."

"Do you?" Rose asked him.

"I do. Except that I never dwell on what might have been. It's my only rule. I live life in the moment, whatever it may bring. And this evening, it's brought me to you."

"Shall we take a walk by the shore?" Frasier asked her, after discreetly settling the bill.

"I feel like I should at least pay for the coffee," Rose said. "Or the mints. I am admittedly a *bit* short on funds right now."

"Don't be ridiculous," Frasier said. "My father was an army man. He never got over the fact that I didn't follow him into the profession; the very least I can do is to adhere to his standard to take care of a lady at all times."

"You are a dying breed," Rose said as she took the arm that Frasier offered and let him escort her down to the shore, feeling all at once supremely happy and excruciatingly awkward to be entwined with him, even so formally.

They stood for a moment listening to the soft lap of the waters, Rose tracing where the crest of the mountains blacked out the starry sky. Rose discreetly extricated her arm from Frasier's, content just to stand next to him in such a perfect moment. Perhaps this might be the thing that kept her going for the next seven years.

"This place is beautiful," Rose whispered. "I don't mean just this spot, although it is. I mean the whole area. When you live in a place like this, surrounded by a landscape like this, all your earthly problems should seem so insignificant."

Frasier smiled. "Does that mean you might settle here, then? Your father would like that."

"I don't know," Rose said. "Part of me thinks that now is the time to travel, to see and go places, be free at last. But tonight, I think it would be very hard to leave."

"And yet, leave here we must," Frasier said abruptly. "How about I take you for a quick drink in Millthwaite on the way back?"

"Don't you have to get back to your girlfriend?" Rose asked him. "Doesn't she mind your taking another woman out to dinner?"

"Cecily and I have planned a tryst in the early hours," Frasier assured her. "And you are not another woman, you are Dearest Rose. It's practically my going to dinner with the Mona Lisa."

"How about I take you for a drink?" Rose asked him. "I can stretch to that, at least."

"It's a deal," Frasier said with a smile. They stood and looked at each other for a moment longer, and then with a shrug Frasier took her hand again as they walked back to the car.

• • •

Rose hadn't really given much thought to the likelihood of Ted being behind the bar when she walked into the pub with Frasier, and not even when his dark eyes met hers did she think for a moment that it particularly mattered. Leaving Frasier to take a seat by the window, she went to the bar, smiling at Ted as she approached.

"What you doing here with him?" was his conversation opener.

Slightly taken aback, Rose looked over her shoulder at Frasier, who smiled at her from beside the window.

"He took me for dinner, and now I'm buying him a drink," she said. "Red wine for me and a single-malt Scotch for him, please."

"So you've been on a date, then, with him?" Ted questioned her.

"It's not a date," Rose said. "It was just dinner." Their journey back through the dark, twisted country roads had been conducted in silence, allowing Rose to make a call to John, who assured her that although Maddie showed no signs of wanting to sleep, she was perfectly happy, and for Rose to ponder how to adjust to knowing and liking the real Frasier, as opposed to the one who'd lived in her head for so long.

"It's just it's . . . it's Frasier," Rose said, belatedly aware that that wasn't much of an explanation to Ted. "He's been very important to me."

"Rose," Ted said suddenly, his expression intensifying.

"Yes?" Rose said, glancing over her shoulder to where Frasier was studying a print of some Victorian children with baskets full of apples.

"I know we said the kiss was just kissing," Ted said. "But the thing is, I think I might like you, Rose. I mean, *like* you."

Rose blinked at him. "No, you don't."

"Yeah," he said, holding her gaze. "Yeah, I do. I want to kiss you again. Tonight."

"No," Rose said, not sure what else she could say, not sure how to feel. "You don't."

"Meet me later," Ted said, as if he hadn't heard a word she said. "After Mr. Sappy over there's gone home."

"Ted . . ." Rose was uncertain, caught off guard. "I've just . . . I've got so much at home to deal with now. I'm not sure I can deal with you too. It's too soon."

"You can," Ted insisted. "If you really think about it, you want to. I'll take care of you. I won't hurt you or do anything you don't want. I just want to be near you, Rose. From midnight, I'll be downstairs in the B and B. I've got a key, I'll let myself in. There's a whole annex which no one ever goes in. I think there might still even be a bed."

"Ted!" Rose gasped, knowing full well that Ted's late granny's bed was still *in situ*, even though Jenny had nagged Brian to take it to the dump.

"You are so lovely," she told him. "But I'm . . . I'm a mess. I'll be no good for you."

"Then let me be good for you," Ted said. "I'll be there, I'll wait, all night if I have to." He leaned closer across the bar so that she could feel his breath on her cheek. "I want to kiss you again so badly, Rose. And that's all it will be, I swear."

It took quite some doing to get the drinks back to Frasier without guzzling them both.

"Good night, then," Rose said as Frasier escorted her to the B & B door. She couldn't be sure that Jenny and Shona were hovering on the other side of it, but she got the distinct feeling she and Frasier weren't entirely alone.

"Thank you for a lovely evening," Frasier said. "You really are the most charming company."

"Thank you," Rose said, wondering what the protocol would be on kissing him good night. Could she reasonably kiss him on the cheek, she wondered, discovering that she would really like to know what that golden stubble would feel like beneath her lips—an image that was rapidly followed by guilt and anxiety.

"You know, I must introduce you to Cecily," Frasier said, smiling fondly at the mention of his girlfriend's name. "She would absolutely love you. And you'd probably like her too. She's awfully funny."

"Oh, oh, well, yes, of course. That would be nice," Rose said.

"Good night again." Frasier shook her hand. "See you very soon."

"Bye!" Rose said as she slid her key into the lock, the door opening before she had a chance to turn it.

"He shook your hand, didn't he?" Shona said. "I saw it through the peephole. It was all sort of funny and far away, but he did actually shake your hand, didn't he?"

"Yes!" Rose said briskly, shutting the door and crossing her arms. Jenny was on the second stair, this time in a fire-engine-red nightie trimmed with black lace.

"Disappointed?" she asked Rose, sympathetically. "I expect you fancied a nice kiss."

"No, not disappointed, and no, I did not expect or indeed 'fancy' a nice kiss!" Rose protested far too much on both counts. "Frasier is an acquaintance, with a girlfriend called Cecily, and I am barely single. It would have been awful if he'd kissed me, dreadful."

"Shocking," Shona said. "Almost as bad as if he'd taken you to a remote spot and kissed your face off."

"Shona!" Rose cried, feeling two hot spots of heat flare on her cheeks. "Stop talking rubbish!"

"Now, now," Jenny said. "Let's not tease the poor lass. You're quite right, love. Best all round that he didn't kiss you. It would have only muddled the already very murky waters. Still, you wished he had, though, don't you?"

Rose lay awake in the dark for a long time, missing the sound of Maddie's breathing and the hump of her body under the covers. She had phoned John again before getting into bed, and he'd told her in rather irritated tones that Maddie was now fast asleep in her fortress, which was what she'd decided to call the book- and box-lined room that she was ensconced in. She'd eaten cheese on toast, drawn a good deal, tested him on color theory, and eventually asked to go to bed. There had been a moment when the sound of the wind rattling the window gave her pause, but John had told her not to be so ridiculous and she had complied.

"OK," Rose had said uncertainly, both peeved and proud that Maddie hadn't had her usual meltdown and demanded her mother. "Well, I'll be round first thing to get her then."

"This presumably means I can now get some sleep, does it?" John asked her testily.

"Yes, sorry. And thank you," Rose said. "Night, John."

John did not reply.

Midnight had come and gone almost an hour ago and she still hadn't moved from her position, lying flat on her back with the bedspread pulled up under her chin. Rose had been utterly determined not to be tempted by Ted's proposal, had pulled on a nightshirt with the image of a fluffy yellow cartoon chick on the front of it, and decidedly climbed into her single bed, which she would not be moved from for any reason whatsoever, particularly not making out with her landlady's son.

And yet sleep evaded her, her busy brain a tangle of circling thoughts and images. Was she really simply over Richard and the things he had done to her? It could not be so simple. Perhaps Shona was right, perhaps she did have more to face than she was able to admit, and maybe the euphoria—yes, because that was what she was feeling now—was really just a manifestation of relief. She didn't have to be afraid anymore. Not tonight, anyway.

She could be anyone she wanted to be. Maybe even the sort of woman who lets herself be kissed by one man when she isn't sure of her feelings for another.

Rose knew, as she lay there staring up at the ceiling, that the way she felt about Frasier was real and not imagined. Even if it happened seven years ago, she had fallen in love with him, and that wasn't going to go away soon just because of the inconvenience of real life and beautiful girlfriends called Cecily.

But that didn't stop her from thinking about Ted, her mind drifting back to him again and again, waiting for her. Wanting to kiss her and touch her, like he had done before. And Rose wanted that feeling again, she realized with a surge of adrenaline as she sat up in bed.

Deciding that it was best not to allow herself too much time to examine her motivations, Rose climbed out of bed. Pulling Haleigh's nightshirt down over her bare behind, she paused for a moment in front of the dressing table mirror, noticing with a frisson of satisfaction the fine contours of her body just visible under the clingy material. It had been a very long time since Rose had considered herself as a woman, one who might genuinely be attractive to men. It was exciting and scary to do that now, like learning to walk all over again.

Going to see Ted was another step on her journey, she told

herself as she tiptoed down the stairs, her quest to find herself, discover more about what it meant to be a woman. Ted was part of the key to unlocking the woman she really was.

Rose held her breath as she crept into the living room, which was silent and dark, save for the ticking of the clock on the mantel. Ted was not there. For a second she felt foolish and disappointed, and a little relieved. But then she remembered the annex, where Ted said there was a bed. Her heart rattling against her ribs, she tiptoed across the carpet, feeling the grime and grit between her toes, made her way through the tiny dark hallway, and opened the door to the shadowy annex. There were no curtains up at the window, so the moonlight flooded in, throwing mysterious shadows and cutting a silvery pathway right to the bedroom.

Silently Rose repeated again and again exactly what she planned to say to Ted, if she could find the courage.

Sitting on the edge of the stripped bed, Ted sat up sharply when she came in through the door, catching his breath at the sight of her, which was when Rose remembered that she was mostly naked. Hiding as much of her body as she could behind the doorframe, she waved, which on reflection seemed rather odd, even in what was a rather odd situation.

"Hi!" she squeaked nervously, her resolve in great danger of evaporating into thin air.

"I thought you would never come," Ted said, standing up and taking a few steps towards her.

"So did I," Rose said. "Ted . . ."

"It's OK," Ted said, closing the space between them, taking her hand and drawing her out into a pool of moonlight. "I know you are nervous, and I promise I won't try anything else. Wow," he said, taking the sight of her in. "Bit freaky that you're wearing my sister's nightshirt."

"I'm not sure if you understand," Rose said, turning back

towards the door. "I need to say that . . . You need to know that I . . ."

But before she could move, Ted put his hands on her hips and pulled her close to him so that their bodies were almost, but not quite, touching.

"I know," Ted whispered, his hands gently resting on her hips. "And I don't care. I just want the chance to feel the way I did the other night. That's enough for me, I swear it."

"Ted," Rose said, looking him in the eye. "You are such a lovely man. And I'm . . . I'm pretty sure I'm broken. I don't want to break you too."

"It doesn't matter if you do," Ted said, cupping her face in his palms. "Don't you get it? *I've fallen for you.*"

Rose caught her breath as she finally understood that Ted really meant it when he said he was in love with her. It was overwhelming to know that somehow she'd touched this lovely, sweet man so deeply, without ever meaning to. The way he looked at her, the way he held her made her pulse quicken and her chest tighten, but was that anything like love? Surely the best thing she could do now would be to leave, to clear her head and her heart, and not do anything rash. And yet, Rose found that she didn't want to go.

"Oh, Ted," she whispered. "I don't know what to say."

"I was rather hoping you wouldn't say anything," Ted said. "I was thinking there would just be more kissing. More kisses for me to think about again and again every second that I am not with you."

Rose gasped, the suppressed passion in his voice, the intense look in his dark eyes threatening to sweep her off her feet. She wasn't equipped to deal with this, she didn't know how to, only that for a man to look at her that way was both new, exhilarating, and terrifying all at once. And yet she had to be honest with him, she owed him that much.

"The thing is, Ted, do you remember on the mountain when I told you I loved someone else? That person was Frasier. And I do love him. I have for a long time. I wish I didn't—everything would be so much simpler if I didn't—but that feeling won't simply vanish. Not even for someone as totally, wonderfully amazing as you."

For a moment Ted said nothing at all, and as he turned his gaze away from her, Rose thought that now might be the best time to run away.

"Shall I go? Say something," she urged him.

"Can't." Ted shook his head. "Don't know what to say, except that even knowing all that, I'd still give anything to kiss you again. Look, you were in love with Frasier then, on the mountain and you still kissed me. Why not now?"

"Because that was different," Rose said, struggling to clarify exactly why. "It didn't mean so much."

"That's not what it felt like," Ted said earnestly. "It felt like it meant a lot to you. Not in the same way that it did to me, I realize that, but you said kissing me chased away the darkness, it cleansed you. So what if you love someone else? He's not here tonight, he won't be here tomorrow night or maybe ever at all. If one more night of kissing me can make you feel good and me happy, just for a little while, what harm can it do?"

Ted took a step closer to her, resting the fingertips of his right hand on her cheek.

"Please, Rose," he whispered, bending his lips to hers. "Please."

Rose meant to stop him, she meant to stop him as soon as she felt his soft warm breath on her cheek, the second his lips met hers, the moment his arm snaked its way around her waist and pulled her close to him. She meant to, but perhaps it was because she knew she could trust Ted to stop whenever she told him to, and because the feeling of love, tenderness, and kindness that enveloped her as long as she was in Ted's arms was really so wonderful, that the moment when she wanted him to stop kissing her never came.

Chapter Twelve

"But I really don't want you to go home," Rose said, as Shona packed her bags. "Please, Shona, stay a bit longer."

"I can't, babe," Shona said with a regretful smile. "It's been over a week, Mum's fed up with the boys, and anyway, I miss them! I need to go home, get my life sorted the way you are."

Rose wasn't at all sure she was getting her life sorted in any sense of the word. It had been four days since she'd woken up in the annex, with the dawn light streaming in through the uncovered ground-floor window, and found herself naked and wrapped in Ted's arms. Having left her watch upstairs, she'd been unsure of the time, but, aware that it wouldn't be too long before Jenny was up and preparing breakfast, she knew she had to get back into her own bed pronto.

The events of the night, which really had stopped only about an hour earlier, were something that Rose was going to need a good deal of time on her own to process and to make sense of. But the short story was that Ted had swept her into a passionate momentum that seemed to have an impetus outside her control. When it came to it there had been no need for talking, or any rationalization at all, for that matter. And Rose had let herself get deliriously lost in his embrace, delighting in his pleasure just as much as her own, forgetting everything for those few hours except the wonderful discovery of what it was like to be with a man who didn't want to hurt or humiliate you. Ted had been so gentle, so hesitant at first, and caring. He knew that Rose was very far from ready for sex, and he'd never pushed it that far, instead only layering pleasure upon pleasure until, for several wonderful hours, Rose forgot herself and her crazy life that lay just outside the door, completely.

In the cold light of day, though, she had found it hard to believe that she and the woman who'd spent the night with Ted were the same person. This small, nude, flimsy individual had no idea how on earth she had managed to be quite so passionate, and whilst mainly sober too. Quietly, she had extricated herself from under the exhausted and spent young man's arm and, pulling on her nightshirt, raced as quickly and as quietly upstairs as she could, falling into bed with a good deal of relief, waiting and watching the clock until it was an acceptable time to get up again.

Ted must have woken up to find himself alone and sneaked out sometime before Jenny started breakfast, because when Rose did come down Jenny seemed as bright and breezy as she ever was, with no idea that her precious son had been all but seduced by her paying guest. Rose could not know for sure that Ted had said nothing to his mum, apart from the fact that Jenny had not murdered her, because she had neither seen nor heard from Ted once in the days since their tryst. And it wasn't because she was avoiding him, apart from not going to the pub. In fact, it had started to look a lot like he was avoiding her, which threw Rose into all sorts of paroxysms of anxiety. What if she'd done it all wrong, what if she'd disappointed and appalled him, and what if what was meant to be her moment of carefree womanly blossoming had actually been a career-ending disaster, which she, as stupidly naïve as she was, had been too ignorant to notice?

And now Shona was going home.

"Yes, but . . . what if the kids came here? What if you moved here? What if we got a place, you and me, and moved here? Think how brilliant that would be!" Rose clapped her hands together like a small child confronted with a shop window full of toys, but Shona didn't seem nearly as taken with the idea.

Frowning, she rested the back of her hand against Rose's forehead, its skin cool against Rose's brow as she looked into her eyes. "Are you sickening for something? Look, babe, I'm not moving up here. For one thing, I don't do sheep, with their devil eyes and funny walks, and for another I am not going to move the boys from their home and their school, and leave my mum and the place I grew up for a load of yokels. I love you, and I'll miss you. And I'm so proud of you for coming this far, in both senses, including literally coming *this* far to *here*!" Shona grinned at her. "I came up here to hold your hand, and you barely needed me at all. And now I've got to make a start at working out what *I* want to do next."

"It's just . . . well, what about Ryan?" Rose asked reluctantly, afraid of the answer.

"What about him?" Shona asked her, dropping her gaze as she stepped away from Rose and returned to her packing.

"Are you going back for him?" Rose said.

Shona said nothing, busily folding a bra as she attempted to ignore Rose.

"Sho? I heard you talking to him on the phone!"

Rose was referring to the hushed conversation she had strained to overhear as it drifted in, along with Shona's cigarette smoke, through an open window. Shona's voice had been soft and gentle, full of tenderness and affection, something that even Rose, who knew only too well how easy it was to find yourself trapped in an impossible relationship, found hard to understand. How Shona could bear to talk at all, let alone with such care and kindness, to the man who always let her down was beyond her.

"Are you going back for him?"

"No!" Shona said, adding quietly, "I don't know yet."

"Shona, you *can't*. You can't let him back in your life, you have to see that, don't you?" Rose asked her desperately. "I mean, what if I announced that actually, now I'd had a chance to think about it, Richard wasn't all *that* bad and was maybe just a bit misunderstood and that after all I *would* go back to him, what would you say? You'd kill me!"

"It's different," Shona protested. "Completely different. Ryan isn't a psycho. He's just an arsehole. And he does love me. He really does."

"So you *are* going back to him, then," Rose said, knowing this was an argument that she was unlikely to win, hoping desperately that things would work out the way her friend wanted them to.

"I'm not going back to him straightaway." Shona shrugged defensively. "But perhaps in time, if things work out. If he can show me he's really changed. I'm not an idiot—I'm not going to just run into his arms like nothing's ever happened—but I love him, babe, and really that's all there is to it at the end of the day, isn't it?"

"Then there's nothing I can say, is there? Except that I hope you are right about this, Shona, I really hope that you and Ryan can make a go of it. If anyone deserves another chance in life, it's you."

Shona's smile was tinged with sadness. "Thank you, darling."

"But please, please, stay one more night?" Rose begged her.

"No! Look, I'm not going until later. I promised Jenny I'd help put the finishing touches on the annex so she can decide what to do with it next, and then I'm going to drive through the night. Be back in time to hug and kiss my little men. I've missed them, for all the fun I've had up here with you. It's you, you know, that's made me see what I have to do next. I know now I have to do whatever it takes to try and be happy."

"I'll miss you," Rose said, finding tears suddenly standing in her eyes. "I don't know why, but this feels so final."

"Don't be so stupid, it's not like it's forever, and besides," Shona said, reaching out to ruffle Rose's hair, "don't you see? This is where your life is now, and it's written all over your face how much freer you feel here, how important getting to know your dad is to you. Even mooning after that idiot you think you're in love with."

"I *do* love it here," Rose said, reaching out and hugging her friend as she sat on the floor. "But your going means that my staying feels less like a temporary thing and more like, well, a decision."

"That's good, isn't it?" Shona asked her. "Starting again, that's what all this is about. Although how you are going to choose between Frasier and Ted I don't know."

"There is no choice!" Rose insisted. "There is no Frasier *or* Ted."

That Rose hadn't seen or heard from Ted since their hours in the annex she supposed was probably for the best. He'd said a lot of things to her that night, things she hadn't said back. Some distance between them now was a good thing, some time for her to feel less bad about how she'd let him kiss her when she knew that it meant very different things to both of them.

"I wouldn't be so sure about that," Shona said. "Frasier's been down here twice this week already, and he's taking you and Maddie to Edinburgh tomorrow. That's an awful lot of effort for a man who lives in another country, with another woman."

"It's just Frasier being nice. You said it yourself, he's one of those people who can't help being good to everyone they meet. He knows I'm going through a tricky time and he's decided to try and help me through it, probably to keep Dad on an even keel more than anything. He's a friend," Rose said, feeling a warmth spreading inside her every time she said his name. "And that is really much more than I could have expected, when I came here armed only with a postcard and a crazed look in my eye."

It was true that Frasier had arrived at the B & B on Monday evening just before tea and offered to take Rose and Maddie into Keswick for fish and chips.

After showering herself of all traces that her night with Ted might have left on her, her skin aching with tiredness and an excess of touching, Rose had gone to collect Maddie early that morning to find both grandfather and granddaughter already at work in companionable silence in the barn, so at ease in each other's company that she felt a little guilty for interrupting them. Maddie had looked up from her work as she heard the barn door creak open and beamed at Rose.

"Oh, hello, Mum. Come and look at this."

John had been in good spirits too, although he looked a little tired, and perhaps paler than Rose thought was good. She wondered if he really did live on a diet of moldy cheese and bread.

"Did she keep you up?" Rose asked him, but he shook his head.

"No, she was asleep by midnight. Age kept me up. It's a funny thing that the longer you live, and the more tired you become, the less your body is inclined to grant you sleep."

"If you like I could go and pick some things up for you," Rose offered. He looked worn thin, and she suspected that it was her daughter's fault.

"No, thank you. I have a person for that."

And so, politely rebuffed, and none the wiser as to who this mysterious person might be, Rose had spent the morning in the barn, watching Maddie work, feeling the warmth of the sun beating through the skylight on to the back of her neck, surreptitiously watching John laying the groundwork for the piece that he'd said he was not ready for her to see yet, and feeling all in all really rather peaceful despite last night's tempest. And then later Frasier had come and taken them out for fish and chips, saying that he was just passing and thought why not spend the evening with the two loveliest ladies in the village, although Rose couldn't think of a reason why he would be just passing, unless . . . well, unless he had gone out of his way just to see her.

They'd had a lovely laid-back evening, like none that Rose could ever remember having with Richard, not even in the early days. Maddie had quizzed Frasier endlessly on what he knew about art, gave him a test in color theory, which he failed deliberately in order to let her explain it to him, and he had patiently spent a great deal of time checking her fish for bones, when she remembered that she was afraid of choking on one. It was rare to find a single man prepared to be so patient with any child, let alone one as relentless as Maddie, and the more Rose watched him go out of his way to engage Maddie, the more she hopelessly adored him. The real Frasier was every bit as lovely as the imaginary one that she had loved for so long, which was a comfort in a way, knowing that she hadn't wasted all those years of pining for someone who turned out to be terrible in real life.

"You are good with her," Rose had said quietly when Maddie went to refresh her glass of colored pens. "It's kind of you. A lot of people find her difficult to get along with."

"She's not difficult at all." Frasier shook his head. "A little eccentric, perhaps, and unusual, but not difficult. Besides, she is decidedly, preciously talented at drawing, which is fascinating. I like her a lot. She reminds me that I would have liked to have had children once."

"Well, there's still time, you're not over the hill yet!" Rose exclaimed, although the idea of Cecily full-bellied with Frasier's child was quite a painful one.

"Cecily is not keen on children," Frasier admitted, perhaps with a touch of sadness. "She prefers it to be just the two of us."

"Funny," Rose couldn't stop herself from saying, "that's exactly what Richard said to me. So she's the one, is she, Cecily? The one you will settle with forever?"

The question, so loaded with longing and double meanings, slipped out before Rose could control her tongue. Frasier turned to look at her, inclining his head slightly to one side, clearly trying to discern exactly what she meant.

"I haven't really thought about not being with Cecily," he said. "We've been together nearly two years now, and she's really quite wonderful."

"Right," Rose said, forcing her mouth into a brittle smile. "Not that it's any of my business. I think some of Jenny's natural curiosity must have rubbed off on me. Look, anyway, thank you so much for coming to take us out when you still have that long journey all the way back again."

"Oh, no," Frasier said. "Not tonight. Tonight I'm staying over with John, mostly against his will. His third painting will be ready for shipping tomorrow, so I thought I'd oversee the loading and then he might let me talk to him about his next commission. I'll be free in the afternoon—if you like we could go for a walk? I could show you some of my favorite views."

"A walk? Thank you, that would be lovely," Rose said, surprised and confused once more. Just when she finally thought she knew where she stood, Frasier changed the rules all over again. "You really are being very nice to me."

"It's not exactly hard," Frasier said, smiling perhaps a little coyly, "to be nice to you. I'm rather glad to have the chance at last. And I was thinking on Friday I might come down early, pick you and Maddie up, and take you to see my gallery for the day. You can see some of your dad's work, and I thought Maddie would like to see other art—we could even brave the National Gallery, if she's keen."

"Really?" Rose looked at him. "Are you sure? Shouldn't you be discovering artists or doing something with Cecily?"

"Oh, Cecily is far too busy to bother with me on a weekday." Frasier grinned affectionately. "As long as I'm present and correct from six p.m. Friday onwards we get along just fine, and, well, look . . . you've been through some tough times recently. I know you don't want to talk about it, but I also know that you could do with a friend or two at the moment. The way you are handling this, handling John . . . it's admirable. I don't pretend to know how things were with your husband, but I do know that when I saw you on that day seven years ago, you looked so unutterably sad and lost and so . . . trapped. And if I'm honest I've never stopped thinking about you since that moment, wondering how you were and where you were. I hoped that I'd simply caught you on a bad day, and that you were truly happy. It pains me to know that for a good deal of the time you were not."

"I wasn't that day." Rose remembered, pain flashing across her face. "When I met you, it wasn't long after I realized just how awful my marriage was, and yet I had no idea how to escape from it. That time I spent with you, it gave me . . ." she paused, intent on not loading what she said next with too much meaning, ". . . a glimmer of what life could be like."

There was a silence between them as Maddie returned to the table with all the pens she had been able to gather with two fists, deposited them, and went off to retrieve the rest, much to the disapproval of the waitress.

"Spares," she said by way of explanation.

"I can't bear to think of you feeling so desolate," Frasier said, mustering a smile to cheer both of them. "And yet now suddenly here you are, and you look so full of life and promise," he continued as Maddie began to arrange the pens into color groupings. "And although I know that we know each other very little in reality, I can promise you that there aren't many people in the world who are more pleased to see you that way than I am."

"I actually think that might be true," Rose said with a smile, thinking of her limited pool of friends. "And if it is true, then I am very lucky to have such a good friend waiting for me, just when I need him."

Frasier smiled. "So you will indulge me and let me show you my empire?"

"Have you got an empire?" Maddie asked him, as she sat down now in possession of every single felt-tip pen that the restaurant owned, completely oblivious of the scandalized looks of the waitress, as she began to draw.

"Well, I've got a gallery, some offices, and a shop," Frasier said modestly.

"Not really an empire, is it?" Maddie said, rolling her eyes. "An empire is a ton of countries, enslaved by your mighty power. Not a shop and an office."

"Fair point," Frasier said.

• • •

Afterward, when he drove them home, Maddie fell asleep full of chips in the back of the car and was still slumbering as Frasier drew up in front of the B & B.

"I look forward to seeing you tomorrow, for our walk," he said, leaning across and kissing Rose ever so lightly on the cheek.

Their walk the next day had been pleasant, under the sunshine, buffeted by the warm winds, with Maddie talking nonstop, inventing goblins and trolls and whispering ghosts around every turn and behind every weather-stunted tree. Rose had not said much, and neither had Frasier, but she had been content to be in his company as they made their way to one of the lesser peaks, he offering her his hand when they came to any tricky inclines, holding onto her fingers for perhaps just a moment longer than he needed to. And when they finally parted outside John's house, everything had felt just as it should.

Yes, Rose discovered that she was rather happy to be confused and beguiled by Frasier McCleod, because even if Frasier was just being especially nice to the daughter of his best client, and Ted had just been in the midst of a passing crush, it was a good deal more pleasant and exciting than being the person she had been before. Than being Richard's wife.

"See that dreamy look in your eye?" Shona declared mischievously, drawing Rose back into the present. "You've had that a lot recently. That's definitely a thinking-about-a-man look. Which one is it? Ted, all young and keen; or Frasier, all unavailable and hand-holdy?"

"Don't try and change the subject," Rose said firmly, although the hint of a blush crept in her cheeks. The funny thing was Shona thought she had two men at her beck and call, and the real truth was that actually she had neither. "The point is, I'm not sure I can cope without you."

"Don't be a silly sod," Shona said. "Don't you get it? You've been coping without me since I got here. Rose, you don't need anyone anymore."

"Mum," Maddie said with some gravity as Rose went downstairs to find her daughter waiting by the front door with her sketchbook tucked under her arm, "can we go now?"

"Go where?" Rose asked her, still out of sorts from hearing the news that Shona was leaving. Leaving her to live her life alone, for the first time since she was eighteen.

"To Granddad's!" Maddie exclaimed.

"But we haven't made a plan to go to Granddad's today. He's not expecting us," Rose said. "I thought that really you and I haven't seen each other that much since we got here. The weather looks like it might hold, so I thought we might go for a walk, or drive to one of the lakes, maybe get a boat?"

Maddie stared at her as if she'd just suggested taking a trip to the moon.

"We don't need to arrange to see Granddad," Maddie said. "We just need to go, and besides, we did walking yesterday. I want to go and see Granddad and paint."

Rose sighed, uncertain what to do. The truth was she wanted to go and see John too. Their odd, both new and old relationship had reached a plateau of polite friendliness over the last few days, which she knew she would have to fight against if she wanted anything deeper from him. Rose hadn't asked him any more difficult questions and he hadn't appeared to mind her being there, which was about as close as they had come to any sort of obvious affection. When all of this had started, and Rose had found John here in the middle of nowhere, she'd thought that maybe that was enough. Now, though, with Shona about to leave her and sensing that the time she had to ignore Richard and his demands was quickly running out, Rose needed someone, and she discovered that she really wanted her dad.

The truth was, just being near him was reassuring in a way that Rose hadn't experienced for so many years. She'd been so long without a parent that she'd underestimated her desire for that one person who would always be there to lean on, and yet that worried her. She didn't want to start expecting more from John than he was able to give, and she didn't want to start to need him in her life, not now, even though this was perhaps the time she needed him most. It was too dangerous to rely on a man like John now, when everything was so precariously balanced and when she was supposed to be standing on her own two feet. Shona had told her that she didn't need anybody else, but Rose wasn't at all sure about that. If anything, for most of the time she felt like a fraud, like a headless chicken who wasn't so much getting her life together as just careering around making snap decisions based on very little common sense, mainly in an effort to avoid the fact that her old life, her dark, difficult bad life, had not vanished into thin air and would need to be confronted and concluded one day very soon.

And yet John *was* her father, and he *was* here, and he didn't mind her coming. He especially didn't mind Maddie, and in an odd way the developing relationship between the old man and the seven-year-old had improved Rose's own connection with her daughter as well as her father. The pressure between mother and child to support each other had been eased, and both of them sensed that release of tension and welcomed it.

John was part of her life now, and whatever came next, whether he would let her know more of him or not, Rose knew that she wouldn't want to go back to the way things were before she found him.

"OK," Rose said, smiling at the thought of another afternoon in the barn with her family, "let's go and see Granddad and see what he's up to today."

They had been about to get in the car when Rose spotted Ted striding down the street towards them. Thinking that he might have been about to come and see her, Rose lifted her hand and waved at him.

"Hello!"

Ted stopped dead, examined her standing with her hand waving hesitantly in the air, and, turning on his heel, walked purposefully in the other direction without even acknowledging that he'd seen her. That confirmed it, then: he definitely was avoiding her, and Rose couldn't really blame him.

You silly fool, Rose thought to herself, letting yourself get carried away on the spur of the moment, and now you've upset Ted.

"Ted pretended not to see you," Maddie said with her usual inclination towards clarity. "He must not like you anymore. It's just like when Lucy and Caroline stopped playing with me at school, and then everyone else did too."

"Horrible Lucy and Caroline," Rose said, feeling jangled and confused as she watched Ted walk away. "Who wants to be friends with them anyway?"

"I wouldn't have minded," Maddie said, a touch wistfully, before adding, "Oh, well, come on, then, let's go and see Granddad."

Maddie was rattling the barn door and finding it locked.

"He's not in here!" Maddie said with some consternation. "Where is he, then, if he's not in here? He's always in here."

"Well," Rose said as she reached the locked barn door, "I suppose he can't live in the barn. Let's go and see if he's in the cottage. You know, we didn't check with him that he would be in. He might have gone out."

"Granddad doesn't go out," Maddie said firmly, very sure of the facts, and Rose had to admit that he had certainly given that impression since she'd first visited him. She had only ever seen him outside the confines of Storm Cottage once, when he had come to see her at the B & B, and for some reason she couldn't imagine him just deciding to take an impromptu trip.

Maddie raced up the path, discovering at once that the door to Storm Cottage was unlocked, which didn't mean anything. Rose hadn't known it to be locked since she'd arrived, and she was fairly sure that if John had gone out he would still have left it that way. When they walked into the kitchen and living area, the cottage was still and silent, a pattern of leaves, their shadows cast by the midday sun, dancing cheerfully on the flagstones. A half-empty pint of sour milk sat on the table, and a pair of ancient-looking paint-spattered boots stood at the foot of the stairs.

"He's in! Granddad!" Maddie yelled, pointing at the boots. "Granddad!"

"Shhh," Rose said, getting the distinct feeing that she was trespassing as she looked around for any signs of her father.

"Why?" Maddie said, the pitch of her voice seeming at odds with the dusty quiet of the little house. "If he's not here he won't know I'm shouting, and if he is he will hear us."

"Well, I don't think he is in, so—" A dull thud came from above their heads.

"Granddad!" Maddie said, on the verge of racing up the stairs.

"Hold on!" Rose said, halting her in her tracks. Something wasn't right. She wasn't sure what it was, but whatever it might be, she didn't want Maddie to be the first person to find out. "He might be in the loo, or in bed or . . ." dead drunk, after realizing that finding his daughter again was just too much for him to take, Rose thought with a sense of foreboding. "Wait here and I'll go and have a look."

"But I don't want to." Maddie started for the stairs.

"Maddie!" Rose must have said her name with more authority than either of them was used to because instead of bolting up the stairs as she usually would, Maddie came back and plonked herself down at the kitchen table, folding her arms and pouting.

Taking a breath, Rose climbed the rickety, steep staircase, all sorts of visions of what she might find up there racing through her mind: her father passed out with a bottle of vodka cradled in his arms; or in bed with the "someone" who did his shopping and goodness knew what else. Or maybe not John at all, maybe just some particularly big and carnivorous rat.

"John?" Rose called out in barely more than a whisper, as she got to the top of the stairs. "Are you in?"

There was no reply, no further thuds or scrapes that might have been her father or outsized rodents. Advancing slowly, Rose pushed open the door to the bathroom. It was empty. Briefly she peered through the crack in the boxroom door. Almost all of the clutter that had been in there when she'd first arrived was gone, and the little room, although still only just big enough for a single bed, seemed bright and airy. Certain that John was not here, and that the thud had just been the old house making its presence known, Rose pushed open John's bedroom door, just to be on the safe side, before going back downstairs.

It was then that she realized John was in bed, or half in it, at least. Rose clapped both her hands over her mouth as she allowed herself a moment to take in what she saw. He seemed to have fallen—no, collapsed—out of bed, his long legs still tangled in the sheets, while his torso lay twisted on the floor, his head turned away from her towards the wall, his skin starkly white in the buttercup summer sunshine.

"John!" Rose whispered, falling to her knees on the floor next to him, feeling like the little girl at her mother's bedside again. "John?"

Rose let out a long, audible breath of relief as John turned his head to look at her, but the feeling didn't last for long. His face was sallow, his eyes sunken, ringed in black. How long had he been there?

The sharp scent in the air, the dampness on the edge of his rumpled sheet, made her worry that it was for a very long time.

"Are you drunk?" Rose asked him, withdrawing her hand in a moment of mistrust.

"Rose . . ." John winced, and Rose could see it hurt him to breathe and to talk. "Dizzy spell, useless old bones. I tried to get up, fell, I think I've hurt my back. Can't move."

"Your back? How long have you been here?" Rose said, her hand fluttering above her father, not sure where or how to touch him, or what to do next. "Why did this happen? Have you been drinking?"

"No!" John said with as much energy as he could muster. "Not even water. Thirsty . . . Been here since about five, feel so bloody stupid."

"Let me help you up." Rose tried hooking her arms under his, used to picking up her wisp of a mother from an early age, but even though he looked so thin and frail, she couldn't budge him. The more she tried, the more it hurt him.

"I'm so sorry, John, I can't do this alone," Rose said desperately. "I need to get help."

"There's a number . . ."

"I'll call an ambulance—" Rose began.

"No, no!" John used what little strength he had to be insistent. "There's a number on the pad by the bed. Call that."

"Who is it?" Rose said, kneeling up and reaching for the pad. She knew enough to know it was a Keswick number. "Your doctor?"

"No," John wheezed. "No goddamn doctors. They never do anything."

"Who, then?" Rose asked him anxiously. John seemed to hold his breath for what felt like the longest time, before he answered on a painful outward gasp.

"Tilda," he said, breathing the name on a long ragged outward breath. "She knows. She knows what to do."

Chapter Thirteen

The sight of Tilda standing at her father's front door brought Rose up short, catching her breath as she was confronted with the villain of so much of her life. How many nights had she gone to sleep blaming this woman for ruining her life? How many mornings had she woken up wishing her ill? For most of her life Rose had thought of Tilda as the thief of her happiness, and yet here she was, John's first port of call in an emergency, and looking no more menacing than any other slightly bohemian woman in her sixties.

"How is he?" Tilda asked as Rose awkwardly stood aside to let her in, then followed her to the foot of the stairs. Even if she hadn't had such limited experience in handling awkward social situations, Rose was pretty sure she would still have found this almost impossible. After her short, surreal telephone conversation with Tilda, which did not seem to rattle the older woman at all, Rose had carefully lifted John's legs out of the bed and put a pillow under his head to make him at least a little more comfortable. She'd sat on the floor next to him, neither of them speaking as she fed him sips of water from a glass by the bed, just as she had done so many times for her mother, stroking her hair as Marian sobbed herself dry of tears, even though she could scarcely remember why anymore.

"When Mum was very bad," Rose said, "sometimes I'd find her out of it on the floor—so often, actually, that it sort of became normal. Get in from school, have a drink of juice, pick Mum up off the floor, put her in bed. I could do it with her; there was nothing to her. I'm sorry I can't lift you."

"You really have nothing to be sorry for," John said, looking a little better now that he'd had a drink. "I'm the one who should be sorry. I want to be the one to look after you for once, not the other way round."

"I don't need looking after." Rose said it reflexively, exactly as she had said it to her mother, discovering only after she had spoken the words that they felt true. "I just need to be with you, to be part of a family. That's enough for me, more than enough. Now's the time of my life when I should be standing on my own two feet at last, making a future with Maddie. Looking after myself."

It had seemed like an age that they had sat there, side by side, but the knock at the door had still come all too soon for Rose.

"Don't hate her," John said as she got up to answer the door. "None of this is her fault."

Rose had said nothing.

"As well as can be expected," Rose said to Tilda now. "What's wrong with him? Has he been drinking again? He doesn't smell of it, but . . . I just want to know what's going on. I am his daughter."

Rose looked over to where Maddie was sitting on the sofa, her eyes watchful and wary.

Tilda did not reply, her hand on the banister, clearly eager to be with John, to help him. She stilled herself, though, knowing that she couldn't just ignore Rose.

"It's nice to see you, Rose," she said carefully. "I appreciate that this must be hard for you. I know John hadn't told you that we are still . . . in touch. If it helps, I can tell you that having you back in his life has made him happier than I've seen him for a long time. Not that it's that easy to tell the difference."

Tilda hazarded a tiny smile at her attempt at a joke, but Rose found it impossible to reciprocate.

She opened her mouth to speak, then swiftly closed it again. No words would come out. There was nothing that she could think of to say, her mind still too busy processing all this new information.

Tilda, it seemed, was still her father's secret, his bit on the side. Rose had never asked what had happened to her because she had assumed that her father's most destructive lover had fallen along the wayside with all the other detritus that he left in his wake. But she had been wrong. He had merely kept Tilda's presence from her. He'd lied to her again after all this time.

"Well . . . so." Tilda looked horribly uncomfortable. "If you don't mind, I'll go up now. The nurses, when he first had this trouble, taught me a special lifting technique. It should do the trick." Rose watched as Tilda hurried up the stairs, feeling cut out of John's life all over again, that little girl sitting on the bottom stair, as Daddy kissed her goodbye.

Of course it wasn't the first time she had met Tilda, if meeting was the right word to describe the first time that Rose had encountered the person who had somehow endured throughout John's life. Rose first and last set eyes on her when Tilda had been posing for John in his studio, and, sensing her mother's discomfort about what might be going on at the bottom of the garden by the way she stood and stared out of the kitchen window, drying the same mug over and over again, Rose had decided to go and investigate.

As she had crept in through the studio door, she was confronted with Tilda reclining, nude, on an old chaise longue that Rose remembered John buying as a prop specifically for this piece of work. Rose had been so fascinated by her first sight of a naked person, excluding herself, that she had forgotten to be frightened of the wrath that would rain down on her if John discovered her presence. He had told her very clearly that she was not welcome in the studio while he was painting Tilda. The instruction had stung just as badly as one of John's rare but wicked slaps across her legs if she angered him. Rose had been perfectly well aware that John preferred his daughter to his wife—after all, he made no secret of it, often pitting the two of them against poor Marian—and the thought that there might be a new favorite on the scene had piqued her childish jealousy. And yet when she had looked at Tilda, lying there on the black velvet, Rose had understood, even at that tender age, why John had become so fascinated with this otherworldy woman.

Tilda's body was altogether different from her mother's. It was opulent, luxuriant, an excess of milky white flesh that curved and undulated, flowing out from beneath her mass of dark hair almost like a waterfall flowing over rocks. John had never troubled himself with life models before Tilda, and even then, even when she was so young, Rose suspected that his newfound interest in figure painting had more to do with this one subject than anything else. Rose couldn't take her eyes off Tilda and neither could John, that was until he spotted Rose in the corner and, roaring with fury, he'd picked her up and thrown her out of the studio and into the dark and rainy afternoon. Rose had hated Tilda from that moment on. And that iconic image that had for so long been imprinted on her mind seemed to have very little to do with the person who had stood at her father's door a few moments before; it had nothing to do with this old lady.

The black hair, though still thick and long, had been replaced by a wiry gray, which fanned out over her heavy-set shoulders, and the fleshy glamorous body she'd once had had thickened and filled out so that her impressive bosom seemed to take up most of the loose embroidered top she was wearing. Her black eyes were still lined with kohl, and her face, though a little heavier and a touch jowled, was still clearly recognizable. Those heavy lids, the straight nose, and full mouth that had proved so alluring to John were all still there. Not as alluring as the drink, though, Rose reminded herself. John had chosen vodka over Tilda in the end, and that too showed in the lines around her eyes and mouth. And yet, she was still here. She was undoubtedly the mysterious person who brought his food, cleaned his house, did his washing. Were they together or not? Frasier had never mentioned Tilda to her, and John had told her that Tilda left him years ago. What did it mean that she was still so involved in his life, and right now, when her father was lying in bed, ashen gray and weak as a kitten, did it matter? It came as a shock to Rose to realize that she never imagined her father would still have Tilda in his life now. Knowing him, she'd expected him to fail at that relationship, just as he'd failed at everything else. Tilda still being around, in whatever capacity, meant that Rose had been wrong about John in one fundamental way: he hadn't lost or discarded everyone who'd ever meant anything to him.

Rose paced back and forth at the bottom of the stairs, anxious to know what was going on up there.

"Why can't we go up?" Maddie said impatiently. "Who is that strange-looking lady, anyway?"

"She's a friend of John's," Rose said, staring at the ceiling.

"Granddad doesn't have any friends," Maddie said. "Except us and Frasier."

"It appears he does," Rose said.

"Well, we're his relatives," Maddie said. "We are more important. I want to see what's wrong with him. I've been good, staying down here all this time. Why can't I go up?"

"Wait just a little," Rose said, guessing that John wouldn't want either of them to see him needing help to get clean and change. They sat there for another half an hour, in silence, listening to thumps and scrapes over their heads, the sound of running water rattling down the pipes and then, finally, Rose heard Tilda call her name from the top of the stairs. Seeing that she couldn't hold a worried-looking Maddie back any longer, Rose beckoned for her to follow.

"Come on, then," Rose said, putting her arm around Maddie's shoulders. "But no questions. John is tired and poorly. I'm sure he'd like to see you if you don't wear him out with talking."

"I wouldn't!" Maddie protested, following Rose up the stairs, perhaps a little nervously. After all, she didn't know what to expect either, after everything that had gone on around her.

When they got to the bedroom, Maddie holding onto Rose's waist from behind, they found Tilda sitting on the edge of the bed, John's arm hanging loosely around her waist, as she brushed the wisps of hair from his forehead. It was a picture of tenderness and love, full of an easy affection. They sprang apart at Rose and Maddie's approach like illicit lovers, which was, Rose supposed, what they were, even now. Set out on the bedside table were three blister packs of pills, all half empty. Smiling reassuringly at Maddie, who peered out from behind Rose's legs, and glancing at Rose, Tilda popped one out of the packet and gave it to John, holding a glass of water to his lips to help him wash it down.

"What is that?" Rose asked her, advancing into the room, leaving Maddie hovering uncertainly by the door. "What are you giving him?"

"Pain relief," Tilda said, covering John's hand protectively, which infuriated Rose for some reason she couldn't quite fathom, perhaps because with Tilda around he seemed like suddenly half the man, as if she literally diminished him.

"What for? What's wrong with you, John?"

"A year or so ago—" Tilda began, but John cut across her.

"I've got arthritis. I hate it, it's ruining my life. I try not to talk about it. Sometimes I forget to take the meds—so many now, I've got to take. I get bored with it. And then I pay the price, fall out of bed and can't move again, silly old bastard. Seized up like a rusty old tin man."

"I thought you said it was a dizzy spell," Rose said, biting her lip. What wasn't he telling her?

"It was: withdrawal from the damn meds. I'll be fine, a little rest, some food and water. Are you worried?" John held out a trembling hand to Rose and she crossed the room to sit beside him, ousting Tilda from her position on the bed. As soon as she sat down, Maddie came to join them, looking up at the curious-looking Tilda with naked distrust.

"Why didn't you tell me before about the arthritis?" Rose said, glancing back at Tilda, who now stood by the door. "I could have got your pills, made sure you didn't forget to take them!"

"I don't expect you to come here after all these years without a father and nurse me like I'm your child," John said firmly. "And besides, Tilda knows what to do. A few hours' rest, let the pills kick in, and I will be fine and everything will be back to normal."

"You look gray," Maddie said from the crook of her mother's arm. "Are you going to die?"

"One day," John said, smiling weakly as he reached out, briefly touching Maddie's cheek. "But not today, I promise you."

"Or tomorrow," Maddie said. "Or until I've finished my paintings?"

"Deal," John said, a twitch of a smile lifting his mouth.

"I'll go," Tilda said. "I brought groceries, some juice. Maddie, shall I make you a snack? Let Mum and Granddad talk."

Maddie twisted her mouth into a knot of rebellion, and Rose braced herself for a classic Maddie moment. Amazingly, though, it did not come. Rose watched astonished as Maddie visibly controlled what she longed to say, sensing it would not be right, and nodded.

"OK, but I don't like butter in my sandwiches."

Rose waited until she heard Tilda and Maddie descending the stairs. Looking at John's hand, which still rested in hers, so old and, now she came to think of it, beginning to be misshapen and twisted by arthritis like a gnarled old tree, she had to force back the tears that threatened in her throat.

"It's just arthritis, nothing else?" Rose asked John.

"I'm fine," John said. "Or I will be. I am very touched that you care."

"Of course I care!" Rose said. "How could I not? We still barely know each other—I couldn't stand to lose you again now."

John squeezed her fingers hard, unable to say anything more.

"So you and Tilda, are you still together?" Rose asked him quietly, not taking her eyes from his hand.

"We are . . . married," John said, "although we haven't lived together for a very, very long time. Ten years at least."

"Married!" Rose looked up at him sharply, shocked by the news. It never occurred to her that he'd married Tilda. "When?"

John withdrew his hand from hers. "As soon as the divorce came through. I think we both acknowledge that we married at the wrong time, for the wrong reasons. I barely remember the wedding day, or the first year of marriage, for that matter. Tilda left me when the drinking became too much and she couldn't take any more. She hoped I would change for her, that there would be children, a home, a normal life, but none of that happened. She gave up a lot for me, and in the end I gave her nothing in return. I killed almost all the love she ever had for me. She couldn't even bring herself to come back to me after I sobered up and, once sober, I wasn't sure that she should anyway. I'd hurt her too much too, you see. And I don't blame her for not wanting to risk that again. She lives in Keswick now, runs a little jewelry shop. She still thinks enough of me to get me food once a week, clean up now and then. Help me when I become . . . ill. We are friends, I suppose. I'm sorry I didn't tell you. I didn't know how to."

He looked down at his hands, lying limp on top of the sheets.

"I just can't take it in," Rose said, aghast. A few hours ago Tilda had been a ghost from her past, an unwelcome memory, and now she was here, very present and, more than that, her father's *wife*. "All this time I thought you and I were making progress, and you were secretly discussing me with her."

"No, not at all. All I said was how pleased I was that you were here, and how I didn't want to chase you away by telling you about her, which hurt her, but she understood. I know how much you must hate Tilda, with good reason, I suppose. But she is not a bad person, Rose. I've damaged her as much as I've damaged you. Don't hate her now, please. I . . ."

Rose waited for him to finish his sentence but no more words came, as he leaned back into the pillow, looking suddenly exhausted.

"I'm sorry," Rose said, shocked by his frailty. "Tilda being here isn't going to chase me away and I don't want to hate her. I'm just . . . I didn't expect her to still be in your life and I didn't expect you to be so . . . old."

The faint ghost of a smile hovered around John's graying lips.

"I suppose I deserved that," he said.

"I didn't mean it in a bad way," Rose said. "I just mean that in my head you've always been this big lion of a man, invincible. And now, now I see you are not."

"I am very far from it," John said, his eyes drooping with tiredness.

"You need to sleep, Dad," Rose said.

"Say that again," John said hazily.

"You need to sleep," Rose repeated.

"No, the other part."

"Dad," she said, smiling as he drifted off to what looked like a restful sleep at last.

When Rose got to the bottom of the stairs, Maddie was staring suspiciously at Tilda over a large glass of juice, each regarding the other silently.

"Rose, I'm sorry about the circumstances," Tilda said as she got up a little stiffly. "It is really nice to see you here. It means so much to your father."

"He's said more than enough to let me know how he feels, thank you," Rose said, mindful of Maddie listening intently.

"This must all be so strange for you," Tilda said, smiling pleasantly. "I know you must have mixed feelings about meeting me, to say the least. I don't blame you. So, cards on the table. I'm not going to try and make you be friends with me, I don't want to stand in the way of you and John getting to know each other, but if John wants or needs my help I will come, just as I always have. And I'd ask you not to try and come between us and what little we have left. Does that seem fair?"

"Who are you again?" Maddie asked her.

"It seems fair," Rose said, relieved that she wasn't to be forced into some reunion with a woman she'd last seen naked and who had loomed over her life like a shadow for so long. This Tilda, this sixty-something woman, seemed almost like a separate entity from that woman who had haunted her life up until now. At least now that specter could be exorcised for good. Still, Rose did not feel like throwing her arms around Tilda and forgiving her. After all, she was a very significant part of why Rose's life had disintegrated so rapidly, her fragile sense of security washed away with one single tide.

"Who is she?" Maddie persisted, looking at Rose.

"I'm Tilda," Tilda said. "I'm a good friend of John's. I look in on him sometimes."

"Well, you don't need to anymore," Maddie said, perhaps picking up on the tension in the room. "He's got us now. We're related to him."

"I know, and that's lovely, but John and I—"

"Anyway," Maddie said, "he won't need you now, will he, Mum? Now that we are going to live here."

Tilda looked at Rose, who hurriedly covered up the surprise in her face as she met the older woman's gaze.

"Is that right?" Tilda asked her. "Only John didn't mention anything."

"Oh, so he doesn't tell you everything, then?" Rose said, sounding more cruel than she meant to. "We'll stay for today and tonight, make sure he's OK. But we don't have plans to exactly live here. Not yet, anyway."

"Right," Tilda said. "I brought the ingredients for shepherd's pie; it always tempts him when he's been—"

"I can do it," Rose said, looking pointedly at the door, "if you want to go."

Tilda's expression flinched. "Of course, if that's what you want. Tell him to call me if he—"

"I'm sorry," Rose said, suddenly realizing she was being cruel, not to the seductress who stole her father away but to a concerned and very worried older woman. "I don't mean to be unkind to you. It's just . . . I didn't know about you until just now. And it would mean a lot to me to be able to look after my dad for tonight."

"I understand, I do," Tilda said. "Rose, I'm so sorry for everything that's happened. I'm so sorry that I played a part in hurting you."

"Thank you," Rose said. She didn't know how else to respond.

Rose felt a pang of regret as she saw the sadness on Tilda's face as she picked up her bag and left, knowing that she was behaving badly and unfairly, but unable to stop her nine-year-old self from kicking out at the woman who'd hurt her so deeply. There was time enough to reach an amicable place with Tilda. It didn't have to be today.

"Who was that woman?" Maddie repeated, as Tilda left and Rose was staring into a bag of ingredients, wondering if she even knew how to make shepherd's pie.

"That was Granddad's wife," Rose said.

"So my grandma?" Maddie asked her, wide-eyed.

"No," Rose said. "Granddad's second wife. She's not related to us."

After a good deal of guess work, quite a lot of good luck, and some creative help from Maddie, Rose managed to cobble together something that looked like an approximation of shepherd's pie. Maddie took great pleasure in peeling the potatoes, although Rose had to stop her at one point when she became so obsessed with getting them perfectly round that she was peeling them almost to marble size, and Rose guessed what to do with the lamb mince so that it looked rich and brown and just about right.

There were a set number of dishes on Richard's list of favorites that Rose knew how to execute perfectly, from steak and ale pie to calamari. But Richard had not liked shepherd's pie and so Rose had never learnt to make it. Another unexpected aspect to her new life, she thought, smiling to herself as Maddie pretended to wash up but really was just enjoying playing in the warm soapy water. Now she could learn to cook all sorts of exotic dishes: shepherd's pie, toad in the hole, maybe she would even go crazy and tackle a lasagne. When Rose thought about her life, and how very desperate it had been, how almost comically stupid her narrow existence was, she found that she wanted to laugh out loud. And she would have, except she was still afraid of Richard hearing her. Richard never did like her laughing.

"This is nice," Maddie said, filling a milk bottle with water and pouring it over the back of her hands. "I mean, I know Granddad is sick, and that is bad, but he's not going to die so then this can be nice, can't it? You and me and cooking. I like it."

"Me too," Rose said. "I don't know why we haven't done it before."

"I want to live here, Mum," Maddie said quite suddenly, turning away from the sink to look at Rose, washing-up liquid bubbles garlanding her wrists. "Like I said to that lady, I want to live here with Granddad, and cook together and paint every day."

Rose put the finished pie into the creaky old oven, unsure whether it was nearly hot enough, and thought for a moment.

"If we lived here, or near here, there would be a lot to think about."

"Like what?" Maddie asked her.

"School," Rose said. "It will be a new term before you know it. We'd have to find you a school place."

"But why?" Maddie sighed unhappily. "I don't like school. Teachers don't like me, children don't like me, and I don't like them. I'm not the sort of child who suits school. You could keep me at home and let me be a genius."

Full of compassion for her poor awkward, cast-out little girl, Rose went to Maddie and put her arms around her.

"That's not true," she said. "It's not true that people don't like you. It's just that you are different from most children, and they find you a little hard to get to know. I mean, how many other seven-year-olds know so much about Ancient Egypt? Or want to paint instead of play with dolls or watch TV? But you should have friends your own age, and if we did stay around here you would have to go to school. This time, though, I'd be a better mummy. I'd help people understand how lovely you really are because I know they'll like you when they do."

For once Maddie relaxed into Rose's body, letting herself be hugged.

"I would try school again, if we stay here," Maddie said.

"And what about Daddy?" Rose said tentatively. "Living here would mean you were very far away from him."

"It doesn't matter," Maddie said, drawing back to look up at her mum. "Daddy is a bad man, isn't he? He hurt me and you, and he makes you cry a lot."

Rose stared in Maddie's face, which seemed so certain, and wanted to weep.

"I don't know," she said. "I don't know if Daddy is a bad man. I thought once that Granddad was bad, and he certainly made a lot of mistakes, but we're getting to be friends now—good friends—and I don't think he is bad anymore. I think Daddy and I don't belong together. We make each other very unhappy. But I would never want to take you away from your dad, Maddie. Even after he scared us as much as he did." Rose's mouth went dry as she spoke out loud the words she could hardly bear to think.

"He was never unkind to me before," Maddie said. "He used to always smile at me, and let me read to him, and take me out for trips to learn things. But he's stopped being like that now. He's turned into a troll." Maddie's face folded inwards in dismay as she remembered once again what happened. "He hurt me. He stopped being Daddy and he hurt me."

"I know," Rose said softly, struggling to explain what she did not really understand herself. That Richard had turned his inner fury, even if without malicious intent, on Maddie had shaken her to the core, and she was terribly afraid that, having hurt her once, having broken that taboo, albeit accidentally, it would be easier for him to hurt her again. For all this time she'd thought about leaving Richard, of escaping him, she'd never worked out if that meant cutting him completely out of Maddie's life too, severing her from her father, just as she had been from hers. "I am sure that Daddy is very sorry for what happened. I am sure about that. Maybe one day you'll be able to talk to him about what happened," Rose said uncertainly. "If you want to, that is."

"OK," Maddie said. "As long as we can stay here."

"I'm not sure we could actually live in Storm Cottage," Rose said. "For one thing there is only one other very small bedroom—you'd barely squeeze in there! And for another, John likes living alone. I don't think he'd want us."

"I would," John said. Maddie and Rose looked up to see

him coming slowly down the stairs, clutching the banister. "I would like you to live here. And there is room. Through there." He nodded at a door that Rose hadn't noticed before, because there were a large number of boxes piled up in front of it. "There's a good-sized room in there. I've been holding off making it into a bedroom for me, putting in a shower room, because I didn't want to admit that the time was coming when I wouldn't make the stairs. But it would do for you, Rose, until I can get it modified. So there is room, if you want to live here."

"There, you see?" Maddie said happily. "And now it is settled. Are you ready to paint yet, Granddad?"

"Maddie, hang on a second," Rose said, going to help her father down the last two steps. "Dad, should you even be up?"

"I feel fine," John said. "I told you, all I needed was a rest and my medication."

"You don't look fine, though," Rose said, examining John's grayish and waxy skin.

"I'm fine," he said, brushing her helping hand away. "I heard you two talking down here. It was a nice sound. I would like to live with you, Rose. Not to be my nurse or take care of me. I will be on my feet for a good while longer yet, and when . . . if I'm not, I'll sort out care." John looked at her, taking a breath as he obviously needed to gather some courage to say the words he'd clearly prepared. "I would like you to live here because you are my little girl. And I've missed you all these years. Because I'm selfish and weak, and the older I get, the more I would like the chance for redemption."

"And because you like me," Maddie reminded him, keen not to be left out.

"And because I like *you* very much," John told the child fondly.

"Live here?" Rose looked around the tiny cramped room. "But what about Tilda?"

"Tilda is important to me," John said. "More than I am able to say. But our friendship is what it is. I can't ever mend what I took from her: the chance to be happy, have children, grandchildren. I don't want to lose her, so I'd have to ask you to find a way to accept her, maybe even befriend her one day."

Rose ran her fingers over her face. This felt so soon, so sudden. Wasn't it only last week that her father was all but ignoring her? Could things really change so quickly, in the blink of an eye? There was so much to consider, to worry about, if it didn't work out. Not least, uprooting Maddie again just as she got settled into a new home, but worse, the hurt that both of them would feel if in the end John couldn't live with and care for them in the way he hoped to. Rose wasn't strong enough to stand another rejection, not from her father, not again.

And then she remembered how her mother went out one morning and never came back, how Richard walked into the café one day and took over her life, how she had cut away her old hair and dyed it blond, how she had let a man she barely knew kiss every single inch of her. This was what life was like, hanging on a thread, balanced on a knife edge. Life was a precarious existence full of uncertainty, and it was only her marriage to Richard that had kept her from understanding that until now.

"OK," Rose said, much to Maddie's delight. "Perhaps we could move in over the weekend? On a trial basis, see how it goes? But yes, yes, Dad. Yes, we would love to live here with you."

"Good." John smiled, sinking rather abruptly onto a chair, causing both Maddie and Rose to rush to his side. "Oh, for

God's sake, stop clucking around me like I'm an invalid. Keep this rubbish up and I will change my mind."

"You're going to live here with your old man?" Shona said, looking up at the outside of Storm Cottage. "Has it got an inside loo?"

Shona had stopped by on her way home to say a proper goodbye after Rose had called her to tell her their plans. It was getting late, close to eleven, but still the sky was awash with light, even though the moon had risen and the stars had begun to pierce through.

"I'm going to try," Rose said cautiously. "Who would have thought it? I came here with some half-cocked plan to get Frasier, and I found my father, a home, friends. A place where Maddie feels like she belongs. It really couldn't be much better, could it? Do you think this could be it, Shona? Do you think this is our time to be happy?"

"I do," Shona said. "I think it's our time to be happy for both of us. Not just you, but me too. I feel that, Rose, I really do."

The two women hugged each other for a long time, Rose reluctant to let go of her friend.

"Jenny's going to be put out when you tell her," Shona said, rolling her eyes. "For a minute this afternoon it looked like she had another guest. This bloke turned up, reckoned he was a rambler, although if he was, the only place he'd ever rambled to was the pub. But anyway, he had a look around, decided he didn't like it, and was on his way. When you move out she'll have no guests again."

"There's got to be something I can do to help her," Rose said. "She's scary, but she's been nice to me."

"Help her figure out how to make money out of that annex, that would be a start," Shona said. She nodded at the car. "I'd better be on my way."

"Drive carefully," Rose said. "Stop if you get tired. Don't drink and drive."

"Because I might spill it." Shona giggled. "As if I ever would. Who are you, my mother? Oh, no, that's the angry woman stranded at home with my kids. See you, babe."

"See you," Rose said. She stood in the yard until the light of the little Nissan finally disappeared into the advancing gloom. Now it was time to start to live her new life for real, no more rehearsals. This was it.

Chapter Fourteen

"Will I need a passport?" Maddie said as she and Rose set off in Frasier's car early the next morning. Goodness only knew what time he'd got up to pick them up, but he'd arrived at eight on the dot on Friday morning, concerned to hear that John had had a funny turn.

"Do I need to call the specialist?" he'd asked John almost as soon as he'd walked in through the door of Storm Cottage, pulling out a chair and sitting next to him. John regarded him sideways with a distinctly disdainful air; he was definitely feeling better.

"It's just the old trouble," John said carefully. "The damn arthritis, the pills, the withdrawal if I forget to take them. I'm fine now. Rose stayed here with me last night, and tomorrow they are going to come and stay here perhaps for good, if I'm lucky."

"Really?" Frasier beamed at Rose. "That's wonderful news. Someone to answer the phone at last!"

"I shan't be turning the phone on," John said drily, raising a menacing brow. "So where are you taking my daughter today, and why?"

"Oh! Er . . . just thought I'd take her to look at the gallery, have a day trip, see some of your work, you know," Frasier had said, shifting a little uncomfortably in his chair, like a teenage boy having met his girlfriend's angry father for the first time. "You're more than welcome to come along. It's just when I've asked before—"

"I'd rather gouge my eyes out with a rusty nail than go anywhere near that den of commercialism," John said, pursing his lips in what might have been a gesture of disapproval or a repressed smile, Rose wasn't sure.

"We don't have to go," Rose stepped in. "Not if you're not up to being alone?"

"I am perfectly capable of being alone," John said. "In fact, I shall enjoy it, a little period of calm before my life changes forever. And besides, Tilda said she'd pop in to see how I am."

Rose noticed how Frasier's eyes had widened, and he glanced at her, no doubt to gauge her reaction to the news that Tilda was still a part of her father's life. So he had known about her all along too. What other secrets did her father have that Frasier was keeping for him? The truth was that Rose hadn't really had much time to think about it. She'd spent the previous night squashed into the single bed in the boxroom with Maddie, in case John wanted her in the night. Encircled in her arms, Maddie had drifted off to sleep at once, but Rose wasn't sure that she slept at all for any of the night, as everything that had happened circled round and round in her head. Tilda, her father's wife, still his friend, and what else? It was hard to tell from their brief meeting, and Rose supposed that if she'd never met Tilda before, had no idea who she was, she would just have seen a kind, concerned older woman when she opened the front door to Storm Cottage, and not the home wrecker she had always believed Tilda to be.

That was part of it, Rose had thought, part of coming to terms with what had happened and finding a way to love her father again. Accepting that he too was as responsible as anyone else—if not more so—for what had happened to Rose and her mother including Marian and even Rose herself. Realizing that he was as flawed as every other human being. Wouldn't Maddie have to do the same to love her father again, one day soon? And when the time came, Rose would have to steel herself to help her do it. There wasn't any alternative.

"Just bear in mind that you are not to touch my daughter in any way I do not deem appropriate," John had said, this time a definite smile twitching around his mouth.

"Never, ever, I would never . . ." Frasier had said, a little disappointingly, until he realized that John was joking and broke out into a smile. "Without Rose's say-so."

Rose had grinned all the way to the car.

"You won't need a passport," Frasier told Maddie. "Not yet, anyway. Maybe in a couple of years' time you Sassenachs will find it harder to get across the border, but today you should be OK."

"What's a Sassenach?" Maddie asked him.

"It's a sort of rude word that Scottish people use to describe Englishpeople," Frasier said, winking at Rose, who was repressing a smile as she looked out the window.

"Well, that's not very polite, is it, Mum?" Maddie said, huffing. "Not very polite at all."

There was a moment or two of awkward silence. And then Frasier piped up, "So anyone for a game of I Spy?"

Poor Frasier McCleod, he'd lived his whole life long without ever before playing a game of I Spy with Rose's daughter. Little did he know it was going to be a long, long journey.

It took almost two hours before Frasier finally pulled up in front of McCleod's Fine Arts, which, as Rose peered out the window, seemed to take up all four stories of an impressive-looking Regency gray stone house on Queen Street, opposite ornamental gardens enclosed with decorative wrought-iron railings, and in the middle of an elegant-looking terrace. Coming round the car, Frasier opened the door and helped Rose out, then lifted Maddie down onto the pavement.

"It looks foreign," Maddie said, staring up at the building with interest. "How far away is the Loch Ness Monster? Will I need to speak Scottish to understand anyone? Will they try and arrest me for being a sassa-thingy?"

"How about we start off with some tea and cake?" Frasier said, taking Maddie's hand and leading her into the gallery. "And no, no one will try and arrest you, I promise. I must say, young Maddie, I have never played such an expert and intricately complicated game of I Spy before."

"I'm not an expert," Maddie said proudly, clearly thinking that was exactly what she was. "I just like to describe things accurately, which does mean that sometimes I do have to use a lot of initials."

"I would never, ever have got that the bluish, greenish, tinted-with-pink thing was C for cloud, one that we last saw about thirty kilometers ago!" Frasier said with remarkable goodwill, considering that Maddie had spent most of the journey testing him to his limit. Rose smiled; it was nice that Maddie had another adult to call her friend. Her next task must be to find her someone of her own age who would understand her.

"That was because you weren't concentrating properly," Maddie said, content to leave her hand in his as he led them into the gallery. "I did keep telling you to!"

Behind the reception desk, a pretty red-haired young girl beamed at Frasier, coming round the desk to greet Maddie and Rose. For one horrible moment, Rose thought that this charming young creature, in the full flush of beautiful youth, might be Cecily, but it turned out her name was Tamar and she was an art student who worked here part time, to help fund her studies. It was clear she had an enormous crush on Frasier, by the way she fluttered her lashes at him and giggled when he asked her to arrange some tea and cake, but happily Frasier was completely oblivious to her admiration. He probably had eyes only for Cecily, Rose thought.

"Come and look at some art," Frasier said after dispatching Tamar. "Maddie, I want you to tell me what you think of my latest acquisitions, which ones will make me money and which I will be reluctantly returning to the artist."

Rose and Frasier hung back as Maddie walked around the large room, which must have once been about four if not five separate rooms and which Frasier explained he'd gone to great trouble and expense to open out into his main showing area, with a few smaller rooms leading off it.

"It's really very impressive," Rose said in hushed tones, feeling that for some reason she ought to be whispering. "Did you have all of this when you came to see me in Broadstairs?"

"Good Lord, no." Frasier shook his head. "I barely had two pennies to rub together when I came to see you. Not that I would have wanted you to know that. I was very keen to impress you. I knew you wouldn't want to talk to just any old two-bit con man—which I wasn't, by the way. I was just . . . starting out on my own after years of working for other people."

Rose stopped as Maddie stood nose to canvas with a painting that seemed to her to depict mainly a large purple blob, and yet her daughter seemed fascinated by it, examining it minutely.

"You certainly did make an impression on me," Rose said, glancing at him shyly. "More than you will ever know, really."

"Me? Really?" Frasier replied softly. "And to think for all those years since, all I've been doing is thinking how crass and rude you must have thought me, turning up like that out of the blue, dragging up all sorts of terrible memories for you, and all so I could chase down a painting and make some money." He turned to look at her and, sensing his gaze on her cheek, Rose met his eyes. "There was so much I wanted to say, to do that day. There was something about you that was so . . . compelling. You'll laugh, Rose, you'll think I'm foolish, but you'll never know how hard it was for me to just leave you there. I didn't want to. I barely knew you, and yet . . . Oh, well, there are only so many times a man can regret a thing. Can regret not saying or . . ."

He stopped himself, dropping his gaze from Rose, who on impulse reached out and took his fingertips in her hand.

"What you don't know," she told him in a barely audible whisper, suddenly spurred on by the look in his eye, the timbre in his voice, and the need to tell him the truth, "is that those few minutes you spent with me on that day have kept me going ever since, all these years, through the hell of my marriage. I was thinking about you and the way you looked at me and spoke to me that day. Every time I thought about you I became a little stronger, and the reason I—"

"Darling, there you are!"

Frasier tugged his fingers abruptly from Rose's hand and turned to greet a tall, slender, perfectly put together natural blonde who was striding across the gallery toward them in a pair of pressed white linen trousers and a lacy white camisole top that left little to the imagination. She had a great body, Rose had to grudgingly concede, one that positively begged to be shown off.

"Cecily, what a surprise!" Frasier said, going to greet her

and seeming a little caught off guard when she kissed him full on the lips. "I didn't expect to see you today. I thought you had that thing—"

"The PR networking lunch, you mean," Cecily said, beaming at Rose and Maddie in turn. "I do have that, but as you were showered and gone before I got up this morning, and I missed you, I thought I'd pop in and say hello before I have to spend hours pretending to care what other much less interesting people than me have to say!" Cecily winked at Maddie, who smiled at her.

"Everyone I know is less interesting than me," Maddie said eagerly, as if she'd just met a soul mate.

"It's a terrible bore, isn't it?" Cecily said, smiling warmly at Maddie. "So, my darling, are you going to introduce me to your guests?"

She turned to Frasier, the questioning look in her eyes enough to let Rose know that Frasier hadn't told Cecily anything about them.

"Of course. This is Maddie, and this is her mother, Rose Jacobs," Frasier said, introducing them formally. Cecily took her hand and shook it once, with firm confidence. "John Jacobs' daughter. She is staying with her father and wanted to see the gallery. Well, as John contributes about sixty percent of our annual turnover, I thought it was only right that I obliged."

"Rose!" Cecily said warmly, taking Rose by surprise by hugging her as if embracing a long-lost friend. "How nice to meet you at last. I've often wondered what it must be like to be the child of a great genius, which your father undoubtedly is. I think in many ways it must be as much a creative struggle for you to be his daughter as it is for him to be an artist."

Rose blinked. "Um, I don't know really. We haven't spoken to each other in about twenty years."

"Oh, of course," Cecily said, dismayed. "I can be so crass. I'm so good at putting my foot in it, I sometimes think I need to employ my own PR company. I hope things work out, for both of you. I know I'm an old romantic, but I'm always hopeful of a happy ending."

"Me too," Rose said, utterly dismayed that Cecily, whilst being a little over the top and inappropriately dressed, seemed to be a very nice, decent, not to mention beautiful, woman.

"One day," Cecily said, putting her arms about Frasier's waist and holding him close, "we will both get our happy endings, I'm sure. I'd like to know what your dad is like when he's happy. He scared me to death!"

"You've met my dad?" Rose asked her, intrigued.

"Well, once. Frasier took me with him once. He made a great show of pretending to loathe me!" Cecily's laugh tinkled like shattering glass. "Who am I kidding? He really didn't like me at all."

"I'm not sure he likes anyone very much," Rose said, feeling a surge of affection for her father for succeeding where she was so far failing. If there was any choice to be made between small, broken Rose and beautiful, overblown Cecily, Rose knew whom she'd choose, and it would be herself.

"Well, endless hours of pointless talking await me. I'd better leave you to it." Cecily hugged Rose once again. "So nice to meet you, Rose. Make sure Frasier takes good care of you. And as for you, my darling, will you really not be home for dinner? I'm making one of my famous stir-frys."

"I . . . no," Frasier said apologetically. "I'll be taking Rose and Maddie back to Cumbria. It will be a really late night, I'm sorry." He kissed the top of her head.

"Well, then, I shall wait with bated breath until you return," Cecily said flirtatiously. "I might even put on my best pajamas."

"You're already wearing pajamas," Maddie said, but Cecily was striding out of the gallery, the sound of her heels ricocheting off the wooden floor.

"So that's Cecily," Rose said. "Frasier, she seems lovely."

"She is lovely." Frasier looked after Cecily as the door swung shut behind her. "Probably a lot more lovely than I deserve."

"Well," Rose said, struggling to compose herself and remember her manners. She had the distinct feeling that before Cecily had appeared and proceeded to be so charming, something was happening between her and Frasier, that in that moment she could have told him anything, and he would have been ready to listen, might even be ready to feel the same way. Now Rose couldn't see any way of getting that moment back again, not when she had seen with her own eyes the kind of woman that Frasier went for. She could not be more different from Cecily, which meant she was light-years away from ever catching Frasier's eye. "What's next?"

Rose tried her best to keep Cecily's visit out of her head as they sat and talked over tea and cake in the middle of the gallery, on a blanket spread out on the floor for an indoor picnic, an idea that Maddie was enchanted by.

Of course, it couldn't be so perfect that in one moment Frasier would look at her, realize he loved her too, and they'd live happily ever after. Rose didn't really know why she'd allowed herself to think that that was even possible. Perhaps too many years of dreaming of Frasier, of always imagining him as the handsome Prince Charming in all of the fairy tales that she had read to a mostly disinterested Maddie, had truly given Rose rose-colored glasses. At least embarking on her own quest to follow her heart, full of folly as it might have been, had freed her from the tower that Richard had kept her locked up in and brought her home to her father. That was what she had to focus on, and that Frasier obviously cared for her a great deal. If she could only get this idea of being in love with him out of her head, and hating his girlfriend, then she would have a really good friend, and Rose knew that she needed as many of those as she could get right now.

It was time for her to grow up, to be the mum that Maddie needed and deserved, to be the best daughter she could be to a man who was trying his level best to be her father, and to stop letting younger men kiss her on a rock under the moon. Rose sighed to herself as she watched Maddie question Frasier on the works that hung around her. It was just as well that she wasn't in love with Ted, she supposed, since he'd gone off her so completely and abruptly, but it was a shame, especially as Frasier was so very taken, that there would be no more kissing Ted, even if she wasn't in love with him. Maybe that was the ultimate test of being a grown-up. Being able to exist from day to day without having to be in love with anyone at all, even if only in your head.

"Come with me," Frasier said, standing and holding a hand out to Rose. "I wanted to save this room until last. It's just for you."

Rose elected not to take his hand this time, deciding that someone had to draw a line between what was acceptable behavior for just good friends, and it might as well be her. Nevertheless she followed him across the length of the gallery to a closed door on the other side.

"It's one of the very few pieces I have by John Jacobs that weren't already sold before they were painted," Frasier told her, his hand on the door handle. "He did it a few weeks before you arrived, which is why I think you are going to love it. He hates it, of course; I caught him trying to burn it in the yard one day. But I told him that if he did that he'd be basically burning money, which made him want to burn it all the more, but I managed to stop him in the end and it's just as well . . . as I've just sold it for a hefty five figures."

Frasier opened the door onto a long, brightly lit white room, the whole of the far end of which was taken up with a John Jacobs painting, a vast landscape, half created from what rose around Storm Cottage, and half clearly from his imagination, giving it a magical, dreamlike quality, which made it feel just a little surreal to Rose, as if she had walked into her father's dream playing out on a screen.

"It's beautiful," Rose said, utterly absorbed by what she was looking at. "I just don't see why he hates this stuff so much."

"There is a very interesting use of orange in the sky," Maddie said. "Granddad is very clever at color. He wrote a book about it you know."

"Look at this," Frasier said. He reached for Rose's hand and then thought better of it after her last rebuttal, beckoning her over to the painting. On the crest of a hill she was just able to make out a tiny figure, the figure of a child, sitting curled up on the hillside, gazing at a view far away. Rose stared at it for a long time, tears filling her eyes, her heart swelling with emotion as she realized what she was looking at. It was an exact reproduction, recreated in miniature, of the painting her father had done of her as a child; it was *Dearest Rose* who was sitting alone on the mountainside, a tiny vulnerable figure abandoned to the elements. It was the way that John pictured her, lost and alone.

"It's me," Rose said quietly as Maddie came to stand next to her, peering at the image that could almost have been completely dwarfed by the expanse and scale of the painting unless someone pointed it out to you. "He painted *me*."

"Or it might be me," Maddie said, a touch jealously. "It looks a bit like me, actually."

Rose turned to Frasier. "That means, even before I came here, even before he knew that I was here, he was thinking about me. He *did* care. He did feel *something*."

"I think he always has," Frasier said, putting an arm around her shoulders, making Rose instantly tense. "I'm so glad that you got to see this before it gets shipped to Texas. It's proof, I think, of what your father might never be able to truly convince you of himself. That he's sorry, so sorry that he lost you, and that you were never out of his thoughts."

"Thank you," Rose whispered, tears sliding silently down her face, as she awkwardly allowed Frasier to enfold her in a hug. "You don't know how much it means to me."

"You don't know how much it means to me to be able to give you this gift, after all this time," Frasier said, wiping a tear from her cheek with the ball of his thumb. Maddie turned round and stared up at Frasier and her mother, in each other's arms, her mother in tears, and yet smiling at the same time.

"Are you *quite* sure you are not in love with Mummy?" she asked.

It was late when they got back to the B & B, where Maddie and Rose would spend their last night before moving their belongings to Storm Cottage. For the rest of the day Frasier had shown Maddie the wonders of the National Gallery, escorted them around the beautiful city, taking in all the sights, and bought them dinner at the world-famous Witchery, where their table must have taken quite a lot of string-pulling to acquire at such short notice, before loading them back into his Audi and making another long drive back to Cumbria, this time, due to mutual agreement, without the tortures of I Spy.

"I'm worried about all this driving that you're doing," Rose said as they pulled up, glancing at Frasier's worn-looking, if very handsome, face. "What if you fall asleep at the wheel? I could never live with myself. Especially as it's all been to ferry me and Maddie back and forth."

"You are probably right," Frasier had said reluctantly. "I am starting to feel a little worn-out. The thing is, Cecily will kill me if I don't show up tonight, but I'm sure she'd rather have me late and alive than on time and dead. Or at least I think I'm sure . . ." He smiled, leaning his head back against the headrest as he looked at Rose, his expression unreadable. "No, when I come to think about it, I think I'd really better stop over."

"If she does kill you," Maddie said helpfully, her head and shoulders appearing between the two front seats, "we will call the police."

"Will you stay the night with Dad?" Rose asked him, reluctant for him to go, even though she knew she had no right to be.

"I could," Frasier said, glancing at the B & B and then back at Rose, some thought process that Rose could not follow galloping across his face. "Or how about I book a room at the B and B and then you and I can talk some more, once this little one is in bed, and perhaps even share a nightcap?" Rose knew that it shouldn't thrill her that Frasier had chosen spending more time with her over getting back to Cecily, and that really he was just being sensible and choosing not to crash into a ditch over getting back to Cecily, but she couldn't help being pleased that her attempts at setting up the boundaries of their friendship had been abandoned as soon as he'd shown her the painting her father had done of her, and she knew it was hopeless to pretend not to love him.

The idea of spending a few more minutes with Frasier, even under the watchful eyes of Jenny, was too lovely to be spoilt by technicalities. And besides, bringing home a new guest, even just for one night, might make up for leaving Jenny tomorrow, which Rose knew her landlady was feeling very sad about, and not just because of the loss of revenue.

Quietly pleased to have an unexpected guest, and clearly bursting to know more about what he was doing, staying the night under the same roof as Rose, Jenny had taken an uncomplaining, dog tired but happy Maddie up to bed, leaving Brian to book Frasier into a single room on another floor. ("We don't hold with no bed hopping here," Jenny had warned him, as she guided Maddie up the stairs, who'd replied, her voice gradually receding, "I bed-hop all the time. And bed-jump and bed-belly-flop . . .")

After completing the formalities, Brian wished them a good night, explaining that it had been a long day, but they were most welcome to sit up in the living room as long as they liked. As they pushed closed the living room door, Frasier and Rose overheard a heated exchange on the staircase, Brian doing his level best to dissuade Jenny from coming back downstairs and sitting in the living room, playing the role of curious chaperone. Even if there was no chance of any kind of romance, Rose was grateful that Brian managed to get Jenny back upstairs, with a few softly spoken words and what sounded like a firm slap on the rump. In any event, Jenny was giggling as she trotted back up the stairs.

"Would you like some wine?" Rose asked him. "I've got a bottle in my room that Shona left me. It's vintage twenty-four-hour garage, but still it's not bad."

"Thank you, yes," Frasier said, taking great care examining Jenny's doll's house as she left. "This is really quite remarkable . . ."

Maddie was already asleep as Rose entered the room, her drawing pad tucked under her arm, a more than passable portrait of Frasier on the open page. Rose picked it up and studied it. The nose wasn't quite right, and she'd shaded under his eyes a little too deeply, making him look older than he was, but the most prominent thing that Rose noticed was that the drawing was done with affection. Maddie really liked Frasier.

Rose picked up the bottle of wine from the dressing table and then thought for a moment. Perhaps, perhaps it should be now that she gave Frasier the gift she had brought with her on that first night. The gift that for more than seven years she had hoped to give one day.

It would be hard to think of a better time than now to show him what she had brought with her all this way. The only thing was that once he had seen it, Rose felt her story with Frasier would be completed at last, and she wasn't sure she wanted that. Nevertheless, she had promised herself that she would never spend another second stuck in a life that did not want her, and Frasier didn't want her, not in the way she'd hoped for. Perhaps now was the perfect time to close that last precious chapter on her hopes and dreams for him, and to start a new one built on friendship and trust, which was the one thing Rose was more than certain of, after the time that they had spent together today. Frasier knew so little of what her life had been like with Richard, or rather he'd asked her so little, and she knew he sensed a great deal about that and more besides. Because only a man who really understood her could possibly have known how much it meant to her to see that painting. Frasier had given her every reason to trust in his friendship, and there could be no greater symbol of her trust in him than giving him this very precious object.

Her mind made up, Rose knelt on the floor and pulled out her package, still tightly wrapped in a blanket, from under her bed and clutched it to her bosom, hugging it just as she would a child, whispering a final goodbye.

Coming back into the room, she found Frasier with the glass cabinet door of the doll's house open, his head deep inside its drawing room. "Do you know I think this might be an original?" he said in muffled tones.

"An original doll's house?" Rose asked him, confused.

"A John Grasmere watercolor," he said, pointing to a tiny painting that hung on the back wall of the house, which Rose could see as she peered over his shoulder. "I'd have to take it down and really inspect it, but it looks too good to be a copy and he did spend a lot of time around here. Could even be worth a few hundred pounds . . . thank you." He took the glass of red wine that Rose offered him and, taking a sip, tried hard not to make a face.

"Not exactly the caliber of grape you are used to," Rose said, smiling as Frasier seated himself in Brian's armchair.

"It's perfectly awful," Frasier admitted. "But luckily the company is sufficiently distracting to make it bearable. I'm glad I decided to stay here tonight. We have spent so little time alone together and I find that . . . I rather miss you when you're not there."

There was an awkward silence, Frasier looking as if he regretted saying those words as soon as he'd spoken them and Rose at a loss as to how to react.

"Frasier, I've got something to tell you," she said eventually, deciding to press on despite the moment of uncertainty, knotting her fingers together as she braced herself. "It's going to sound a bit mad, but please just listen and let me tell you, because it's the story behind this." Rose took the parcel from where she'd propped it up against the sideboard and placed it on Frasier's lap, kneeling on the floor in front of him. He watched her for what seemed like an age in the lamplight, looking as if there were a thousand words on the tip of his tongue, none of which he could find a way to articulate.

"Go on," he said eventually, making an effort to keep the tone light. "How intriguing."

"Right, well." Rose took a breath. "That day, the day you came to my house, the day you wanted to track down that painting of me as a girl? You could tell that something was very wrong, and you were right." Rose shifted a little, taking a deep breath, steadying her nerves for this moment that she had longed for and that now terrified her more than she could imagine. Never be frightened again was her promise, she reminded herself, lifting her chin to complete these last few steps on her journey.

"I was so afraid. I was terrified for every single second that you were there. I was afraid that my husband would come back before you had gone and find you there, and I knew that if he did, it would make him very, very angry, because even then, he didn't like me talking to anyone unless he was present, but especially not men. Even then he kept me in the house as much as he could, made me feel worthless and pointless, and that I wouldn't—couldn't—even exist if it weren't for his approval. He'd never hit me at that point—that didn't come until much later—but he could terrify me without ever having to lay a finger on me. He had control over my mind, you see. And I believed him, I believed him because my father had walked out on me and my mother, well, once Dad left her, she'd faded away day by day until she ceased to exist. And on that day, the day that you arrived, all I had was my unborn child. I was so scared about bringing her into a marriage and a home that didn't have any love in them, or any hope. And I thought you might think I was a little standoffish, closed off and unfriendly. But you sensed that something was wrong, and the truth was I was scared."

"Oh, Rose." Frasier leant forward in his chair. "I knew it. I knew when I saw you how much pain you were in. The first moment I set eyes on you, I wanted to scoop you up and carry you out of there, like some sort of ridiculous knight in shining armor. But you were married, and pregnant, living in a nice home, wife of a doctor. I thought I was being a fool, that of course you must be happy. If only I'd asked you, if only I'd been able to help."

"You did help," Rose said. "You were kind to me, you saw me as a person, someone who was interesting and important, a person with a history, a life and a value. And I . . . I have been so grateful for that hour I spent with you ever since, because as things between Richard and me got worse—and they got a lot worse—I could think back on that time we had together, and the way you smiled at me, and how you looked at me, and I would know that whatever Richard told me about how useless and pointless and stupid I was, he was wrong. I would take out the postcard you sent me and read it and reread it and it would keep me going. From the day I met you I gradually became a stronger and stronger person, until I finally had the strength to leave him. And I promised myself that one day I would find you and thank you in person."

Rose laid her palm flat on the package. "And now that moment has finally come."

Frasier shook his head, and Rose wondered if it was because he knew what she was going to say and didn't want her to say it out loud.

"Rose," he said earnestly, "if I had had any idea that you felt this way, you know I would have come back, don't you? You realize that I would never, never have left you there. For so long I've worried about how I let you down, how I didn't do enough. When I didn't hear from you, the time I tried to tell you that I'd found John, I thought, I hoped, that you must be happy, that you must have moved on. I made myself think that way over and over again. I can't forgive myself if I—"

"Frasier," Rose interrupted him, knowing that if she waited much longer she'd lose the courage to say what she wanted to, "let me finish what I have to say, please."

"Of course, I'm sorry," he said. "It's just that I am really rather overwhelmed. And once you've started to say something that you've been thinking and feeling for such a long time, it's hard to stop it coming out."

"I know," Rose said, taking a shuddering breath. "Which is why I have to tell you—Frasier, I didn't come here to find my father. I had no idea he would be here. I came here because it's the painting on the postcard, my only connection to *you*. I came here to find *you*, to thank you and to give you this." She nodded at the blanket. "I wasn't entirely honest with you that first day. I don't know why, it was the only thing I had of him, I suppose. The one thing I protected from Richard, hid away from him right at the back of my dad's old studio. And now it's yours."

Frowning, Frasier said nothing as she untied the string that held the blanket in place, and then carefully unwrapped what lay beneath. He gasped when he saw the contents, unable to tear his eyes away from what he was looking at.

"*Dearest Rose!*" he whispered. "You had it, you had *Dearest Rose*, the original painting, all along." He looked up at her, his eyes shining with delight. "Oh, Rose, you don't know how long I've waited to set eyes on this. It's beautiful, just as I imagined it, if not better. I never thought I'd see the day." When he looked back up at her he had tears in his eyes. "Thank you, Rose, thank you so much for letting me see it, hold it."

"It's for you," Rose said happily, flooded with pleasure at delighting him so much. "It's a gift, for you, to say thank you for saving me. Even if you weren't there, you still saved me. You saved my life."

Frasier was speechless for a moment, and then slowly, ever so carefully, he got to his feet and, placing the painting flat on the tabletop, he knelt on the floor next to Rose.

"This is not a gift I can accept," he told her gently. "This painting is more than just a work of art, it's the link between you and your father that has kept you united all these years. It's the one thing you wouldn't part with, not for your husband, not for me or for money, and it's the image that he never let go of. I could never take this, Rose. It belongs to you and John, and that's where it must stay. Besides," he said as he reached into his pocket, "there is something I want to show you."

Frasier took a square of folded paper out of his inner jacket pocket and handed it to her. Her hands trembled as she carefully unfolded it. Rose gasped as she realized what she was looking at. It was the copy of the sketch of *Dearest Rose.* The very same one Frasier had shown her on that first day, the day they had met.

"You see?" Frasier said. "You don't need to give me your painting. I've been carrying you next to my heart for all these years."

Rose looked away, uncertain what to say or even think. The hope that Frasier might feel even a little of what she felt for him was so excruciatingly fragile that now, at this critical moment, she almost wanted to turn away from knowing.

"But . . . but I wanted to say thank you," Rose said, "and I can't think of how else to do it. I've planned to give it to you for a very long time."

"I know," Frasier replied, reaching out to cup her face in the palm of his hand. "But I am certain that in your heart you don't want to part with it. And you don't have to. Just to see it with my own eyes is enough. And to know you is more than enough."

Rose leant her cheek into his touch, unable to look him in the eye as she felt him examining her, terrified.

"Rose . . ." Frasier said, struggling to form the words that he himself was unsure of, ". . . I don't understand the way I'm feeling right now. I thought I had everything sorted out and settled in my life. I thought that I knew where I was going, what I was doing, and that I'd put a single hour with a woman I barely knew but could never forget behind me at long last." Frasier moved his hand just a little, lifting Rose's chin so she couldn't help but look at him, and the expression she saw in his face made her catch her breath. "But since I've met you again, all that's turned on its head and I'm back in your house, sitting at your kitchen table, looking at you and believing that, as incredible as it seems, for the first time in my life I've fallen in love. And it's true. I can't hide from it anymore, Rose. I love you. I loved you then, I love you now. I think I always have."

Rose couldn't speak, so she simply nodded, her whole body trembling.

"I'm sorry," Frasier said. "This is the last thing you need now. Me declaring my heart to you when you have so much to face, with your husband, your father. I just had to speak out, Rose, because it's so damn obvious to everyone in the world except you. Even Cecily noticed it. I was doing such a damn terrible job of pretending otherwise, and much as I don't want to hurt her, I'm too tired to pretend any longer." Reluctantly Frasier took his hand away from her face, smiling ruefully. "Please don't feel that you have to do anything to reciprocate."

"Reciprocate?" Rose said, reaching out to touch his arm with the tips of her fingers. "You idiot, how can you possibly not know that I feel just exactly the same? That I've hoped and longed just to be in the same room as you for years and years, and now I just can't believe that it's true. I feel the same way, Frasier, of course I do. I always have, I have always loved you too."

There was a moment, the briefest moment, of separation between them and then Frasier reached out, picked up her hand in his own, and drew her close to him.

Softly, slowly and with infinite care, he kissed her, so lightly that the embrace was barely there, and yet Rose felt it with every particle of her body, years of repressed longing surging through her like a tidal wave. There was no uncertainty here, no fear. This was nothing like the reckless experimental kissing she had tried with Ted. All Rose felt now was the overwhelming sense that finally she was where she belonged. For so long she had thought herself in love with a fairy-tale prince, a perfect creation of her starved imagination, but now, now she knew that the love she felt for Frasier was real, because finally she knew the real man behind her dreams, and he was more wonderful in reality than she could ever have dreamt of.

"I feel like you might break in my hands, you are so delicate," Frasier whispered, breathless with love for her.

"I'm not so delicate that you can't kiss me again," Rose whispered, leaning into his embrace, this time their kisses a little bolder, a little more insistent. Then Frasier withdrew.

"There's no need to hurry this," he said. "Not after we've waited so long."

"Have you changed your mind?" Rose asked him anxiously, always prepared for the worst.

"No, no . . . God, Rose, not at all. There's nothing I'd like more than to take you to bed right now. But you, you've been through so much, and me, I've waited almost eight years to have this moment, this lifetime with you. I don't want to rush it. Everything has to be just right before we are truly together.

There are people who deserve our honorable treatment: Cecily, your father, Maddie. And, most important, you. You are like a flower, a rose, too easily crushed, and I won't let either one of us putting a foot wrong in a rush to be together endanger you or what we might have here." He smiled, drawing her into his arms and holding her tight, kissing her hair. "It's too wonderful, too miraculous, to be able to love you at last and for you to love me back, for me to let any little detail spoil it. So I'm going to kiss you once more, dearest Rose, and then we will say good night, and if I sleep tonight, which is unlikely, it will be knowing that I've fallen in love with the woman I've always been in love with, and in the morning I can start making everything right so that we can be together for the rest of our lives."

"Really? Do you really mean it? Richard will make it difficult, you know. He will still want to hurt me, punish me for leaving him."

"He can try," Frasier said, "but with me at your side he won't have a chance. And besides, you are much stronger than you realize, Rose. Look at all you've conquered so far just to be here. I would say that makes you positively formidable."

Frasier climbed to his feet and took Rose's hand to help her up.

"Good night, Rose," he said, escorting her up the first flight of stairs.

"I feel happy," Rose said, her brow wrinkling as she took the first step up to her room. "I always worry when I feel happy, something always goes wrong."

"Not this time," Frasier said. "I swear it to you. Good night, my love."

"Good night, Frasier," Rose said.

When, at last, she slipped under her covers, feeling the

cool sheets against her skin and knowing that Frasier was only one floor beneath, and Maddie was sleeping peacefully at her side, Rose did indeed feel happy. Happier than she could ever remember feeling before in her entire adult life, because for the first time, at last, she had a future she could truly look forward to.

Chapter Fifteen

"You are humming, Mum," Maddie said as Rose did her best to brush her hair into some sort of style before breakfast. "Why are you humming?"

"I don't know," Rose said happily, thinking of the last few seconds when the tips of her fingers had touched Frasier's on the banister last night. "It's a beautiful morning, we've moving up to Storm Cottage, you are a wonderful daughter. I feel happy, I suppose."

"Me too," Maddie said thoughtfully. "I feel happy too, although I *will* miss Jenny's cooking."

"Come on, then," Rose said, holding her hand out to Maddie. "Let's go and get one last Jenny special breakfast."

Rose and Maddie were chattering happily away to each other as they walked into the dining room to find Frasier already sitting at a table. Seated opposite, much to Rose's surprise and dismay, was Ted. Instantly Rose's quiet contentment transformed into repressed anxiety. What was Ted doing here? What did he want and, more important, what was he planning to say and to whom?

Keep calm, Rose told herself. This, after all, is where Ted's mum lives. He's got every right to be here and probably it's got nothing at all to do with you.

Both men looked up when they saw Rose and Maddie, smiles breaking across their faces.

"Rose," Frasier said simply, keeping his promise to keep their attachment a secret until all obstacles had been resolved, not that he needed to say a word: it was in his eyes and as clear as day. It was rather thrilling, Rose thought, like being in an Austen novel, two secret lovers exchanging nothing more than longing looks and the occasional touch. However, Ted sitting right across the table from Frasier did rather put a dampener on the thrill. Rose could sense that he had come with a purpose, and that it had something very much to do with her. It would be all right, Rose told herself. Ted was her friend, he wouldn't set out to hurt her.

"Hi, Rose," Ted said, half getting out of his chair as she approached. She would have sat at another table but Maddie went straight over and sat next to Frasier. "I'm glad I caught you before you left the B and B to move in with your dad."

"Oh?" Rose said, doing her best to appear unconcerned about why that might be.

"Did your girlfriend kill you?" Maddie interrupted Ted, talking to Frasier with genuine curiosity.

"Not yet," Frasier said, glancing at Rose and smiling. "Perhaps later. Almost certainly later."

"I hope not," Maddie said. "I quite like you."

"I was hoping for a quick word," Ted said, as Rose sat down reluctantly next to him, instantly drawing Frasier's interest away from his bacon. "In private, please?"

"And what have you got to talk to Rose about in private, young man?" Jenny asked him mistrustfully as she appeared with a pot of fresh tea.

"Well, if I told you it wouldn't be private, would it?" Ted told her, winking at Maddie, who giggled. "Have you got a minute, Rose? Maybe we could have a quick chat in the annex."

"In the annex?" Jenny exclaimed, irritated. "In the annex? You know what you are, Ted? You are no better than you should be."

"Yeah, right, Mum. Still got no idea what you mean by that," Ted said, clearly keen to say whatever it was he had come here to say. "Rose? If you don't mind?"

"Um, OK . . . well, just for a minute," Rose said, smiling weakly at a concerned-looking Frasier, whose brow furrowed as he watched Rose disappear with Ted.

"Mum's always going off with Ted," Rose heard Maddie say as Ted followed her out of the room, indulging in her habit of saying things just for the dramatic sake of it. "It's like they've got a secret or something."

"Ted, look . . ." Rose began as soon as they were alone, eager to get this sorted and to return to Frasier. "It's fine. You don't have to say anything."

"I do," Ted insisted. "I have to say I'm sorry." Rose waited for him to say more, but he faltered, gazing up at the battered fringed lampshade for inspiration.

"OK, great. Never mind, let's forget about it," Rose said, but before she could turn back, Ted was talking again.

"I'm sorry that I walked in the other direction the other day and pretended that I hadn't seen you when I obviously had. And I'm sorry that I haven't got in touch since the other night. You must think I'm a right dick."

"It's OK," Rose repeated, edging towards the door. "You don't have to be sorry, you don't have to explain. I get it. We got a bit carried away—I got a bit carried away—let's just forget about it and move on, right?"

Ted stared at her aghast. "That's not what I'm trying to say at all."

"What?" Rose asked him, looking longingly at the exit, which Ted was blocking. "Pardon?"

"You've got to me," Ted said simply. "That's why I never got in touch, after . . . the last time. I was trying to get my head round it. And to be honest, it's taken me this long to pluck up the courage to tell you."

"Oh," Rose said, reluctant to hurt someone who'd been so kind to her. "Oh, Ted. I'm so sorry . . ."

"Please don't tell me you don't feel it too," he said unhappily. "I know you did, because it would be impossible for me to feel something so strongly that was only one-sided, I know it would."

"For a moment I did," Rose said as carefully as she could. "I thought I might feel something for you too. And I do really *care* about you, but the truth is I *don't* feel the same way. I just don't."

"I know," Ted went on as if he hadn't heard her. "I know what you're going to say: you're older than me, still married, and you've got a kid to think about. But if you do think about it, Rose—I mean really think about it—those are just excuses. You're going to live with your old man, so you'll have a permanent base near me. Just right for us to get to know each other, with no pressure whatsoever." Ted spread his hand flat in the air to emphasize his point. "And you won't be married forever. I can help you start divorce proceedings, even take care of your ex if he annoys you."

"Ted," Rose tried again, wrought with guilt and regret. Never, not once, had she thought that perhaps the first ever moment of spontaneity in her life would come to this, that she'd somehow end up hurting Ted. "We can't, I don't want to, you see. Because I—"

Before Rose could utter another syllable, Ted had grabbed her by the arms and was attempting to kiss her. Panicking, and suddenly very afraid, Rose twisted her head away and tried her best to wriggle out of his grasp, overwhelmed in that moment by her need to get away from him, away from any man intent on forcing himself on her.

"No," she cried. "No, no, no!"

Just at that moment, Jenny and Frasier walked into the room.

"So you think it could be like a studio, like an artist's, perhaps for traveling painters . . . ?" Rose was dimly aware of Jenny saying just as she and Frasier came into full view.

"Edward!" Jenny shouted, horrified. "Put that girl down at once, do you hear me?"

"What the hell is going on here?" Frasier asked, as Rose backed away, taking a breath, her heart racing as she struggled to shrug off the memories of Richard pinning her down and refusing to let her go. This was nothing like that, she told herself, this was just Ted refusing to hear what she was saying. But still, she couldn't stop herself from trembling, from wanting to bolt from the room and find a safe place to hide as suddenly she was drenched in that sickening sense of shame once again.

"It's nothing," Rose said, all the tremor in her voice clearly indicating otherwise as she struggled to collect herself, her terrified body defying her. "Nothing. Just some crossed wires. Ted thought, he thinks that he likes me . . . but I've explained to him that it wouldn't work. That I'm with you now."

Too late Rose realized how cold and blunt her efforts to seem coherent must have sounded to Ted, who had done nothing really, other than offer her his heart on a plate, only to have it trampled on in front of an audience. He stared at her, his face a picture of pain and rejection.

"Ted, you idiot," Jenny said, slapping him smartly across the back of the head. "Whatever were you thinking, forcing yourself on Rose like that? She's practically old enough to be your mother, for one thing, and for another I've taught you better manners than that, you silly boy."

"It didn't look like Ted was really getting the message, it has to be said," Frasier added, going to Rose and putting a protective arm around her, inflaming Ted's already heightened color even more. "Are you OK?"

"I'm fine," Rose said, sensing that Ted was about to explode with the buildup of rejection and humiliation, that he was on the brink of lashing out, and now it would be very unlikely that Rose would be able to stop him. "Seriously, none of this is Ted's fault. It's all mine."

"Yeah," Ted said, his demeanor becoming suddenly cold and fraught. "Damn right it's your fault. Women who kiss men behind other men's backs are usually to blame when things get out of hand. Anyway, who are you to ask?" Ted demanded of Frasier. "Because I wasn't *forcing* myself on her. I'd never do that. I was trying to kiss her like I have done a hundred times before, since she got here, and she didn't complain then. Far from it. She loved it, and more besides. You name it, Rose and I have done it."

"Ted!" Jenny gasped. "How could you say such things?"

"You are skating on very thin ice, young man," Frasier said, his jaw clenching tightly, his skin blanching along his clenched knuckles.

Then first Jenny and then Frasier caught sight of the look of excruciating guilt that must have been writ large across Rose's face, and the penny dropped for both of them at precisely the same moment: that Ted was not lying, at least not entirely.

"Rose?" Frasier asked her, his voice void of emotion. "Tell me that's not true."

"It's not," Rose said hurriedly, unhappily, unable to keep up with the turn of events. "Not the way that Ted's saying it is. We did kiss, yes. But it was . . . it was because . . . it's hard to explain, really. But it was just some kissing, and it never meant a thing."

"Oh, really?" Ted asked her angrily. "So we've not hooked up a couple of times, then, Rose? We didn't spend most of a night together, naked in that bed?" He nodded at the stripped mattress behind them, and Rose felt Frasier's arm slip from around her shoulders and fall heavily to his side.

"It wasn't like that, Ted," she said. "And you know it."

"I know exactly what it was like." Ted leered at her, all trace of the man she had grown to like so much gone from his face. "I know exactly what you were like."

"Please, don't lie, not about this," Rose pleaded quietly. "Please, I know you're hurt, but—"

"I'm not hurt," Ted said bitterly. "I couldn't care less."

"You went after my boy, after everything I said to you?" Jenny said, stopping Ted from saying more that his mother probably knew he'd regret. Until she spoke, Rose had forgotten Jenny was there, so intent was she on stopping Ted from ruining everything with Frasier. It didn't occur to her that he could ruin everything with Jenny too.

"No!" she insisted. "I didn't go after him. It just happened, and we both knew it was stupid . . . and actually not very much did happen, did it, Ted?" Rose said, looking again to Ted to tell the truth: that really all they had ever done was kiss, even though some of it had been without clothes on.

"Oh, I wouldn't say that," Ted said, crossing his arms and lifting his chin in defiance, directing his comments at Frasier.

"She was really up for it. You want to watch yourself, mate. This one's a really live wire, take it from me. That's if you know how to get her going. I could give you some tips if you like."

Rose gasped as Frasier crossed the room in one step and, grabbing Ted by the collar, shoved him against the wall, his fist hovering in midair.

"Go on, then," Ted spat at him. "Take a shot at me. I promise you it will be your last one, old man."

With some force of will Frasier dragged his hand down and let Ted go, releasing him as if he were some objectionable piece of rubbish.

"Frasier," Rose began to try to explain, watching her happiness crumble away before her eyes, "it was when I was still very confused, before I thought that there was any chance of anything happening between you and me, and Ted's twisting it because he's angry and hurt—"

"So you're saying that's what I was? A way of passing the time?" Ted asked her. "I'm not angry and hurt, I'm just pissed off that I wasted any of my time on you."

"You'd barely got here, Rose," Frasier said softly, his expression stricken. "We hardly had a chance to say hello, let alone work out how we felt about each other. I thought . . . I thought you felt the same about me as I did about you, that coming here was to finally make all those feelings we had for each other a reality. That after we'd both waited for so long you would be able to wait just a while longer. I didn't think you'd opt to hedge your bets and jump into bed with someone else while you were waiting to see how things turned out."

"I didn't jump into bed with him!" Rose protested. "Not in that way!" she trailed off as she looked at Ted's grandma's bed where she had more or less done just that. What a fool she had been, how stupid not to see where her curiosity would lead her. It turned out that Rose had picked exactly the worst moment of her life to be spontaneous.

"I've had enough of this," Ted said angrily. Clearly upset, he left, slamming the door so hard behind him that it opened again.

"Well," Jenny said promptly, her face clenched as tightly as her fists, which were balled at her sides. "You'll be wanting to settle your bill and be on your way. I'll go and make it up for you now. Oh, and if I could have my daughter's things washed and folded and returned by tomorrow, that would be much appreciated. Thank you."

Rose watched, bereft, as two of the people who had been so kind and so welcoming to her when she'd arrived in Millthwaite, friendless and alone, walked out of her life, most likely for good. One or two moments of allowing herself to stop thinking and just feel had led to this, to her fledgling happiness descending so quickly into chaos and recrimination. It was her own fault, and now she had to deal with the consequences.

Rose turned to Frasier, who was standing rooted to the spot, unable to look at her. This couldn't be happening, could it? She would be able to fix this, wouldn't she? The universe wouldn't take Frasier away from her, the moment that she found him, over one silly mistake that she hadn't even known was a mistake until just now?

Slowly Rose walked over to Frasier and reached out a hand, letting it hover in the air for a moment before it fell, dejected and rejected, to her side.

"You have to understand," she attempted to explain. "I've been bricked up in my marriage for so long, I just wanted to taste what it was like to be free, to be normal. I *did* come here for you. Everything I told you last night *was* true, but when I got here . . . I felt like a fool to have even thought that you might feel the same way about me, and you had Cecily, and a life that looked already complete and perfect. I was reeling, trying to find my feet, trying to work out who I was, if I wasn't married to Richard. Ted was kind to me. I know that's hard to believe, but he was. He made me smile and laugh. He made me feel . . . human and . . . new. I told him right from the start that it was you I loved, and I'm sure that when he's had a chance to calm down and cool off, he'll tell the truth."

"And so do you always have sex with everyone who is kind to you?" Frasier asked her stiffly. "Are you really that pathetic?"

"I didn't sleep with him!" Rose said, finding her full voice at last, physically hurting from Frasier's cruel words as they fell home, sharp end first. "But, you know what, I wish I had, I really do. Because I am *sick* of men telling me what I can and can't do, what I can and can't think or feel. And of treating me like I'm just some . . . some possession to be boxed up and put on a shelf, and to stay there until I'm wanted." Rose found herself marching up to him, her face in his, so overtaken was she by a sense of injustice and fury. "Seven *years* I waited for you, Frasier. Seven years, and you *never* came back. And I *never* stopped loving you, not for one second, not even when much worse was happening to me than being kissed by some boy." Rose had to pause to catch her breath, tasting the salt of her own tears on her tongue. "And even then, even where the chances of finding you were so small, I still looked, I looked for you the *first* chance I got, the first *second*. Doesn't that count for anything with you? Or is all you can think about that, because I kissed another man, everything we said and shared last night is null and void? Because if that's true then I really have been in love with a fantasy all this time, and you are not the man I thought you were."

Frasier still could not look at her.

"I don't know how to feel," he said, his tone cold, remote. "Last night I was ready to give my whole life for you, to end it with Cecily, do my best to win over your father, and Maddie. I thought that what we had was special, unsullied. But now . . . now I don't know."

Rose stared at him in disbelief. "Frasier, I know I didn't behave very well, I know I didn't think things through. I rushed into something with Ted, but that doesn't change who I am, how I feel about you. At least not yet it hasn't."

Frasier shook his head. "Then I'm sorry, Rose," he said. "I'm not the man for you. It seems I am not the man I thought I was. I wanted to be strong for you, but this . . . I'm sorry."

Rose watched aghast as he walked out, leaving her alone, in the bare, sorry little annex, all her hopes and dreams dismantled in an instant. Completely dumbfounded, she sat on the edge of the bed where she and Ted had shared so many fevered kisses and tried very hard to make sense of it all.

It was true, that for a moment she thought something could happen with Ted. Even though she'd known in the pit of her stomach that the more she let him kiss her, the more complicated it would become. But when she had been in Frasier's arms last night, she had known for certain there was only one man for her. There had only ever been one man. One man who, after years of longing for her, had suddenly changed his mind.

If the way he feels about me is really so fragile, Rose thought, then Shona was right: all of this was an illusion, one that he was drawn into too, for a while. And now it's blown away into the thin air again.

"What are you doing, Mum?" Maddie asked her, wrinkling her nose as she came into the annex, which still smelt a little musty. "I don't like it in here, but I don't like it in there more. Jenny's cross for no reason and she's put all our bags outside the front door. I asked her why and she told me to ask you."

"Really?" Rose sighed, feeling suddenly a lot less at home in Millthwaite, her new beginning in tatters. Steadying herself, she did the only thing she could do, which was to pick herself up and carry on.

"Right, then, well, come on," she said, mustering a smile for Maddie. "Let's go and live with Granddad."

"I'm excited about living with Granddad," Maddie told her as they stopped in the hallway where Jenny was waiting, her arms crossed, an envelope, presumably containing Rose's bill, crumpled in one hand.

She offered it to Rose. "Your bill is in there. You can post payment through the door when you're ready. No need to knock."

"Or I could just pay you now?" Rose offered, beginning to reach for her bag. "If you'd just give me a minute to sort out the cash—"

"I'd rather you just went," Jenny said, thrusting the envelope into Rose's reluctant hand.

"Goodbye, Jenny," Rose said, sighing. "You've been a good friend to me. I hope that soon you realize that I haven't done anything nearly as bad as you think I have."

Jenny ignored her as Rose took the envelope and went outside to find her bags slung on the ground, her carefully rewrapped painting lying in the street for anyone to trample on. With a heavy heart, Rose carefully picked the bundle up and laid it on the backseat of the car.

"Why is everyone in such a bad mood, Mum?" Maddie asked her, as she climbed into the back of the car alongside the painting. "What's happened? This morning you were humming and Jenny was cheerful, and now Frasier has gone off without saying goodbye, Ted kicked a chair on his way out, and Jenny won't look at me. Have I done something wrong again without realizing? Have I said something I shouldn't?"

"No!" Rose said, completely unprepared for the possibility that Maddie might think all this sudden bad feeling had something to do with her. "No, darling, no. It's just me. It's all me. I've done something stupid and managed to upset everyone who I thought were our friends. I'm sorry. It's all my fault, again. I haven't been a very good mummy, have I?"

"I think you have been fine," Maddie said, sincerely enough to bring a tear to Rose's eyes.

Suddenly feeling drained, Rose sat on the edge of the backseat next to her daughter.

"Don't worry," Maddie said, clapping her on the back and rubbing her shoulder. "I do that all the time: fall out with people when I don't mean to. It hurts for a bit when people don't talk to you and stop liking you, but if you act like it doesn't matter and pretend you don't care, they leave you alone after a bit, and then at least you can pretend that you are OK even if that's not how you feel inside."

Rose rested her palm against Maddie's cheek, stunned by the revelation that suddenly put her troubles into stark perspective. "Is that what it was like for you at school?" she asked. Maddie had never said anything about what life was like for her before, never in so much detail, at least.

"Yes," Maddie said, matter-of-factly with a small shrug. "I annoy people, I always do. I am really unlikable, I just am. I don't even have to try. Sometimes I think there is no point in starting to be friends with people because they will only go off me eventually. So a lot of the time I don't bother."

"Oh, Maddie," Rose said. "I had no idea that you felt that way, because it's not true, you are a lovely person."

"Don't worry, Mum," Maddie said. "I don't mind, and anyway we live here now. And I feel different here. I feel . . . nicer. I'm sure it will be fine when I start school again, and whatever you've done to upset everyone we know, just pretend that you don't care. Eventually you will stop caring for real and they'll get bored and leave you alone."

"That's good advice," Rose said.

"And we've always got Granddad," Maddie said. "That's what I like about him the most. He likes us even though we are very unlikable."

Feeling closer to her daughter in that moment than she ever had before, Rose climbed into the front of the car, knowing that now she needed to begin again from scratch to rebuild what she had thought she was already halfway to rebuilding. Somehow, although she was sure the hurt and disappointment would come crashing in later, it didn't matter as much as she had feared, just at that moment. Now for the first time in her life she understood what it felt like to be her daughter, and that insight was priceless. *And* she was going home to her father.

Above and beyond anything else, she had a place to call home.

Chapter Sixteen

Maddie scrambled out of the car as soon as it came to a stop, racing to the barn first and, finding it locked once again, back to the cottage. Rose smiled as she watched Maddie, as happy as she had ever seen her, her thick hair flying behind her, her feet barely touching the ground in her hurry to be the first to announce that they were home. Taking some of their luggage out of the boot, Rose paused for a second, allowing herself a moment to breathe in the air, admire the scenery around her, knowing with a small sense of pleasure that soon the majesty and wonder of the mountains would become commonplace to her, just like every familiar scene should.

Maddie had left the front door swinging on its creaky hinges, so Rose had only to shoulder it open, without the need to put her bags down. It was when she came across the scene in the living room that she dropped them, frozen for a moment by shock.

Maddie was sitting crossed-legged on the floor next to John, who was lying sprawled on his front, completely still. From what little Rose could see, his face lay smashed against the tiles, white and waxy. There was an acrid smell of urine in the air, and Rose knew with a dark, grim certainty that whatever was wrong, it was far more than arthritis.

"He's dead," Maddie said, looking up at her, clearly in shock. "He's not breathing."

"Yes, he is," Rose insisted, suddenly galvanized from shock into action. There was a small pool of vomit by his head, which meant that it was a good thing he had collapsed on his front, Rose thought as she rolled him onto his side, into the recovery position. Frantically she tried feeling for a pulse and then, realizing she was panicking too much to be able to concentrate, she rested her head against his chest and waited. After what seemed like an age, his ribs creaked, rose and fell beneath her head.

"He's breathing," Rose said, shaking him quite firmly by the shoulder, just the way she had used to with her mother. "Dad! Wake up!"

Unable to rouse him, Rose reached for a dusty cushion from the chair and put it under his head, rolling up a blanket that was strewn on the sofa and propping it against him to stop him from slipping onto his back.

"Maddie, it will be OK," Rose told her daughter, who sat perfectly still in her original position, quiet and contained, her eyes big with fear. But she wasn't about to panic—Rose knew that. Maddie had lived long enough with fear, even if she wasn't entirely aware of it, to know that panicking didn't help.

Taking her phone, Rose touched John's forehead, checking for a temperature and finding him cold as she dialed 999. It was a brief call, in which she explained, as calmly as she could, the symptoms and, having sent Maddie to fetch them, read out the names of the pills that were stacked by John's bed. None of it felt real, and as the dispatcher told Rose that an air ambulance was on its way and would be with them in minutes, Rose felt utterly detached, separated from what was happening just as she had on the day she found out about her mother. Only this wasn't happening now, she told herself. No one was dying now.

Seeing her opportunity to get her away from the scene that she was so afraid would turn to one of loss, Rose sent Maddie to the yard to keep an eye out for a helicopter. Then she dialed Frasier's number, unsurprised when it went straight to voice mail.

"Frasier," she said as calmly as she could, determined not to let him hear the tears and panic that threatened in her voice behind the false façade of calm, "John's collapsed again. It's worse this time. He's not conscious. I've called an ambulance. Please, please, for Dad's sake, please come. He needs you. We both do."

Hanging up and without a second thought, Rose called Tilda next, thankful that she'd decided to put the number in her phone after all.

"Hello, Tilda's Things?" Tilda answered the phone breezily, happily unaware of the words she was about to hear.

"It's Dad," Rose said, her voice breaking into sobs at last. "I've called an ambulance. Tilda, it doesn't look good. I think . . . I think he's dying."

"I'm coming," Tilda said, hanging up the phone.

Tilda's car swept into the yard, stopping on its far side, as Rose watched her father, his face now obscured by an oxygen mask, being loaded into the helicopter, its blades making a tremendous noise as they swooped round.

"We can't take you with us," a young woman paramedic told Rose, shouting to make herself heard over the din. "We're taking him to Furness General. They've got all the right care there to see what the trouble is. We'll be there in minutes, so you don't need to worry, OK?"

"OK," Rose said, dumbfounded, as Tilda, her arms covering her head against the whirlwind the blades created, jogged as best as she could to her side.

"He's got cancer," she told the paramedic, out of breath, in such a hurry to deliver the vital information that she had clearly forgotten it was the first time that Rose was hearing the news about her father's condition. "Liver, bowels, pancreas. He's had treatment—chemo- and radiotherapy, and a bowel reconstruction."

"Right," the paramedic said, her eyes widening as she took the information in. "Thank you. When you arrive, ask at the main desk. They'll tell you where to go."

She ran back to the helicopter, and Maddie clung to Rose's legs, cowering, as the aircraft lifted into the air, buffeting them with powerful winds. Rose did not move from the spot she was standing in until she could no longer see it. Then she turned to Tilda.

"Will you drive?" she asked her. "I'm not sure I could concentrate."

Tilda nodded. "Rose, listen—" Tilda began to attempt to explain, her face ashen with worry.

"No." Rose shook her head, indicating Maddie, who was listening intently to every word with wide, scared eyes. "Don't say anything now."

Rose smiled at her daughter, hoping to look reassuring. "Maddie, I'm taking you back to Jenny's, because I don't know how long I'm going to be with Granddad, so I think it would be best if you stayed there tonight."

"But Jenny doesn't like us anymore," Maddie protested anxiously. "I don't mind waiting. I'll be fine. I'll bring my sketchpad."

"Jenny is cross with *me*," Rose said, gently firm, "not you. Come on now, Maddie. We don't have time to argue. Please do as I ask."

Reluctantly, Maddie nodded, climbing into the back of the car as Rose picked up her bag of things.

"Do you have a key?" she asked Tilda, realizing she had no way of locking the cottage.

Tilda shook her head. "No, John never locks it. I'm not sure he even knows where the key is."

"Well, then," Rose said, looking at the rough, shabby door, "we'll leave it just exactly as it always is for when he comes home."

It had been an awkward moment, the persistent ringing of the doorbell, and having to put her foot between the door and the frame to stop Jenny from slamming it in her face.

"Jenny," Rose had said urgently, all too aware that Maddie was watching her intently from the car, "please, just listen. Dad's collapsed and an air ambulance came. He's got cancer. I've only just found out. Please, please take Maddie. I don't know when I'll be back and I've got no one else to ask. Please. None of this is Maddie's fault. Don't make her suffer because I've been an idiot."

Jenny had opened the door at once, her features taut but not completely unkind.

"Of course I'll take her," she said. Rose beckoned for Maddie to come out of the car, which Maddie did reluctantly, eyeing Jenny with a good deal of mistrust.

"Are you going to be unkind to me?" she asked Jenny.

"No, dear, of course not," Jenny said, upset by Maddie's wariness.

"Thank you," Rose said, hugging Maddie briefly to her chest as she looked at Jenny. "I'll pay for another night of board, of course."

"No need to do that," Jenny said stiffly. "You're a local now."

"Jenny, you were so good to me," Rose said sincerely,

"when I had no one else. I never did anything to deliberately hurt you or your family, I promise you."

Jenny nodded, sucking in her bottom lip. "Well, I dare say you didn't," she said. "But Ted is my boy, and I know him. I know he feels things more deeply than he'll ever let on. I expect things will calm down. Go and be with your dad, and, Rose, I hope it's not too bad, lass."

Grateful for that one word of affection, Rose gave Maddie another kiss goodbye and ran back to the car, pulling on her seat belt as Tilda drove away.

"Now, you can talk," Rose said to Tilda as soon as they were out. "Tell me everything."

"He was ill for a long time, of course," Tilda began slowly, telling a story that she wished she didn't know by heart. "Not that he would ever admit to it, or even go to a doctor. Not until the pain got so bad he couldn't stand it. Frasier took him the first time. Marched him into the surgery like a naughty schoolboy, he was *so* furious." Tilda smiled faintly at the memory, her eyes on the ever-twisting road as Rose watched. "Frasier was the only one that could make him go, though. Thank God he did."

"And they diagnosed it straightaway?" Rose asked, feeling strangely detached from the devastating news, aware that news like that, news that cannot be easily recovered from, takes a very long time to filter through the body's defenses and hit home. It had been the same when they told her they'd found her mum's body. It had been days—days of people being kind to her, speaking in hushed tones and bringing her hot meals in oven-warmed dishes—before any of it sunk in. Experienced in loss, Rose knew that she had to use the period of numbness to learn what she could, to try to understand why her father had never mentioned to her that he was dying.

"Well, I think the doctor knew, yes. But there were tests. Lots of tests, biopsies. I went with him. Frasier and I both did when the consultant gave him the news. Bowel cancer, serious, and it had spread to the liver and beyond. They said that whatever they did now it was about prolonging his life, not curing him. I half expected John to say don't bother, it's fine, I'll just die, but he didn't."

Tilda didn't take her eyes off the road, but Rose could tell by the tension in her throat and the thickness in her voice that she was fighting off tears.

"Why not?" Rose asked her. "For you?"

"For you," Tilda said simply. "John had long since given up any hope of seeing you again. In fact, after the cancer he told me it was the last thing he wanted: to see you, to find you again, only to lose you so soon. But for the last few years all the work he's been doing, it's been for you. All the money, almost all of it, has gone into a trust fund for you. He knew money didn't make up for the father that he failed to be, but he said it made him feel a little better, knowing that after he'd gone, you'd realize that he had thought about you, had missed you. Even if you never touched the money or gave it away, he didn't care. Just as long as you knew. So when they told him that he only had a couple of years at best, with surgery, radiotherapy, chemo, drugs, he took it. He wanted to make as much money as he could for you."

"Christ," Rose said quietly, "it's so unfair. Why now? Why now, after everything I've been through, when I've only just found him?"

"At least you have found him," Tilda said. "Even if it's for a short time, it's better than no time at all. Keep thinking that. And, well, I'll bet you any money you like he's sitting up in bed complaining when we get there."

• • •

But after a frustrating hour of driving and several minutes of trying to find somewhere to park, not to mention tracking down exactly where John was, Tilda was proved wrong. John had been given a private side room, and his face was still covered with an oxygen mask. A nurse took them to his side, telling them he hadn't been conscious since they arrived, but that a doctor would be with them as soon as possible to let them know what was going on.

Rose sat down on the odd pink plastic chair by his bedside and looked at him. He looked so frail, so weak. As if the force of nature that made him who he was had all but evaporated, leaving just a shell behind.

"I'll get us some tea," Tilda said, putting a hand on Rose's shoulder. "Try not to worry, Rose. Your dad's been down before. And almost out too, but if I know him at all I know he won't give up fighting for every second more that he can squeeze out of life, and he'll do that for you and Maddie. I promise you."

Rose nodded. "Thank you," she said quietly, adding with just as much calm measure, "I'm glad you're here."

"Oh, Rose, dear," Tilda said, patting her once again on the shoulder and then rubbing it briefly, "I'm glad that *you* are here."

They were standing in the corridor outside John's room.

"His main problem right now," said the doctor, who looked to Rose like he should still be at school and not managing the life and death of someone that she loved, "is that he's dehydrated and malnourished. I think he's probably been in pain for a long while, not eating properly. From our initial examination we suspect an obstruction in the bowel, but I'm reluctant to investigate further until we've got his stats back up.

We'll know more tomorrow, but for now you should probably go home, rest."

"If it's a bowel obstruction," Rose asked him, her face drawn and pale, "what then, another op?"

"I don't know," the doctor admitted reluctantly. "We need his notes from Leeds. We need to see what has already been done, if surgery is the way to go or . . . if a more palliative approach is required."

"Oh God," Rose sobbed, burying her head in her hands, making the young doctor shift awkwardly from one foot to the other and look longingly for an escape.

"How am I going to explain this to Maddie?" she asked Tilda, turning to gaze at her father through the slats of the blind at the window of his room, where he was lying silent and still, oblivious to everything that was going on around him.

Wake up, Dad, she pleaded silently. Please, please, wake up. Don't give up now.

For the first few seconds after waking, it took Rose a little while to work out where she was. There was dim gray light filtering in through the thin hospital curtains and the rhythmic beat of the heart monitor, but still it took awhile for the realization to dawn on her that she had spent the night in hospital. When it did, the worry that had had a continuous grip on her heart since yesterday squeezed hard again.

Forcing her stiff neck into an upright position, she winced as pain shot down into her shoulder. She remembered that she'd decided to stay the night by John's bedside, waiting for him to come round. It had been John squeezing her fingers that had roused her.

"Bloody hospital," John said, his mouth dry. "Why am I here?"

"Here." Rose tried to hide her relief as she picked up a beaker of water from the bedside table and held it to his lips. "I imagine you're here because you've been doing your level best to ignore that terminal cancer you've got."

John directed his gaze upwards, his dark sunken eyes studying the ceiling tiles for some moments, Rose sitting paralyzed at his side, finding it impossible to express all the emotion that had built up in her, suspecting that a crying, wailing daughter would be the last thing he would want.

"I don't want to be here," John said eventually. "Want to go home. I have work to do."

"Dad." Rose leant on the bed, resting her forehead on his hand for a moment. "Why didn't you tell me?"

"No time," John rasped. "You've only just got here. I suppose this is my just deserts. To lose you now."

"You're not going to die," Rose told him emphatically, even though she didn't know it was true. "Well, not yet, anyway. Not for a very long time. The doctor seemed to think you've been ignoring symptoms. I bet they'll patch you up and we can still do what we planned. Live together at Storm Cottage, be a family."

"Perhaps," John said wearily, "perhaps."

"Don't leave me, Dad," Rose begged him desperately, her determination to contain her emotions crumbling away. "Please, not again."

"I'll try my best," John said. "Rose . . . you know how sorry I am, don't you?"

"You don't have to say it again." Rose shook her head, turning her face away from him.

"I do, not for you, for me. I need to say I am sorry over and over again as many times as I can. Please allow that. Allow me to ease my conscience just a little."

"Morning!" A large and altogether too cheerful male nurse

bustled into the room, trampling over the moment before Rose could say anything in reply.

"Look who's up and about, then?" he said brightly to John. "You're nil by mouth till the doctor's seen you, but I can bring you a cuppa if you like, love?" he said, looking at Rose, who nodded gratefully.

"I will be leaving shortly," John told the nurse, waving his hand at the door. "If you could bring me the form . . ."

"Dad!" Rose shook her head. "No, you will not. You will not leave. You will see what you can do to stay with me for as long as possible."

"She's right, you know," the nurse said, still sounding breezy. "These last few weeks you'll have with your loved ones are the ones that will mean the most. Don't be in a hurry to give up whatever time you can get."

John sighed, leaning his head back against the pillow. "Very well."

"Now stay there. I'm going to phone Maddie, tell her how you are," Rose said.

"Don't tell her about . . . " John said anxiously.

"I won't, not yet," Rose replied, wondering how she was going to explain any of this to her daughter. "Not until we know more. But Maddie isn't like most children. The more she knows the less she worries. So when we know something, then I'll talk to her. Now stay put."

"It's not like I'm about to abseil out the window," John said.

"How is he?" Frasier's voice stopped Rose dead in her tracks as she walked down the hospital corridor. Slowly she turned round to set eyes on him, standing a few feet away from her, his face etched with concern. Forcing herself to stay put, and not run to him and beg him to put his arms around her, which is what she wanted most in all the world, Rose drew her shoulders back and lifted her chin just a little.

You are not that woman anymore, Rose reminded herself in her father's voice. You don't need a man to look after you, not even Frasier. You can and you will stand alone.

"They don't really know yet," she said, the exhaustion sounding in her voice. "I've only just found out about the cancer. I'm not sure—no one seems to be—what this latest collapse means . . ." She stopped talking as her voice came dangerously close to breaking.

"Rose," Frasier kept his distance, running his fingers through his fair hair, "I'm sorry that I knew and didn't tell you. Your father really didn't want you to know. He didn't want you to feel that you had to stay, had to forgive him."

"I know." Rose nodded wearily, too exhausted to be angry. "I understand that. I can't say I wouldn't rather have known. But I understand why you did what you did."

"Thank you," Frasier said, carefully mannered, distant again. More of a stranger to her in that moment than he had been all those years ago on the first morning they had met.

"Rose?" The nurse who had offered her tea called her name. "The doctor's ready to talk to you and your dad now."

It was a long and silent drive back to Storm Cottage, and Rose would rather have done it with Tilda, but she had had to leave at some point late in the night, to make arrangements for her shop today. So it was Frasier who volunteered to take her back home, so she'd have a night to prepare for John's return.

"So he's coming home," Frasier said, as he opened the front door of the cottage for Rose, switching on all the lights. "That's good news."

"He's coming home to die," Rose said bleakly as she walked into the small still room, which seemed so empty without him in it. "Inoperable, that's what they said. Untreatable now. All they can do is give him pain relief and the best quality of life possible. I'm losing him all over again."

She leant against the kitchen table, trying desperately to stop her shoulders from shaking, longing to be touched, comforted. But the only other person there stayed exactly where he was.

"I know it must seem that way," Frasier said, clearly struggling to know what to say now that their relationship had been reestablished once again, "but try to think of it as time, precious time to—"

"Frasier," Rose cut across him, exhausted, mustering only the will to turn and face him. "Please, don't try to tell me to think of this time we have together as a gift. It isn't a gift, it's a punishment, it's a cruel trick, but it's *not* a gift. I was foolish enough to think I'd found a new start in life, a place to be happy, people to be happy with, but I was wrong, wasn't I?"

"No," Frasier insisted. "Rose, I . . . got swept up in the moment, between you and me. I suppose I wanted to believe the fairy tale as much as you did. And that was wrong. I shouldn't have done that to you, and I shouldn't have blamed you for what happened with Ted—"

"Nothing happened with me and Ted!" Rose exclaimed, a brief burst of anger propelling her forward a few steps.

"It doesn't matter anyway," Frasier said, backing away. "It's none of my business. I was stupid to let myself get carried away, to get involved with you when I knew in my heart that you weren't ready. You've been through so much, you have so much yet to face."

"Isn't it up to me to decide what I can cope with?" Rose asked him tightly. "This isn't about me, Frasier, it's about you, changing your mind in the cold light of day."

Frasier did not contradict her. "I think it was the painting, and seeing you again, and, oh, I don't know. I'm just an old romantic," he said, remorse on his face. "I'm sorry if I hurt you. But I want you to know that I am here for you and John. I will be your friend as long as you will have me."

Rose stared into his handsome face, desperate to slap him smartly around it. But she couldn't. There was no time to be self-indulgent. Now she had to think of John, and Maddie, whom she'd promised to pick up from Jenny's before bedtime.

"Come with me," she said, taking a bunch of keys from a drawer in the kitchen.

Frasier followed her to the barn, where she unlocked three padlocks until they came at last to John's room of private work.

"Dad needs something to focus on," she said, wavering at the last moment over what she was about to do. "Something to keep him going. His private work is in here. He doesn't want me to see this yet, so you go in. You look at it and see if it's good enough and if there is enough."

"Enough for what?" Frasier asked her.

"Enough to mount an exhibition," Rose said, "of the work that means the most to him and gives him his true identity as an artist. I want you to exhibit him in your gallery, show the world what a truly great painter he is, at last. I want you to give him back his self-respect."

"Right," Frasier said, looking at the closed door uncertainly. "He would rip my head off if he knew what I was doing."

"Well," Rose said, finding the ghost of a smile, "there's always a bright side."

It seemed like an age that Rose was waiting in the vast empty middle room, staring up at the shafts of late afternoon sun that streamed in through the skylights, as she watched the particles of dust that danced and spun in its wake. Then at last she heard Frasier emerge from the room behind her, pulling the door closed and shutting the padlock firmly.

"No?" Rose asked him.

Frasier was silent for a moment, and then quite without warning he scooped her up in his arms and twirled her around twice, before setting her, a little unsteadily, back on her feet.

"Sorry," he said, realizing too late how inappropriate he'd been. "I just had to—"

"Um, just tell me," Rose said, angered once again by the way he was with her.

"Brilliant," Frasier said simply, happily. "Brilliant, epic, personal, emotional, ground-breaking, cutting edge, true, true works of genius. It will be the greatest exhibition that I have ever mounted, and I'm going to make sure that the whole world is there to see it."

"Good," Rose said. "That is wonderful. Now we just have to work out a way to break it to Dad."

Chapter Seventeen

It had been three days since John had been allowed home, and when he arrived, chauffeured by Frasier, his house was considerably different from when he'd left it. The study, which was to have been Rose's room for the time being, had been cleaned from top to bottom, his bed had been brought down, and a commode sat discreetly in the corner, which Rose knew that John would hate, so she asked Tilda to explain it to him so that he wouldn't have to think he was a burden to Rose. Rose had ordered a new bed, which had been delivered and installed in her father's bedroom, and she and Tilda had spent quite some time transferring all of his belongings, the piles of books and magazines, the photos, pictures and prints that he surrounded himself with, down from the bedroom to the study. It wasn't exactly that they had developed a friendship, or any particular warmth between the two of them, it was more that they had a common purpose: to make John's last weeks with them as comfortable and as peaceful as possible. No, there was no growth of affection between Rose and Tilda, more just an absence of animosity, which both of them seemed content to live with for now.

The doctors had made it quite clear that there was no further treatment now available to John, that all they could do for him was offer him pain relief and therapy to make his life as comfortable as possible. They'd removed the obstruction in his bowel while he'd been in hospital, and Rose was pleased to see that helped ease the constant expression of pain that seemed engraved on his face. He had some color again and had looked more at ease when she'd gone to see him the previous night to explain that she'd moved the rooms and done her best to make everything just as she thought he would like it.

"I rather thought I'd get to say when I decided I couldn't make the stairs," John said a little churlishly. "But thank you, I know you are trying to help. What helps me the most is knowing that you will be there. It's more than I deserve."

What neither Frasier nor Rose had mentioned to him was their plan to exhibit his private work. Frasier said there were things he had to get in place first. He'd have to clear the gallery of its planned events for the next couple of months, which meant placating other painters and mobilizing an army of PR and marketing executives. They couldn't risk waiting until there was a window in the schedule or for the usual lead time of publicizing an event like this, but neither could they afford to open without as much fanfare as possible. Between them, Rose and Frasier had decided, late one night, over a glass of wine in the kitchen at Storm Cottage, that they would tell John only when most of the work had already been done.

Tensions had eased considerably between Rose and Frasier, his anger at discovering her liaison with Ted now neatly tucked away behind his polite, concerned smile and friendly attentions. Not since the moment that Frasier had brought her back to Storm Cottage had either one of them mentioned the words they'd said, the promises they'd made to each other in those few idyllic hours that night. The hope that there had been, the happiness—it was as if none of it had ever happened, as if Frasier had cut those twenty-four hours out of his life without a second thought, his life with Cecily, and the gallery, and worrying about John closing over that one night and the following stormy morning with cool, calm waters.

Whenever Rose had had a second to think about herself since then she even questioned whether any of it had ever happened, or if it was just a figment of her fevered imagination, a dream so vivid, so longed for, that she had believed it to be real. In any case, it seemed like the best policy was simply to leave things as they were. If indeed she had been within touching distance of a life with Frasier, then the moment had passed, and perhaps it had less to do with her misdemeanor and much more to do with his waking up with cold feet and looking for a way to back out.

After some wrangling, she decided finally that she had to tell Maddie what was happening before John arrived home. It seemed too unfair not to, to expect the child to be robbed quite suddenly of someone she had come to care about, without a moment to prepare. Rose had been a lot older than Maddie when her mother had died, but still she remembered how she would have given anything to know that Marian was playing out her last days. To know, to savor every last moment with her, and to not waste a second on boredom or bad feeling. Perhaps it would be too much for Maddie to bear, but Rose had come to realize over the last few weeks that her daughter was really a remarkable person, coping with a world that must seem almost impossible to live in with a stoicism beyond her years.

"Granddad's coming home," Rose said to Maddie, who'd been making him an excessively colorful welcome home card earlier that morning. "Frasier and Tilda have gone to collect him. Want to help me make him some soup?"

"Yes!" Maddie said, jumping up, her hands smothered in

poster paint. "And then Granddad and I can get back to work again, and you can sort me out a school, and I can practice being good at friends."

"I'm not sure he'll be up to working, not in the barn," Rose said. "He's had an operation, so he's still very sore and he's very, very sick, Maddie."

"I know," Maddie said. "Ambulances don't come for you unless you are very, very sick."

"The thing is," Rose said, handing Maddie some potatoes to peel, with no idea how to phrase what she needed to say, other than just saying it. "The thing is, Granddad won't ever get better."

"Well, he is old," Maddie said. "Old people are slower."

"No, I mean, he's not ever going to be like he was before the ambulance came. He's very ill, and . . . I thought you should know, you should be ready when he . . . because quite soon he . . ."

Rose had been unable to finish the sentence, sobs constricting her throat and tears streaming down her cheeks. Turning away from Maddie, she tried to hide her own grief, to keep it in check until there was time for it, but she failed.

"Granddad is going to die," Maddie stated, rubbing the palm of her hand across Rose's back. "How soon?"

"Soon," Rose said. "We don't know exactly. Hopefully he will have a few weeks, months even. I'm sorry, I shouldn't have told you."

"It's OK," Maddie said quite calmly, picking up the potato peeler and setting about skinning the potatoes. She hadn't spoken more than two words about it to Rose since, certainly not about how she felt, and Rose worried that she'd done the wrong thing in telling her, but when John arrived back, leaning heavily on Frasier, Maddie had gone directly to him and put her arms around his waist.

"I'm sorry about you dying, Granddad," she said. "I love you."

"Me too," John said, masking his surprise with a gruff cough. "Me too."

"Still," Maddie said, taking his hand and holding it as Frasier helped him over to his armchair, "we've got weeks and weeks, months even, so let's not think about it. OK?"

"OK," John said, as he settled painfully into the chair and took the still wet card that Maddie handed him, a portrait of him, painting in his barn, looking exactly as grim and gruff as he did when he worked.

"It says get well soon," Maddie said apologetically. "I didn't know you were going to die when I made it."

"It's lovely," John said, repressing a grim smile as he looked at his granddaughter. "Just like you."

"Thanks," Maddie said. "I've made you some soup too. Mum helped, slightly."

Frasier and Tilda stayed, spooning the soup out of bowls, seated around John in his armchair. John ate very little, and at one point almost spilt what was left in his lap, as he nodded off, listening to Frasier talking about the value of exhibiting new work and how it enriched an artist's life and reputation.

"Granddad!" Maddie's voice roused him, as she saved the bowl from tilting too far on his tray and lifted it off his lap.

"I think perhaps I'd better go to bed," John said, leaning his head against the back of the chair. "It's these pills they've given me, I expect. I'll give it a day or two and then see how I get on without them."

"Dad, you can't just stop taking them," Rose said.

"She's right," Tilda said anxiously. "You can't just ignore the doctors, John."

"I can do what I bloody like. It's my body," John snapped. "I know I'd rather spend what time I've got left awake and not snoring my head off."

"Granddad," Maddie said, biting her lip, "if you go to sleep, you will wake up, won't you?"

"I will do my best," John promised her as Frasier helped him to his feet.

"I'll watch you, then," Maddie said. "Poke you if you stop breathing or anything."

"Maddie," John said gently, resting his palm on the top of her head, "what happened to not thinking about it?"

"I'm not thinking about it," Maddie said. "I'm just being vigilant."

"Here." John reached into his pocket and pulled out a key. "You can have the barn as your studio now. I'm giving it to you. You go over there now and start working for both of us. That will be the best way to make sure I wake up again. I'll be worrying about the mess you'll be making in my barn too much not to."

"OK!" Maddie said with delight, racing off at top speed without even pausing to close the cottage door behind her.

"I'm not really sure a seven-year-old should be given free rein over an entire barn," Rose said anxiously, caught between her maternal worry and the look of joy on Maddie's face.

"Nonsense," John said, as he made his way into the bedroom with Frasier's assistance. "Children are too coddled these days. Besides, running riot in a barn is better than sitting vigil over my deathbed, don't you agree?"

"I really thought I was doing the right thing, telling her," Rose said, making John comfortable as Frasier and Tilda discreetly left the room.

"And so do I. Children deserve honesty and respect. Another lesson I've learnt too late." He leant back on the pillow, gazing out of the window to a view of almost solid rock, broken up only here and there with patches of growth. "Strikes me that child's grown up in a house so full of lies and artifice she's hungry for truth, even if it is difficult. She's learnt to shut herself away, disconnect herself from the world, like you have. Like I did. And it's partly my fault she's lived through what she has and believed it to be normal. I want you to protect her, Rose, but don't lie to her. Don't let her be shut away from the world like we were. There is too much joy in it to be missed. And that is the last thing I wanted for either of you."

"Do you think I've ruined her?" Rose asked him. "I let her live that way. I believed she was immune to it all, because everything that happened, happened out of sight. It's only since we got here, since I've seen her stop living constantly on the edge of her seat, that I've realized she went through it just as much as I did. I should have left so much earlier, the day she was born, long before she was born. Why didn't I? Why wasn't I strong enough?"

"I don't think you should dwell on that," John said, studying her face. "Maddie's damaged, yes, and so are you. But you have a lifetime to repair that damage, and that's what you need to focus on now. That's what I need to know that you will be focusing on after I'm gone."

Rose nodded. "I promise," she said.

"I had hoped to die looking at the mountain peak," he said drowsily, returning his gaze to the window. "Not its grubby roots."

"I'm sorry," Rose said.

"Don't be." John smiled at her, reaching for her hand. "I can't manage the stairs all of a sudden and there it is. There's nothing to be done about it. Thank you for making this neglected old room as pleasant as you have."

Rose said nothing, sitting on the edge of the bed as she looked out the window at the wall of rock outside.

"Feeling trapped?" John asked her. "You know you don't have to stay, don't you? I don't expect you to. You are under no obligation."

"Yes," Rose said, "I do feel trapped, but not by you or your mountain. I'm just trying to come to terms with the life that I have, the one that closes doors as soon as it opens them. That's what I feel trapped by: my fate to only ever have who or what I want for the shortest of times. You, Mum, a happy marriage . . ." Frasier, she added silently.

"Don't say that," John said. "You have Maddie, and she is quite the most interesting child I've ever met. And although your mother is gone, and I soon will be, you will always have us. I wonder if I'll see her again, afterwards. I do hope so. I would very much like to apologize to her for being such an arse."

"I don't think you'll have to," Rose said. "Mum forgave you long before she died. It was her own frailties that she never let up on."

"Then I'll apologize for that," John said drowsily, his eyes fluttering. "I never met a finer woman than your mother. If I could have just loved her enough then I would have been a very happy man."

He breathed out a long rattling breath as he drifted into sleep, and Rose waited for his chest to rise and fall again twice before she felt able to get up and go back to the living room.

Tilda was gone. Only Frasier remained, standing by the kitchen sink, looking out the window, the afternoon sunshine lighting up his face with golden promise, making him look very young, just exactly as he had the first time Rose had met him. She stood for a moment watching him, wishing she was free to go to him, touch his cheek and kiss him, just as she longed to do. Perhaps her feelings for him had been nothing more than pipe dreams when she arrived, but now, oddly perhaps, since he'd withdrawn romantically she found she still loved him so much it ached and pulsated in every limb, every fiber of her body.

"Hello," she said for want of anything better to say and needing to make her presence known somehow.

"Hello." Frasier turned to her and smiled. "Tilda went. She said to call her if you needed anything. I think she finds this all rather hard, keeping her distance, being stalwart. She's trying awfully hard to do the right thing by you."

"I know," Rose said. "I know I need to do the same for her, and I will."

"I told her about the exhibition," Frasier went on. "She thinks it's a great idea and on that front I have cleared the schedule and got the PR people ready. So now we need to talk to your father, to get him to allow me to remove the work, photograph it, frame it, hang it, get it ready to be discovered." He hesitated, smiling ruefully. "I was thinking that perhaps that part would come better from you?"

"Me?" Rose said, feeling daunted by the prospect. "I'm not sure. I promised Dad I wouldn't look at his work before he was ready to show it to me. And I haven't broken that promise yet. I think it should come from you."

"Or how about both of us," Frasier said warmly, "presenting a united front. And we can recruit Maddie too. He's bound to be less angry with her as a buffer."

Rose grinned. "He'd be glad to know that we are still intimidated by him."

"I always will be," Frasier said fondly. "I've never met another man like him."

The two of them stood there in the late afternoon sunshine, smiling at each other for a moment longer, sensing the gulf of years stretching between them, now seemingly impossible to bridge.

"I should go," Frasier said. "I've got this dinner."

"Cecily will be waiting," Rose added.

"No." Frasier hesitated. "I ended things with Cecily. It wasn't right to string her along. I didn't love her, not as much as a man should love a woman. And judging by her reaction, I don't think she loved me more than life itself either. If anything, she was almost relieved."

"Oh," Rose said, uncertain how to react. "It's just I thought after . . . what happened."

There was a difficult silence, neither of them knowing quite what to say next.

"I'll be down tomorrow," Frasier said finally. "I will be here every single day that I can be for your father, for as long as it takes."

After a moment, Frasier came to her and kissed her lightly on the cheek. "Goodbye, Rose."

Rose waited for his car to disappear round the track before she let herself cry.

At some point after Frasier left, she must have fallen asleep, if only for a few minutes, sitting in her father's chair, the sunshine dappling on her cheek. Rose woke up with a start, certain she had forgotten something and, more than that, that something was terribly wrong. Sitting up abruptly, she felt her heart pounding fiercely in her chest, gripped by an instinctive fear that she knew was real.

Her first instinct was to go to John's room, where, after a moment's inspection, she reassured herself he was just still sleeping, his chest rising and falling steadily. And then she heard it, just a snatch of voice carried by a breeze through the open window. It was Maddie's voice, and although Rose heard it for only a second she was certain that Maddie sounded afraid.

Remembering that her daughter had been in the barn alone for over an hour, Rose panicked, racing toward the building, but Maddie was nowhere to be seen. The open door, swinging on its hinges in the increasingly brisk wind, slammed shut in a series of nerve-shattering bangs. Turning wildly on her heel, Rose scanned the empty yard, whipping round frantically to study the hillside for any sign of Maddie in her brightly spotted sundress, afraid that the little girl had taken her newfound freedom to heart and gone by herself for a walk.

"No!" Rose gasped. Maddie's shout came from inside the barn, but not from the first room; that had been empty. She must be in the room where John dried his work. Her heart in her mouth, Rose rushed back, pausing for a fraction to see the padlock that normally kept the door locked had been forced open, but the door was pulled shut.

Sick with fear, Rose flung the door open to see her daughter staring defiantly up at her father, who was standing in front of her, his hands on her shoulders. He was speaking, but so quietly Rose didn't catch a word of it before he looked up and saw her. He turned towards her smiling, one hand still possessively gripping Maddie.

Rose took a ragged breath, her body urging her to run as fast as she could, her heart keeping her rooted to the spot where, a meter away, she was certain her daughter was in danger. Richard had finally found them, and he was very, very angry.

She stood for several seconds staring at him, the set of his shoulders, the incline of his head as he talked to Maddie, trying to decipher his mood as she had a thousand times before. To anyone who didn't know him the way Rose did, watching him now, he seemed completely relaxed, at ease.

But Rose knew better. She knew that no one could do a

better job of hiding away his rage behind a pleasant smile and a polite tone than her husband. Maddie, on the other hand, was harder to read. She looked calm, determined even, but her fists were tightly clenched, and although she was standing perfectly still, Rose could see that every sinew of the little girl was repelled and desperate to be away from her father's touch.

There was nothing for it, Rose realized, struggling to control the fear that gripped her. She could not run away; there was nowhere to hide. This was the moment when she had to face him. Now she would find out if she really had what it took to stand on her own two feet, to protect her daughter, to be the woman she needed to be finally to be free of him.

"Rose," Richard greeted her, no doubt seeing the look on Maddie's face as she approached. "I found our daughter alone and unattended in a barn, a building literally chock-full of death traps. Not the most responsible of parenting, if you don't mind my saying. Not that I'm in the least bit surprised. By the look of what you've done to your hair you really have lost it this time. You look ridiculous."

"Why did you break into this room?" Rose asked him, keeping her gaze locked on him, afraid that if she stopped looking at him, even for one second, something might happen that she couldn't prevent.

"I didn't," said Richard, while Maddie's flinch as the tips of his fingers whitened on her bare shoulder revealed the real truth. "The door was already open."

Why did he come here and, instead of coming to find and confront her, take Maddie somewhere he thought no one would see and hear them? What dreadful way had he been planning to take his revenge on her?

"Maddie, come here," Rose said as calmly as she could, holding out her arms to her daughter, who took a step towards her but was prevented from coming farther by her father's hand.

"What are you doing?" Rose asked him as calmly as she was able, drawing on her years of practice of not letting him see she was afraid, even if he already knew it.

"I've missed my little girl," Richard said, his tone so cold, so devoid of any affection that Rose wondered if he'd ever loved their daughter at all, if all that too had been just another charade to add to his carefully constructed replica of the perfect family man. Her maternal instinct flaring fiercely, Rose went to Maddie and took her arm in one hand, the other detaching his hand from her shoulder with relative ease. Richard seemed amused by her efforts, but not intimidated.

Rose backed away towards the door, sheltering Maddie against her body, noticing the red fingerprints on her skin that would soon turn to bruises.

"What do you want, Richard?" she asked him.

"I'm rather surprised that you have to ask me that," he said, his smile icy. "You run away, for no reason, with *my* child, without telling me where you are or how she is. Am I expected just to give up without looking for you, when you know I love you both so much and that your place is at home with me?"

"I didn't run away for no reason." Rose forced herself to speak, despite feeling paralyzed by the fear that came from knowing what her husband had been, and was, capable of. The longer she kept him talking like this, the better chance she would have of finding a way out, of getting Maddie away. Rose knew that this polite conversation was a thin veneer, scarcely concealing the fury that simmered below, and if Richard was willing to intimidate his daughter to get his own way, there was no telling what else he would do. It seemed that her bid for freedom had eroded what little self-control he'd had. Now he felt justified in doing what he must to regain control, and Rose knew with heart-stopping certainty that he was waiting for his chance to crush her in whatever way he could. She also knew that there was a very real chance she might not be able to escape him.

Think of Maddie, she told herself, tensing every sinew of her body, refusing to allow herself to shake in front of him. Save Maddie.

"I left you, Richard, and you know perfectly well why," she said.

Richard's eyes narrowed almost imperceptibly, and then he smiled that awful smile so laden with menace that Rose knew only too well. It was her final warning.

"I've missed you too, Rose, I can't wait for the chance for us to get reacquainted," Richard said, walking slowly towards them.

"Maddie, go to Granddad," Rose said urgently, pushing her daughter towards the door, putting her body between the exit and Richard. "Go and tell him where I am."

"But . . ." Maddie hesitated by the door, torn between wanting to run and a reluctance to leave her mother.

"Go!" Rose told her, as steadily as she was able to, unable to muster a smile. "I will be fine." The last thing Rose wanted was to be parted from her daughter, but she could not use her as a human shield and they could not stay here in this stalemate forever. If Richard was going to strike, it was best that it was when Maddie wasn't there. Maddie took one last look at her mother and ran, the outer barn door slamming shut in the wind that raged outside, rattling the rafters and beams of the barn.

Rose turned back to Richard and braced herself for what was to come, her relief at getting Maddie out of immediate danger short-lived. The rational part of her mind told her this was her husband, and she'd been married to him for years; it wasn't as if he was going to kill her. But another, more primal part of her knew with awful certainty that something had broken in Richard, that what little restraint he'd had before was gone and now he was capable of anything.

"Shall we?" he said, gripping her arm the moment that Maddie left, dragging her farther inside the room and pushing the door shut again.

"Don't touch me," Rose said fiercely, shaking free of his grasp with some effort, feeling the imprints of his grip on her tender arm. She glared at him, gratified to see that her show of temper surprised him, not that it would do her much good. In one maneuver, he had her trapped inside the room and was blocking her way to the door.

"You don't get to touch me anymore, Richard," she said boldly. He wasn't used to her standing up to him, being anything but compliant and meek. Perhaps if she showed him how strong she had become he would back down. It was a faint hope, but the only thing Rose could think of at that moment.

"Don't I?" Richard said, watching her and seeming to take a great deal of pleasure in her predicament. "We'll see about that, won't we?"

"Look," Rose said, fighting to keep her composure, her voice strong and loud, struggling to say anything, *do* anything that would defuse the situation, "if you just think, for a minute . . . see what you are doing. It doesn't have to be this way. We don't have to hate each other. Let's just do the right thing. Let's get divorced and you can see Maddie. I won't stand in your way. I just want—"

"Nice try," Richard said, slowly closing the gap between them. "It's too late for that now. I want my family back in my house. I want you and my daughter back in my home where you belong. And when I'm ready, you'll go inside, you'll pack your things, and we'll leave. But first, I think it's time we had a little reunion, don't you?"

"No." Rose shook her head, pressing her lips together to stop her teeth from chattering. "No, Richard, please don't—"

"Don't argue with me, Rose," Richard said, dangerously close to losing his cool.

"Why?" Rose asked him desperately, trying to circle round him toward the door. "Why do this? When you haven't loved me for years, if you ever did. When all you do is trap and torment me, even hurting your own child, because you can't wait to punish me for something I will never understand. Why?"

"How many times do I have to tell you?" Richard asked her angrily. "You belong to me. You owe me. I rescued you, Rose. I picked you up at your lowest, most pathetic point, and I gave you a life, a husband, a family, a home. And now you are going to repay me for all the strain and stress you've put me through. You're going to make me feel better, like a good wife should."

Richard backed her against a wall, his sour breath filling her nostrils, making her want to gag.

"Just do exactly as I say," he murmured as he closed the gap between them.

On the last two words he closed in on her, trapping her against the wall of the barn with an arm either side of her head.

Gritting her teeth, Rose was determined not to show him fear, not to show him even a glimpse of the sickening dread she felt coursing through her, knowing all too well what would come next.

"No," she told Richard, determined to meet his eye. "I will *never* do what you want me to, never ever again."

With whiplike precision Richard hit her sharply across

the face, sending her cheek smashing into the barn wall with the force of the blow. Rose blinked, fighting the darkness that suddenly crowded the edge of her vision, stumbling sideways, momentarily dazed as stars swam in front of her eyes. Adrenaline was the only thing stopping her from passing out—that and the knowledge that, no matter what happened, she couldn't leave Maddie and John to Richard's mercy.

"See what you made me do?" Richard asked her. "Me, who has never laid a finger on you in anger. And now you've made me hurt you. I hope you are ashamed, Rose. You should be."

Despite the pain that seared down her neck, Rose brought her gaze up to meet his.

"You are pathetic," she told him, quietly defiant, finding a will to fight him that she didn't know she had. "Nothing more than a bully. I'm done being frightened of you, Richard. You bore me."

"You are my wife," Richard said, fury twisting his face as he pushed her hard into the wall, pinning her shoulder with one hand, and pulling at the buttons of her jeans with the other, dragging the waistband down over her hips. "And I think it's about time I reminded you of that. I've missed you, Rose."

"No!" Rose shouted, using every scrap of strength she had to push him backwards with just enough force to break his grip on her for a few moments. She twisted herself away from him, pulling up her jeans, as she raced for the closed door. But Richard grabbed her arm before she could make it, throwing her, sprawling, onto the hard concrete floor. Rose felt the back of her head reverberate with the pain on contact, as he stood over her, his image blurring before her eyes.

Do not pass out, she told herself furiously. Do not pass out!

"You are my wife," Richard repeated as he knelt down between her legs. "You belong to me."

Furiously, Rose pushed against his weight as he lay on top of her, one arm pinned across her throat, pressing hard against her windpipe, the other dragging down her jeans once more, until she could feel the cold, rough floor rasp against her skin.

Unable to talk, barely able to breathe, Rose struggled for as long as she could, until it hit her with a sudden cold clarity that she could not win this fight. If she kept trying to push him off, he would only hurt her more, perhaps more than her body could bear, and even though in those last few seconds before Richard got what he wanted, death seemed like a haven, Rose could not allow it to happen. She knew she must do whatever it took to survive.

Turning her head away from him as she ceased to struggle, she fixed her eyes on the wall, where once she had stood and gazed at one of her father's beautiful paintings. And she tried with all her might to recall it in every detail, every brushstroke, every color, to free herself from shame, the knowledge that no matter how her heart and mind might be strong enough to repel him, her body never would be, and that was why he would always win.

"Good girl," Richard said, relieving the pressure on her throat a little. "See how nice things can be when you only do as you are—"

"Get up." Rose heard a familiar voice echoing inside her head as if from very far away, and she wondered if she was imagining it. "Pull up your trousers and get up, I said, you disgusting piece of filth."

Turning her head with some force of will, Rose saw Jenny standing in the doorway of the room, her hands on her hips. As clouded as her vision was, Rose could tell that Jenny's face was white with horror, and there was fear there too, uncertainty that she could really do anything to help. Seizing the moment of distraction as Richard sat up to examine this intruder, Rose dragged herself painfully as far away from him as she could, pulling her disheveled clothes back on.

"Get out," Richard told Jenny, his eyes glittering with contempt. "She is my wife and this is none of your business."

"She is my friend," Jenny said, her voice finding strength and volume with every word. "*My* friend, and I won't have the likes of you pawing her. Where's your self-respect, where's your manhood?"

If Jenny was attempting to bait Richard away from Rose, she was doing a good job, as Richard clambered to his feet, wiping the back of his hand across his mouth as he steadied himself, his attention fixed on this interfering woman.

Dizzy and sick, her head clamoring with pain, Rose used the wall to help herself climb to her feet, taking a couple of unsteady steps forward, intent on getting to Jenny, on getting to the exit.

"I've called the police," Jenny said, keeping her eyes on Richard, focusing his attention on her. "They'll be here any minute. And do you want to know why? Your daughter. She phoned me. She told me that the father who had hit her was up here at Storm Cottage. Your *daughter* asked me to call the police. What kind of man are you?"

She spat the words with such naked contempt that for a moment Richard was caught off guard, unused to strangers seeing his true colors. Then, realizing himself exposed anyway, and with nothing to lose, the old fury caught light, and Rose gasped as he flew at Jenny, hearing her friend cry out as he raised his fist to strike her.

It was only after it had happened that Rose could make sense of it. One moment Richard had been poised to hurt her friend, the next he was sprawled prone on the floor and Rose was standing over him, a length of wood in her hand, the sirens that had been sounding in the distance growing steadily louder.

Rose and Jenny stared at each other across Richard, who rolled onto his back, groaning.

Rose blinked at the image that was gradually coming into focus, searching for reason in the confusion of shadows and flashes of light.

"You clocked him good and proper," Jenny said, her eyes wide.

"Maddie?" Rose managed to ask her, swaying dangerously on her feet, the wood clattering to the floor as her fingers lost the ability to grip.

"Inside. She's safe," Jenny said.

"You came," Rose sobbed, the words tearing out of her throat with a rush of gratitude. "You came."

"Yes," Jenny said, as a policeman entered the room, followed by another, "but it was you who put him in his place."

Rose wasn't really sure about everything that happened next, only that somehow she was seated on the stool in her father's studio, a concerned young police officer holding some gauze to her head and reassuring her that everything was going to be all right. Scanning the room, Rose saw her husband being escorted away by another officer, who had a firm grip on his arm.

"I'll be in touch," he said, stiffly, desperate to regain his composure. "This isn't over. I'll be having you charged with assault."

Before Rose could shape a response to this, Jenny cut in with a mirthless laugh from where she stood at Rose's side. "You'll be charging her? I don't think so. This time you've gone too far, son. Ever tried being a GP with a criminal record?"

Rose didn't allow herself to breathe until Richard was out of sight. Only then did her knees buckle, her body trembling uncontrollably as she slid off the stool and sank back down onto the floor.

"I've called an ambulance," the police officer said, kneeling beside her. "Just hold on a minute more."

"No." Rose's voice shook, but she was adamant. "I'm not going anywhere. My dad is sick."

"I think we'll let them take a look at you, anyway," he said, examining the graze on her cheek.

"I'm fine, really," Rose insisted just as the barn swirled around her and all the lights blinked out at once.

"I'm not going to hospital," Rose insisted as soon as she came to again, certain that, despite the sharp pain in her neck and blurred edges that still surrounded her vision, she didn't want to see the inside of a hospital ever again. "I'm fine."

"Hmm." The female paramedic who had arrived shortly after Richard had been escorted by a policeman into another ambulance, shone a light in her eyes. "Well, I can't make you come with me, if you don't want to."

She glanced up at Jenny. "Keep an eye out for signs of concussion. If she's sick or incoherent, take her to hospital immediately. And let the police take their photos and a statement. Make sure this goes on record, at the very least."

"That's what I said," Jenny said, peering at Rose, who was propped, much to her shame, against a barrage of cushions on the sofa, her father sitting in his armchair, staring anxiously at her. "But she won't have it."

"I'm fine," Rose said. "Really. I'm just glad it's over."

"It's not that over," the young policeman, PC Brig, said uncomfortably. "Your husband is saying you assaulted him, that it was unprovoked."

"Well, that's a wicked lie!" Jenny insisted immediately. "I was there, I saw it. I'm a witness!"

"Which is why you need to let us take statements, collect evidence. I strongly advise that you press charges."

"Talk to them," the paramedic said kindly. "You should at least put what happened on record, even if you don't want to take it further. I see this all the time, too much: the woman just wants it all to go away, the man ends up getting it all his own way. Show him now that you mean business, otherwise he'll just keep coming."

Rose glanced over at Maddie, who was sitting on the arm of John's chair, her arm around his neck. She had yet to approach Rose, as if she was scared of touching her. Instead she sat staring, no doubt trying to take in what had happened, what her father had done now. These were conversations that Rose did not want her daughter to hear; she'd been through enough today.

"I will," Rose promised, looking at PC Brig. "But not now, please. My little girl . . . I am fine, honestly." She turned to John. "I'm so sorry, this is the last thing you need now."

"If I could have got out of bed . . ." John said, his face set with fury. "I felt so weak, so useless. Maddie was the one who knew what to do. Maddie called for help."

Maddie said nothing, still staring at her mother as if she were trying to take it all in. Rose held out her arms to her, but Maddie stayed where she was.

"Thank you," Rose said to Jenny. "For everything you've done for us. Since we got here, I mean, not just today. But really, thank you for coming, especially when . . . well, after what happened. If you hadn't come . . . I really do thank you from the bottom of my heart."

"Hmph," Jenny said, pursing her lips. "Never could stand a bully."

"Hello?"

Rose looked up to see Ted's head appearing round the

front door, his expression a combination of shock at the drama, the number of official personnel, and embarrassment. He clearly wasn't too sure how Rose would take to seeing him, and honestly neither was she.

"I just got your message, Mum, I'm sorry." He looked at Rose. "Can I come in?"

Rose nodded, dropping her gaze as he came into the room, just as the paramedic was packing up her bag.

"Here comes the cavalry," Jenny said, "about an hour too late. Still, never mind."

"It was on silent!" Ted said guiltily, unable to look at Rose. "Did you call Dad?"

"Yes, and his was on silent too, no doubt," Jenny said. "Doesn't matter. We handled it, didn't we, love?"

Rose nodded, still unable to believe that she had somehow found the physical strength to lay Richard out on the floor. She glanced at Maddie, wondering if she knew what Rose had done, and that was why she was reluctant to come to her. What if Maddie was afraid of her too?

"He was about to hit me—me, your mother—and this one"—Jenny pointed at Rose—"she just picked up this massive lump of timber like it was a matchstick and—"

"Jenny," Rose said, nodding at Maddie.

"Here, Maddie," Ted said, fishing his car keys out of his jeans pocket. "Go to my car and look in the glove compartment. I'm pretty sure there's a Mars bar there. You can have it if you want."

"Thanks," Maddie said, taking the keys without enthusiasm and then handing them back to Ted. "I don't really like Mars bars, but I don't mind going upstairs for a bit and looking at my book if you want to talk about things without me."

"Oh, Maddie," Rose said, trying to sit up and then regretting the impulse as the room swam around her, annoyed that

Ted was trying to manage a situation he'd had nothing to do with, "you don't have to go anywhere if you don't want to."

"I do want to," Maddie said, sliding off the kitchen chair. "I'm tired."

"Maddie?" Rose stopped her. "Are you OK? Everything that's happened, it's a lot to take in."

Maddie eyed her for a moment longer. "I'm fine," she said.

Rose watched anxiously as she clumped slowly up the stairs, her head bowed heavily.

"I'll go up," Jenny said. "Keep the little mite company for a bit. She might chat to me."

"We'd like a word too," PC Brig said, catching Rose's expression. "Not now, when she's ready. Just need to get all the angles."

"Right," the paramedic said. "I've got to go. But I'm serious, if it gets worse, go to hospital. And don't let whoever did this to you get away with it."

"Thank you," Rose said painfully. "I appreciate your help."

"I could sort him out for you." Ted paced behind the sofa. "I could, you know, have a proper word. With my fists."

"I'm going to pretend I didn't hear that," the policeman said. "Look, if the hospital lets him go, there's not much chance we'll be able to hold him tonight. I don't think he'll come back here—he's not an idiot, he's already trying to make out he's the victim—but just keep an eye out, OK?"

Ted saw them out while John and his daughter gazed at each other across the small space between their chairs, their expressions mirroring one another as they took in the full extent of each other's injuries and ailments.

"I'm not the one who's ill," Rose said brightly, unable to bear to look on her father's face. "This is so silly. There really is no need for all this fuss."

"I did this to you," John said. "It was my neglect that

pushed you into the arms of a man who would . . ." he faltered, unable to say the next words out loud. "I can't bear it. I can't bear that I put you through this."

Rose watched him silently for a moment, wishing she could say that none of this was his fault, but she couldn't find a way to do that, not even for this man whom she had slowly begun to love again.

"I don't suppose I would have got married at eighteen if I'd had parents around," she said slowly. "But this is my life, Dad, and it was my choice to marry Richard. I knew, somewhere, in some tiny part of me, right from the start, that something wasn't right with me and Richard. It was just that I had nothing to compare it to, and to be honest I didn't want to listen to those doubts. I wanted to be married, I wanted to be in a family, I wanted to be safe. And I could have left him. There were a hundred times I could have left him and didn't because . . . I didn't have the courage." Her voice broke as the realization of what she had so narrowly escaped broke over her. "Not even today. I thought I was strong now and I was free. But I wasn't. I gave up. I gave up fighting him off, and if Jenny hadn't come he would have . . . In those few seconds I was willing to go back to how everything had been just to save myself. I wasn't brave at all."

"You are a remarkable young woman," John said, his jaw set. "More brave than anyone in this room."

"Then why don't I feel it?" Rose wept into her hands, her tears hot and painful. "Why do I feel like he's won, again?"

"Rose." Ted crouched down before her, touching her arm, which she withdrew with a flinch, unable to look at him. Ted stared at his spurned hand and then, seeing the expression of stony disapproval on John's face, stood up, backing away to what seemed like a safe distance.

"I need to say how sorry I am," Ted said unhappily, looking anywhere but at Rose. "How really, really sorry I am for the way I behaved, the things I said, the way I tried to . . ." He faltered, remembering how he'd tried to make Rose kiss him, only now realizing exactly why she'd been so repulsed by his clumsy advances. "I'm not like him, Rose. You do know that, don't you? I was hurt and stupid and wrong and a liar, but I would never . . . I'm not like him, and I'm so, so sorry."

"Sorry for what?" John asked, determined to be the one to step in this time.

"Nothing much," Rose said sharply. "Something that got blown out of proportion." Finally Rose looked at Ted. "I know you are not like him," she said. "You frightened me, though, Ted, and you lied about me. You were the first man I'd met in a long time that I thought I could trust, and you lied about me."

"I hate myself," Ted said miserably. "I do."

"I can see that," Rose said, her will to be angry at Ted in the midst of everything else crumbling easily away. She looked at him. "It wasn't all your fault, and really I'd rather just forget about it, if that's OK?"

"Thank you," Ted said, and then seeing John glowering at him added, "Look, you might not like this idea, and I know the last time I saw you I behaved like a bit of a dick, but anyway, I've decided, and I won't change my mind. I'm going to stay on the sofa tonight, make sure that you lot are OK, be on standby in case he comes back."

Rose was uncertain about having Ted stay the night after everything he'd done, and yet it would be reassuring to have him here. The police officer didn't think Richard would come back, and a sane man wouldn't, but Rose wasn't sure what little, if any, sanity Richard had left.

"Thank you, it would make me feel better knowing that you are here."

"Good," Ted said, looking relieved to have this chance to make amends. "Great."

"What's this?" Jenny said as she came down the stairs. "What are you planning, Edward?"

"I'm staying the night, that's all," Ted said. "To keep an eye on them."

"Well, if you're staying, I'm staying to keep an eye on you," Jenny said. "I'll have the sofa, you can have the chair."

"Mum . . ." Ted began to protest.

"Don't argue with me, young man, I've decided," Jenny said, crossing her arms.

"Neither of you has to stay," John said, clearly resenting this well-meaning invasion of his home. "I can take care of my daughter."

"You couldn't take care of a kitten," Jenny said with the same characteristic bluntness that fortunately John appreciated. "We're staying and that is that. I'll just call my Brian and let him know, else he'll think I've run off with the cowman again."

It was some time later, whilst Jenny was settling Maddie to sleep, and John had nodded off in his chair, that Rose found herself more or less alone with Ted again for the first time since the incident in the annex. Neither of them spoke. Rose was really at a loss as to what to say to this young man who'd both become a friend and wrecked her dreams within a matter of days.

"You must hate me," Ted said suddenly, unable to look at her, his voice tight with emotion. "For trying to make you kiss me like that, like that . . . that animal did. I knew you'd been through something awful, something dreadful to make you so afraid but, Rose, I never guessed it was that. And now I know I'm no better than him. No wonder you hate me."

"I don't hate you," Rose said softly, leaning forward a little towards him. Her neck was still sore, the back of her head and cheek were bruised, but her mind felt clearer now, at least. "I don't have the energy to hate anyone anymore."

Ted shook his head, hurriedly wiping away the tears that had sprung to his eyes, keen that Rose shouldn't see that he was crying.

"Ted," Rose said, making him look at her, "you are a million times better than him, a gazillion. Yes, you behaved like a moron, but you've been so kind to me too. If anything, I'm at fault. I shouldn't have let things go so far between us. You got tangled up in the problems of a very confused and stupid woman."

"You really can't feel about me like I do about you?" Ted asked her earnestly, his dark eyes fixed on her so intently that Rose almost wished that she could, almost thought that perhaps if she tried the feelings might come eventually. But if life had taught her anything, it was to listen to that small quiet voice that told her when something wasn't right for her, no matter how perfect it might seem.

Rose shook her head, a tear of regret sliding down her cheek. "I'm sorry."

Ted nodded, turning his face from her for a moment, as he took a breath.

"But we could try being friends again. I need one of those now. And so does Maddie."

"I never ever thought it would be me getting the let's be friends speech." Ted sighed ruefully. "But friends it is, then. Look, do you want me to have a word with that Frasier, tell him how things really were between us?"

Rose shook her head. "I think that door has rather closed," she said. "It's probably for the best."

"Yeah," Ted said sadly. "You're saying the words out loud,

but your face is telling another story. You're still hurting for him. Trust me, I can spot the signs."

Rose didn't bother denying the truth. "Well, if it wasn't meant to be, what can I do?" she said. "I've got far too much else to think about now than a man. I've got Dad and Maddie, and making a life for myself here. And honestly, even if what happened with Frasier does hurt, it is better this way. It's about time I was my own person."

"Are you two OK now?" Jenny asked tartly as she returned downstairs, causing John to stir a little in his chair.

"Sneaking around behind people's backs like a pair of teenagers. I've never seen the like," Jenny growled. "Still, I don't suppose I should really have gone quite so overboard on being cross about it as I did. I forget that Ted is a grown man most of the time, mainly because he acts like a child. But still, there it is."

"There what is, Ma?" Ted asked her, winking at Rose.

"What I said," Jenny said. "There that is."

"Mum?" Ted prodded her.

"Fine, I'm sorry too," Jenny snapped before bustling off to the sink where she began to wash up very noisily, muttering, "What sort of civilized human being doesn't have a dishwasher in this day and age I really don't know."

Chapter Eighteen

It was clear that neither Frasier nor John really knew how to deal with the aftermath of Richard's visit, each of them feeling powerless and detached in his own way. Frasier was clearly irritated that it had been Jenny, and especially Ted, who were already there taking care of Rose when he arrived. But beyond that Rose had no idea what he was thinking. He was just as polite, charming, and friendly as he had been before, except now there was a kind of barrier around him, a reserve Rose felt indicated that he found it difficult to be near her. Which was hardly surprising, she supposed. It was never easy to be near someone who'd been through something like she had, the constant fear of not knowing what to say or how to be. If things had been different, Rose would have begged him to be like he'd always been with her, but now there was that distance. They could work together, quietly plan the exhibition together, spend time with John and Maddie, all of them in the same room quite comfortably, but they could never really say anything to each other that mattered.

What worried Rose most, though, was how John reacted to Richard's brief but destructive invasion into his life.

Sinking into himself, wrought with guilt and anger, he didn't seem to want to get out of bed the next day, unable to look Rose in the eye, not willing to eat, just lying in bed staring at the blank whitewashed wall across the room. Not even Frasier's arrival sparked his usual mischievous intent to wind his friend up as best he could. It was clear that John blamed himself, despite what Rose had said, and now he was angry and frustrated with his illness, his weakness, all too aware that soon he would be leaving her alone and unprotected.

Rose was desperate that this not be the way that John spent the rest of his time with her and Maddie, and yet it hurt to realize that she did not know him well enough to be able to bring him out.

When Frasier saw the bruise on Rose's cheek, as she stood in the kitchen trying to make lasagne, his face was unreadable. Ted had already left, but Jenny, who was still there bustling about, dusting under and behind things, taking every opportunity to peer into drawers, told him the short version of the story in her usual blunt and to-the-point way in five seconds flat, which Rose had been grateful for. The last thing she wanted was to have to explain to Frasier what had happened.

"And where is he now?" Frasier asked, his expression very still.

"I don't know," Rose said, shaking her head. "Gone home, the police think. They rang to tell me. He hasn't pressed charges against me—he's probably realized he wouldn't get away with it—and if I press charges there'll be a scandal. His reputation, his life, his practice will all go up in smoke."

"So why don't you, then?" Jenny asked her.

Rose shrugged. "I just want him gone. Not to have to go through months and months of legal stuff, and even if they do find him guilty, he's got no record, no previous offenses. He'll probably get a slap on the wrist, and he will still be out there, angry. I can't see the point."

"If you want him gone, you need to show him that this is over," Frasier said. "The police is one way of doing that."

Rose said nothing, silently resolute.

"Well, I'll stay here until we can be sure he's not still in the area," Frasier said, his eyes fixed on Rose's cheek.

"Ted stayed last night," Maddie told Frasier, midway through the process of sifting flour, a job Rose had given her to keep her busy. "But I'm not scared of Dad," she told Frasier, as if she was working out her own thoughts aloud. "Mum beat him up. He should be scared of Mum."

"Well, good for Ted," Frasier said, his voice taut. "But he's gone now, and in the meantime, I'll stay here." He looked at Jenny. "If you have a moment before you go, I brought some examples, brochures that I sent for. I'd almost forgotten what we'd been talking about until they arrived. I thought you'd like to look at them."

Before Rose could find out what business Frasier could possibly have with Jenny, there was a muffled call from the study.

"Dad," Rose said. "I'm so worried about him, he's so down. Do you think you could maybe make him cross or want to throw something at you, or chuck you out, even? I'd do anything to see him his old grumpy self again."

"Well, breaking the news of the exhibition to him is bound to distract him," Frasier said a little warily. "I'll give it my best shot."

Rose followed Frasier as far as the study door, hoping to be out of earshot of Jenny, who was muttering to herself about *E. coli* as she returned to cleaning out the fridge, while Maddie steadfastly spooned flour through the sieve.

"He has taken what happened with Richard very badly, blaming himself," Rose told Frasier.

"He's not the only one," Frasier said, reaching out and gently touching her face just below the bruise. "I should never have left you."

"What reason did you have to stay?" Rose asked him. "None of us knew that would be the day Richard turned up. I'm worried about Dad. I'm worried that if he feels this deflated now, then he'll stop trying to . . . stay."

"Why are you whispering?" Maddie asked them, appearing at the bottom of the stairs, her hands and face covered in flour.

"Because it's private," Rose told her daughter, a little more firmly than she meant to. "Which reminds me, you and I are going to look at the local school in a couple of days. The nice head teacher is letting us in specially, even though they aren't back from the summer holidays yet."

"Oh," Maddie said, utterly uncheered by the news. "Well, I suppose that will be OK. I'm not going if I don't completely like it, though."

"Are you coming?" Frasier asked Rose as Maddie returned to her sifting.

"No, you go in first. Whenever he looks at me he looks so sad," Rose said, biting her lip. Frasier touched her briefly on the shoulder, in a moment of consolation, and then closed the door behind him.

It was almost an hour later when Frasier called Rose in to see her father. John was sitting up in bed, with a writing board resting on his lap and a selection of official-looking papers spread out across the bed. Obviously Frasier's visit had had some effect on him, Rose thought gratefully. Whatever he was doing, it was better than just lying there staring into thin air.

"Good," John said purposefully when she arrived. "Frasier and I have been dealing with your situation. That man will only ever get near you and Maddie again over my dead body, and as that situation is imminent, I have taken measures to ensure you are protected when I'm not here."

"Measures?" Rose said uncertainly, sitting on the bed.

"I have telephoned the police station in Keswick. They are sending out an officer to take your statement about what happened. They'll want to speak to Jenny too. They took photos last night of your injuries, and they'll take some more today."

"Dad!" Rose protested. "This isn't what I want. What about Maddie? Did you stop to think about how it would affect her, knowing the police are chasing her father?"

"This *is* for Maddie too," John said firmly, with more life than she had seen in him since yesterday. "It was Maddie who asked for the police. I don't know what motivates a human to behave as your husband did yesterday, and I know that he is Maddie's father, but still, he has to be stopped. Like Frasier stopped me from drinking by locking me up for months. Richard has to be stopped before he ruins lives beyond repair, including Maddie's. And this is the first step to that. I know it is extreme, but perhaps official involvement is one way of making him see what it is he's been doing, the sort of person he's become."

Rose bowed her head in thought. "OK, perhaps you're right. But I don't want to speak to them here. I don't want Maddie to know. If they're talking to Jenny too, I'll go to the B and B, meet them there."

"Good," John said. "Now, I wasn't going to tell you this just yet, but I think you need to know now. A few years ago I set up a trust fund for you. It's not supposed to be realized until I die, but under the circumstances, I've asked Frasier, who is the executor, to arrange for a portion to be paid to you immediately, pay legal fees, help you set up your new life, and make sure you don't want for anything. And he's arranging for a solicitor to see you, to help you get divorce proceedings started.

Her name is . . . ?" John looked at Frasier, who'd been standing obediently at his side all this time.

"Janette," Frasier said, "Janette Webb. She's excellent."

"Really?" Rose said, looking at Frasier, a little breathless, not to mention just a little irritated by how speedily her life was being organized for her. She knew that both men wanted, and even needed, to help her, but this felt a little too much like control over her—that her own destiny was being taken away from her just as she was beginning to regain it.

"This is all a bit too fast," she said. "I'm not sure that I'm ready for this yet."

"Rose," John spoke her name urgently, "I have no choice but to act fast, don't you see that? I'm not trying to railroad you, but I can't leave you knowing that I haven't done all I can to make things safe for you and Maddie. I'm sure I don't deserve that peace of mind, I know you blame me . . . but please let me be a father to you."

Rose bit her lip, torn between her desire to make her dad happy and her determination to control her own life for once. This wasn't about manipulation or control, she told herself. This was just a father trying to help his daughter.

"All right," she conceded. "I'll talk to the police and the Janette person. But after that I make my own decisions, OK?"

"Very well," John said, seemingly content that he'd got her to take that first step to making her break from Richard permanently, and in her heart Rose knew he was right. A prolonged stalemate between her and her husband would only make things messy and uncertain. Richard did need showing, by official means, if necessary, that her life as his wife was finished for good. Miles weren't enough to keep him away, and if she left things as they were, sooner or later he would be back. Rose knew she couldn't let that happen.

"Very well," she said. "Dad, I'll do what you want, for you and for Maddie."

"And for me," Frasier added, so softly that Rose wasn't sure she'd heard him right.

"But I want you to do something for me too," she continued, glancing up at Frasier, who knew exactly what she was about to say. "Something that would mean more to me than you can imagine."

John looked at her suspiciously over the top of his glasses.

"Frasier and I want to exhibit your private work, and we want to open in two weeks' time," Rose rushed the words out all at once, hoping that the quicker she said them the less likely John was to have time to react negatively. She hoped in vain.

"Absolutely not," John said with such vehemence that his face flooded red and Rose feared for his heart, on top of everything else. "I don't know how you can ask that of me! That work is not for sale. It is not for anyone else but me. It's my . . . diary, my legacy, my gift to you when I am gone, and I will not, I repeat, I will *not* let this man turn it into a three-ring circus, just so he can cream his percentage off the top." He pointed an accusing finger at Frasier. "I won't, Rose. I'm sorry, I won't. I never wanted you to see them while I was alive; if there was a way I could stop you seeing them afterwards, then I would. They document the side of me I hate the most."

Rose watched dismayed as John bowed his head, sweeping his glasses off his face and pinching the bridge of his nose, as tears squeezed out between his tightly shut eyes.

"Dad," she said, sliding off the edge of the bed to kneel next to him. "Please, don't cry. This isn't at all what we wanted. All we wanted was to show the world what an incredible artist you are. And I *haven't* seen the paintings yet. I promised you I wouldn't and I haven't. Frasier looked at them, and he thinks they are amazing, brilliant, wonderful."

"It's true," Frasier said, taking Rose's place on the bed. "John, don't deprive the world of what you have here. This work is important. It needs to be seen."

"And I don't suppose your concern," John said, gaining his composure, "has anything to do with how much a painting goes up in value once its creator is dead?"

Frasier looked hurt, turning his face away from his friend.

"I know," he said quietly, "that is not what you really think of me. I know you know that I am your friend, that I always have and always will do the very best I can for you." When Frasier turned back to face John, his face was set with determination. "I will take a good deal of your vitriol, John, but not that. Besides, this exhibition wouldn't be about you, it would be *for* Rose. A way for you to show her your soul. Rose listened to you, now you listen to me. Do this one thing for your daughter. And if it helps, we don't have to put the works up for sale. It could be for viewing only. A retrospective and an unveiling of a great undiscovered British talent in one fell swoop."

"I will be a laughingstock," John said, a little less vehemently. "Some foolish old man who's made all his money painting chocolate-box-pretty pictures and now is praying for some validation from the critics on his deathbed. How they will mock me. I'm sorry, Rose, I don't want to disappoint you. But no, I don't want to."

"Can I show you something?" Rose went to a bookshelf in the corner of the room and from behind it retrieved an object that Frasier recognized as soon as he saw the familiar blanket wrapping. "I was going to put it on the wall for you before you got back, but I couldn't find a hammer," Rose said as she unwrapped the painting. Carefully, she set it at the foot of the bed, standing behind it, holding its edges very carefully.

John gazed at the painting, saying nothing as his eyes roamed over it, looking as if he'd just been reunited with a very dear friend that he had no idea how to react to.

"This painting," Rose told him over the brim of the canvas, "or at least the sketch for this painting, is the reason why Frasier looked all over the country for you." She glanced briefly at Frasier, before returning her attention to John. "The reason why I met him, the reason that I came here, the reason that I ever found you. This painting that I *know* you never forgot, because you painted it again."

Father and daughter held each other's gaze, saying more in that moment of silence to one another than they could with a thousand words. This was Rose's proof that she had never forgotten John, and his symbol to prove that she had always been in his thoughts, even when he himself had been lost.

"This isn't chocolate-box art, Dad," Rose said. "This wasn't painted for money, or fame. It was a moment between this little girl and her father. I've always kept it. No matter what else was happening, not even when Frasier wanted it, and most of me wanted him to have it. I kept this safe because I looked at it and I felt the love you had for me when you painted it. It was the one thing that I couldn't ever bear to part with because it was the one little bit of you that I had."

John stared at the painting for a long time before speaking. "You were sitting on the windowsill, looking out the window with the sunlight in your hair. I did a quick sketch to remember the tilt of your head, the way you crossed your legs and posed your hands, but most of that came from memory and from the emotion, the love I felt for you in that second. You're right, I never forgot that moment between us, even though sometimes it was unbearable to recall."

"And this image is repeated," Frasier told Rose, risking John's wrath, "again and again, not just in the work I showed you at the gallery but in the works in the barn too."

"Is that true, Dad?" Rose asked him softly, carefully lifting the painting off the bed and setting it against the wall.

John nodded, dropping his gaze from her. "It's hardly enough, though, is it? One memory of love to live with in an entire lifetime. I am so ashamed, Rose, so very ashamed of the life that I have led. I don't want to turn that shame into glory."

"But what if you turned it into a story?" Rose said, returning to his side. "A path for me to follow. A path that will lead me to a better understanding of you? And think of all the organizing and deciding you'll have to do. You'll be able to boss Frasier around mercilessly and be as difficult and as obstinate as you like, and I just think the more you have to occupy your mind, the . . ." Rose stumbled to a faltering stop, realizing what she was about to say.

"The longer I will live," John finished for her. "Is that what this is about?"

"I've only just found you," Rose said. "Maddie barely knows you. I want every second I can get."

"Well, then," John said, taking her hand, "why didn't you just say that in the first place?"

It had been a very long day, which Rose was looking forward to seeing the back of by the time she finally said goodbye to Jenny, tucked Maddie up in the boxroom, and ushered Tilda, who'd arrived late afternoon, probably in a bid to give Rose time with her father, into John's room for time alone with her husband.

After everyone had sampled Rose's lasagne together, and Tilda was in John's room, Rose came downstairs to the heart-aching sight of Frasier sitting on the sofa, his arm slung along the length of the back, as if he were issuing an invitation for her to nestle in the crook of his arm. He wasn't doing that, of course, she thought sadly, he wasn't doing any such thing, so taking a glass of wine that Frasier had poured for her from the sideboard, Rose went and sat opposite him, in her father's armchair.

"How was it, talking to the police?" Frasier asked her. Just after lunch, Rose had been as good as her word and gone down to meet the officer at the B & B, telling Maddie she was popping out for some boring old shopping.

"It was difficult," Rose admitted. "The hardest part is seeing the expression on people's faces when you try to explain to them what life was like. I can see exactly what they're thinking: poor stupid cow, why didn't she leave him at the first sign of trouble? What they don't know is there isn't a first sign of trouble. It's like that experiment you hear about when you are a child. That if you put a frog in a pan of cold water, and gently heat it, you can boil it to death without it ever noticing. That's what it was like. Richard was ever so slowly smothering me, and I got so used to the lack of oxygen, I didn't notice." Rose took a deep gulp of wine. "Still, she has my statement now; it's on record. And Jenny's too. Thank God they didn't feel the need to talk to Maddie. And I do feel better. I feel like I have really made a start on taking back control of my life again."

Rose smiled at him across the small space between them, which represented such a huge gulf. "Thank you for being here."

"I honestly don't have anywhere else to be," Frasier said. "Although I might just have to spend a little money on a new sofa if I'm going to be here for a while. I might even go crazy and make it a sofa bed."

They were both silent for a moment, Frasier lost in his own thoughts as Rose allowed herself secretly to wonder what it would be like to take Frasier by the hand and lead him upstairs to her bed.

"You never really said what it was like," Frasier said, when Rose finally found the courage to look up at him. "I knew your marriage to Richard was a bad one, and that you felt trapped and unhappy, but I didn't realize quite how awful it was, the things he . . . put you through."

Rose shrugged, looking deep into the glass of wine. "It's not something you really want to talk about. I feel so stupid, so weak, so pathetic."

"Pathetic is the last thing you are," Frasier said. "You are strong, impressively so. Resilient, stoic, amazing."

Rose's smile was rueful. "Oh, stop trying to be kind, Frasier. They are not the qualities you'd normally put on an Internet dating profile, are they?"

"Are you thinking of Internet dating?" Frasier asked her, alarmed.

"No! Look around you. If Dad has got this mythical laptop you speak of, I've yet to find it. And no, no, no to Internet dating or indeed dating. If I know anything now, it's that I'm nowhere near ready to have anything to do with men. Kissing Ted proved that."

Frasier nodded, his expression unreadable.

"And kissing him was all that happened," Rose said, deciding she might as well grasp the nettle while she had the benefit of most of a glass of wine inside her. "And I'm not sorry I did it, even though it . . . changed things between us. Ted was good to me, and kind. He understood. He gave me back something I'd lost and didn't need anything in return. I'm sorry his feelings got caught up in it all, and most of all I'm sorry that I messed everything up between you and me. But I'm not sorry I kissed him, Frasier. Ted reminded me that kissing is actually really wonderful."

"I'm glad," Frasier said, adding ever so slowly, "I would have liked to have been the one to give you that gift."

Rose looked up at him sharply. "Don't do that again," she said, suddenly angry.

"Don't do what?" he asked, taken aback.

"You are impossible to know how to be around," Rose told him bitterly. "One minute you're holding my hand, the next talking about how great Cecily is. Or saying you've always loved me and then actually sorry, no, that was a terrible mistake. That we can only ever just be friends, and *now* that you wished you'd kissed me instead of Ted. It's not fair, Frasier!" Rose got up, walking over to the sideboard where the rest of the wine was. "I know where I stand now. You made it very clear. And that's how I want it to stay. You, there on the sofa, me upstairs in the bedroom, working together as friends for Dad. If I ever could handle anything more, that's gone now. You made sure of it. Now I just want to be alone and let my heart rest for a while."

Frasier leaned back on the sofa saying nothing. Two bright spots of red were coloring his cheeks.

"Rose, I didn't mean to upset you . . ."

"Good night," Rose said, picking up her glass of wine, and, even though it was barely nine, "see you in the morning."

It took until Rose had reached the bottom stair for Frasier to speak.

"Rose," he said, "for what it's worth, I'm sorry."

"For what it's worth," Rose said sadly, the anger draining out of her, "I know."

Chapter Nineteen

"So?" Rose asked John, who now, two weeks after his operation, was at least able to get out of bed for most of the day, even though he looked thinner, grayer, and more gaunt than ever. "It's opening night, are you excited?"

"I'm a quivering wreck," John said drily. "Can't you tell?"

"I'm excited." Maddie hopped from one foot to the other. "I'm the most excited of everyone, because Frasier told me that there is a surprise for me. And I am the most excited about that. I don't know what it is going to be. It might be a television for my bedroom, that would be good. Or an iPad."

"It's not either of those things," Frasier said, coming down the stairs, his hair wet, a towel around his neck. Despite the lingering awkwardness between Rose and him, he had been good to his word and moved into the cottage, running his business as much as he could from his laptop, even going so far as to have a sofa bed delivered and a wireless router fitted, just as he had threatened, and much to John's disgust.

"I've had that sofa for fifteen years," John had said unhappily as it was moved out of the living room and into the barn, for the time being at least. "I got it at a house clearance. It had belonged to the woman who died for fifteen years before that. She died on it. Never heard her complain about it being bumpy."

"Maybe that's why she died," Maddie had said thoughtfully. "Maybe the bumpiness killed her."

"It's only temporary," Frasier had reassured John. "As soon as things are settled, I will put your old sofa of doom back and take this one with me. I'm going to need to find a new place to live anyway. Cecily seems to have decided that she's got rights to my flat in our separation, which doesn't matter so much, it was only a rental, but it does rather leave me homeless, and the office at the gallery isn't ideal."

Frasier was obviously stretched to the limit, running his business from the cottage, making regular round-trips to the gallery and back, supervising the removal of John's secret paintings, which Rose still had not seen, determined to honor her word to her father until they were hanging in the gallery. Even though Rose did her best, on scant experience, to help him organize the marketing, the guest list, the news and media, at the end of every day he looked tired out and more besides, as if he were carrying some other unknown burden. He probably missed Cecily, Rose thought. It would be only natural. And he probably wondered why and how his life had become so completely intertwined with theirs. Secretly Rose worried that they had become a burden to him, but she said nothing, supposing that as soon as the exhibition was over he'd be able to quietly withdraw, and in many ways she would welcome the peace that would come from not having to see him every day and know she'd lost him.

Frasier had managed to drum up quite a storm of interest in the show. Not that they mentioned that to John, who was certain that anyone who came would be there only to mock him, and who was in fact working on the basis that no one would come at all. As that seemed something of a comfort to him, neither Rose nor Frasier had done anything to change his opinion.

What he had clearly enjoyed, though, was spending time with Frasier, talking over his work with another living human being for the first time, explaining what he felt inclined to, remaining silent on what he did not. As it wasn't practical for him to travel to Edinburgh before the opening, Frasier brought the plans to him, including a scale model of the gallery, with numbered squares of cardboard, each representing one of almost thirty works. Rose would watch as John and Frasier argued constantly about which work should go where, Frasier always acquiescing in the end. It was a trait that made Rose love him all the more, as futile as that was. Frasier was always going to let John have his way, but he knew that John enjoyed the argument and the discussion, the back and forth and the debate. And Rose suspected that John knew he knew it too. This was simply a demonstration of two very good friends, telling each other how much they cared for one another in the best way they knew how, with sustained disagreement.

Tilda had been there too, for much of the time, not every day, although Rose knew she would be if she could. The running of her business, which didn't turn over enough to employ staff full time, demanded that she could not be absent from it as much as she would like. And although they never spoke of it, Rose was sure that she had taken a conscious step back, to allow Rose the time she needed with her father, uninterrupted by the demands or needs of another. Whenever Tilda was there, the love she still felt for John, despite everything he'd put her through, and the equal affection he felt in return was palpable, as clearly written in their expressions and gestures as it would have been in black and white on a page. With supreme politeness, Tilda would always ask Rose what she could do to help, and Rose would respond by always having something ready. The laundry mostly, which could not be done at the cottage because John had never acquired a washing machine, entertaining Maddie sometimes while Rose and her father talked, and always Rose would make sure that John and Tilda had time together alone, usually in John's room.

One afternoon she had ventured in there to ask them if they wanted tea, to find them both asleep on John's bed, Tilda's head resting on his chest, his arm wrapped around her. It was such an intensely personal moment that Rose had quickly backed out of the room, quietly closing the door behind her. Nevertheless, Rose was glad that she had seen it.

As soon as the opening night of the exhibition was out of the way Rose was going to ask Tilda to come and stay with them, to use some of the great deal of money that John had released to her to pay for someone to run the shop for as long as was needed. This, Rose realized, was not a time when John should have to choose between the people he loved and cared for, and if she had unwittingly become the cause of that, she was determined not to be for one moment more.

Rose was quietly optimistic about Maddie's chances of settling in at her new school. The head had enjoyed all of the seven-year-old's many questions as she showed her around the small school, seeming undaunted by Maddie's trademark bluntness and lack of tact. Maddie had liked what she'd seen and even been on a successful playdate with a local girl who would be in her class, managing to go a whole afternoon without offending or upsetting anyone.

Rose had taken the opportunity to drive to Carlisle again and buy herself some more clothes, including something for the opening. It had been a strange experience, walking around the shops with money in her pockets and no one to please but herself, and she had spent several minutes wandering about before she realized that she had just begun to get a sense of her own style. She knew it wasn't Richard's idea of what she should look like, or Haleigh's haphazard approach to youthful fashion, it was just wearing what made her feel good inside. Initially lost, Rose had laden herself down with item after item, gradually working her way through shop after shop until she found clothes that she liked, that she felt comfortable in, and finally choosing a knee-length, sea-green pencil dress for her father's exhibition, which set off her slender figure and contrasted with her blond hair. As Rose examined herself in the dressing room mirror, she ran her fingers through her hair, which was longer now and dark at the roots, discovering that she was very keen that her old hair did not come back, not yet. It was still too much of a reminder of who she'd once been.

Still wearing the dress, she sat down on the little stool provided in the cubicle and dialed Shona's number.

"Will you come and do my hair again?" she asked, making Shona chuckle.

"No, go to a bloody hairdresser or sheepshearer or whatever it is they have up there. So you're keeping it blond then?"

"Yes," Rose said, looking at herself in the mirror. "Yes, I like Blond Rose. Blond Rose is the one that hits husbands with planks."

"How are you now, about all that?" Shona asked her. "I told Mum, Mum's told the town all about it. And after the police visited him at the surgery for a chat, it's been brilliant. It was in the local press and everything. 'Local Doctor Quizzed over Domestic Abuse!' I'm sending you a copy."

Rose already knew, but she didn't say anything. She knew because despite her reservation about pressing a charge against him, she had been left with no choice but to go ahead with it when Richard continued to call and text her, becoming increasingly menacing. Finally she had asked the police to intervene, and then, after only a moment's hesitation, she had left an anonymous message on the local paper's news desk answerphone, tipping them off about the scandal. Her only weapon against Richard returning was to show him how she could destroy his precious reputation, and for once in her life Rose did not hold back.

"It's Dad's exhibition coming up," Rose said. "That's all I'm thinking about. I wish you could be there. Things OK your end?"

There was the briefest pause. "I've left Ryan," Shona said. "For good this time."

"Oh, no," Rose said, her heart sinking. "What's he done now?"

"Actually, nothing. Not yet," Shona said. "It was the waiting I couldn't cope with. He was being lovely, sweet, nice to the kids—but I knew, I just knew it wouldn't last. And I didn't want to go through that again. So I decided not to. I left him. Well, kicked him out on his arse to be exact. And you know what? I feel great about it. Free. It's fucking brilliant."

"Really." Rose smiled as she spoke. "You and I are pretty wonderful, aren't we?"

"You said it, mate." Shona laughed. "We kick arse."

The visit with the solicitor that her father insisted on had gone as well as could be expected. Frasier had accompanied her for moral support and Rose had felt a curious mixture of fear and exhilaration as she took the first steps to filing for a divorce. What she did not feel, though, she noted, as the solicitor tried in vain to persuade her to claim maintenance and child support from Richard, something she absolutely refused to do, was regret. No, there wasn't even a trace of regret.

"But it's your house," the solicitor said.

"And I've never been happy there," Rose said. "Let him have it. I want nothing to do with it or him."

"Are you OK?" Frasier had asked her on the drive back afterwards.

"I think so," Rose said. "I think I have a lot of things—thoughts, feelings—I need to untangle. I still haven't really thought about everything that Maddie and I have been through. Haven't processed it, as the Americans would say. I suppose I probably will need to do that, won't I, to really move on, and make a fresh start?"

"I suppose you will," Frasier said, "yes."

"Well, today was a start," Rose said, smiling at him. "I'll take that for now."

At least things between Rose and Frasier were manageable, and she was glad to have him in her life at this crucial time, even though it was not how she had spent so many unhappy hours imagining it.

When it came time to leave, Frasier, Tilda, and Maddie were already outside, Maddie fussing over who sat where in Frasier's enormous car. It was the first moment that Rose had had alone with John all day.

"How are you feeling, though?" she asked him. "I mean really."

John shrugged. "Like a man on the point of imminent death, I suppose."

"Stop joking!" Rose protested. "I can't talk to you about anything important without you wanting to brush it off, make light of it."

"My dearest Rose," John said, smiling fondly at her, "a man does not want to spend the last days of his life dwelling on the last days of his life. He doesn't want to spend it sitting for hours in a car going to the hellhole that is Scotland either, but as you have made me do one of those things, then the very least you can do is let me get away with the other."

"I suppose that is fair enough," Rose said, impulsively covering his hand with hers. "It's just there is still so much I want to say to you, Dad, so much I want to talk about. All those years that I missed—I can't help wanting to try and cram them all in now."

"But that would be no good," John said, putting his arms around her and hugging her to his frail chest, "because for most of those years you missed I wasn't a good enough man to be your father, and now, now that I finally am close to being good enough, the best that I can do for you, and you for me, is to live in the moment, with you and Maddie, and Tilda, and even Frasier, I suppose. You are my family, and that is so much more that I have any right to hope for."

Rose nodded, leaving her head where it was for a moment, enjoying the rare embrace.

The car horn sounded outside, signaling that Maddie had finally chosen her seat and that Frasier was ready to take them to Edinburgh.

"Ready to meet your public?" Rose asked John.

He sighed heavily. "With a little bit of luck I might die on the way," he said.

Chapter Twenty

Fortunately it was a warm evening when they arrived at the gallery, strong sun giving the dour gray stone of the building a rosy glow. Frasier helped Tilda and John out of the car, Maddie racing ahead to find Tamar waiting in the doorway, waving madly at her with a youthful enthusiasm that almost matched Maddie's.

"We're all ready," Tamar said excitedly as John and his entourage mounted the steps. "Everything is exactly as you wanted it, Mr. Jacobs."

"Not exactly, my dear," John said, smiling at her, "given that I wanted it all locked up in my barn until after I was dead, but still, I appreciate your efforts."

"Oh," Tamar said, uncertain whether or not John Jacobs was joking and at a loss as to how to respond.

"Ignore him," Rose said, smiling at her. "*I*, for one, can't wait to see it."

"John," Frasier said, "why don't you take Rose and Maddie round now? Show them your work yourself, before anyone else comes. I feel that the first time Rose sees it, it should be a private moment among the three of you."

"And my surprise," Maddie insisted. "Which is most important. Where is that, by the way?"

John looked into the gallery with no small amount of dread on his face, an image of vulnerability that made Rose want to bundle him into the car and take him home again in that instant.

"Come on, then," he said, offering Rose his arm and then leaning on her when she took it. "But I must warn you, I painted all these sober."

The buzz of the crowd, the clinking of glasses, and the low background of classical piano music filled the gallery, which was packed with people from the art world, who, it appeared, had traveled far and wide to see her father's work. Having had her own private viewing, Rose was content to watch from the very edges of the room, her back against the wall, as she saw her father laughing and talking with great animation and energy to a group of people he'd never met before, with all the confidence of a man who knew he had every right to be in that place at that time. Tilda stood at his side, quietly proud, and Maddie danced about his feet, leading any adult she could catch, which had been several, to the very heart of the exhibition and her surprise, which she was deeply proud of.

Rose and Maddie's journey through the gallery with John, before the doors had opened and all of these people had streamed in, had been a journey through years of her life, her life that she had not even been aware of, her life as it had been kept alight in John's imagination, heart, and memory. Or rather, both the life he regretted destroying so wantonly and the one he imagined could have been, if he had been a different man.

As he led Rose from painting to painting, saying very little about each one, she understood why he had been so reluctant to talk to her about the past this morning, why he hadn't wanted to waste any more precious moments on it when it was all here for her to see. Every memory he'd clung on to, every regret and mistake, the image of Rose as a child, the same image, over and over again, it was all here, laid out with brutal, affecting honesty.

Tilda was part of the tapestry too, appearing often, sometimes on her own, sometimes with Rose. It had been his depiction of Marian, Rose's mother, as the beautiful, confident girl he'd first fallen for that touched Rose the most. Marian, whose hair had been light blond, and whom Rose always tried to remember as she was when Rose was very little, always laughing and full of joy. When Rose looked at John's painting of her mother, she saw not only that precious memory of her mother brought to life, but most touchingly of all Rose saw herself as she was now, the image of her mother then. And perhaps that had been the greatest gift that John could have given her, the sense that by surviving Richard, by coming through this, she had picked up the torch of her mother's life, which had once burnt so brightly, and was carrying it forward into the unknown, living her new life for both of them.

The very last painting by John featured Maddie too, flying amongst the clouds, her arms outstretched above the mountains that surrounded Storm Cottage. And it was there that they found Maddie's surprise.

Her own painting, mounted and hung right next to John's portrait of her. It was an image of John at his easel, his granddaughter sitting at his feet, drawing, and Rose, complete with her short spiky blond hair, sitting on a stool reading a book, waiting for the artists to finish. It was about as close to a depiction of perfect, if untraditional, family life that Rose had ever seen, and it meant more than she could say that it was Maddie who recognized and captured the moment.

After that, Rose had been more than content to let her father go, walking into a world that was waiting to greet him, and to take quiet pleasure from seeing how very much he enjoyed a constant stream of people telling him how wonderful he was. Which was exactly how it should be, Rose decided. He'd lived too much of his life believing the opposite, and though that once had been true, it wasn't anymore.

"This is all a bit wonderful, isn't it?" Frasier said, appearing at her side.

"Yes," Rose said, turning to smile at him. "More wonderful than I could have imagined. Look at him, after all that fuss he made, he loves this!"

"I always thought it was a shame that he insisted on hiding away for so long," Frasier agreed. "But to be honest, I don't think he could have done this until he had you back in his life, until you'd been reconciled. Thank God you found him when you did. If you hadn't, I think we would all have missed this moment."

"Yes," Rose said, smiling thoughtfully as she watched her father throw his head back in laughter at something Maddie had said. "I was following love when we came here, after all. I just didn't know which love it was."

There had been talk of staying overnight in a hotel after the show, but John had been insistent that he wanted to go home, telling everyone that if he was going to die, he damn well wanted to do it in his own bed.

Not long into the journey Maddie had drifted off to sleep, leaning against John, who soon followed her, his chin drooping to his chest, his eyes closing. Neither Tilda, Frasier, nor Rose spoke a word on the way home, content to sit in silence because there was simply nothing that needed to be said.

"Here," Frasier said, as he turned off the engine outside Storm Cottage. "I'll carry Maddie up to bed. Tilda, would you mind turning on the lights for me, turn down the bed for John? I'll be back in a second, Rose, to help with John."

Rose stretched her arms above her head as she got out of the car, taking a second to look up at the blanket of stars that shone so brightly here in the countryside, extending right across the sky. Weary, but happy, she went around the car and opened the passenger door.

"Dad," she whispered, gently tugging at John's arm. "Dad, we're home."

"Are we?" John said, opening his eyes with some difficulty. "Good. I'm glad, I've been waiting."

The evening had obviously taken it out of him. He had to lean heavily on Frasier all the way into the house, and he collapsed gratefully into the bed as soon as he saw it. Rose discreetly left as Tilda helped him wash, undress, and get ready for bed, returning when she came out to pick up her bag.

"Why don't you stay the night, Tilda?" Rose asked her, putting her hand on her wrist before she could pick up her bag. "Stay with Dad. I know that he'd like it if you were here with him in the morning and from now on. I could help you get someone for the shop, and we can collect what you need from home tomorrow. I want you to be here, we all do."

Saying nothing, Tilda nodded, her eyes filling with tears. Rose sensed not to say any more, that Tilda needed a moment to collect herself after the emotional day.

At last Tilda sniffed and said, "I'll make some tea. Milk no sugar, for you."

Rose went into John's room, where the light was already turned out and he was almost asleep again.

"Well, it's official," she said, sitting on the edge of the bed and taking the hand that he reached out to her. "The whole world loves you and thinks you are a genius."

"That's what they say to your face," John said, but there was pleasure in his voice.

"And that's what they will always say," Rose said, adding casually, "Look, I know you won't mind, but I've asked Tilda to stay with us until . . . well, for as long as she wants. That's OK, isn't it?"

"Yes," John said, squeezing her fingers in the dark. "Thank you."

They were content to sit there for a moment or two, neither speaking until John broke the silence.

"Do you love me, Rose?" he asked her. "I feel like a damn fool for asking, but I think perhaps that it's all that matters to me now."

"Yes," Rose said with certainty, kissing the papery skin on the back of his hand. "I've always loved you, Dad. Never stopped, not even when I hated you. And now I know why: it turns out you are *quite* good at painting."

John smiled. "I want you to know that I always loved you, even in my darkest, most selfish hours. Even when I didn't know my own name. My love for you never went away. Thank you for coming back, Rose. And thank you for tonight."

Rose sat with him for a moment longer, the two of them watching the moon through the window as it sailed behind the peak of the mountain.

"Tilda will be back in a minute," Rose said, getting up. "Don't overdo it."

"Marian had hair that always smelt like honey," John said suddenly, causing Rose to pause by the door. "And a laugh so bright, she could light up the brightest corner. You are like her, Rose. You are her legacy. I look at you and I can see her again. Bright and brave and strong, the girl I first met all those years ago. You are her now. You will do her memory justice, I know it."

"Thanks, Dad," Rose said, her voice thick with emotion. "I hope so. See you in the morning."

"Yes," John said. "See you in the morning."

It had been almost three weeks after the exhibition, the morning that Rose woke up and knew, as soon as she opened her eyes to the very first light of dawn, that John was gone.

The house just felt different, emptier and bereft of the life that had inhabited it so fiercely for so long. Uncertain how to feel, because nothing seemed real, she got up and padded downstairs in her bare feet, which were numb to the icy-cold flagstones, to find Tilda sitting perfectly still at the table, staring blindly at its rough surface.

"Tilda," Rose said, putting a hand on the older woman's shoulder.

"He's . . ." Tilda looked up at her, her eyes brimming with tears.

"I know," Rose said. "How long?"

Tilda shook her head. "I'm not sure, I just woke up and he was gone. I stayed with him, held him until he was . . . cold."

Rose took a seat next to her father's wife and held her hand. "This was exactly the way that he wanted it," she said, filled with a sense of calm and peace. "At home, in bed, with you by his side, and me and Maddie in his life. This is exactly what he would have wanted."

"Yes," Tilda agreed, a tear tracking its way down her face. "But it doesn't change it, does it? It doesn't change how very awful it is that he's gone."

"No," Rose agreed, feeling the sobs rising in her own throat. "And it doesn't change that however much time I had with him, it would never have been enough."

And with their arms around each other, Rose and Tilda sat at the kitchen table and cried until the gray light of the early dawn turned into golden later summer sunshine, and the first day that John Jacobs was no longer in the world rose up to meet a perfect blue sky.

Epilogue

Rose had discovered that she loved watching the crackling fire of a winter evening, when the cold nights were drawing in, and Maddie, weary after another successful day at school, was tucked up happily in bed.

Her life in Storm Cottage had settled into a comfortable, contented routine over the last few months, one in which she had finally found the time to let her heart and her mind settle and heal, as she gradually made sense out of everything that had happened to bring her to this point.

In the weeks that followed John's death, Rose came to realize that he had left her an exceptionally wealthy woman, and that, if she wanted, she never had to work or worry about money again. Rose had been both overwhelmed and terrified by the responsibility. With the help of Janette, she'd set up a trust fund for Maddie, doubled the already very comfortable settlement that John had left Tilda, and after a great deal of discussion with Jenny, bought into the B & B—just the business, not the property—ensuring that Jenny and Brian's family home was safe, and they were also, at long last, free of both debt and worry.

Then together Rose and Jenny set about implementing the plan that Frasier had first come up with on that dreadful morning when he'd found out about her kissing Ted.

It was a brilliant idea, really, as clever as it was simple. With Rose's investment they set about completely redecorating the entire establishment, to make it modern and fresh, and gutting the annex to turn it into a light, airy studio, after which they began the process of remarketing the B & B as an artists' and writers' retreat, its association with John Jacobs doing it no harm at all when it came to attracting trade.

Rose had even managed, after some stiff debate and the promise of hired help, to persuade Jenny to extend the hours when breakfast was served and introduce coffee. Her next plan was to convince Jenny to offer her excellent home cooking in the evening, but she was waiting for the New Year before she suggested that, having learnt from Brian that Jenny took much better to new ideas if she believed them to be her own.

It had been a happy few weeks, seeing the B & B coming back to life again, going for the odd drink in the pub, watching from a distance as Ted's flirtations with several girls eventually petered out to just one: Tamar from the gallery, who'd begun to come down once a week to catalog and value all of John's remaining work for the insurers, a gesture that Rose had been glad of, knowing that Frasier would have come himself, if she hadn't told him how much she needed time alone, not only to get over what had been for her a lifelong love but also to find her feet in this brand-new world, where she was the mistress of her own destiny. Tamar had caught Ted's eye the first time he saw her, and Rose was fairly certain that something of a romance was blossoming between the two.

On the rare occasions Rose did see Frasier, that special closeness between them, that easy joy they had once taken in each other's company had slowly returned. And perhaps, Rose even allowed herself to think from time to time, just for a fraction of a second, just maybe . . . there might be a second chance for them both.

She'd been thinking exactly that when a sound by the door interrupted her thoughts. Turning round, she noticed that a long white envelope had been slid underneath the door. Intrigued and a little alarmed, Rose went to pick it up, anxiety flaring in her chest as she recognized Frasier's handwriting.

Dearest Rose,

I will never forget the first time I saw you, you took my breath away. But it wasn't your beauty that I fell instantly in love with, it was your courage, the fire in your eyes, even when you sat so still and talked so quietly. I told myself I was crazy for falling for a woman who was not only married, but pregnant, a woman I'd only just met, and I tried to forget about you. But I couldn't stop myself from writing you that note, from trying to say so much without saying anything at all.

The second I met you again, all of those feelings came back, not that they had ever really gone away—you have always been the woman of my dreams. I loved your father very much, but I confess I hoped that by knowing him, I would get the chance to see you again one day. As our friendship grew, I discovered more and more reasons to fall in love with you, but I never believed that you might feel the same way as me. When you told me about the note, and the real reason you came to Millthwaite, I was so happy, everything was perfect. I'm not proud of what happened after that, of the way I behaved, and how I slighted you, you who deserve it least of all. I believe I was overwhelmed and I realize how it must have looked, but I wasn't running away from you. I was running away from the terrifying prospect of having a dream come true and of somehow failing you. If only I had an ounce of your courage.

I can only hope that by now you have had the time to forgive me my foolishness and to realize once again that if you give me another chance, I will do all I can every day for the rest of our lives to deserve you.

Dearest Rose, you are the bravest, most beautiful, funniest, cleverest woman I have ever met, and you make my heart race as much now as the very first time I saw you. And just so we are clear, I love you, Rose.

Yours always,

Frasier

P.S. I'm standing outside the door.

Rose clasped the letter to her chest, knowing even in that moment that it would be one she would read over and over again, for the rest of her life. And then, with tears of joy brimming in her eyes, she put her hand on the latch and opened the front door.

Acknowledgments

Firstly I want to say a special heartfelt thank you to the hundreds of women who were brave enough to share their stories of domestic abuse with me during the course of researching this book. I never imagined, when I asked for people to contact me with their stories, that I would receive such an overwhelming response, each experience as desperately painful and shocking as the last, and so sickeningly common that surely more must be done to stop the routine abuse of women in their own homes.

The publication of *The Runaway Wife* marks the tenth anniversary of the publication of my first novel in 2002. A lot has happened in those ten years, including birth, divorce, marriage, and (a lot) more birth, but one thing has always remained constant through all the ups and downs, and that is my writing. I've been exceptionally fortunate and grateful to the team at Simon & Schuster, over much of that time, and now seems like a good time to thank everyone who has contributed to and supported my work, both past and present.

Special thanks to my editor, Emilia Pisani, who has helped make this book as good as it can be.

Thank you also to my agent and friend Lizzy Kremer, who has been at my side for every one of those years, is always in my corner, and sometimes is the only person in the world keeping me sane!

I'm so lucky to have become good friends with many other writers, in a community that is unfailingly supportive, and I want to thank especially Katy Regan, Katie Fforde, Trisha Ashley, Caroline Smailes, Serena Mackesy, Cally Taylor, Elle Amberley, Keris Stainton, Tamsyn Murray, and so many more who inspire, cheer, and make me laugh on a daily basis.

Also my dear friends Jenny Matthews, Margi Harris, Catherine Ashley, Kirstie Seaman, Claire Winter, Rosie Woolley, Cathy Carter, Sarah Darby and, yes, you again Katy Regan. I love you.

The world of social networking means I now get to meet and get to know readers from around the world, some of whom have become friends and all of whom have kept me motivated with their good wishes and appreciation, so thank you to all of you, you don't know how much pleasure it gives me to get a message of support from Texas, or Thailand, or Twickenham on a Monday morning!

Finally, thank you to my family: my husband Adam, whose belief in me and love means so much, and my incredible, beautiful, talented, funny, adorable children, Lily, Fred, Stanley, and Aubrey, and my stepson, Harry. You keep us busy and tired but life would be so boring without you.

G A Gallery Readers Group Guide

The Runaway Wife

ROWAN COLEMAN

Rose Pritchard has fled her home with her seven-year-old daughter Maddie, arriving at a B&B in a remote village in the middle of the night. Rose is not just running away from something but running toward a new life that she hopes exists, in search of the person who once offered her hope.

Almost immediately Rose wonders if she's made a terrible mistake—if she's chasing a dream—but she knows in her heart that she cannot go back. She's been given a second chance—at life and at love—but will she have the courage to take it?

Questions for Discussion

1. Coleman unfolds Rose's story one layer at a time, slowly uncovering the reasons for her hasty getaway. How did learning more about Rose's past influence how you perceived her in the present-day narrative?

2. Rose sees herself as a vulnerable and fragile person, but her inner strength becomes more and more apparent as the storyline progresses. What are some examples of Rose's bravery? What are the turning points that help her learn to assert herself?

3. Both Shona and Rose have endured abusive and unhealthy relationships. Compare and contrast how each woman copes with her situation. How did they end up with these men, and what does it take for them to walk away?

4. Rose shocks everyone—including herself—by cutting off all her hair and dyeing it blond. How significant is her dramatically different appearance? Have you ever undergone a physical transformation to help you make a change in your life?

5. After nearly eight years of anticipation, how do you think Frasier lives up to Rose's expectations? In what ways is he not quite who she imagined he'd be?

6. Rose not only reconnects with Frasier in Millthwaite but finds her estranged father as well. Discuss the different ways in which each of these newfound relationships impact her. What do Frasier and John provide Rose that she's been missing all these years?

7. How are Maddie and John able to build a relationship despite both of them having difficulty connecting with others? What are some of the ways in which Maddie and John are similar?

8. *The Runaway Wife* has a diverse cast of secondary characters, from brash and outspoken Shona to Jenny, whose bark seems much worse than her bite. Who was your favorite secondary character?

9. Maddie is an eccentric and precocious child. What are some examples of Maddie being wise beyond her years? What are some of your favorite Maddie-isms?

10. Discuss Frasier's reaction when he finds out about Rose's liaison with Ted. What was your reaction to his behavior? How does his attitude reflect his perception of Rose?

11. Frasier and Rose made an instant connection that sustained itself for years. Would you call this love at first sight? Do you believe that it's possible to feel this way about someone you've met only briefly?

Enhance Your Book Club

1. Frasier and Rose show the world John's true identity as an artist with his final exhibition. Visit a local art gallery or museum with your book club and discuss your favorite works.

2. Research England's Lake District (www.golakes.co.uk/) and choose which B&B you'd most like to stay in. Bring photos to your next meeting and describe your ideal getaway in the English countryside.

3. If you like this novel, check out other books by Rowan Coleman, such as *Lessons in Laughing Out Loud, The Home for Broken Hearts,* and *The Accidental Mother.* You can learn more about the author and her work at www.rowancoleman.co.uk and follower her on Twitter @RowanColeman.